Merry Christmas
Deanna,
– And the American
Dream. Enjoy!

Ann Cullen

Emma Parchen

Twelve Years Of Her American Dream

ANN CULLEN

BOOK MONTANA HELENA

This is a work of fiction, but the major events, people with names, and many details are real. The characterizations and the interaction between people were fabricated to facilitate the story line.

Published in the United States of America

ISBN 0-9670759-1-2

Book Montana: First Edition

Foreword

The following story is a fictional account based real people, places, and events. To tell the story of the Parchens, it was necessary to accept that the name "Henry" occurred a minimum of four times within the family circle. To offset confusion, the family nicknamed Emma Parchen's brother and her son "Harry", while her husband, Henry Parchen, and his nephew, Henry Duerfeldt, continued to be referred to as "Henry" throughout. Two "Jennys" also occurred. Emma's sister's name was spelled with a "y", while Jennie Paynter's name was spelled with an "ie".

In writing this story, no point of fact was intentionally negated or ignored, and is based on the records found in:

Benton Avenue Cemetery
City of Helena, Recording Office
Forestvale Cemetery
Lewis & Clark Public Library
Montana Historical Society Library
Montana Historical Society Photographic Archives

Characterizations and interaction between characters were fabricated to facilitate the story line.

ANN CULLEN has a degree in American History from Pacific Lutheran University.

Also the author of:

Lilly Cullen
Helena, Montana 1894

Chapter One

"I am marrying a man from Helena, dear aunt, and we shall go there to live," Emma wrote. "My brother, Harry, introduced us last June when he brought him home one evening for supper. You see, Mr. Parchen is Harry's boss, and he has a business house in Deer Lodge City that my brother now runs."

Emma thought for a moment, and then continued her letter.

"Mr. Parchen is not a painter nor a musician like grandfather, nor a doctor like my father. He is not French, nor catholic. But we are in America -- he is American -- and I love him with all my heart. Mother, of course, regrets his religion, but in all other ways is content with him. I wish you to feel the same. Henry Parchen is an honest, hardworking, fine man, and promises me that before we die we shall have a proper wedding trip and see the sights. The statement is not to be taken lightly. Everyone who knows him, says his word is gold."

A smile emerged on Emma's face as she thought how wonderful it would be to see the shiny waves of the Pacific Ocean. She continued her letter.

"My brother, Harry, has not struck it rich yet. For all the fuss he made about finding gold in Montana, we are financially unchanged. I am afraid he has grandfather's enthusiasm, and his lack of luck. He has continuously panned for the allusive nuggets since we came, but has found nothing substantial enough to make a claim on, despite his hopes. Once, he actually hired on with a gold extracting company to see if he was going about it right. All he learned was that he hated the hard, dirty work of hydraulics and mine shafts. This last fall he took a month off with a couple of buddies to go on a 'long tramp', as he calls it, looking for placer gold around western Montana. They had a grand time, but found nothing of consequence. He has now resigned himself to make his fortune in other ways."

Emma scanned her handwriting, added a comment or two, and dated the letter February 7th, 1872, the day of her wedding. She folded the pages, and stuffed them into the waiting envelope that she addressed to her Aunt Renard in Missouri. This she set it against her lamp so they would not forget to mail it.

Her mother came through the door. "You better get dressed. People will be here in less than an hour."

Emma rose to her feet. "Is Jenny getting ready?"

"Yes, she's dressing in my room," Emma's mother replied as she noticed the new letter setting on her daughter's small table. "You wrote to Aunt Renard, good. I was hoping you would," she commented as she now helped Emma into the undergarments of her wedding dress. "Your Aunt Renard has been after me and after me to send you to her. It is quite beyond her imagination that you could find a decent man so far out west. She thinks all the males out here are shiftless prospectors, trappers, and worse." Emma's mother smiled. "My sister needs to hear the news from your own pen." She pulled the lacing of her daughter's corset tight.

"I still don't understand why all these undergarments are fastened in the back," Emma complained. "I need a maid to help me dress."

Her mother smiled as she held the underskirt open for her daughter to step into. "It's tradition," her mother responded as she pulled the fabric up over Emma's hips, "one of the few we have left. Your grandmother wore a gown like this when she married. I wore hers when I married your father, but it was passed to your aunts, and I never knew what became of it. True this dress is rather old fashioned. Mine was too. But while grandmother always said she might not always know everything she should about the world, she was infallible when it came to weddings. 'Wear this dress,' she said, 'and it will bring you and your husband closer together on your wedding night. It will bring you luck.'"

"How can any dress bring two people closer together?" Emma replied. "It's just yardage."

Her mother smiled knowingly as she now retrieved the dress itself, and helped her daughter into it, lacing up the delicate silk ties in back and adjusting the folds of fabric and lace.

Emma reached for her chapel veil as her sister appeared at the door.

"Wow, Em, you look gorgeous," Jenny exclaimed.

Emma's attention shifted to her sister. "The dress needs something at the neck. Can I borrow your crystal beads?"

"Hasn't your Henry Parchen given you a locket?" Jenny cried as she waltzed into the room.

"No, not yet," Emma replied.

"Hmm, he's so proper about things. I would have thought he'd given you one by now." She came to a stop in front of her sister as she scrutinized the neckline of the wedding gown. Then she turned to their mother. "What did you wear?"

"My silver crucifix," she answered.

"Ugh, not for your wedding," Jenny retorted in distaste. "The thing is gruesome."

"I never thought so," their mother responded, a bit hurt.

"Never mind," Jenny remarked. "How about the necklace daddy gave you after Em was born?"

"It's a bit long," their mother responded, "but we can try." She disappeared momentarily, and came back with her late husband's gift. She fastened it around her daughter's neck.

"There, see," Jenny proclaimed. "It's beautiful."

"If Emma bends her neck, it will virtually drop down out of sight," their mother worried.

"Exactly," Jenny laughed, "and her Henry will wonder if the pendant's been lost, and look a little closer."

Emma was glazing in the mirror, oblivious to her sister's words. She had always loved the necklace, and her fingers touched it appreciatively. "I would like to wear it," she responded. "I wish daddy was here."

Her mother's expression softened. "I do too, dear. He would be so proud." She glanced up at the arrival of her son, Harry, thankful that they had long ago given him the nickname that had kept the boy's name distinct from the father's. Now years later it would also serve to keep Harry distinct from Emma's new husband, Henry. The practice of handing down family names could get confusing.

"Where is Jenny?" Emma's brother called as he appeared at the bedroom door that had inadvertently been left open. "Mrs. Wilcox is here."

"I have to run," Jenny responded as she quickly kissed her sister's cheek for luck. The young woman rushed out into the hall.

"How is Henry doing?" Emma's mother asked as her son lingered momentarily.

"Parchen? He's a bunch of nerves," Harry laughed. "His hands are shaking so badly, he's dropped Emma's wedding band a half dozen times."

"Just so he doesn't loose it." Their mother smiled.

"No chance of that," Harry proclaimed. "I have it now."

"Don't you loose it," Emma replied.

"Me? Who fixed you up with old Henry in the first place, sis?" her brother chuckled. "I would hardly mess things up now."

Emma smiled. Her brother had encouraged her relationship with Henry Parchen from the very beginning. Half the time she wondered if it was just her brother's affable nature that had sped things along, or if he was hoping a marital union would cement his rise within the druggist's business. Emma knew Harry had an ambitious streak, and there was no denying the economic advantages of becoming family with Mr. Parchen. Still, Emma could not begrudge her brother this. He had been instrumental in facilitating the match, a match Emma would never have thought possible. Henry Parchen was so quiet and strong, not the sort who would even talk to her on his own. So what was wrong if everyone gained from the arrangement. It wasn't as if her family wasn't due for a change of luck.

Emma could hear voices drifting up from the front room. Her mother had moved most of the furniture from the two adjoining rooms downstairs to make space for all the chairs. Numerous rows now occupied the floor as they all faced the front window where Reverend Stoy would marry them. Emma felt a wave of nervousness rush through her. Could it really be happening? She could hardly believe that she would be Mrs. Henry Parchen before the evening was over.

"You wait here," her mother instructed. "Henry must not see you before the ceremony. Your brother will come and get you when it's time."

Emma watched her mother follow Harry from the room, and sat down at the table, nervously fidgeting with her newly written letter. Piano music now masked most the conversation of the arriving people. From the foot of the stairs she heard Reverend Stoy's voice with her mother's, and then these faded. Her attention returned to the letter in her hands.

Her mother had written to Aunt Renard weeks before. Her brother had advised against it, citing the woman's incessant claim on Emma ever since the time his sister had stayed with her during Jenny's small pox. But their mother had insisted that Aunt Renard know of the upcoming nuptials, she was after all family. Their aunt had written an explosive reply that had Emma's mother in tears for two days. Emma had wanted to read the letter, but her mother had refused, burning it on the spot in the wood stove. This was, as her mother put it, one of the many sacrifices a mother willingly makes for her children. She would not allow Emma to be upset by her aunt's words. From that point, she put on a cheerful face, and only asked that Emma write her aunt a few lines, announcing her marriage as if nothing had passed between them.

Emma sighed. She liked her Aunt Renard. She had been very nice to her back when Jenny had the small pox, but she knew her mother was right. Aunt Renard would want her to marry back East, some stifled young man with a stuffed shirt. It would be a marriage of forbearance from the very start, without even a spark of what Emma already had with Henry Parchen. Emma smiled. She and Henry had sparks, that was certain. There was so much heat between them, at times Emma felt she would melt on the very spot. The whole world faded into nothingness when she was with Henry. All that mattered was Henry. During these occurrences Aunt Renard was not even a thought.

Her brother appeared at the door. "Are you ready?" he asked quietly.

"Yes," Emma responded as she instantly rose.

A warm smile appeared on Harry D'Acheul's lips. "You know, Em, I have often wondered if I made a mistake bringing Parchen home for dinner that first time. The moment he set eyes on you, he could hardly take them off. And if you hadn't liked him, or he hadn't been true, it could really have ended badly." He held out his hand to his sister. "But now I know it was all worth it. You have never looked more radiantly beautiful. If this isn't love, nothing is."

Emma smiled, took her brother's hand, and walked down to the front room with him. There, all their friends were gathered as Jenny accompanied Mrs. Wilcox on the piano, and together they sang the processional hymn.

Slowly and deliberately Emma walked with her brother down the narrow aisle through their friends to where Reverend Stoy and Henry Parchen waited. The reverend stood in his solemn black robe. Henry was in his best wool suit. Emma glanced down at her fiancé's hands folded in front of him. She noticed the quiver of his fingers as the top hand gripped the bottom one harder.

Emma smiled. She was nervous too. She wanted to be Henry's wife so badly, yet she had never been a wife before. Could it really all be happening today, right now? It was a dream...and yet it was so solemn with vows before God and all their friends. Emma took a deep breath.

Harry left his sister standing beside his boss, and took his place to one side. Jenny rose from the piano, and took her place on the other side of the couple.

The ceremony lasted only minutes. Emma listened intently to Reverend Stoy as her heart pounded within her. It always did when she was in the presence of Henry Parchen. Henry smiled as he caught her eye momentarily, and then his attention shifted back to what the reverend was saying. Henry made the appropriate responses, as did Emma, but suddenly a panicked look took hold of the bridegroom as Reverend Stoy asked for the ring. Harry immediately offered the requested item as he turned to smile at his boss. Henry Parchen immediately relaxed, and suddenly he and Emma were presented as man and wife.

A soft tumult of approval radiated from their family and friends, and the couple officially kissed. The ceremony then transpired into a warm reception, so fully enjoyed by those assembled that they did not leave until nearly midnight. Henry and Emma danced and ate and unwrapped gifts to everyone's delight. They had received some handsome presents, many from Missouri and Nebraska where the couple's extended families resided. Emma noted her Aunt Renard had sent a silver soup toureen. Her mother must have written back to her.

As their friends slowly left late that evening, Henry turned to his new bride. "We have to be up early in the morning. The Overland Coach leaves for Helena at eight."

"Yes," Emma murmured softly. It was time to finish their farewells, and turn in for the night.

Emma followed her new husband up the steep rear steps away from the family. They were supposed to have the downstairs room for the night. It had the largest bed in the house, but it was too close to all the clean-up. Instead, Henry led Emma up to her old room. Jenny had already left for the evening to spend the night with a girl friend, and so they would be undisturbed. Henry led his new bride through the door, and secured it shut by leaning a straight chair in under the knob.

"Our night things are all downstairs," Emma noted as her new husband encircled her with his arms.

"They are, aren't they," he responded as he watched her expression.

"Don't you want them?"

"No, do you?" he asked.

"The beds are awfully narrow up here," Emma noted.

"Do you care?" He kissed her. "Do you?" he repeated now as he paused, looking into her eyes. His embrace pulled her closer against him.

Emma felt the heat rising from her skin. Her heart raced. Her attention sharpened, but not on her surroundings. The love of her life was with her, touching her, stirring the fire within her. The room faded from her mind.

"Do you care?" Henry repeated with a smile.

"No," she whispered back. His mouth was on hers, hers on his.

Henry reached behind her, and suddenly the bodice of Emma's wedding gown loosened around her. The surprise was met with sheer relief on Emma's part. Alone she would have remained a prisoner of her garments.

"Emma, wake up," Henry called as he reached over and gently kissed her the following morning. "It's nearly six. We have to pack yet."

Emma's arms slid around her new husband's neck, and they kissed again.

"No, no we have to get up," he insisted softly as he now pulled away. "There will be time enough for that later." He smiled happily, and pulled on his trousers.

"The clothes that I was planning to wear, are all downstairs," Emma noted as she sat up in bed.

"Well I don't think the family is up yet, if you want to sneak down and get them," Henry replied, "but you better hurry."

Emma stole from bed, pulled on some old things of her sister's, and crept out the door. Within moments she was back. "Mom's already starting breakfast," she reported.

Henry looked up as his new wife deposited herself in his lap. They were instantly kissing.

"Emma, it's getting late," Henry retorted with a smile. "Eight o'clock waits for no one, and with the snow, neither will the Overland Coach."

"All right," she replied begrudgingly. She got up, and stripped off her sister's clothes, purposely displaying her scantily clad body before her husband. Her wantonness startled him, and he rose to embrace her passionately.

Ten minutes later, Henry again re-gained self control as the two of them now dressed for the trip. As Henry went down to breakfast, Emma hastily straightened the room, and then followed. Her mother was dishing up a hearty meal, setting the plates before them on the table.

"Morning Henry, Emma," she greeted with a smile. "How did you two sleep?"

Emma flashed her mother a defiant look.

"Harry and I packed up your gifts last night after everyone left," her mother continued, undaunted. "We thought you would want your new things with. He has already taken the boxes down to the station."

"What about my trunk?" Emma asked as she ate.

"Taken care of," her mother answered. "All you need now is your husband."

Emma glanced at Henry who smiled between bites. It seemed strange to hear the term used in their regard.

"And wear the warmest cloak and garments you have," Henry added. "The trip is going to be long and cold, I'm afraid." Then he turned to Emma's mother. "Marie, thank you for breakfast, the wedding, and your daughter." He smiled briefly, and turned to his bride. "Emma, we have got to go."

"I'm coming," she responded. She followed her husband from the table.

Within five minutes, they were heading down the snowy street to where the Overland Coach already waited. Emma's mother and brother hurried with them, and lingered as they boarded, saying good bye and wishing them a good journey.

As the stagecoach lurched into the street on its winter runners, Emma's attention finally left the family she was leaving behind, and focused on the one other passenger. She was an older woman in her late sixties. Deer Lodge City disappeared outside, and a half mile beyond the horses pulled to a stop as the woman got out, shouting her thanks to the driver above. Within moments they were underway again.

Emma snuggled up to her new husband. "Did you hire a private coach?"

Henry smiled. "You would almost think so, aside from that woman. But no, this long, cold journey is not one people take unless they have to."

"Is that why you took it? Because you had to," Emma teased.

"Yes," he confessed. "I could not live without you." His head bent to kiss her.

She willingly responded, becoming lost in caress as the horses carried them farther and farther away from Deer Lodge City.

"It's snowing again," Henry noted after several moments. He brushed a few flakes from Emma's cheek. The coach slowed accordingly. Both looked out at the weather. The scenery was wrapped in the white fog of falling snow.

"This trip could get long," Henry commented.

"I don't care as long as I'm with you," Emma declared happily.

Henry responded with a loving smile. Then his eyes shifted outside again as concern rose in his eyes. They had the mountain pass ahead of them.

"What time is it," Emma asked.

Her husband pulled out his pocket watch. "Almost twelve," he answered as the Overland Coach pulled off their route and headed for a corral. They came to a stop.

"Ten minutes," the driver shouted as he swung down from his seat. "You have ten minutes to stretch your legs while we change the horses, and not a minute more. We are running behind schedule."

Henry opened the coach door, and got out. Emma followed. They walked hand in hand through the soft snow, heading toward the river where the trees towered above and the underbrush rose to give privacy.

"There is so much ice in the river," Emma noted quietly. She looked around her. Their surroundings were pristine with no trace of human existence.

Emma's pace slowed to a stop as her eyes settled on her husband. A soft winter breeze hissed in her ears. Her arms reached up to embrace his neck. "It's very private here," she stated quietly.

Henry Parchen's heart quickened, just as it had the first time he set eyes on Emma. Unknown to her brother, Henry Parchen had known Harry had two sisters long before the invitation to supper came. It was the overriding reason why Henry had accepted the invitation. Emma had caught his attention on the street the week of her arrival. She had caught a small child before it ran out in front of a passing wagon. In the commotion she hadn't noticed him. But Emma's beauty, her seductive beauty, was something Henry could not erase from his mind. It haunted him. It plagued him. It followed him wherever he went, and through whatever he did. Then when Emma's brother, Harry, had proposed his “long tramp” for late August, Henry Parchen had welcomed it. It gave him the excuse he needed to spend more time in the Deer Lodge store.

Henry took his bride into his arms, his lips finding hers, their bodies collapsing into the soft snow.

Chapter Two

Emma ran with Henry back to the Overland Coach. They had lost track of time until voices had awakened them from their preoccupation.

Henry quickly helped his wife into the coach, and followed. They had hardly settled into their seats before the vehicle lurched forward, and they were underway.

"How long until the next stop?" Emma inquired as she dusted the snow off her clothes, and reached for the basket her mother had sent with. Lunch emerged.

"Probably another four hours," Henry replied.

"That long?" Emma responded. "How far is it then to Helena?"

"A long way," Henry answered.

"Will we make it by nightfall?"

"It doesn't look like it." Henry began to eat.

Emma stared at him.

"We still have MacDonald's pass ahead of us," Henry continued. "We will probably hold up at the Frenchwoman's ranch."

The coach slowed. A deep snow drift covered the road. Tediously they made their way through it.

Silence stole over the couple as their eyes focused outside. If this was any indication of the pace ahead, they would be lucky to reach the next station before dark.

Time marched on as the horses pulled them at varying speeds toward their destination. They reached the Frenchwoman's ranch at 4:40 that afternoon.

"We will be spending the night," the driver informed them as he opened the coach door.

Emma followed her husband outside, quickly surveying her surroundings. "Primitive" was the only description that came to mind as she noted the small graveyard a short distance away.

"It's just for one night," Henry responded with a soft smile at his wife's sudden shyness.

"I can't wait until we get to Helena," Emma stated.

She followed her husband into the rough dwelling where a hospitable welcome was accorded them. They ate dinner with the residents and the driver. Their bed was a blanket on the floor in front of the fireplace.

Emma did not sleep well that night. The floor was hard, and snoring woke her whenever she did manage to drift off. She envied Henry. He slept through it all.

Daybreak did not come soon enough for Emma. She was exhausted and bored as she watched the driver head outside at the first hint of light. Johnny was not gone long. It had continued to snow during the night; and as the house roused itself, there was serious talk of whether it was feasible to continue traveling. Six inches of new snow blanketed the land, and the pass was before them.

But by eight o'clock Emma and Henry again found themselves seated inside the Overland Coach, heading up the grade. The snow was deeper now, the air more brisk, and clouds again threatened precipitation. Johnny urged the horses on, pressing them as fast as he dared. The ascent up the pass was the critical leg of the journey.

Henry Parchen noted how much shorter the trees lining the road looked than during his summer trips. The snow had accumulated considerable depth. He glanced at Emma. She had taken the seat opposite him on this part of the journey.

"You realize I haven't a house for us yet," Henry stated.

"Yes, you told me," Emma replied. "You live above the store."

"It's not fancy."

"But comfortable. You said it was comfortable," Emma responded.

"Comfortable enough for me," Henry replied. "I don't require much."

Emma focused on her husband. "Do you think I require extravagances because I used to live in St. Louis? My mother's house is not extravagant."

"But..." Henry Parchen's face turned abruptly. "We're stopping."

The driver swung down off the top of the coach, grabbing the ax. Henry opened the door, and peered out. A large chunk of tree lay in the road.

"Have you got a saw?" Henry called to Johnny.

"Yeah, behind the seat," he answered.

Within moments both men were hard at work on the tree limb. They worked furiously. Snow was beginning to fall. The sky was dark.

Emma glanced at the splintered tree trunk where a main branch had broken away under all the weight of the snow. She pulled out her watch. It was nearly nine.

It took an hour and a half for the men to drag the smaller chunks of tree from the road so the coach could continue. During that time a new half inch of snow settled over them. The horses pawed the ground restlessly.

"How far is the station?" Emma asked as Henry finally climbed back into the coach beside her.

"We are probably about a third of the way up the grade. The station is on the other side of the summit," her husband informed her as the vehicle lurched forward again. The snowfall increased, turning the air white.

"You look cold," Emma noted.

Henry smiled, rubbing his hands briskly together.

"Here, let me help," Emma offered as she took off her gloves. The air was so chill that she seemed to be making little progress until she pulled his hands in under her cloak. "There, that's better."

"In more ways than one." Henry smiled.

"We are alone," she replied.

"And newly married," he agreed. He pulled her toward him, kissing her as his fervor warmed him. Suddenly his attention shifted, and he turned once again to the window.

"What's wrong?" she asked.

"Our progress has slowed again."

"It's no wonder. You can't even see the trees," Emma exclaimed.

They came to a stand still. Within moments Johnny came through the coach door, finding a seat opposite Henry and Emma.

"I hope the snow doesn't last long. We may have to turn back," he commented as he dusted the white off his shoulders. "I trust you don't mind sharing your compartment, but we aren't going any place until this weather lets up, and it's cold out there."

"It's not much better in here," Emma offered.

"But with three bodies instead of two, it could improve," Johnny chuckled as he let down the leather window flaps, and then pulled out a worn deck of cards. "Do you play poker, Ma'am?" he asked in the dim light.

Emma glanced at Henry. Johnny had already handed him the deck of cards to shuffle. "No," she answered quietly.

"What do you play?"

"Rummy."

"Then Rummy it is," he declared. "Ante in everyone."

Henry reached into his pocket for whatever trifle he might be carrying, and placed it on the floor in front of them. Emma followed suit. A bent cigarette, an agate, and Emma's handkerchief became the prize. Henry distributed the cards, and they all settled into the game as they waited out the weather.

"What if the snow doesn't stop?" Emma asked as she drew a seven of hearts.

The men glanced at her.

"It always does," Johnny answered. "It's just a matter of time."

"But what if it gets dark?" she continued.

"Then," the driver replied with a smile, "we sleep here until morning."

"Won't we freeze to death?" Emma cried in alarm.

"Not if we snuggle up together," Johnny chuckled.

Emma turned to Henry with bewildered eyes.

"You asked," he responded lightly.

Emma scooped her cards together, and placed them under the pile on the floor. Then she opened the door against the men's complaints, and stepped outside. The snow was still falling heavily as she made her way along the coach to the horses. A thick pile of snow already blanketed their backs. She patted the closest one on the neck.

"How long are we going to be stuck here," she asked quietly as she offered the horse a piece of hard candy.

The animal took the gift, crunching down on it, enjoying the sweetness.

Emma looked up into the sky, but all she could see were the flakes of snow against a gray-white background. She shivered. Her toes had become numb long ago, and she could only hope the temperature would not drop much more.

Then suddenly the sun broke from the clouds, and Emma realized she could see down the road. She ran for the coach door.

"It's stopped," she cried as she whipped the door open. "The snow has stopped."

"All right, who has the best hand?" Henry demanded.

"I do," Johnny declared. He snatched up Emma's handkerchief with a smile, putting it in his pocket with the cigarette. As he headed out the door, he placed the agate in Emma's hand.

"I didn't even play," Emma protested.

"It doesn't matter," Henry responded as he helped his wife in. "Whoever announces good weather, after we've been waylaid a while, always gets a prize of one sort or another. I got a half smoked cigar once." Her husband smiled.

"Ugh," Emma responded. "Sometimes I think my Aunt Renard is right about the West."

"Actually it was a darn good cigar," Henry chuckled. "It would have been a shame to waste it."

Two hours later they made the summit of MacDonald's pass. Here the driver stopped, checking the brakes and making adjustments. The snow had frozen into an icy crust in the shade of the hills, and Johnny wanted all the traction he could get. Slowly the driver urged the horses down the grade.

For an hour and a half their progress was good. Then suddenly one lead horse slipped as his counter dropped to his knees. Only Johnny's quick response kept further damage from happening. Stopped in their tracks, the two horses were able to regain their feet without injury as Johnny shouted for Henry to come take the reins. Meanwhile he was strapping cleats to his boots, and heading to the lead horses. He took a horse's bridle in hand, and began slowly and carefully walking them forward.

Emma was now alone in the coach as she watched the passing scenery. Their pace was pathetically slow, so slow she could walk faster. With the passing minutes, a certain restlessness grew in her. This was the second day she had been confined inside the vehicle. It was cold; it was boring; and she longed for action. Without a second thought, Emma emerged through the coach door to walk beside it. Anything had to be better than its confinement.

Emma's foot struck ground and instantly slid, pulling her off balance. She found herself on her backside sliding past the coach, past the horses, heading for the side of the hill. She was vaguely conscious of Henry screaming hoarsely as a wave of helplessness struck her. She could not stop. She was at the mercy of the frozen snow beneath her, and suddenly she imagined the drop-off on the other side of the road -- the trees, the rocks, the danger. In panic, she strained to see where her momentum was taking her. She dropped into a crevice along the foot of the hill, and there she grabbed a frozen bush, praying it would not break under her weight. This stopped her momentarily as she grabbed a better handhold. Her weight shifted. Emma held her breath. She did not want to slip away again.

"Parchen, stay put," Johnny shouted. "I will get her."

Carefully and tediously the driver made his way down to where Emma clung to her bush, too afraid to move. Johnny's heels crunched through the icy crust of the snow, step by step, as he made his way toward her.

"Don't move, Mrs. Parchen," he instructed. "Let me get below you."

Emma made no response. She did not dare move even that slight bit.

"There," Johnny announced. He lifted Emma into his young, strong arms, and turned back to the coach. "Bring the horses down, nice and slow," he shouted to Henry.

Within moments the Overland Coach pulled up alongside, and Johnny placed Emma inside.

"Are you hurt," he asked now, "aside from your skinned cheek?"

"I don't know," she answered. "My left ankle hurts a little."

Johnny took hold of it, carefully checking its soundness. "I think you just wrenched it. Keep it warm," he admonished. He shut the door, and looked up at Henry. "She's okay. Just a little shaky." He glanced at the grade ahead. "Parchen, wait until I get up front, and then we will start down again." He pushed in the leather window flap. "Are you all right, Mrs. Parchen?"

"Yes."

"Well, stay away from the door. We don't want you racing down the mountainside again. We'll check the latch at the station."

Their slow pace down the grade commenced once again as Emma leaned back in her seat. She could have been killed...or seriously injured. She knew that. Why hadn't she realized the reason for their slow pace was the icy road. Her stunt was so stupid, so thoughtless.

For the remainder of the afternoon, the stagecoach inched its way down the eastern grade of MacDonald Pass as Emma smarted from the rebuke she poured out on herself, from the sting of her skinned cheek, and from the ache of her ankle. If she thought she was uncomfortable before, it was nothing compared to now. Yet she sat and endured it all, grateful for the security of the coach.

After about an hour, Emma dozed off, weary from her lack of sleep the night before, the excitement of her embarrassing accident, and from the trauma of her ankle. She woke as Henry climbed in beside her.

"Are you all right?" he asked anxiously.

"Yes. Why are we stopped?"

"We are at the bottom of the grade. Johnny doesn't need me to drive any more."

"How far is the station?" Emma asked as her husband shut the coach door carefully behind him. It was getting dark outside.

"Oh maybe ten to twenty minutes yet. It's not far." His attention focused sharply on her. "You scared me to death! How did you fall out the door?"

"I didn't," she answered quietly. "We were going so slow, I wanted to walk."

"Walk," Henry exclaimed. "You wanted to walk? Even the horses were having trouble doing that. Why do you think we were going so slow."

"It was a stupid stunt," Emma acknowledged. "I'm sorry. Do you hate me?"

Henry Parchen's countenance softened. "No, of course not. Just don't ever do it again. I don't want to be a widower."

The coach turned off the road at the MacDonald station, and pulled to a stop in front of the heavy timbered house. Henry opened the door as Emma tried to rise to her feet. A soft cry escaped her lips as she suddenly realized how sore her ankle had become.

Henry backed out of the coach as he supported much of Emma's weight. Outside, Emma stood gingerly on one foot as she tested the hurt one. It was fine as long as she did not lean to her left, and the leather of her boot did not press into her flesh.

"Can you walk," Henry asked anxiously.

"I think I can once I get my boot off. It must be bruised, and the leather is so stiff."

The men got her inside where her husband helped her off with the boot. Alexander MacDonald provided a warm foot bath of Epsom salts.

Dinner was simple basic food, and Emma was provided with a bed for the night. Here she would haven gotten some good sleep if her ankle had not tormented her every time she moved. By the time morning arrived, Emma was more than ready to complete her journey to her husband's home.

Emma knew Helena's City Drug Store was bigger than the one at Deer Lodge, and she looked forward to seeing her new quarters, and getting to know her husband's partner.

The Overland Coach left with fresh horses at eight. There was little concern about the ten miles into town, but the distance did not pass with ease. Deep snow covered the road on the east side of the pass just as it had on the west side, and progress was slow, though constant.

It was 2:45 when the coach arrived in Helena. The driver leaned over the side, and yelled at Parchen. "You want to be dropped off at the drug store?" He knew Emma did not find walking pleasant, and they weren't on schedule anyway.

"I would appreciate it," Henry shouted back.

"In the front?" Johnny called.

"I'd prefer the alley."

Within minutes they stopped behind the drug store. Johnny unloaded the Parchen luggage as Henry helped his wife out.

"How about if I take the trunk on up for you," Johnny offered as Emma tested her foot.

"It's the first door on the left," Henry instructed. He followed the man up with their boxes.

Emma carefully began to walk, impatient to see her new home. The stairs proved to be the largest obstacle. The leather of her boot folded into her bruise with the rise of each step.

"Thank you," Henry responded as the two re-appeared in the hall.

"Don't mention it," Johnny replied as he headed back down. He slowed as he passed Emma. "I hope your ankle feels better soon."

"Thank you," she stated quietly. Emma finished the climb, and entered Henry's rooms.

"We are home at last," Henry commented as he turned to lay a fire in the wood stove.

Emma surveyed the barren room. The ceiling was high with plenty of light from the several windows, but no wallpaper graced the rough plaster walls, no paint cheered the raw wood casings, no varnish shone from the plank floor. It was just a warehouse with a single table, two straight chairs, an ice box, and… Emma looked at the stack of crates dividing off one end of the room. Behind them she could just make out the bed.

She turned to her new husband in shock. Wallpaper, paint, and varnish were things he carried in the store. He could have them for a fraction of the price anyone else could.

"I apologize for the dust," Henry continued now as he finished with the wood stove. "It tends to gather when you are gone a few days."

Emma looked around her again. She saw no dust, no dirt, just nothingness.

"I don't generally spend much time up here," Henry added. "I would show you the store, but…" His eyes dropped to her sore ankle. He hastily grabbed a wood chair and offered it to her.

Emma declined, taking a step as she winced from the pain. She felt trapped and confused as if she had somehow made a terrible mistake. Where was the evidence she had married well? Where was this fine man she had bragged about to her aunt? A proper wedding trip, seeing the sights! This man did not know the first thing about wealth.

"Emma, what's wrong?" Henry now pleaded as her silent eyes worried him. "I know the place isn't much. I told you I hadn't secured a house yet."

"I thought I had married well," she noted aloud.

"You married me for my money?" he retorted.

Her eyes swung to him. "I married you for love, but I thought you at least had comfortable rooms. You didn't tell me you lived in a warehouse."

"So we live in a warehouse," he responded quietly, "it saves money so we can get ahead. How else do you think I was able to open the Deer Lodge store?"

"I thought your business was profitable," she answered.

"It is, but only because I watch every penny."

"Obviously," Emma agreed as her eyes again swung over the bareness of the room, "but you surely don't entertain Governor Potts here."

"I don't entertain at all. It costs too much money," Henry Parchen replied.

Emma turned, looking behind her at the make-shift bedroom. She did not know where to go or what to do. The fact frustrated her. It made her feel helpless.

"Why don't you go and change out of those boots," Henry now encouraged. "Johnny put your trunk in the bedroom."

Emma's eyes swung momentarily back to her new husband as she marveled at the use of such a term for the crate partitioned space. Then she obediently headed for the bed. The room was already growing warmer as she took off her cloak, and then her boots.

Henry left their warehouse apartment without a word, and Emma did not know if she cared. In her stocking feet she went over and opened her trunk, pilfering through until she found her summer shoes. These at least would allow her to walk without pain.

Emma wandered back out to the table, wondering what to do. She opened the ice box. It was empty. She wandered over to the window, looking out across the alley and the back areas of the city. This was not a view to invite her friends to see. It was embarrassing.

So maybe the luck of her family had not changed, Emma decided with chagrin. Her mother had often told her of the hardships she had endured, that her grandparents had endured when they came to this country. Money was always at the root of their problems, or rather the lack of it -- that was why they had stayed in St. Louis with all its endless epidemics. Her father was after all a doctor. The fact that her mother had lost more infant children than had lived, the fact that her father, the doctor, had also died in St. Louis, well, her brother was right to bring them to Montana. So he hadn't found any gold! At least he had gotten them out of that nest of contagion.

Emma looked around the empty room again. She now lived in a warehouse, so what! It saved money, and by the looks of things they did not have much to spare. Still, the reality of everything was a bit of a shock. Emma felt emotion rise within her breast. She thought she had married well, just like her grandmother had thought…and her grandparents had left France, enduring all kinds of trials and hardships. Maybe it was just their family's lot in life.

Emma's thoughts lingered on her mother. She had endured so much – the aftermath of the French Revolution, crossing the ocean, sub-standard housing, and the illness and death of so many she loved. In contrast, what was this bare room to endure? It was warm and dry.

Tears rose in Emma's eyes. She knew she was being selfish. Henry Parchen was a fine man, a careful man, a smart man. If he lived in a warehouse, then it was with good reason.

Tears spilled over her lashes as sobs broke from within. Emma's hopes for a comfortable life lay shattered before her. She had not married well. She had just married, that was all. Now all the hardships of life lay before her, all the hardships her mother had already endured, and she honestly did not know if she was up to.

Yet at least they were in Montana where everything was fresh and new, and where it was said the cold winters killed many of the germs that caused disease. Malaria wasn't even a threat here -- just freezing to death. The breath choked within her as Emma retreated to the crate room. She couldn't hold back her emotion any longer as she fell onto the bed. Time lost meaning as wretched sobs broke from her heart.

Henry Parchen entered their rooms quietly. In his arms were the makings of a fine dinner, but his attention was on the mournful sobs coming from the bedroom. He crossed silently to where he could observe his young wife. She did not know he was there. She was too distraught.

Henry considered going to Emma, but he did not know what to say or what to do. He had never spent much time with women, and frankly they had a way of mystifying him with all their carrying on. Still, he had never intended for Emma to feel this way, this despondent. He loved her. It hurt to think he might be responsible for this outbreak of tears. What had he done?

After several minutes passed, Emma quieted. But she did not get up, she continued to lie on the bed. Henry turned quietly away, and headed to the table.

In deep thought Henry unwrapped the thick steaks he had bought. He placed them in his new, big frying pan, and put it on the pot bellied stove. Then he prepared the roasting potatoes, and placed them on his special fitted racks inside the fire chamber. Now he turned to the table cloth he had borrowed from his partner's wife, and spread it neatly across the table. On this he set the fine French wine he had saved for the occasion, and got out the dishes.

Chapter Three

"Emma, are you hungry?" Henry asked quietly as he sat down on the bed beside her. A dinner plate rested in his hand.

His young wife rolled toward him, her head groggy with the deep sleep she had fallen into. Her eyes lifted momentarily to Henry, and then dropped to the supper he held in his hand. The food was neatly placed on the plate, a slice of fried onion setting on the steak, a baked potato resting on the other side, sliced and dripping with butter.

"I thought you would want it before it got cold," Henry offered quietly.

"What about you?" Emma asked.

"Mine is out on the table."

"Then let me join you," Emma responded as she got up. She followed her husband from the crate room. Henry set the plate of food down, and helped his wife with her chair. Then he poured the wine.

Emma watched all in silence. Her husband's thoughtfulness touched her. This was the man she had fallen in love with.

Henry sat down. They took a moment to give thanks, and then in silence began to eat. Henry said nothing, his eyes lifting to observe his young wife from time to time.

"I didn't realize you were fixing dinner," Emma commented finally. "I should have done it for you."

"You were sleeping," Henry replied simply.

Several moments elapsed.

"I would like to see your store," Emma began again. She took a sip of wine.

"I would like to show it to you," Henry responded.

"Maybe after supper?" Emma asked.

"We'll wait until the store closes for the night," Henry answered.

"What time is it?"

"Nearly six," he replied.

They finished their meal in near silence.

Emma took the last of her wine, pausing as she noted its amazing palate. Her eyes lifted to her husband. "This is good."

He smiled softly.

Emma's brow furrowed. How could a man who lived in a warehouse without a trace of decor, know a decent wine, let alone a good one?

"What's the matter?" Henry asked.

"The wine, it's really good."

"I've been saving it for you," he responded.

"For me?"

"I know your family is from France. It doesn't take a genius to guess you would appreciate a fine wine."

"But my brother is always complaining he can't find anything better than rot-gut."

"Harry doesn't deal with the wine merchants," her husband replied.

Emma stared at him. "You do?"

"Regularly." He paused. "Listen Emma, I'm sorry I've made you so miserable. I thought you understood about not having a house yet, and I never dreamed the trip back would be so prolonged, or that you would try to walk on downhill ice… I'm really sorry."

Emma's eyes watered despite her attempt at self-control. "I'm sorry too. I don't mean to be such a baby. The rooms here are fine. I just didn't expect…" Her voice fell off.

Henry looked away, again at a loss. Then he turned back. "I will look for a house on Monday, all right?"

"There's no rush," Emma responded quietly. "There is nothing wrong with these rooms."

"They are too plain," Henry decided gruffly. "I didn't realize how plain they really are. I guess I just never noticed."

"They are fine. Don't do anything rash," Emma replied. "Please Henry, they are fine."

His eyes settled on her. He loved Emma, now as much for her fortitude as for her beauty. He knew she was unhappy, but she was trying hard not to let it show. But her sorrow tore at him. He would gladly go out and find a house, anything to make her happy. But he also knew that to get ahead, they had to be frugal. He just hadn't realized how hard frugality rested on his new bride.

"Things mean a lot to you, don't they," he commented softly.

Emma looked down into her lap. "I suppose they do," she answered quietly. "I never thought they did, but then I have never been without at least a few."

"You are not without them now," her husband responded. "You just haven't unpacked them yet."

Emma looked up. "That's not what I meant. The walls haven't any paper or paint or anything. You don't even have curtains on the windows."

"Never thought I needed any," Henry retorted. "I dress behind the crates."

Emma's jaw quivered. "I want curtains."

"All right," Henry agreed, "that can be your wedding gift."

Emma stared at him. She had always imagined receiving something fine, something beautiful, something expensive – not something household, not from her husband.

"You don't want curtains?" he asked as her expression puzzled him.

"I want curtains," she repeated.

Henry pulled out his pocket watch. "Everyone has probably gone by now. Would you like to go downstairs and pick them out?"

"You have curtains? City Drug in Deer Lodge doesn't."

"We are bigger here, and occasionally we have a demand for them." Henry smiled. "It is usually women who want curtains." He rose from his chair.

Emma followed her new husband downstairs, glad that her summer shoes allowed her to descend without pain. He opened a door, and lit a lamp. This he carried with them as he led her to the shelves housing ready-made curtains.

"I don't know what size we need," Emma commented.

"The largest we carry," Henry responded. "I had to replace a glass in a sash once. It took me a year to get in a piece big enough."

"What did you do in between?"

"Used a board," he answered as he turned to smile at her. "You would have loved it."

"I doubt it," she replied.

Henry forced another smile. "It looks like we have enough white ones...or did you want rose?"

"White, then I can dye them whatever color we want," she answered.

"We want?" he questioned with a small grin. He picked out the appropriate number of rods and hardware. These he took over to the counter, and began to tally them up.

"We have to pay for them?" Emma cried.

"Of course. Did you think they grew on trees?" he replied.

"No," she answered as she laid the curtains next to the rods. "Does paint cost very much?"

He turned. "What do you want to paint?"

"The walls, the woodwork, the floor," she responded. "Nothing is finished upstairs."

"And that is the way it's going to stay," Henry Parchen retorted. "If we spend all our money on that room, we won't ever get that house you want."

Emma fell silent, waiting while her husband finished his tally.

"The curtains are something we can use when we get a house," Henry explained as he now handed her the fabric and picked up the brass rods. "Did you want to look around any before we go back upstairs?"

"No, I'll just find something else I want," Emma replied.

Henry noted her comment, and led the way to the stairs. He spent the next two hours putting up the rods, and helping Emma hang the freshly ironed curtains she was working on by the light of the single kerosene lamp. Then he blew it out, and they went to bed.

It was late the following morning when Emma woke. Henry did not lie beside her. He had not touched her all night. She rose from bed, slipping on a wrap over her nightgown. She wandered out to the table. Henry was not present. She didn't know where he was.

Emma glanced at her new curtains. They helped the room feel a little better, but it still felt empty. She noticed a sack of rolls on the table. This evidently was breakfast. She helped herself to one as she turned to the pot bellied stove, and decided to add another chunk of wood. Where was Henry, she wondered.

Finishing the roll in the crate room, she dressed. Then she went in search of her husband. She found him downstairs in the back, stirring a mixture of strange smelling liquids in a huge barrel. She watched him unobserved for several minutes, noting his trim physic, his masculine strength. But this morning he had a distant air about him, a preoccupation.

"What are you doing, Henry?" she asked finally.

He started violently as he spun to face her. "Working," was his automatic reply. "We have an order of varnish to get out. I didn't think our trip would take so long."

"Who is building this time of year?" Emma asked.

"Actually, the carpenters are working on the inside of a bank. They are putting in some beautiful paneled walls and casing."

"Can I help?"

"No, Emma, not with this. The varnish drips and splatters."

"Is this the only thing you have to do?" she asked.

"No, it's not," her husband answered. "I was away longer than I expected."

"Then let me help with something," she offered.

"There is a can of complexion powder on the shelf behind you," Henry instructed after a moment of thought.

Emma turned.

"Yes, that one. If you take it out front, you'll find small, flat boxes on the counter. Fill them from the can, and then weigh them on the scale. There should be a few boxes of powder left in the lady's beauty section so you can see how to do everything. The woodcut for printing the label should be with the office supplies below the counter."

Emma took her can of facial powder out to the front of the store where she found the numerous, little boxes. Then searching the beauty section, she found her example and retreated to the counter to work.

A rattle occurred at the front door, and within moments a man entered. "You must be Emma," he greeted.

"Yes," she responded hesitantly.

"I'm Wood Paynter, Henry's partner."

"Oh yes, it is nice to meet you," Emma replied as she held out her hand.

Woodman Paynter took it momentarily.

"How is your wife?" Emma asked now. "I understand she just had a baby."

"Yes, yes, we have a new daughter," Wood responded with a smile. "She is eleven days old today."

"Oh how wondrous," Emma replied. "Both baby and mother are feeling fine?"

"Yes," he agreed as he noted Emma's task. "You have been married barely four days, and Henry already has you hard at work?"

"He said he was behind, that our trip home took longer than he had anticipated," Emma explained.

Wood reached under the counter, and retrieved the woodcut and ink pad for Emma. "Henry always says he's behind on his work. You'll get used to it. The fact is, he is one of those people who doesn't know when to quit. If there is money to be made or people to please, Henry is there. It doesn't matter what time of the day or night it is." He paused. "How do you like your rooms?"

Emma glanced momentarily to the back of the store before she answered. "They're a bit sparse," she answered quietly.

Wood Paynter smiled. "Jennie and I told him to rent a little house. We told him his quarters upstairs weren't fit to bring a bride home to, but he wouldn't listen."

Wood opened the ink pad, and wet the woodcut as he showed Emma how to place the design on top of the box. Then he took a pen, dipped it in ink, and labeled the contents and the price. Emma picked up the wooden block to do the next one.

"Henry says he lives upstairs," Wood Paynter continued, "so that in case of an emergency during the night, people can find him and get what they need. Frankly, I'll be amazed if you ever get him out of this building."

Emma looked up from her work. This was not what she wanted to hear. "He won't let me paint upstairs. He says we're going to find a house."

"Paint? Of course he won't let you paint. It costs money. As far as finding a house, I'll believe it when I see it." Then he smiled. "But then Henry is in love, and that could make all the difference. He seems to listen to you and your brother more than me, so who knows. I think I'll go back and find that husband of yours."

Emma printed all the empty boxes, and reached for the pen as her eyes periodically wandered after Wood Paynter. She could hear his voice mingled with her husband's. Henry was evidently catching up on the news he had missed during his absence.

Her conversation with Wood bothered her. It was not what she was used to hearing from her brother and the Deer Lodge City store. There was discontent here, discontent between partners. Yet she knew Paynter had already been Henry's partner longer than anyone.

Emma opened her tin of complexion powder, and began filling the boxes. Within the hour Wood Paynter left, and Henry appeared with Emma's next task.

Monday morning, Emma again woke to find herself alone in bed. She got up, ate the breakfast roll Henry had again provided along with a cup of coffee from the stove, and dressed. But before she headed downstairs, she turned her attention to their rooms. The curtains were a start, but only a start. She knew her mother had several rolled up paintings of her grandfather's. The next time she saw her, Emma would ask if she could have one or two for the walls. It was time Henry Parchen got used to living with a little class.

Emma picked up her sweater, and headed down to work. She was introduced to William Eichler, their apothecary, and then returned to stocking the shelves, supplying them with items she packaged from the store's bulk goods in back. The following day she turned to cleaning -- washing the glass, dusting the merchandise, and oiling the woodwork to make the store sparkle with cleanliness. Her meticulous husband readily approved.

It was mid afternoon when a nicely dressed woman of about forty entered the drug store. Henry immediately approached her.

"Mrs. Chumasero, it's good to see you."

"Mr. Parchen, hello," the woman responded.

"Is there something I can help you find?" Henry inquired politely.

"Oh no, I just came in to pick up a pair of shoe laces for my husband, and I know where you keep them," she replied pleasantly. "But I understand, Mr. Parchen, congratulations are in order."

Henry smiled warmly. "Yes, I was married last week."

"So when do we get to meet the young lady?" Mrs. Chumasero asked.

"Right now, if you wish," Henry decided. He turned, and called his wife's name.

Emma stopped what she was doing, and joined her husband.

"Emma, I would like to introduce Mrs. Chumasero. Mrs. Chumasero, my wife Emma."

"Oh my dear, you are a lovely thing," Mrs. Chumasero gushed. "Your husband was indeed lucky to find such a jewel. How do you like Helena? You are from Deer Lodge City, aren't you?"

"Yes, I am," Emma responded.

Henry's attention diverted to a new customer who had entered the store. Wood Paynter had disappeared momentarily into the back, and Henry excused himself.

"Will you be working in the store here, alongside your husband?" Mrs. Chumasero asked.

"Yes."

"And I understand your father was a doctor," Mrs. Chumasero continued.

Emma's attention settled squarely on the woman now. "How do you know that?"

"Oh I must have overheard someone talking," Mrs. Chumasero replied. "Is it true?"

"Yes," Emma answered.

"Then you know a little bit about pharmaceuticals," Mrs. Chumasero concluded.

"A little," Emma agreed.

"Oh good," Mrs. Chumasero responded with relief. "You see I have this little problem, but I didn't want to trouble your apothecary about it."

"What kind of problem," Emma asked politely.

"Oh, nothing big. I've just been a little irregular since my daughter was married, and I wondered if there was something I could take for it."

"Just eat some extra fruit," Emma replied.

"Oh no, dear," Mrs. Chumasero laughed. "I'm not irregular like that. It's a woman kind of thing. You know."

"Oh. ...oh," Emma responded as she suddenly understood. "Yes, I do think we have something." Emma left the company of her companion, retreating to the tonic and herb section where she had been cleaning. Scouring the shelves, she finally spotted a few small bottles randomly mixed with others on the upper shelf. She seized one, and returned to Mrs. Chumasero.

"Just follow the directions," she advised, "and in a month or so, you should be right back on schedule."

"Oh thank you, I am so relieved," Mrs. Chumasero responded. "Can I pay you for this?"

"Yes, of course," Emma replied as the two women walked over to the counter.

Mrs. Chumasero noticed the displayed Valentine candy, and picked out three, medium sized boxes, adding them to her purchases. "For my daughters," she commented. She tucked away her change and the small bottle of tonic in her bag.

Henry joined his wife at the counter with another customer. Emma returned to her task. Five minutes later, Henry appeared at her elbow.

"Did Mrs. Chumasero find her shoe laces all right?"

"Shoe laces?" Emma replied. "She didn't say anything about shoe laces."

"She only bought candy?"

"And some herbal drops," she answered.

"Herbal drops?" he repeated. "Did she talk to Eichler about them?"

"William? No, Henry, she didn't."

"Why not?" he responded.

"There is such a thing as modesty, you know." Emma smiled softly.

"But we're professional here. We deal with all health issues the same," Henry objected. "She should have talked to Eichler."

"But she didn't want to," she replied. "Would you want to ask a woman about a problem with your genitals?"

"Oh." Henry stared at his wife momentarily. Her frankness on the subject was surprising, even intriguing. It was almost like the morning after they were married when she had purposely exposed her nudity to him. "It wasn't anything serious, was it?" Henry asked as he returned his thoughts to Mrs. Chumasero. "We have to be careful about promising too much when people should see a doctor."

"No, it wasn't anything serious," Emma replied. "Mother has the same problem occasionally. That's when she asks Harry to bring home a little bottle of something. She won't even go into your drug store for it."

"Well at least Mrs. Chumasero got what she needed," Henry decided. "Her husband is a judge in town, and we definitely want to keep that lady happy. It's good for business."

"Henry," Wood Paynter interrupted as he joined them, "I got the rest of the candy unpacked. I have the Valentine boxes stacked just inside the back partition so they'll be handy. The crates I stacked by the back entrance. We're getting too many. We will have to make a trip to the garbage dump soon."

"Crates," Emma responded, "how big are they?"

"About two feet by two feet," Wood answered. "Why?"

"Are they sturdy?" she asked.

"You could stand on them," Wood replied.

"I can use about three," she decided.

"For what?" Henry cried.

"Upstairs," she answered.

"Don't you have enough crates upstairs," Wood retorted in disbelief.

Emma smiled. "This is for something besides Henry's wall." She turned to her husband. "May I have them?"

"Yes," he answered, but the look in his face held reservation. He turned to Wood. "Why don't you take three nice ones up for her. It will get them out of our way."

Paynter shrugged in agreement, and disappeared as Henry now turned back to his wife. "What are you going to use them for?"

"A divan, up against the wall," she answered. "I'll cover them with the quilt Mrs. Wilcox gave us for our wedding, and then I'll have some place to put my feet up and read."

"What's wrong with reading at the table?" Henry asked. "I do it all the time."

"Oh Henry, don't be so boring," Emma responded with a smile. "A person can't be straight laced all the time. It stifles the spirit." With that, Emma returned to her cleaning.

Henry stared after her. There were times he really didn't understand his young wife. She seemed to hate their crate partition upstairs, and yet here she was claiming more wood boxes. She seemed so contradictory. Yet he loved the way she smiled, her energy, her enthusiasm. If a few crates would buy back some of that, some of the spirit she had lost since she came to Helena, then he would give her all the crates she wanted. Besides, they didn't cost him anything.

That evening, Emma tied the crates together, securing sisal packing for cushioning over the top surface and any rough spots. Then she spread Mrs. Wilcox's quilt over it, and shoved the whole thing against the wall. "That will do," she exclaimed triumphantly as she tried it out. She reached for the book she had brought upstairs with her.

"What are you reading?" Henry asked from the table where he worked on the store accounts.

"Culpepper's Herbal Physician," she answered carelessly. "I found it stashed under the counter. It was kind of dusty."

Henry turned in his seat. "That was Dr. Wernigk's. I can't believe the book survived the fire three years ago. With everything I lost, that survived? Amazing!"

"Who was Dr. Wernigk?" Emma asked.

"He and Louis Keysser were my partners when I first came to Helena. We opened up a drug and grocery store, but it wasn't working. I ended up buying out their shares, and closing down the grocery. It was loosing too much money."

"This isn't working either," Emma decided. "I need another crate, maybe two. I have to have some place to put a lamp so I can get enough light to read by."

"Why don't you come over here and share mine. There's no use burning up kerosene in two lamps," Henry noted.

Emma scowled at her husband, but he didn't notice. He had already returned his attention to his accounts. Still, Henry was right. Kerosene did cost money. She rose to her feet, and joined him at the table.

Wednesday morning Emma found a small gift resting beside her breakfast roll. She picked it up, musing over it as she poured herself a cup of coffee. It was Valentine's Day, and the one week anniversary of their marriage. She set the package back down on the table, and turned to breakfast. Henry had not forgotten Valentine's Day. It would be pretty hard to with the increased candy sales downstairs. But her present was not candy, or at least it did not appear to be from the shape and size of the box, it was too small.

Emma thought about it as she ate. Then as she finished her meal, she reached for the gift and unwrapped it. Inside was an ivory comb to ornament her hair. She picked it up appreciatively, noting the intricate lace carving on the end. It was beautiful. She instantly stuck it in her hair, and rushed over to Henry's shaving stand to take a look in the mirror. It definitely complimented her looks. A large smile rose to her lips, and she turned to go downstairs. Henry had more taste than he liked to let on about.

Emma found her husband in the back sorting miscellaneous merchandise between several crates. She reached over and gave him a quick kiss on the cheek. "Thank you for the gift," she stated.

"Oh you found it," he responded with a smile.

"Yes, and it's beautiful," she replied as she put on her store apron.

"Well it's just a little something to let you know how much I enjoy having my valentine here."

Emma stopped. Her husband's love was real. It was touching. "I love you too," she stammered.

"It should be a busy day," Henry continued as he abruptly changed the subject.

Chapter Four

Henry Parchen was right about Valentine's day. Customers streamed into the store in twice the volume of a normally good day. The boxes of candy disappeared one after another as men came in looking for something to take home to their sweethearts. Women came as well, buying treats for their children along with their more practical items. Henry and Wood were constantly with customers.

"Ma'am, excuse me, but could you help an old man?"

Emma climbed down off her step stool.

"Ma'am, I've got this problem," the fellow explained as he showed her his dirty bandage. "The cable snapped down at the mine last week. It was hot from friction, and I got a nasty burn that just doesn't want to heal. Do you have something strong?"

"Have you talked to our apothecary?" Emma asked.

The older man glanced toward the pharmaceutical counter. "I would rather talk to you."

"If you will come over here," Emma responded politely as she recoiled from the man's smell, "I will show you our burn ointment."

"No, I have tried your salve already. It don't do no good. Haven't you got something else?"

Emma picked up the ointment, and read its label. "What seems to be the trouble?" she asked as she mentally noted its contents.

"It just don't do no good," he repeated. "I could describe things, but you's a lady, and I really don't think you would appreciate hearing the details."

"Nothing has turned black, has it?" Emma asked.

"No, but it don't smell so good," the man replied.

"First, you have to clean it thoroughly, no matter how it hurts," Emma instructed. "You have to get rid of anything that stinks."

"All right," he responded slowly.

"Then…" Her voice fell off as she scoured the shelves for what she was looking for. "Hmm," she decided, "let me look over here."

Emma retreated to the tonic and tincture aisle, and picked out two bottles. The injured man followed her.

"Okay," she noted as she turned to her customer, "when you have your wound good and clean. Take this comfrey tincture and mix four to six drops with some soft butter. Spread this over your burn twice a day. Then take this tonic," she continued as she held up the second bottle. "A teaspoon in a glass of water, three times a day. If your burn does not look better in a day or two, you had better find yourself a doctor. You don't want it to go bad."

"Thank you, ma'am," the man responded.

Emma handed him a roll of new bandaging from a nearby shelf. "And keep a clean dressing on it."

"Yes um," he acquiesced. He took the items to the cash register where he waited in line.

Emma turned to find a woman asking for a pair of scissors.

By six o'clock the number of customers had not diminished. But just as soon as the lines at the cash register cleared, Wood Paynter removed his store apron and got ready to leave.

Emma watched her husband's jaw clench in reaction, but he said nothing. Wood smiled as he walked out past her, a box of Valentine candy tucked under his arm.

"Don't work too late," he whispered. "It is Valentine's."

"Do you and your wife have something special planned?" Emma asked.

"I'm spending a quiet dinner with my family," he responded. "Jennie's been working all week on the cutest little Valentine dress for our new daughter. I've got to run."

Emma glanced at her husband. He and William Eichler were both waiting on customers as Wood's comments came back to mind. Was it true that nothing would pry Henry loose when there was money to be made and people to serve? It definitely appeared that way. Yet a new house was going to cost some substantial money, and maybe he was just working all these long hours to help achieve the goal.

Emma went back to work.

It was six forty-five when the store finally cleared of people. Henry locked the front door behind Eichler, and pulled down the window shade. He paused on his way past her.

"It will take me about twenty minutes to count the cash and do the tallies."

"Can I help," she offered.

"Well you could count the money," he decided.

Emma followed him to the counter, and pulled out the cash drawer. By seven they had finished and were heading up the back steps.

"We'll grab our wraps and go over to the International Hotel for a bite to eat, all right?" Henry proposed now.

Emma turned. "Really?"

"We had a good day, and a long one. We'll let someone else do the cooking tonight." Henry put his arm around his wife. "It is really good having you here," he whispered in her ear.

Emma woke with a light heart Thursday morning. She felt good as she rose from bed, a smile lingering on her lips. Dinner at the International Hotel had provided something she had sorely missed from the days of her courtship to Henry Parchen. It had provided an opportunity to talk the way they used to. For a few brief hours they had shared their hopes and dreams apart from the everyday demands of life, apart from the everyday realities.

Emma's heart soared. She had not made a mistake marrying Henry Parchen. She knew that now. She knew that what he had or didn't have was not for his lack of trying, or his lack of business sense. The fire three years before had destroyed much of Helena, including their City Drug Store. It had hit her husband hard, and he was just now starting to see daylight again. The financial blow was something he would never forget, and it made him cautious and fearful lest it should happen again. It was this fear that made him work the extra hours. He had three hard years of progress to make up for, and if another inferno should ever strike, he never wanted to find himself in such hard striates again.

As money allowed, Henry was taking measures to protect what he had. This is why he had instructed Emma's bother to go ahead with his idea of building a fireproof building behind the Deer Lodge City drug store. There they could keep their explosive paint materials, and the back stock of their particularly costly merchandise. Wood Paynter had opposed the idea. He was more interested in investing in things that were not threatened by fire, like mineral rights. But Henry Parchen had seen the wisdom of Harry's idea, and had instructed Emma's brother to go ahead with the project, taking financial responsibility. The brick warehouse was constructed the previous summer, and Henry was constantly considering how to go about protecting his Helena interests as well.

Emma dismissed her dreams of a house. Unlike the impression Wood Paynter had given her, Henry wanted a residence as much, if not more than she did. He had a particular pride in having a family and all its amenities, but experience had taught him the hard lesson of reality, and he would never forget it.

Emma headed downstairs. She found Henry in the back near his desk. He was reaching above his head for an account book in the shelves. Emma glanced quickly around for Paynter and Eichler, but they were nowhere to be seen. She crept up behind her husband, sliding her hands into his apron pockets and pulling herself snugly against him. "I enjoyed last night," Emma commented softly over his shoulder.

"Me too," Henry responded as he now forgot the account book, and twisted until he held his beautiful, young wife in his arms. He kissed her briefly, and then his eyes looked beyond, searching for the others. "We had better stick to work down here."

"As long as you promise that later we will have more of last night," Emma demanded with a grin.

"I promise," Henry replied as his face brightened.

"All right then, I will get to work. I should be through with spring cleaning by tomorrow at quitting." With this Emma waltzed away, spotting Wood Paynter sweeping the front sidewalk as she put on her apron and picked up the furniture oil. She now headed for the office supplies.

Emma finished the store's spring cleaning the following day, and Henry gave her Saturday off to catch up on their laundry and to pick up a few groceries. But this was not all Emma concentrated on. She had now resigned herself to living in the warehouse space, and pinching every penny she could lay her hands on, but her instincts for feathering their nest would not be denied. With their few wedding presents unpacked, she endeavored to decorate their home as best she could, utilizing crates and boxes and anything that would transform the dire empty space into one that suggested ease and comfort. By six that evening, the laundry was done, the groceries purchased, and the room transformed into the product of her energies. When Henry walked through the door that evening, dinner was ready and waiting, candles lit, kerosene saved, and Emma appeared in Henry's favorite dress. His mouth dropped open in surprise.

"Where did all this come from," he gasped as the door fell shut, and his young wife nestled into his arms.

"Mostly from the garbage pile," she answered as she laid her head proudly against his chest.

"You didn't spend any money?" he exclaimed.

"Just for the groceries," she replied. "I have twenty-three cents left."

Henry pulled physically away from her. "This didn't cost anything?"

"No. The new things are our wedding gifts, remember?"

"Ah, yes of course," he responded as he stepped away, surveying the room in its entirety.

Then suddenly a smile broke across Henry's face, and he laughed as he caught up his young wife, sweeping her back into his arms, kissing her passionately. "If you can do this much with nothing," he commented joyously, "just think what we can accomplish! We're going to be rich."

Emma made no reply. Her husband's praise was all she needed. They were going to be rich. One day they would have money – enough for a house, a wedding trip, children...maybe even a big house. Her thoughts were far from organized now as her husband became increasingly passionate.

Suddenly Emma remembered their supper. "Henry… Henry, what about dinner?"

"We'll move it to the floor and have a picnic," he decided with a grin. "It smells good, too good to eat straight and formal-like when we can share it with a whole lot more fun."

Sunday morning Emma did not wake to find herself alone in bed. Her husband was nestled up close to her, and she could feel his body rise and fall with each breath. She rolled over so she could look at him, and suddenly his eyes were open as a smile grew on his lips.

"Good morning," he stated quietly.

"Morning," she replied.

His forefinger rose to trace the lines of her face. "I thought maybe sometime today we might go for a walk. I want to show you the property Wood and I own in partnership. I'm thinking of buying him out. We initially bought the lot with thoughts of another store or warehouse, but it looks like the new commercial buildings are going in on the north side of Broadway if they go in at all. But it would be a nice corner to build a house."

"I would like to see it," Emma responded.

Henry's words were followed by a kiss, and the two lost themselves in the warm passion of the bedcovers. This morning there were no demands from the store, and church wasn't until eleven. With the leisure of their day off, they had time to enjoy more of the intimacy they were discovering in each other. Their passion, however, was not just physical. They shared everything …their thoughts, their dreams, their trust…as they welded their futures solidly together.

"What shall we name our first child?" Henry asked as Emma rose to dress for church.

"Henry, of course," she responded, "but you have to be a little patient, Parchen. It takes nine months for a baby, and in the mean time my belly is going to look like I swallowed a watermelon whole. It's not like I can help in the drug store then."

"No, not then," he agreed, "but we will manage." His thoughts drifted. "Maybe I should bring in some fir boughs to put under the bed."

"Fir boughs? What for," Emma retorted. "It's not Christmas."

"So we'll have a boy," Henry replied.

Emma's dressing stopped. "What?"

"Fir boughs under the bed spawn the male gender. Everyone knows that," Henry responded. "The old country Black Forest firs are best, but as long as the branches are fir, it generally works."

"Not everyone knows that, or believes it," Emma retorted.

"Prussians do," Henry replied.

"Then it's an old Prussian wives' tale," Emma scoffed as she returned to her dressing.

"No, it's true," Henry countered as he now got out of bed. "My father made sure there were fir boughs under the bed for a whole year before I was born. He didn't want to take any chances, though usually people just bring them in when the baby is about to be born."

"Well then you better hope we have a Christmas baby, because I am not Prussian, and I am not cleaning fir needles out from under the bed. It's hard enough to dust under there as it is."

The conversation digressed into general teasing as Henry and Emma ate a quick breakfast, and headed downstairs to church. Henry held the back door open for his wife as she spotted an envelope lying on the floor. She picked it up on the way out.

"What's this?" she asked. "It's addressed to you."

"Who's it from?" Henry inquired cheerfully. Church bells rang in the distance.

"Kleinschmidt," she answered. "Doesn't he own the grocery in Deer Lodge City?"

"Yes, it's a branch of his business here. Open the envelope. It's probably notice of some businessmen's meeting," he replied.

Emma's pace slowed as she took out the message.

"Don't slow down," Henry complained. "If we get to church early enough, I can show you that property before services. It's only a block or so farther."

"No, not today," Emma responded quietly as she came to a stop.

"Why not," Henry demanded.

Emma looked up. "There's been a fire."

"A fire? Where?" her husband cried as his throat went suddenly dry.

"Deer Lodge City," she replied quietly, and handed over the message.

Henry Parchen's face paled as he quickly read the note. Kleinshcmidt had received a brief telegram early that morning, and had passed on what information he had. Both men had stores in Deer Lodge.

"Kleinschmidt is taking a wagon of supplies out at eleven," Henry noted. "That's twenty minutes from now. I'd better talk to him."

"What about Wood Paynter?" Emma asked.

"He should be told," Henry decided as he handed back the message. Parchen bent over the dust of the street and drew a quick map. "He lives here," Henry pointed.

"I'll try to catch him before he leaves for church," Emma immediately declared. "You go catch Kleinschmidt." Emma again mentally noted the map, and set off at a hurried walk. Ten minutes later she climbed the steps to the front porch of Paynter's house, and knocked on the door. Jennie Paynter answered.

"Mrs. Paynter?" Emma asked.

"Yes," Jennie replied hesitantly. The two women had never met.

"I'm Emma Parchen," Emma responded. "I need to see your husband right away. It's important."

"Who is it, dear?" Wood asked as he appeared in the front room, holding their new daughter.

"Emma Parchen," Jennie repeated. "She says it is important."

Wood Paynter joined the ladies as he handed his daughter to his wife. "Emma, what is it?"

Emma handed over Kleinschmidt's message. Wood Paynter immediately read it.

His eyes lifted. "Henry's at the store?"

"What is it, Wood?" his wife asked.

"Deer Lodge City," he answered, "it's burning."

"A fire? Jennie Paynter cried. "No!"

"I'm afraid so. It looks like our interests there are probably ashes by now."

"Henry should be with the Kleinscmidts. They have a wagon heading out at eleven," Emma offered.

Wood's eyes flashed instantly to her. "I have to talk to him." He grabbed his coat off the wall hook, and rushed out.

"Would you like to come in, Emma," Jennie invited now awkwardly. "I was hoping we would get a chance to meet. I just didn't expect these circumstances."

"It is nice to meet you at last," Emma responded, "but with Deer Lodge City in flames… I have family there."

"Oh, of course," Jennie replied. "How stupid of me! Perhaps another time."

"Perhaps," Emma agreed with a gracious smile. "Thank you." With that she turned and left.

Emma's mind was on Deer Lodge City as she walked home. Kleinschmidt had said the fire apparently started in the livery stable next door to City Drug. Had her brother Harry's fireproof building saved at least part of the store, she wondered. Was Harry all right? Why hadn't he sent a telegram? Had the telegraph office gone up in flames too?

Questions upon questions rose in Emma's mind as she hurried on. She knew the Kleinschmidt grocery in Deer Lodge was just down a few buildings from City Drug. Was it in flames? Was her husband still with Kleinschmidt now? Emma let herself into the store, finding another envelope slid under the door.

She opened it, and found a brief telegram from her brother. He was safe. The message stated the facts briefly, and requested a list of supplies be sent immediately.

Emma breathed a huge sigh of relief. The inferno holocaust had not taken lives, only one block of town. She set to work immediately gathering the needed supplies as she heard a wagon pull up behind the store. Within minutes her husband entered with Wood Paynter, their voices carrying loudly to the front of the store.

"You leave my share of goods here," Wood Paynter instructed. "I am through with Deer Lodge. I never wanted a store down there anyway. That was your idea. And now everything I had has gone up in smoke. I'm not putting out another penny for that store. Not a penny, do you hear! Deer Lodge has been nothing but a thorn in my side since we opened it. Enough is enough!"

"But we have insurance this time, and the fire didn't take everything," Henry Parchen objected. "We have the fire proof building."

"You and Harry D'Acheul have the fire proof building. It was your money. I have nothing, and if the insurance company comes through with anything for me, you can bet I'm not going to throw it away on Deer Lodge City again. I want my eggs in a basket I can watch, not somewhere miles away."

There was silence as Emma considered the words she heard. Her brother had requested a list of supplies. Henry would not deny him this, and she went back to work.

When her husband appeared from the rear of the store, he was alone.

"Where is Wood?" Emma asked as she got down off her ladder.

"He's gone to church to see if they have any relief goods they want to send to Deer Lodge."

Emma offered her brother's telegram.

Henry read it. When he looked up, there was relief in his face. "At least we didn't loose everything," he responded, "thanks to your brother."

"It sounds like the fire only took one block of town," Emma commented.

"Yes," Henry agreed. Then he forced a smile. "How would you like a trip back home?"

"I would love it," Emma answered. "Do you think it will take as long as when we came?"

"It could," Henry replied, "depending on the weather, but we won't be the only wagon going. The Kleinschmidts have decided to wait and go with us."

"I have most of the supplies Harry wants," Emma noted.

"Good. How much did you leave us? We won't be getting any regular shipments until late spring."

"I took about a third of the stock on hand," Emma answered.

Her husband nodded his approval. "I wish we had kept more merchandise out with the paint in Deer Lodge. Thank goodness we built that brick building."

"How soon do we leave?" Emma asked.

"We're going to try and make the pass by nightfall," Henry Parchen replied.

The journey to Deer Lodge City was not as demanding as Emma's trip to Helena. The wagons arrived the following evening as dusk settled over the town. Henry drove directly to the house as the fading light reflected off the snow.

"Emma, Henry," Jenny greeted with a shriek of joy. "Mother, they're here." The family descended on the newly married couple with hugs.

"I didn't expect you so soon," Harry D'Acheul told his boss.

"The pass was reasonably good," Henry replied without expression.

"I'm glad," Harry responded. "Come in. Come in. It's freezing out here."

Emma and Henry followed the family into the warm house.

"So tell us about the fire," Henry Parchen urged as Emma's mother offered him a cup of hot coffee. "We came directly here. We haven't seen the store."

"There isn't much to see," Jenny imparted, "except for the charred building in back you guys built last summer. Otherwise, the whole block is pretty much leveled."

"The fire started in the livery," Harry explained. "It was all locked up of course, but a couple of boards had been broken out in back. I noticed the hole about a week ago, but I was in a hurry and didn't investigate. It wasn't very big. I never dreamed anyone could crawl through."

"Anyway," Emma's brother continued, "it was about two o'clock Sunday morning when someone noticed flames popping out of the roof, and sounded the alarm. Everyone came running. But by the time we got to the fire, it was already starting to burn City Drug, and the heat was so intense we couldn't even get close. I did go around back, and I managed to get a few things out...our account books and the cash box, not much more."

"The wind was blowing so hard," Emma's mother offered, "everyone was afraid the flames would leap across the street and set the businesses there on fire too. Those that weren't hauling goods out of the buildings were on the bucket brigade, throwing water to keep the flames from spreading further. But despite the convenience of water from all the melting snow in the street, the heat was so terrible, it was like a wall keeping us from getting too close and doing the good we might have."

"And the goods in the fireproof building?" Henry Parchen asked.

"Still in the building," Emma's brother answered. "Everything seems all right. The problem is, the streets around that section of town are so bad, it's hard to get to. You see all the water churned into mud close to the fire, and then froze with all the foot prints and wagon tracks five or six inches deep. It's almost impossible to walk on. And then out farther, where the water ran over the cold ground, it froze into a sheet of ice. It's just as well you didn't try to see what's left of the store tonight. It's hard enough to manage in daylight."

"So we're not doing business?" Henry Parchen asked in quiet gravity.

"I have several pharmaceutical orders, especially from Dr. Whitford. He is interested in what medical instruments we can order too, since his office faired worse than our store. But he has a couple of patients that really need medicine, that's why I sent the telegram. You brought the digitalis?"

"Yes," Emma answered.

"Good," her brother responded in relief. "Dr. Whitford will be overjoyed." Then he changed the subject. "Why don't we get the horses and wagon into the barn for the night."

The following morning Emma accompanied her husband and brother to the remains of their store. Carefully they picked their way across the ice and frozen mud until they entered the fireproof building. The contents seemed unscathed.

"I'm certainly glad we moved what we did out here," Emma's brother commented. "I've been working on a preliminary order list. Maybe you'd like to review it."

"Yes," Henry Parchen responded as he surveyed the contents of the building. "Have you opened any of the paint? Did the heat damage it?"

"Yeah, I did. I took a small can from the shelves I figured got the hottest, and painted a sample board. It looks fine. You can see it when we go home."

Henry Parchen nodded approval. "Have you contacted the insurance company?"

"Yes, I telegraphed them first thing this morning," Harry replied. "The claims man will be out next week."

"Good." The statement was not in Henry Parchen's usual tone. It was hoarse and soft, and Harry suddenly realized how hard his boss was taking the catastrophe. Henry Parchen wandered outside without another word.

Harry turned to his sister. "We are going to rebuild, aren't we?"

Chapter Five

Emma did not answer. Her eyes were resting on the open door.

"Emma, what's going on?" Harry cried. "I understand this is a bit of a shock. It is for everyone in town. But Henry's been through this before, and we have insurance. We are going to rebuild City Drug, right?"

"I think so," Emma replied as her attention shifted momentarily to her brother. She now followed her husband outside. Henry Parchen had made his way around to where the front of the store used to be. She picked her way through the charred debris.

Henry noticed his wife's quiet approach, and smiled softly. "I never dreamed Harry's idea of the fireproof building would save us so soon."

"He is worried you aren't going to rebuild the store," Emma stated.

"Oh, we'll rebuild. One way or another," he replied. A scowl crossed his brow.

"You're worried about Wood Paynter, aren't you," Emma responded.

"Harry has made repeated innuendoes that he wants to become a partner in City Drug," her husband noted quietly. "Should I take him seriously?"

"I think so," Emma answered.

"If wishes were horses, paupers would ride," Henry quoted.

"Oh," she responded, "I see. You're wondering if Harry has any money."

"New stores cost plenty," Emma's husband replied quietly.

"My brother does go on about things," she admitted, "and he never did find any gold. But I think maybe that's why he is ready to settle down to a business, and his training in New York makes this one particularly fitting for him."

"But the money," Parchen repeated.

"Perhaps you should ask Harry if he has any," Emma suggested.

Her husband pondered her momentarily, and then turned. "Give us a few minutes, will you?" Henry Parchen walked back through the debris, and disappeared inside the brick structure.

Emma looked down the length of the leveled city block. The ground was gray with ashes. A few heavy timbers lay charred and scattered with only foundation stones and debris for company. Everything was desolation.

Across the street the paint of the buildings was blistered and discolored from the intense heat of the fire. Deer Lodge City did not look like the town she had left a few weeks before, but beyond lay the magnificent scenery of Montana, dusted in snow with Mount Powell rising just above the horizon. Fire or not, Emma was glad she had left St. Louis.

Emma walked back toward the fireproof structure that now concealed her husband and brother. A piece of metal glimmered in the sunshine as a light snow began to fall around her. She bent down and pulled up a piece of embossed tin. The ceiling tile was hardly bent. She looked around, and found a dozen more. However some were pretty badly bent, and with the ice, she could only get two or three good ones loose.

"What do you want those for?" Harry stood before her.

"I think they're pretty," Emma responded.

"Pretty well beat to pieces," her brother retorted. "Henry has asked me to buy into the new store. I need three thousand dollars. Do you think mom will loan it to me?"

Emma looked up. "I don't know. Maybe."

"I think we should build a brick store."

"Don't you know people over at the bank by now?" Emma asked.

Her brother smiled. "I do, don't I? What a good idea!" He offered his hand as the two walked back out of the debris.

"What is Henry doing?" Emma asked.

"Gathering some information he needs to fill out the insurance claims, and to settle things with Paynter." Harry smiled. "I guess Wood wants out of Deer Lodge City."

"And you want in," Emma responded as they returned to the building.

"Damn right," her brother replied. "I see how much things really cost, and it doesn't even come close to what gets pocketed around here. There's gold in Montana, but you aren't going to find it laying around in the streams and rivers any more."

Henry Parchen stood in the doorway. "Harry, we need a board walk out to the alley if we are to conduct business here. I think people can get to us then."

"It shouldn't take much to build a walk. We can go over to the mill and get the lumber right now if you want."

"After we see Emma home," Henry replied. They closed up the brick building.

"I often think how much worse the fire would have been if our paint stock had been vulnerable," Emma's brother related on the way to their mother's. "There would have been explosions, and I don't know if anyone could have gotten control of things then. People might even have been hurt."

Henry Parchen paused in his tracks as he thought about his brother-in-laws words. He knew the Helena store had no such protection of its paint stock, and he had personally seen the explosions in the '69 fire. They had been tremendous and fearful, and those on the bucket brigades had scattered like the wind.

The men left Emma at the house, and headed to the mill. Emma's mother met her at the door. "Where are they going?" Marie asked.

"To get lumber. Henry thinks with a broad walk, people can get to the store from the alley."

"It's almost lunch time," her mother noted.

"Well hopefully their stomachs will bring them back home. Shall we lay it out?" Emma offered. They headed for the kitchen. "Where is Jenny?"

"She and Mrs. Wilcox are practicing for a church function," Marie answered. She pulled the needed items from her cold box as Emma retrieved the necessary kettles.

"Emma, how do you like married life?" her mother inquired carefully.

"It's fine," her daughter replied.

"Is it what you expected?"

Emma reached behind her for a paring knife, and took up a potato to peel. "In some ways it is," she responded.

"And in others," her mother prodded.

"In others, it's not," Emma admitted. "I didn't expect the flat above the store to be so…Spartan."

"You married a Spartan man," Marie noted with an encouraging smile.

"Yes, I suppose I did in a way," Emma agreed, "but he is horribly frugal."

"That's not all bad," her mother countered kindly. "It's a shame your grandfather didn't have a little more frugality in him. The money he let me waste… I don't think he even realized what was lost."

"You mean when he sent you to sell the cows in France?" Emma asked.

"Yes, and my stupidity when it came to the pigs. If I hadn't given them so much salt they probably wouldn't have all died."

"Maybe a little Prussian frugality is a good mix with the French blood in our family," Emma decided.

"Couldn't hurt," Marie chuckled. "It wouldn't hurt if a little rubbed off on that brother of yours either," she added. "Your husband is a good influence, I think."

"He has asked Harry to buy into the store here in Deer Lodge City," Emma offered.

Her mother's face lifted. "Really. Mr. Paynter is okay with this?"

"Mr. Paynter, I think, wants to sell his share."

A smile crept into Marie's expression. "What a stroke of luck," she responded quietly. "Maybe something good is going to come out of that inferno after all." Then she turned to her daughter. "The fire about broke my heart when I realized it had taken City Drug. You with your new husband, and Harry… You just didn't need such tragedy so soon."

"God gives us the strength to survive," Emma replied as she quoted her mother's often spoken words.

Henry Parchen and Harry D'Acheul got the lumber, and built the walk to what was left of City Drug. The following day Henry and Emma returned to Helena.

For the next couple of months Emma took on more of the customer responsibility at Helena City Drug while her husband and Wood Paynter poured over the account books, talked to different banks, and basically laid out their plans for the future. Wood Paynter was only too happy to sell what was left of his share of the Deer Lodge City store to Emma's brother. With a small amount of insurance money coming to Paynter's pocket, Henry Parchen now prevailed upon their need to protect their Helena interest. Wood Paynter was reluctant, though he showed some interest in improving their location. This, Henry Parchen encouraged, knowing that they would need a new site if they were to erect a proper brick store.

"Emma, how many bottles of chasteberry tincture have you sold?" Henry Parchen asked as he looked up from his books.

"Probably a dozen or two, once I found the stock in back," she answered. She began sorting the miscellaneous items that had accumulated on the counter during the day.

"The tally says we're down nineteen bottles. Are we really that low?"

"Yes," she agreed. "I have been meaning to ask you about it, but you and Wood are always so busy."

"Nineteen bottles! A case of twenty-four usually lasts us two years or more," Henry responded.

Emma shrugged. "Women want it. It works."

"But they never asked for it before," Henry replied.

"They ask me," Emma countered with a smile. "They ask me for other things too."

"Like what?" he inquired.

"Like what is good for lung congestion, sore throats, cuts and scraps, even indigestion."

Henry focused on his wife. "And what do you tell them?"

"I recommend tinctures of hyssop and nettle for lung congestion, anise and marshmallow for sore throats, plantain and chickweed for skin abrasions, and yellow dock and dandelion for the stomach."

Henry stared at Emma. "You do?"

"Yes."

"And these people come back for more?"

"Sometimes," Emma replied as she turned back to her sorting. "We are getting low on most of them. How long do orders take?"

"A couple of months anyway," he answered, "though there's plenty of dandelion growing wild now that spring is here."

"True," Emma agreed as her task was completed.

Her husband pondered her. "You learned all this out of that book upstairs?"

"From that, and from my father. He worked with a lot of poor immigrants."

"Maybe we should start making our own preparations," Henry suggested.

"I don't know where to get many of the plants," Emma replied.

"But if we had them, you would know how to make the preparations?" her husband asked.

"Sure, tinctures are easy. All you need is drinking alcohol, plants, bottles, and a little sunshine."

"Sunshine?" Henry repeated.

Emma nodded. "Tinctures are aged in a window for two weeks."

"Two weeks, is that all?"

"Oh you have to shake them twice a day, and then strain off the plant, but all the ingredients pass to the alcohol base and are preserved."

A large smile grew on Henry's face. "No kidding?"

"No kidding," she replied. "It's not hard."

"Do you know how much we pay for tinctures?" Henry asked.

"No, are they expensive?"

"Cases of little bottles, bumped and bounced along in ox wagons across half a continent, yes they're expensive." He paused momentarily. "I think maybe we've found you a new occupation," he noted as a twinkle rose in his eye. "One you can even do when you don't want to go out in public."

"You mean when I'm expecting," Emma grinned as her husband now slipped his arms around her waist.

"Yes," he answered as he placed a soft kiss on her cheek.

Wood Paynter appeared from the back. "Made that delivery," he announced cheerfully. "The two of you make a big sale or something?" he asked as he noted their embrace.

"Emma knows how to make tinctures," Parchen offered. "It could save us a bundle."

"She won't have the time if you are planning on a family right away," Wood replied with a smile. "I wouldn't even be surprised if there isn't a little one on the way already, the way you two are."

"The way we are?" Parchen repeated as he let go of Emma. "Emma and I make far less display of ourselves than you and Jennie."

"I'm not implying anything, Parchen," Wood chuckled. "I'm just saying that everyone knows that the two of you are crazy about each other, and when that happens babies aren't far behind. That's all."

"So you aren't interested in starting a new line of business?" Henry Parchen asked.

"A new line of business?" he replied. "Heck, I just got rid of the Deer Lodge fiasco."

"But you wouldn't be adverse to buying from a new source, particularly if the product is less expensive with a higher profit line?"

"Of course not," Wood responded, "but Emma won't have the time. It won't be long, and you won't see her in here any more than you see Jennie."

On April 20th Emma's husband and brother let the contract for the rebuilding of the Deer Lodge City store. It was to be brick and fireproof; and Emma's brother was so excited, it flowed out in every letter and every telegram they received. Henry Parchen meanwhile maintained a cool reserve, calmly making the necessary decisions and reviewing the progress of the proceedings.

"You are happy about the building in Deer Lodge, aren't you?" Emma asked that evening as they finished closing up the Helena store.

"Yes."

"Then why don't you show it?" Emma demanded as she headed up the stairs with her husband.

"I used to get excited about such things," Henry noted as they entered their rooms. He shut the door. "I guess now the financial responsibility looms out at me more."

"Well, I think it's exciting," Emma declared as she spun around and landed in his arms. "A new brick building, wow."

Henry led his wife over to a box setting under the window. "I am more excited about this."

"What is it?" Emma inquired as she bent down. "Dandelion?"

"Dandelion and plantain," he confirmed as he bent beside her. "And underneath is a crate of little bottles. What kind of drinking alcohol do you need?"

"Rum or gin will do," Emma responded as she pulled off the top box, and opened the one of glass.

"Good, I think we have an extra case downstairs I can charge off to us. Do you need to make the tinctures while the greens are fresh?"

"No, I can use fresh or dried," Emma replied. "It just takes more of the fresh plants, that's all."

"If this works, Emma," Henry stated as he again wrapped his arms around her, "we will have our house in no time."

"I doubt a crate of dandelion will bring in that much," Emma laughed.

"We're not talking about one crate," Henry countered with a growing twinkle. "We are talking about crates and crates of dandelion and plantain and chasteberry and whatever else you want. This one is just the beginning. If it works, I will get you the plants, the bottles, the booze, the help, anything you need – because this is something that not just our store needs, but every drug store from here to the Pacific Ocean. There is money to be made, Emma, big money."

"The Pacific Ocean," Emma repeated. "We would ship clear to the Pacific Ocean?"

Her husband smiled. "You wanted to see the Pacific someday, didn't you?"

"Yes," she exclaimed.

"Well I did promise you a wedding trip," Henry responded. "If this works and we expand our market to the coast, we will be able to afford a trip to the Pacific Ocean, and maybe even a mansion." His eyes sparkled with life.

Emma loved to see the joy in her husband's eyes. She loved to imagine having the means her mother had only known as a child. Her hands reached to Henry's face. She wanted to touch this moment of happiness between them. The warmth of his eyes settled on hers as his words now ceased. His lips sought hers and within moments they forgot the room around them as they became lost in each other.

The following morning Emma and Henry went to church. Reverend Stoy from Deer Lodge was preaching at the Methodist/Episcopal Church in Helena for the second week in a row. His sermon centered on overcoming the old sin nature, comparing it to subduing the elements of nature. The recent fire in Deer Lodge City provided ample illustration.

The sermon was an uncomfortable one for Henry Parchen. The reverend's graphic description did much to dampen his spirits, and it wasn't until Emma turned her attention to making tinctures that Henry's mood improved. He helped by constructing temporary shelves in front of their windows. By the time he finished, Henry was again focused on their future hopes and dreams…and the children they wanted.

The following week Emma shook her dandelion and plantain tinctures morning and night, and she stole more and more time to read Culpepper's book. Henry approved as he began to calculate just how much of the various tinctures and tonics the two stores could sale.

Then on Saturday as Emma headed upstairs at the noon hour, she spotted another telegram slid under the back door. She picked it up, anticipating that some calamity had arisen with the construction of the Deer Lodge City store. She returned to Henry as she opened the message.

"What do you have there?" he asked as he finished with a customer.

"A telegram from my brother," she answered. "It's addressed to me, but I suppose it has something to do with the construction of…no, it's mother. She's sick." Emma's face lifted in surprise. "They want me to come home."

"Then it's serious," Henry surmised.

"Typhoid, apparently," Emma responded as she read the telegram again. "Harry wants me to bring medicine."

"Which medicine?" Henry inquired.

"It doesn't say, but Dr. Whitford did loose all his supplies in the fire," Emma replied.

"I suggest these," a familiar voice offered as Dr. Ingersoll appeared from the tincture aisle, and placed several bottles on the counter. "But Dr. Whitford will probably disagree," he stated with a smile. "These two are the homeopathic approach. These three are for the nausea, the infection, and strengthening the immune system. He probably won't object to them."

"Emma, you have met Dr. Cyrus Ingersoll, haven't you?" Henry Parchen asked.

"Yes, briefly. I had a customer at the time," Emma responded with a smile. "How is it you are here precisely when I need you?"

Dr. Ingersoll grinned through the dark hair of his goatee beard. His schoolboy eyes twinkled with pleasure. "I always like to be of service to pretty ladies," he replied.

"Pretty ladies, ugly ones, little children… His competitors say he preys on the weak of heart," Henry Parchen chuckled.

Dr. Ingersoll glanced up. "I have acquired a lot of patients while my competitors have been away doing heroic deeds," he grinned. "But if the truth were to be know, I would wager my recovery rate is better than theirs."

"Perhaps," another voice offered as Dr. Glick brought some supplies up to the counter, "but then you treat the milder cases, don't you? When was the last time you did an amputation without chloroform and got it done before the patient had time to scream?"

"And your patient lived?" Dr. Ingersoll asked.

A disgruntled look rose in Dr. Glick's face. "Of course he lived."

"I didn't know," Dr. Ingersoll responded. "You hear a lot of things."

"Things?" Dr. Glick demanded.

"Well you know, sometimes infections set in." Dr. Ingersoll shrugged.

Dr. Glick looked down at the bottles on the counter. "What are you trying to cure this time, Cy?"

"Mrs. Parchen's mother has typhoid, and Dr. Whitford's office burned in the Deer Lodge fire. I thought these might help."

"Humph," Dr. Glick responded, "the quack approach, I see. Mrs. Parchen, if you really want to help your mother, stay away from these two bottles. They are like giving poison to the sick."

"Like cures like," Dr. Ingersoll retorted. "It works. I have proof."

Dr. Glick did not turn away from Emma. "Mind my advice." Then he paid Henry for his supplies; and without another word, he walked out of the store.

"I had better get what I came in for," Dr. Ingersoll decided. Within minutes he had conducted his business, and left.

"What do you think?" Emma asked as their apothecary passed the counter. She pointed to the bottles of tinctures and tonics still setting on the counter.

"Typhoid, is it?" William Eichler inquired as he slowed to a stop.

"Yes," Emma replied.

"I probably do more business with Dr. Ingersoll than any of the others, and he does have a good recovery rate," William offered, "but the other doctors don't think much of him."

"The Overland Coach doesn't leave until Monday morning, you know," Henry stated quietly.

"I know, that's what worries me," Emma responded. "Perhaps I should telegraph Harry and see how bad she really is."

"Write out your message. I need to go out for a little bit anyway," her husband replied. "Paynter mentioned a downtown lot that is coming up for sale, and if it is any good I think we should jump on it. There isn't a prayer in heaven he'll consider rebuilding this place in brick."

Emma reached for the back of an old envelope, and wrote out her brief message as William Eichler returned to his work. With a worried expression Emma handed it to her husband.

"Your mother's probably not that bad," Henry offered encouragingly. "It's probably the medicine they want."

"But if she doesn't get it until Monday…" Emma didn't continue.

"Let's see what your brother says," Henry responded as he gave her a quick kiss. He took off his apron and grabbed his coat.

Henry Parchen was gone about an hour as Emma helped their various customers. Worry was setting heavy on her shoulders as she pondered her mother's illness. With all the poor health her family had survived in St. Louis, her mother had fared better than most. How was it she was now combating typhoid? Surely she had been exposed to it in St. Louis. Why had she caught it here?

Emma thought about the members of their family that had succumbed to one illness or another over the years. She had lost more brothers and sisters than had survived. She had almost lost Jenny to small pox. She had lost her father to a stomach disorder. Her mother had lost the man she remarried, and both their babies. Emma did not want to loose her mother.

"Emma, the Kleinschmidts are taking another wagon over to Deer Lodge City," Henry announced as he burst through the front door of the store. "If you can be ready to go in ten minutes, you can go with."

"Yes," Emma responded as she tore off her apron. She grabbed the five bottles Dr. Ingersoll had selected, and headed upstairs. Throwing a few things into a carpet bag, she then turned her attention to packing the medicine so it wouldn't break.

"How long do you think you will be gone?" Henry asked as he appeared at the door.

"I don't know," Emma replied. "A couple weeks, I would guess. Did you send the telegram?"

"No, I was waylaid by our neighbor next door. He had a crate fall on his foot. I was helping him when Kleinschmidt stopped by on his way to finish loading the wagon he's taking to Deer Lodge City. I asked Ted if you could ride along."

"There, I think I'm ready," Emma decided as her eyes turned to her husband.

"I will miss you," he stated softly. He took her into his arms.

"I will miss you too," she replied. "Don't forget to shake the tinctures twice a day, and then pour them through a clean white muslin a week from tomorrow, and throw the residue away." She kissed him briefly, and left.

The trip to Deer Lodge went smoothly. The snow that fell on Wednesday had melted, and the horses had no difficulty with the journey. Colonel Kleinschmidt pushed his team and made the Frenchwomen's house by nightfall. Emma found herself at her mother's by noon the following day.

"Jenny, how is mother," Emma cried as she set her bag down inside the door. The young women briefly embraced.

"She is quite miserable," Jenny responded. "Dr. Whitford came by this morning. Did you bring the medicine?"

"Yes," Emma replied as she knelt to her bag. She brought out three of the five bottles.

"Oh good," Jenny breathed in relief. "Harry has been beside himself, simply beside himself. He can't believe that with the loss of the store we simply don't have the necessary medicine."

"Can I see mother?" Emma requested.

"Oh sure, and we'll take her these," Jenny replied as she held up the bottles. "Just let me get a teaspoon."

Emma followed her sister into the kitchen, and then to her mother's room. Marie lay resting in bed. Her face was pale. Her eyes were exhausted.

"How are you feeling, mother?" Jenny asked as she filled the teaspoon. "Emma's brought you something to make you feel better."

The woman took the medicine silently as her eyes swung slowly to Emma.

"She is pretty weak," Jenny explained as she read the next bottle. "Her stomach has been giving her fits, and making her head hurt terribly."

"What does Dr. Whitford say?" Emma inquired.

"Well according to him, mother doesn't actually have typhoid. But it is similar. She has almost all the symptoms. That's what puzzles him." She gave the older woman a teaspoon of the second medicine.

"Let me sit with her for a while," Emma offered.

The medicine did ease the typhoidal symptoms, but Marie's fever and chills persisted into the following week. Dr. Whitford didn't have any answers even though he came by to check on her daily.

Emma sat on the bed beside her mother, and laid a hand on the woman's brow, noting it's heat.

"How is Henry?"

Emma looked into her mother's tired eyes, and smiled. "He is fine, and wishes you a speedy recovery."

"Not much chance of that, I don't suppose," she replied softly.

"Mother, I have some other medicine," Emma offered hesitantly. "Dr. Ingersoll recommended it before I left Helena, but he isn't thought of very highly by…" Emma's words fell off as Marie curled against the misery of her stomach. Typhoid or not, the woman's intestinal discomfort was a fact.

As the misery finally eased, the mother's eyes lifted to her daughter. "Give me the other medicine. I don't care if your doctor is the worst scoundrel this side of the Mississippi."

Chapter Six

Twenty-four hours later Marie broke into a drenching sweat, and she shivered uncontrollably. Her fever had broken. Her headache was suddenly gone. Her stomach while tender, ceased to boil and wrench uncontrollably, and she began her recovery.

A large smile broke across Dr. Whitford's face. "Incredible," he remarked as he closed his bag. "We will keep you on the same medication. It seems to be finally working."

Emma watched the doctor walk out with her brother.

"Why didn't you tell him about the homeopathic medicine," Emma asked as she sat beside her mother. "Harry doesn't even know, does he?"

"No," she answered, "and with good reason. Harry and the good doctor would have me off the remedy instantly. They consider themselves adherents of progressive medicine, and condemn everything else as quackery. No, it's better not to say anything."

"But your recovery is proof," Emma responded.

"No Emma, men like that don't want to hear the truth…unless it upholds their belief system." A soft smile broke across her tired face. "You have brought joy to my life once again."

For the remainder of the week, Emma stayed with her mother, giving her medicine and listening as Marie recalled memories of her past -- of her family's royalist inclinations during the French Revolution, of their magnificent property with its immense garden and large saloon, of her father's financial follies, of the hard work of their French farm with its poor soil, and then of coming to America with all its hardships.

On Monday, Emma returned home to Helena on the morning coach. Without the snow, the trip was over by supper time. Emma grabbed her carpet bag and the rolled up canvas of her grandfather's painting, and set off the few blocks to City Drug Store on foot. By the time she got there, Wood Paynter was just locking up for the night.

With a smile, he let her in. Then Wood turned to shout at his partner, "Henry, guess who's back!" Paynter beamed at Emma. "He's been a basket case, you know, working into the night, being distracted during the day -- a real mess."

"I missed him too," she responded, "and you. How is the family?"

"Fine. Jennie sends her best to your mother. How is she?"

"Better, much better, thank you," Emma replied as her husband appeared.

"Emma," he cried joyously. He caught her up in his arms.

"Well, I'll leave you two alone," Wood decided as he finished locking up. He headed to the back of the store without another word.

"Emma, how is your mother?" Henry demanded.

"She is definitely on the road to recovery," she relayed with a smile. "How is everything here?"

"Fine," Henry answered. "I hear they have the Deer Lodge store's new foundation in."

"Yes," Emma agreed, "and they have started on the brick front."

"Really," Henry cried in delight. He took her bag, and together they headed upstairs. "Wood and I bought a new site for the store. It's just across Broadway. Have you had anything to eat?"

Emma's joy at being home was only exceeded by Henry's joy at having her there, and they strove to make up for their time apart as they talked and touched and soon were caught up in rapturous activity. Emma never knew such ecstasy as her husband simply could not get enough of her, and she could not get enough of him. Perhaps a child would result from their love. She hoped so.

Church, the following morning, was attended with a light heart. Both Emma and Henry hardly heard a word. Their attention was on each other; and as the service let out to the clamor of bells, they walked arm in arm to finally view the lot where Henry planned to build their house. He had already talked to the Paynters, and they were very interested in selling their share. The monetary return had been a major consideration in the purchase of the new site for the drug store.

"What kind of house do you want, Emma?" Henry asked.

"A two story, plus attic. I hate bumping my head every time I make the beds," Emma laughed.

"I suppose you want a large kitchen if you are planning to make tinctures along with our meals," Henry responded.

"Did the dandelion and plantain turn out?" Emma inquired as she remembered their project.

"Yes," he answered with a smile, "and if anything, it is stronger than the stuff we buy."

"Then it will take fewer drops per dose," Emma replied.

"I bottled it. We'll have to get a decent siphon. Pouring is too messy."

"So have you sold any?" Emma asked.

"Not yet. We need labels. But I did let Dr. Ingersoll sample the tincture, and he was pleased."

"The labels shouldn't be a problem," Emma decided. "We can get a woodcut made."

"I thought you might want to design it," Henry responded in approval.

"Yes, I would like that," Emma agreed.

"The engravers will want the design actual size." Henry stopped and turned. "What do you think?"

Emma surveyed the small parcel of land. "Yes," she stated quietly now, "I see a two story house with a porch, and lots of cozy nooks." She left the street and waltzed through the weeds. "Parlor, dinning room, kitchen," she declared, and suddenly turned to the right. "The stair goes there."

"Okay," Henry laughed as he joined her. "Do you want a straight shot up or a stair that turns?"

"One that turns, of course," she replied with a grin. "The front door can go there." She pointed towards Broadway.

"I'll see if the builder has any pictures," Henry offered.

"And we have to have good windows in the kitchen if we're going to make tinctures," Emma added. "I hate gloom anyway."

"I'll remember," Henry promised.

For a full week every time Emma and Henry got a moment to themselves they were instantly caught up in their dreams for the house and the tincture business.

On Friday, Henry even did the unexpected, and took the afternoon off. Driving his wife up through Grizzly Gulch in the wonderfully warm May weather, he surprised Emma with a picnic lunch in a secluded spot by a prattling creek. In absolute privacy, their only intruder was a shy deer who had come from up wind, and had been startled to find two humans in such close embrace. It was a perfect afternoon.

Store work increasingly demanded their attention. Shipments of goods were coming into the store regularly now, and financial questions regarding the construction in Deer Lodge City and the real estate in Helena demanded immediate and full attention. Henry's focus shifted accordingly as Emma noted her sudden lack of energy. Her head hurt and she chilled easily, but she didn't bother her husband about it. He had too much on his mind.

Emma was late arriving downstairs, and wearily reached for her apron.

"Are you all right?" William Eichler asked.

"I think so," Emma responded.

"Have you been sick?" Paynter inquired as he paused on his way past.

"Just once after breakfast," she answered. "It evidently didn't agree with me."

Wood Paytner's expression softened. "So it's finally happened."

"What has?" Emma asked.

"The two of you are expecting," he replied. "You're late, aren't you?"

"Not yet," Emma retorted, a bit miffed by the man's presumption.

"But you will be," he laughed. "Count on it. Congratulations."

"What's the good news?" Henry Parchen inquired as he joined them.

"You're going to be a father," his partner exclaimed with a big smile.

Parchen instantly turned to his wife. "Is this so?" he demanded.

"Not that I know of," she replied in a disgruntled tone.

Henry turned to Paynter. "How do you know?"

A silly grin emerged on Paynter's face. "Morning sickness?"

Parchen spun to his wife. "You were sick this morning?"

"Yes, but I'm not late," she answered as she looked defiantly at Paynter. "I just ate something that didn't agree with me."

"I could be wrong," Wood Paynter admitted, "but it's not like it would be impossible now, is it? Perhaps I should leave you two alone to talk," he decided as he motioned for Eichler to follow him. They headed to the front of the store with some merchandise.

"It is possible," Henry asserted as he looked hopefully at his wife.

"Yes," she replied, "but I told you I'm not late."

Henry scrutinized her appearance. "You're not getting sick like your mother, are you?"

"I have a head ache, that's all," Emma responded as she now slipped the apron over her head and reached to tie the back. "There's stock to get out."

Henry Parchen watched his wife picked up a new crate of tonic, and head for the appropriate section of the store. Emma did look pale and tired, and a certain amount of concern rose in him as he pondered the situation. But coming up with no answers, he turned back to his work.

The ringing pop of shattered glass startled Henry forty minutes later as he looked abruptly up from his purchase orders. He instantly headed toward the sound and his wife. He found Emma staring down at the dropped bottle of tonic as her trembling hand still lingered in the air.

"Emma, you're shaking." Henry reached for her. "Gees, your hands are ice cold."

"I'm sorry. I didn't mean to break it," she responded in a worried tone.

"I know, I know," Henry consoled as he took her into his arms. His hand reached up to brush the strand of hair falling into her eyes, but paused, noting the heat of her forehead. "Emma, you have a fever." He pulled away, studying her face. "If you aren't feeling well, why didn't you say something?"

"There is so much work to be done," she answered softly.

"Yes there is, but you know the funny thing about work is it tends to wait for you...as long as you need." Henry smiled encouragingly. "Go upstairs and get some rest. I'll be up to check on you just as soon as I get the floor cleaned up. Okay?"

"Okay," she suddenly yielded.

Henry headed back with her as far as the steps, and then turned to find a broom, and an old rag. These he retrieved, and headed back to the mess.

"Is Emma all right?" Paynter asked.

"It looks like she's sick, not pregnant," Henry answered. "I hope it's not typhoid."

"Maybe you should get a doctor," Wood suggested. "A bad case of typhoid wouldn't do the store any good."

"I'll check on her just as soon as I clean up the floor," Henry replied.

"Well, I have good news and bad news, Henry," Dr. Ingersoll announced as he emerged from the crate bedroom later that day. "Your wife is definitely sick, but it's not typhoid."

"What is it?" he asked.

"Perhaps a related strain of the illness, but it's not too serious, just uncomfortable. She should be up and around in a week or so." Then he smiled. "But the good news is, you and Emma can expect a little bundle of joy in about eight or nine months."

"Emma's pregnant?" Henry demanded.

"All the indications are there," Dr. Ingersoll responded as Henry's face brightened. "I'd better be on my way," he stated.

After Henry saw the doctor out, he returned to Emma. She looked up at his entrance.

"Doctor Ingersoll told you," she asked softly.

"Yes."

"I guess Wood was right after all."

"I'm glad," Henry responded.

Two and a half weeks later Henry bought out Wood and Jennie's interest in the lot on Rodney and Broadway, and recorded the fact in the Helena's land office. The news no sooner reached Deer Lodge City than Emma received news that her mother and sister were coming for a visit. The women were terribly excited about the baby and the new house, so much so that Harry's move into the new Deer Lodge City drug store was now old news, despite the fact that all of Deer Lodge had only celebrated a mere week before.

Emma met the Overland Coach at the International Hotel, and walked her mother and sister back to City Drug. Both women were duly impressed by the size of the Helena store; but when they were led upstairs, both became exceedingly quiet.

"I told you it was a bit Spartan," Emma responded as she offered them the two chairs at the table.

"A bit?" Jenny's voice fell off.

"Now dear, everyone's priorities differ," her mother replied.

"You and Jenny can share our bed. Henry and I will sleep on the floor," Emma stated as she pulled up a wood crate. She watched as her mother surveyed the room in silence.

"What kind of house is Henry building you?" their mother asked.

"A two story with an attic," Emma answered. "Here, let me get the drawing."

Emma disappeared momentarily into the crate bedroom, and reappeared with a picture and a floor plan. These she submitted to her mother.

"Yes, this looks nice," Marie remarked as Jenny looked on.

"So what are you going to name the baby?" her sister demanded.

"Henry, if it's a boy, and if it's a girl... We haven't really decided yet," Emma replied.

"I always liked the name Celine," Jenny offered, "like our aunt. But you could name the baby Hortense Marie like mother." She grinned.

"Heaven forbid," their mother scoffed. "No girl needs a handle like that. Name her something pretty."

"What name do you like?" Emma asked.

Her mother thought for a moment. “I had a friend I loved very dearly when I was a child. Her name was Adele Chaqual. We took our first communion together, and we each had a wonderful satin ribbon in our hair to match with our white gloves and our beautiful clothes. Oh how I missed her when we moved.”

“Adele, that is pretty,” Emma responded.

“Adele Marie,” Jenny suggested. “That’s much easier to say than Hortense Marie.” She looked at her mother with a teasing expression.

“Yes,” Emma agreed. “What do you think, mother?”

“I will always like the name Adele,” she replied, “but what you name the child is for you and Henry to decide. This is America. Godparents don’t decide such things here, thank goodness. Frankly I always liked my grandfather’s nickname for me better than the one my godparents gave me. ‘Tant pis’, always had a better ring.” She smiled.

“But you wouldn’t want Emma’s baby growing up with a name that means, ‘I don’t care’, would you?” Jenny laughed.

“Oh no,” their mother responded immediately, “but there must be an English word that sounds similar, and means something entirely different.”

“If there is, I can’t think of it,” Emma decided. “But I like Adele.”

Emma’s sister loved the location for their new house, but the Broadway hill troubled their mother. She couldn’t get past the awful climb home after a hard day’s work and/or shopping. However she did have to agree that hills were a fact of living in Helena, and the new neighborhood held promise of much growth.

Jenny and their mother didn’t stay but a few days. Neither liked the idea of Emma and Henry sleeping on the floor, especially considering Emma’s delicate condition.

By the first of July Henry had let the contract for their house. The builders were scheduled to begin on the 8th. It would be finished in five weeks.

“All finished?” Emma cried.

“Not all finished,” Henry replied. “We’re going to complete the inside work ourselves.”

“Yes, I know,” Emma responded, “but we can move in?”

A smile broke across her husband’s face. “Yes, we can move in.”

“I still don’t know how you managed to afford all this,” Emma declared happily. “A new house and the Deer Lodge store rebuilt in the same year!”

“The insurance paid for most of Deer Lodge,” Henry explained, “and City Drug has done pretty decent in the last several months.”

“But you and Wood bought the new site for the store,” she objected.

He smiled. “I took out a small loan at the bank.”

“You borrowed money?” Emma gasped.

“We are expecting a baby,” Henry replied. “I couldn’t very well deny you a house just to finance the new store.”

“But…”

"Don't worry, Emma," her husband soothed. "Our profits are up since you came to town."

"But I won't be in the store this fall," she reminded him.

"You aren't there much now," he retorted with a grin, "not since I brought you all those crates of greens. Do you know how much we're going to make on all the tincture you're making?"

"No," she responded quietly.

"If all goes well, I expect to see enough return by Christmas to clear the loan out completely."

"Really?" she asked. Then she paused. "And what if things don't go well?"

"Then it may take a little longer, maybe spring or even next fall. But that isn't likely if my projections are correct."

It was true. Emma was not lacking for things to do. Plants and jars filled their rooms above the Helena store. Henry had secured crates of dandelion, plantain, clover, yarrow, hyssop, white horehound, and thyme among others. What Emma did not have jars and drinking alcohol for, she dried. Plants straddled drying racks set up end for end through their rooms. Every hour of her day was filled with managing her new industry as she constantly tried to further along the process and maybe regain a little more space, usually for a new crate of plants.

Her pregnancy tired her, and her husband insisted that she indulge herself at these times. Usually she did so by going downstairs and clerking. Her pregnancy wasn't showing yet, and she craved the social interaction. City Drug's women customers desired her feminine advice, and quickly learned when she was most likely to appear.

After supper while Henry worked on the store's accounts, she poured over medical books. Dr. Cyrus Ingersoll now shared much of his library with her, excited over her new preparations. The good doctor was now a regular visitor, checking on her pregnancy and on the progress of her new tinctures. He saw the potential of her many creations for his patients, and he encouraged her at every opportunity.

"Could you make a hawthorn preparation, do you think?" Dr. Ingersoll asked Emma one evening as her husband closed up the store. "I have a couple older patients who have the beginnings of what look to be heart conditions, but they aren't bad enough to put on digitalis. I would like to keep it that way."

"What part of the hawthorn plant would I use?" Emma inquired.

"It's a tree, and the berry is what we're after," he answered.

"I read somewhere that the flower, Lilly of the Valley, is good for heart aliments," Emma responded.

"It is, better than digitalis because it has less toxic properties. But it still has to be carefully supervised by a doctor. That's why I'd like a hawthorn preparation for these patients. They have a need. But if you want to work with

Lilly of the Valley later, I'm all for it. Digitalis has always made me a bit nervous."

"Nervous, what, the other doctors are crying quackery again?" Henry chuckled as he joined them.

"And implicating you," Cyrus Ingersoll replied with a smirk.

"Me? What did I do?" Henry retorted in apparent innocence.

"You're selling potions, aren't you?" Cyrus laughed.

"I'm not selling anything people aren't buying," he stated.

"Clover elixir is really supposed to help a bad complexion?" Cy asked with a raised eyebrow.

"You know it does," Henry answered. "You prescribe it yourself."

"Ah, but it's what cows and sheep eat," Dr. Cy Ingersoll replied.

"I have never seen a cow or a sheep with a bad complexion," Henry offered in fun.

"If they even had a complexion," Emma responded.

"Exactly," Dr. Cy Ingersoll agreed. "But even if the nutrients do help the skin, no one will believe it based on cows, or sheep, or even from human consumption because people eat what they want to eat in proportions that clover couldn't possibly counter."

"That still doesn't make it quackery," Henry replied.

"No? There are those who would beg to differ." Dr. Ingersoll smiled.

Five weeks flew by, and then six. The builder had fallen slightly behind schedule, but the Parchen house was finally ready for its occupants. Emma had entered her fourth month of pregnancy, and she was beginning to show. Henry was elated, fussing over her as he forbid her to carry anything heavy in their move. The weather was hot now, particularly in the afternoons, and Emma found herself confined by her husband to the inside of their new house or outside in the shade.

Emma surveyed the location of their bed in the upstairs room as a refreshing breeze came through the open window. A second small room joined it, utilizing the space above the stair. It would serve as the nursery.

Emma's attention drifted to the door. She had a thousand and one things waiting downstairs as she sat down on the bed. It was hot, and she wanted to indulge in a little preoccupation before she went downstairs. She liked their new house, even if it did need lots of paint and varnish and wallpaper – much like their former rooms. But at least the floors were varnished. With all the dirt that came in on shoes, she had insisted on it. It was the one compromise she wouldn't give in to with Henry. Dirt was ugly when it ground its way into the grain of wood.

Her eyes swung over the dresser, and the new rocking chair that occupied the room opposite the bed. The curtains that had been her wedding gift were already hung on the window. They would need a rug by winter, but she wondered how she was going to manage it. Her time was already so taken with the tinctures, she didn't know when she could spare any, even if she had the rags.

"Emma, I think that does it," Henry announced as he appeared upstairs.

"I should thank Wood and Cy for helping us move," Emma responded as she rose.

"Too late, they are already gone," Henry told her. "I promised them dinner next Sunday."

Dinner did not happen on the 25th of August. Helena was still reeling from the effects of the preceding Friday afternoon. Fire had broken out in the rear of the Northern Pacific Hotel on Main street, and multitudes of residents had turned out to fight the fiendish flames with water buckets, hoses, and axes as they fought to keep the fire from spreading. They guarded neighboring roofs from flying embers, dousing them with water. Sometimes where the threat was too great, firefighters would tear off entire roofs from otherwise fireproof buildings. Merchandise and belongings were pulled from threatened buildings. Nothing was spared to save the structures. But human effort seemed utterly impotent as the fire ravaged a good portion of the business district between Jackson and Warren Streets, north of Broadway. A couple of neighboring sections also burned as the fire spread into the residential district to the east.

"You're tired," Henry noted.

"No, not too bad," Emma replied with a soft smile. "I was just thinking about the baby. We're going to need a crib."

"First things first," Henry laughed. "We have almost six months for that. The kitchen, on the other hand…" He kissed her cheek. "I'll help."

"Yes, you will," she agreed. "My kitchen might as well be the warehouse rooms above the store since you and Wood moved the rest of my tincture supplies home. I hope the businessmen appreciate it. I realize since they were burned out, they have to have someplace downtown to put their stuff, but I can't even find our wood stove."

"It's too hot to cook anyway," he grinned.

Chapter Seven

The kitchen was a mess. Crates rose to a height of six feet as Henry stacked and re-stacked them out of Emma's way. Most of the crates found a home in the empty dining room, and Emma could again find their wood stove, and their table and chairs.

Cognizant of how much tincture was now ready for sale, Henry redoubled his marketing efforts while still availing himself of every opportunity to bring home an abundance of any plant Emma mentioned. Orders for their new products were slow. Bottles were often shipped one at a time, usually to druggists in neighboring towns. Each, however, returned a minimal amount of cash while at the same time freeing up an old space for Emma's new creations. By the end of October, Emma had a dining room warehouse that boasted a nice selection of tinctures and tonics. No one was more pleased than Dr. Cyrus Ingersoll and his wife. Calista was an experienced midwife, and now frequently dropped in at the house. Her visits often turned into informal professional calls, however, as she kept tabs on Emma during her pregnancy.

"There that should do it," Emma stated as she collected the final bottle of tincture Calista wanted. She reached for her account book, and entered the tally.

"And how are you feeling?" Calista asked.

"Fat," Emma retorted. "I feel as if I have a quilt wrapped around my middle."

"That is natural," Calista laughed. "How are your ankles? Any swelling?"

"Oh maybe a little at night," Emma replied.

"You will want to cut back on the amount of salt you use at meals then," she responded. "That should help."

"Did you go to the Rumley's Silver Wedding Anniversary?" Emma inquired now.

"Cy was with a patient last Saturday," Calista answered, "and needed my help, but I understand it was well attended."

"Yes," Emma agreed, "Henry went. He said there were a lot of people there. He regrets I wasn't there to meet the out-of-towners."

Calista smiled. "We weren't the only ones to miss it. Sam Hauser's wife is in her confinement. Her baby is due just a couple of weeks after yours."

"Yes, I met her at the store a while back," Emma offered. "Are you going to delivery her baby? Is she as big as me?"

"No, I believe her doctor is William Steele," the midwife replied, "and I would wager she is probably bigger. Steele fanatically believes pregnant women should stay off their feet. Mrs. Hauser is probably bored to death and indulging in sweets to make up for it."

The weather turned cold, and snow began to fall in earnest so that Helena had a white Thanksgiving. Emma and Henry spent the holiday with Dr. and

Mrs. Ingersoll. Their family was pretty much grown, and there was a nice crowd gathered for the dinner.

Orders for tinctures dwindled to an all time low as the roads became more difficult to travel. Emma turned her attention to preparations for the baby and Christmas. This holiday also would be spent in Helena. The trip to Deer Lodge City was too arduous in Emma's condition, and her mother and sister planned to come the following month and stay until the baby was born.

"Em, are you coming?" Henry called as he lingered at the front door. "I have the foot warmer."

"Yes, yes," Emma replied as she bustled out of the kitchen.

The ground was covered by a thick layer of snow as the couple made their way to the waiting sleigh. Emma got in as her husband placed the coal foot warmer on the floor. Henry climbed in beside his wife, and the sleigh lurched forward.

"Where are we going for our Christmas tree?" Emma asked.

"Just up here in the gulch," Henry answered.

The air was brisk as the horses pulled them, clouds of vapor rising from their nostrils.

"I suppose you're going to insist on a fir tree." Emma grinned.

"Absolutely," Henry retorted. "We want the baby to be a boy, don't we?"

"I don't know," Emma replied evasively, "a girl would be a good baby-sitter for the younger children."

"I need a boy," Henry decided. "Someone who can help out in the store as he gets bigger."

"And a girl couldn't?" Emma countered. "Then what have I been doing down there all these months?"

"I didn't mean it like that," Henry responded. "It's just that eventually a boy could do the heavier work too."

"So all you want is a slave," Emma stated with a teasing grin.

"Emma, no, I want someone who can take over the store someday," her husband replied. "Is that so bad? Our children will have to make their way in the world one way or another. What is wrong with providing that means?"

"Nothing at all," Emma answered. She hadn't meant for Henry to take her teasing so seriously. She leaned against him, laying her face against his coat. He responded by placing a kiss on her forehead.

The horses were pulling the sleigh up the grade, down the narrow road, through the snow laden trees. The sky above was blue between the broken white clouds. Their surroundings were so clean and clear and beautiful. It reminded Emma of the day after their wedding when the coach had taken them through the pristine landscape to their new home.

Twenty minutes more brought them to a small frozen pond. Young evergreen saplings grew randomly beside it.

"I think there should be a tree here somewhere," Henry noted as he turned off the gulch road.

The couple got out of the sleigh. Henry carried a cross cut saw.

"How about that one?" he asked as he pointed twenty-five yards beyond.

"It's beautiful," Emma exclaimed. The ten foot tree was shrouded with snow as it glittered in the sunlight. "Is finding a tree really this easy?"

Henry smiled. "You are in Montana now, not St. Louis."

The two walked the short distance to the fir tree. It was beautifully shaped with branches fanning out at regular intervals.

"I have never seen such a beautiful tree," Emma commented in awe.

Her husband pointed a short distance away. A larger parent tree stood some thirty or forty feet in the air, just as perfectly shaped.

"The mama tree," Emma cried. "No wonder, they're all perfect!"

Henry smiled. "They're not as soft to touch as Douglas fir, but they look good."

Emma took off her mitten, and touched a branch. "Ow," she retorted, "it's not soft at all. It feels more like a short needle pine tree."

"But it is fir," Henry laughed. "We did agree on a fir for Christmas, remember?" he replied. "We'll see if we can find some Douglas fir for smell. You want to make some garlands, don't you?"

"Yes, and I don't want to work with evergreens that bite," Emma remarked, "not when I have to wind string around and around them."

Henry bent down, and began to saw. It was barely more than moments before their Christmas tree fell in a cascade of powdered snow. Henry carried it back to the sleigh. Then he took Emma's hand, and together they went for a walk into the woods, looking for Douglas fir.

"This reminds me of our walk along the creek during our first trip here," Henry stated quietly as his arm wrapped around his wife's shoulders. "We were late getting back to the coach." He kissed his wife's cheek tenderly. Henry's attention then dropped to her bulging stomach. He placed a light hand on it as a smile emerged on his lips. "Little Henry will be a fine lad," he commented as his eyes met hers.

"Little Adele will be wondrous," she replied as she teased him.

He kissed her on the lips.

"Which tree is Douglas fir?" Emma asked after a moment.

"That one," Henry answered as he briefly pointed.

"I think the sex of the baby is already a fact," Emma responded as they kissed again.

"It doesn't matter," Henry confessed as he picked her up, and deposited her gently in the snow beside him. "There's no coach waiting now."

Emma looked at the pile of Douglas Fir on the floor the following morning. It was Christmas Eve, and Henry was at work. She had until six that evening to decorate the house. Henry believed in celebrating Christmas that night. It was a tradition from his Lutheran background. Emma's traditions centered on the following morning, being French and Catholic, but she was a Parchen now. After the baby was born, maybe things would be different with packages appearing in the morning. But for now, they would celebrate Christmas Eve.

Emma looked at their perfect Christmas tree standing in the bare living room. Henry had put it in the stand the night before, and she already had to fill the coffee can twice with water. Their decorations were limited to food items. Emma had two dozen gingerbread cookies to hang, but not until after the popcorn was strung and placed on the tree. She also had a box of crabapples she planned to add. The only things missing were the candles. With all the expenses of the year, she and Henry had decided they could do without the extravagance of candles on the tree.

By the time Emma finished, the room looked a lot less bare. She only wished she had a decent rug to spread before the Christmas tree. She did have two boxes to place under it. Both were for Henry. She smiled.

Emma had spent hours dreaming up something she could give him on their limited budget, but it was no use. Everything she wanted cost too much. So faced with reality, she had come up with a new plan. It had taken hours of extra work, always done on the sly when he wasn't home, and then hidden where he would never look. But the extra effort had paid off, she sent her unique mix of tincture to Deer Lodge for good money, enough to buy Henry a silver pocket knife to attach to the watch and chain his father had given him.

Emma turned her attention to the garlands she was to make. The Douglas fir smelled wonderful as she twisted the dark twine around and through the branches, turning them into lengthy strands of green. As each one was finished, she draped it over the doorways and windows. The rooms looked somehow less empty. The kitchen was almost pretty.

Now Emma took out all the spare candles they had, and fixing them on the window sills with a bit of clay, the decorative look was complete. But of course they wouldn't light them, candles cost too much.

By the time Henry got home, the house smelled of evergreens and dinner. His wife had moved their small kitchen table into the parlor beside the Christmas tree. Henry slid a large box in under the branches as he noted the two smaller ones. Emma had gotten him something for Christmas. It surprised him as he realized he had given her no money for that purpose. Had she managed to save a little out of their grocery budget?

Henry took off his coat, and hung it in the hall. Then he wandered out to the kitchen. Emma was dishing up over the wood stove. He gave his wife a kiss. "Merry Christmas," he told her quietly.

"Merry Christmas," she responded.

"It smells wonderful," he stated as she offered him a plate.

She smiled. "Let's take our dinner in by the tree."

The wine was already on the table as they sat down.

"Did you move the table clear in here by yourself?" Henry asked with concern.

"I shoved it all the way," Emma answered with a smile. "It's light weight."

"Not that light, besides it could have scratched the floor," Henry objected.

"Not with socks tied to the feet," Emma laughed.

"You put socks on the wood legs?"

Emma grinned. "The table was cold."

"I bet," Henry retorted as he relaxed. "The place looks great…so do you."

"I look fat," Emma replied.

"No, you look wonderful, like a plum…ripe and sweet."

"I won't be ripe for another two months," Emma stated.

"But just think, then we'll be parents." Henry smiled. "Shall we say grace?"

The evening was spent quietly together, savoring the evening -- the food, each other's company, their dreams, and of course the presents. Henry opened his first. A look of shock entered his face at the extravagance of the gift.

"How?" he gasped. "I didn't give you any money."

Emma smiled. "Open the second package."

"I don't know if I dare. Did you rob a bank?"

"Open it," Emma encouraged. "It will explain the first."

Hesitantly, Henry reached for his second gift. Warily he began to unwrap it as his eyes often drifted to his wife. "It's a bottle of tincture," he decided as he pulled the item from its box. His eyes turned to Emma as questions furrowed his brow.

"Read the label," she directed.

He scanned the information. "You are combining things now?"

Emma smiled. "It was Harry's idea. I sold two cases of it to Dr. Whitford. He loves it."

"Dr. Whitford? Really," Henry exclaimed.

"If it does that well in Deer Lodge City, think what it could do in Helena," Emma responded.

"And you got enough from selling two boxes to buy this silver pocket knife?" Henry asked.

"There is a mark-up of nearly 800%." Emma smiled, "...and no, I did not rob any bank."

"800%!" Henry exclaimed. "How did you come up with that figure?"

"I asked my brother what it would sell for," Emma responded innocently.

A smile crept into Henry Parchen's face. "And what mark-up did City Drug take?"

"I don't know, but Harry paid me nearly 800%," she replied, "so it must have been somewhat more."

"The stuff is good?"

"Dr. Whitford thinks so. I guess it strengthens the immune system."

"I don't recognize this plant," her husband noted as he pointed to one of the ingredients. "What is it?"

"Well, it's something that Calista brought me one time," Emma answered. "Some miner heard about it from a Piegan woman, and she had heard stories of its healing powers from another tribe. Neither seemed to know much about it, but when I put a little in the tincture… I don't even know what it's called yet, so I just gave it a nickname."

"But it helps, it really helps," Henry prodded.

"Dr. Whitford thinks so," Emma replied.

"So how much supply do you have left?" Henry asked.

"Just the bottle you're holding," Emma answered.

"But you know where to get more of this plant?"

"I can ask Calista," Emma replied. She smiled. "Can I open my present now?"

Henry's attention suddenly shifted. "Of course," he responded as he reached for her gift.

Emma silently opened the present, revealing miniature bedding.

"It's for the baby," Henry offered.

She made no response as she inspected the things. Then her eyes lifted. "How do we know what size the crib will be?"

Henry rose to his feet, and extended his hand for her to grasp. She followed him outside. There on the porch was the crib, newly constructed of oak.

"Oh," she gasped in surprise.

Henry immediately reached inside the crib, and pulled free the mattress and the supporting ropes. These he handed to Emma. "If you will take these inside, I'll bring the rest. I don't want you to get cold."

Within minutes the crib was re-assembled in the parlor, and Emma fit the new bedding on the mattress in the warmth of the parlor stove. Then she stood back to admire the baby bed. "It's gorgeous," she exclaimed in quiet appreciation.

"I don't really think the baby will care what it sleeps in," Henry offered with a smile, "but I know you do. Merry Christmas."

Emma instantly encircled Henry with her arms, and kissed him.

"Only two more months, and our little one will be here," Henry muttered as he buried his face in her sweet smelling hair. "Your mother and sister made up the sheets and things. The crib is from me."

The women of Emma's family arrived in Helena by the twenty-fifth of January, and excitement flowed into every corner of the house. Emma no longer lived in a warehouse, and her mother and sister were very pleased. The two of them shared a room upstairs. Henry had borrowed an extra bed from the Ingersolls, and had purchased an old dresser from Mrs. Chumasero. With two daughters married in the last thirteen months, the judge's wife had decided to clear out her attic. Frugal Henry had even brought home a rug one evening, and so the bedroom had been transformed into the state of acceptability.

Emma spent time visiting with her family as they told her all about the Imperial Masquerade her brother had attended. It seemed Harry had made quite a place for himself in Deer Lodge City. Business was good, and his advice was sought in all things medical, second only to the doctors.

Jenny had also impressed Deer Lodge with her talents and refinement. She often participated with Mrs. Wilcox in vocal events at church, or for the community in general. But years before, small pox had left her face scarred and pitted, and as a consequence not even her brother's friends considered her seriously in matters of matrimony. Appreciated only for her music, Jenny found acceptance at church and took advantage of every social opportunity that came her way. Her mother encouraged her in the latter.

Emma, meanwhile, had extra help around the house as her tincture orders again came to life from around the state. The volume was not great. Orders rather seemed to tickle in, one bottle here, two there. Emma packaged them, and her husband deposited the tinctures on the first coach out.

The weeks passed with wind and snow during the first of February, settling down a bit for Valentines. After that, the weather was hardly noticed around the Parchen house. Everyone's attention centered on the baby's due date.

"Any time," Calista announced as she finished Emma's examination, "but not today. Your contractions were a false alarm, I'm afraid."

"But she is due tomorrow," Jenny exclaimed.

"Yes," Calista answered, "but I wouldn't get my hopes up too high. First babies take their time."

"But she should have the baby sometime tomorrow," Jenny insisted.

"Not necessarily," her mother responded. "She might run late."

"Days late," Calista agreed.

"But that's not good, is it?" Jenny asked.

"Babies come when they want to. You can't rush them," her mother replied with a smile.

"Jenny, it won't hurt if Emma runs a few days over, even a week," Calista explained. "The baby may need an extra day or two. Being born is no small task, and the stronger the little one is, the better. Don't worry. The baby knows when it's time." She smiled at Emma as she patted her arm. "Try not to be anxious."

"All right," Emma responded. She had lived with her bloated body for nine months. She could live with it longer.

Then on the morning of February 28th, Emma's water broke, and mild contractions began, subtle and soft. They were not frequent despite Jenny's rush out of the house to find Henry and the doctor.

"Emma, your contractions aren't close together yet at all," her mother noted. "You might as well get up and do a little light work. It will help things along."

"I want to conserve my strength," Emma replied quietly.

"Your water has broken," her mother objected. "This is not the time to conserve. Anything you can do to speed things along will only benefit you and the baby."

"All right," Emma responded as she got to her feet, "what do you suggest?"

"Walking, anything that includes walking," Marie answered.

Emma walked. Her contractions came harder and harder until they took her breath away, and left her weak and exhausted. Only then did her mother help her into bed, and turn her care over to Dr. Ingersoll. Both Cy and Calista were there coaching and encouraging Emma along. Henry stationed himself in the hall with Jenny. There were already enough people in the bedroom who knew what they were doing, and he didn't want to be in the way.

Emma broke into a scream as the baby's head crowned.

"Don't push, Emma," Dr. Ingersoll objected. "Let the contractions ease the baby out, otherwise you will tear."

"It hurts not to," Emma gasped.

"Breathe. Concentrate on your breathing," Calista advised.

Emma was breathing, gasping for air.

"Here it comes," Dr. Ingersoll encouraged.

The intense contraction eased, and Emma collapsed in utter exhaustion only to have another contraction take control of her. She tensed with the agony. She could not get enough air.

"Easy, Emma, one shoulder at a time," Cy Ingersoll instructed.

Loud gasps were escaping Emma, and then suddenly she felt the baby slide from her, and the contraction eased.

"It's a girl," Emma's mother noted joyfully.

Emma lay resting momentarily. "Let me have her."

"Not just yet, Cy is working with the baby," Calista stated. "He has to cut the cord, and check her over."

"I want to see," Emma demanded as she rose defiantly over herself, kneeling before the doctor and the baby. Dr. Ingersoll had just finished checking for mucous in the baby's throat, and was turning her over on his hand, giving the child a swift but careful slap on the back.

Objection rose within Emma. But before she could voice it, another contraction gripped her, doubling her back with its agony. Emma braced herself against the wrenching labor as Calista helped her through the delivery of the placenta.

"There now, lie back and rest a little" the mid-wife advised.

"My baby," Emma responded weakly.

"Let's get you cleaned up first," Calista countered as she glanced at her husband. Cy shook his head in silence. The midwife took a basin of soap and water, and washed the young woman. Marie appeared with a fresh nightgown, and together they dressed Emma.

"My baby," Emma repeated as her mother now turned her efforts to the soiled bedding. The older woman stole a glance at Calista.

"I'll get Henry," the doctor's wife decided.

Apprehension rose within Emma as she suddenly realized she had not heard the baby cry. She sat up. Doctor Ingersoll was packing his medical bag. "Where is my daughter?" she demanded.

Henry came through the door, but Emma's attention never left Cy. He turned, looking at her with incredibly sad eyes.

"No," Emma screamed as she rose to her feet. "Where is my daughter?"

Henry caught his wife in his arms. "The baby's stillborn. There was nothing anyone could do."

"No," Emma cried as she fought her husband, trying to escape, crying for her baby. Emma saw Dr. Ingersoll finish with his bag, and turn to leave. Calista held a bundle of blankets, the baby's blankets.

"I want to see her. I want to see my daughter," Emma shrieked. The Ingersolls were unmoved, and prepared to leave. "Henry, please," she begged.

Henry's attention shifted. "Cy, she has a right," he stated in a broken tone. The midwife came slowly over, pulling the blanket from the baby's head.

Chapter Eight

"Little Adele…"

"No," Henry objected as he physically came between Emma and Calista. "No, the baby is not Adele. Adele will be our daughter. This baby never lived."

Tears boiled in Emma's eyes, and streamed down her cheeks. "Please, Henry, let me see my daughter."

"She is not Adele," Henry repeated.

"Okay, she is not Adele," Emma conceded quietly.

Her husband then stepped aside, and Emma was allowed to look into her dead baby's face.

"Oh," Emma cried as she beheld the blank look of the baby's expression, "she is so little." Emma reached to touch the small cheeks and the tip of the small nose. "Her eyelashes are so delicate." She reached to pull up the limp, tiny hand with its tiny fingers. "Ohh…"

"That's enough, Emma," Henry decided. "They have to take the baby now."

Emma looked up, tears again boiling in her eyes, but she let the baby go as her husband took her into his arms. Within moments they were alone.

Emma looked around the room. No evidence of the newborn remained. The thought frightened her. She had just gone through physical hell, and nothing remained, nothing spoke of the nine months she had carried her unborn, nothing spoke of the child who had not lived.

She broke from her husband, walking hastily into the nursery. The crib remained, the crib and the rocking chair and the stack of diapers on the small changing table. Emma stood trembling in the doorway.

"Emma, we will have another baby," Henry encouraged softly as he joined her.

She turned. "I don't want another baby. I want my daughter."

"I know. I know." He fell silent.

"Why?" Emma suddenly demanded. "Why did this happen?"

"Cy said it could have been a number of things," Henry replied.

"Like what?" Emma asked.

"You were sick early in your pregnancy. The baby's heart might not have been strong enough to survive birthing, or maybe it had something to do with her nervous system," Henry offered.

"I was sick…" Emma's eyes dropped from her husband. It was true. She had been sick, but it was early on, and the baby had developed just fine along the way. She looked up. "Henry, that was a long time ago, and the baby was alive. It kicked, remember?"

Henry took his wife's face in his hands, tenderly kissing her forehead. Then he looked straight into her eyes. "I remember," he stated softly, "but I also remember the cramps in your legs. What is the difference?"

"What do you mean?" she cried in confusion.

"Your cramps were reflex movement. Couldn't the kicks have been the same thing?"

Emma stared at her husband. "I'm alive. The baby was alive."

"Yes Emma, you are alive, but not the cramps. They had no life of their own. They just happened, a response of the muscles in your legs. The baby in your womb was growing. Its muscle tissue would need to move, to kick. That doesn't mean the baby had life yet, just reflex motility. Cy told me it happens. Babies have to breathe to live. They have to receive their spirit from God in that first breath. Ours didn't take a first breath."

"No," Emma disagreed, "I felt the kicks. My baby was alive." She turned away. She didn't want to think about what her husband said.

"Emma…"

She ignored Henry. She retreated to the bed, and laid down. Suddenly she could not think. She was just tired, so very tired.

Emma felt the bed move beside her as Henry laid down parallel behind her. She remained still for the longest time, feigning sleep as she pondered the catastrophe of her life. Suddenly she became aware of a soft gasping; and as she lay listening, she realized her husband was sobbing, deep in his own grief. It moved her, and she rolled over and took him into her arms. His resistance broke completely apart, and he cried hard.

Emma laid her head on his, dry eyed and stunned. She knew Henry had been as excited about the baby as she. She knew his dreams. But she never expected this.

Two hours later a soft knocking came at the bedroom door. Henry sat up, and then rose to answer it. Emma's mother held a plate of hot dinner in her hand.

"Emma should eat something. You should too," she advised.

"Thank you," Henry responded as he took the plate.

The elder woman smiled softly. Her eyes were red from crying.

Henry shut the door again, and returned to Emma. "Your mother thinks you should eat something." He set the plate down between them.

"Why… Why do you insist our daughter was never alive," Emma demanded in a broken tone.

"Because that's what the Bible says," Henry answered quietly. He picked up a piece of fried chicken and took a bite. The food in his mouth felt dry and rough, and only with effort did he swallow. He put the rest of the meat back on the plate.

"No, that doesn't make any sense. I felt our baby inside me," Emma insisted.

"The Mosaic Law says that if a woman with child is caused to miscarry, the party responsible shall be fined what the husband demands. The Mosaic Law does not consider it murder, therefore there is no life in the womb."

Emma stared in shock at her husband, his words echoing in her ears. "Where does it say that?" she demanded.

"Exodus 21:22," Henry answered.

"How do you know that?" she cried.

"Lutherans memorize scripture," he responded, "tons and tons of scripture. We start as children."

"But Christ canceled the Old Testament with the new," she objected.

"Christ came to fulfill scripture, not to cancel it," Henry replied. "He said so."

Emma took the piece of chicken Henry had discarded and bit off a piece. In silence she ate as she considered everything that had happened.

"Your mother is taking our loss kind of hard," Henry finally commented. "Her eyes were red when she brought up the food."

Emma's attention shifted to him. "She has lost many of her own children." Then she paused. "But only one unborn."

"I pray we never loose another," Henry replied.

Henry never left his wife's side that night, but in the morning he was absent over three hours. When he got back, he returned to Emma. She was in the kitchen with her mother. With one glance at the man, Marie excused herself. Henry sat down at the table with his wife.

"Where have you been?" Emma asked quietly.

"I made arrangements for the baby to be buried," he answered in a still voice. "They will do it Monday morning, all right?"

"The coffin, is it nice?" Emma inquired.

"It's pine," Henry responded.

Tears rose in Emma's eyes. "She shouldn't be buried in a plain old pine box. She deserves better."

"She didn't even live," Henry objected.

"And that's precisely why she should have the best," Emma cried. "It's not as if you and I can give her anything else." She paused momentarily. "She should be laid out in her christening gown, and buried in a beautiful white coffin. Has anyone said Last Rites over her body?"

"No, and they won't," Henry responded, "not over my daughter. She is probably already back in heaven. She never had a chance to sin. We don't need some priest to mouth empty words."

Emma's jaw trembled. Her catholic background was still very much a part of her understanding, even if she and Henry were now Episcopalian.

Henry's expression softened. "Our pastor has agreed to say a few words at the grave Monday morning."

Tears were streaming down Emma's cheeks. "The baby deserves more than a pine box."

"All right," Henry agreed as he took her in his arms.

Monday morning Emma and Henry were joined at the cemetery by their pastor, Emma's mother and sister, Cy and Calista Ingersoll, and Wood Paynter. A few words were spoken over the grave, and then the painted white coffin was lowered into the earth. Emma took the fact hard, refusing to leave until well after the others. Only her mother seemed to understand. The two of them stood side by side in the chill February air as Henry paced and worried. Jenny had returned to town with the Ingersolls.

"Emma, I know it's hard to bury a child," her mother finally commented.

"You have buried so many," Emma replied quietly.

"Yes, six," she answered, "and two husbands."

"I can't do it," Emma told her. She turned to the woman. "I don't know how you did it...but I can't."

"Shh," her mother consoled as she took her daughter into her arms, "this doesn't mean you will have to. The first baby is always the hardest. The next one will be easier, you'll see."

"I don't want a next one," Emma stated. "I don't want to go through this ever again."

"Oh no, Emma," her mother responded, "you never want to be without your children no matter what the cost." She reached up to brush the hair out of her daughter's eyes. "You and Jenny and Harry have been the joy of my life. I would be all alone without you. You need your children, Emma. You need their love."

Her daughter's jaw trembled. "I'm scared."

"I know, darling. I was too. But I will never be sorry that I brought you into this world, never." She paused. "Henry's a fine man, and will make a wonderful father. Don't deny him, Emma. He loves you. He will love your children."

The elder now took hold of Emma's arm, and walked her away from the grave to Henry and the waiting buggy.

Three and a half weeks later Jenny excitedly accepted a young man's invitation to a party. She had met him at church where she had already impressed several with her musical talent.

"You two go out too," Emma's mother encouraged as Henry shyly invited his wife out to dinner.

"I don't know," Emma responded. She really wasn't in the mood.

"Go," her mother insisted. "It will be good for you."

"Please Emma," Henry begged. "We haven't done anything together in ages."

Emma's resolve weakened, and the two took immediate advantage. Her mother quickly helped Emma get ready, and then Henry escorted her to the International Hotel. Hope rose within him. Maybe dinner here would again work its magic on Emma, just like it had the year before.

As the two took their seats at the table, the waiter brought a nice French wine and poured two glasses.

"Drink," Henry encouraged as he took up his own glass.

Emma sipped her wine. It was a good wine.

"So Wood tells me we have quite a stack of orders piling up for tinctures," Henry began. "Do you think you can get started on them very soon?"

"Yes," Emma replied quietly as she surveyed her surroundings. A whole year had passed since they had been at the restaurant. So much had happened.

"Good." Henry smiled. "We have an order of new wallpaper coming in this week. Maybe there will be something in it you would like for the front room."

"Can we afford it?" Emma asked.

"We'll manage," he answered.

"How?" she demanded. "We've had so many expenses already."

"I put off building the new store here in Helena," Henry responded quietly.

"Put off the new store?" Emma cried. "That's your dream, and you need it for fire protection."

"It will wait," he replied. "We have insurance."

"But why, Henry?"

"Because I no longer have the down payment to get a bank loan," he answered as he purposely reached for the wine bottle and began reading its label.

Emma took hold of his arm. "What happened to the down payment?"

Henry's eyes now settled on his wife. "I had to buy a cemetery plot," he told her reluctantly.

Emma's eyes widened, and then she looked quickly down at the table. Her whole demeanor took on a look of shock. She had been so caught up in her grief, she hadn't realized.

"Emma, it's all right," Henry offered. "This way we can afford a few things for the house, and then when we have another good year, Wood and I will build. We still have the land. He wasn't in any hurry to invest in a new store anyway."

"I want to leave," Emma decided as she looked up with tears in her eyes. "Please."

"You want to go home?" Henry asked.

"No," Emma replied as confusion settled over her. "No, I don't want to go home. Mother wouldn't like it. Can't we just go somewhere else, somewhere private?" she begged.

"Certainly," Henry responded as he rose to his feet. "Where would you like to go?"

"Anywhere," she answered.

Her husband left enough money on the table to cover their bottle of wine, and then escorted his wife to the door. "It's cold outside," he noted.

"I don't mind the cold," she replied.

They walked out together, traveling the icy walks. Henry didn't know where they were going. He really didn't care. His attention was on his wife.

"I didn't realize," she began after several blocks. "I didn't realize you were giving up the new store." She turned to him.

"It doesn't matter," he commented.

"It does matter," she responded. "It matters to me." She was staring into his eyes. Her face was pale, trembling with emotion. "You gave up the store for our baby."

Henry said nothing. He did not know what to say. He only knew that what he had done was right. Emma was so beautiful, and yet so very frail. He took her into his arms, holding her against him, treasuring the moment together. Her face turned upward, and suddenly they were kissing. It was as if all the penned up emotion of the past week, of their grief, of their sorrow, had found release right there on the side of the street. Henry looked up in desperation, wondering where they even were.

"We could go upstairs," Emma suggested feverishly.

The two stood in front of City Drug. It was closed. Henry glanced at the empty street, and immediately searched for his key. Letting them in, the two hastened upstairs where stacks of boxes and crates were now encroaching on their old rooms.

Emma's mother and sister stayed until the first of April, keeping Emma company and helping her catch up on the tincture shipments. Incredibly enough, Emma's creations were now more in demand than during the previous fall and winter. Then on Saturday, April 5th, Emma and Henry accompanied their relatives home to Deer Lodge. It was a good change of air for Emma, and Henry wanted the chance to discuss City Drug's spring orders with Harry. It was a brief visit. Emma and Henry were home within the week, and back to their old routines.

"It's good to see Emma in the store again," Wood commented to Henry. "She is almost her old self."

Henry smiled as he watched his wife help Mrs. Stoakes. "Emma seems to draw the lady customers."

"That she does," Wood agreed. "And you are getting almost human." He abruptly broke into a smile. "Come on Parchen, don't take offense. It's just good to see you put something else ahead of all the constant business demands...and you don't want to neglect Emma, not just now." He walked nonchalantly away.

Henry's gaze wandered to Mrs. Stoakes. Cy Ingersoll had entered the store, and stopped to talk to the ladies. Then as the elder woman left, Dr. Ingersoll's attention settled on Emma.

"Is she a patient," Emma asked.

"Who? Mrs. Stoakes?" Ingersoll responded.

"Yes."

Cy smiled. "I have called on both Mrs. Stoakes and her daughter as need has dictated. Her daughter's married to William Cullen, you know. He's served on the legislature."

"So I gathered," Emma replied.

"You are looking good," Cy decided. "I assume you haven't had any complications. I haven't seen you in a while."

"No, no complications," Emma answered softly.

"Good. Now what about the Lily of the Valley we talked about once. Did you ever make a tincture of it?"

"No. Do you need some?" Emma asked.

"I'm afraid so," Cy responded. "A miner from Virginia City has been here two months, and his heart is plaguing him terribly. He thought the change of air would make him better, but I think our altitude is just too high to make any difference."

"I wonder if Henry can get me any of the lily," Emma pondered. "I don't know if it's the right time of year. In any case it will take two weeks for the tinctures to cure."

"As I suspected," Cy Ingersoll replied. "I think I'll load my miner up then with some digitalis, and tell him to get out of the mountains. I really don't want to bury the man."

"Do they ever ignore your advice?" Emma inquired as the two walked down the drug store aisle.

"Too often for my liking," Cy replied. "By the way, Calista would like to know if she can come by the house for some tinctures. Actually, I think it's just an excuse to have a cup of tea. She misses her regular visits, and your little talks. Most women don't understand her technical language." He smiled.

"I will be home tomorrow morning," Emma responded. "I have some shipments to get out. Then I will be stocking shelves here in the store in the afternoon."

"I will tell her," Cy promised.

Calista did stop by in the morning, and Emma enjoyed their cup of tea. Calista left with nearly half a case of tinctures. By two in the afternoon, Emma was back at the store as promised. But as word had gotten out that she would be in, friends dropped by with their various minor complaints, and to personally see how Emma was doing. Even Mrs. Hauser dropped in to pick up some powder for her new daughter. The encounter was brief, but Emma eyed the infant with envy. She hadn't realized how much the mere sight of a baby would affect her.

"Emma."

Emma turned, and looked up from the half box she had managed to empty onto the bottom shelf. The afternoon had been a busy one.

"Emma, you can stop now," Henry told her. "The store's been closed for nearly half an hour."

"Is it that late?" she asked as she glanced toward the windows. The shades were already drawn.

"Yes, it is that late," Henry answered softly as he knelt beside her. "Where have you been?"

"Oh, I don't know. I guess I was thinking about the Hauser baby," Emma replied softly.

Henry took the box from between them, and turned his full attention on his wife. "We can have another. We can even spend another night upstairs, if you want."

Emma smiled. "I love you, Henry, but I really think the charm of that night was its spontaneity, not the cold room with all its boxes."

Henry now sat down beside her, pulling her into his lap. As she gasped in surprise, he laughed, and the two fell lengthwise on the floor. Henry kissed her, and slowly she responded as the passion grew between them.

The next morning Emma and Henry were both back at work as Wood Paynter noted their increased productivity. He pondered it a moment, and then smiled as he turned back to his customer. The miner wanted to talk, and not about the can of talcum he had come in for. He had relatives in Deer Lodge City, and he had just found out his little niece had whooping cough. Many of the school children were already sick with it, and he feared his nephew might catch it too.

When the man left, Wood Paynter went over to Henry. "You should be glad you made your trip to Deer Lodge when you did," he noted. "Whooping cough has just broken out down there."

Henry turned. "Whooping cough?"

"Yes. You better keep Emma home."

"Thanks," Henry responded as his eyes turned to his wife.

Two months went by almost unnoticed as Emma went about her work. Tincture orders had increased dramatically, and many of the spring plants were now available for use. Emma turned all her energies to the new demands, happy to be of use and of the money coming her way. She wanted very much to accumulate enough to secure the down payment on Henry's downtown store. She loved him for his sacrifice, and she would love to give the money back.

Emma sat down one morning with Calista over a cup of tea. She relished the little breaks from her duties that had once again become regular.

"You have been working pretty hard lately," Calista noted as she surveyed the number of medicinal plants drying on racks.

"Yes," Emma responded pleasantly, "I have…and I am enjoying it."

Calista smiled. "You won't be sorry to take a little break, will you?"

"A break, when?" Emma asked.

"Oh, I don't know," Calista replied evasively, "maybe in about six months."

"Well yes, orders do slow down during the winter," Emma agreed. "Yes, I suppose a break would be nice."

"How much weight have you gained?" Calista asked.

"Weight?" Emma replied. She looked down at her waist. "I have gained a little, haven't I? I guess I've been too busy to notice."

"And you're late?" Calista pressed.

Emma face flashed upward. "Yes, I probably am. How did you know that?"

"I'm a midwife, remember. It's my job to know."

"Are you saying what I think you are?" Emma suddenly demanded as her eyes grew large.

Calista smiled.

"No," Emma responded in disbelief, "it can't be."

"Are you sure?" Calista laughed. "You and Henry seem friendly enough."

Emma rose to her feet in confusion.

"Why don't we check for sure?" Calista suggested quietly.

Chapter Nine

Emma shut the door behind the midwife as she pondered their visit. Calista had come for medicine and a chance to talk. She had left with definite news. Emma was pregnant.

Emma did not know how to feel as she picked up their tea cups and deposited them in her wash pan. She returned to her drying plants, taking a bunch to her work space. Here she took the usable parts off the stalks, and placed them on a piece of oil cloth where she began crushing them with a rolling pin.

Emma worked methodically. Her thoughts were elsewhere. Suddenly she left her work, walked out of the kitchen, and headed upstairs. She hesitated in the doorway of the nursery, and then entered, whisking the dust sheets off the crib and the changing table. Her hand reached to touch the presence of the crib, the stack of diapers unmoved on the changing table. She wanted a baby so much, but the experience of the stillborn tormented her with fear. She did not want to loose another. She did not want to be like her mother. She did not want to face any more loss.

Emma sank to the floor as thoughts flooded her mind. She was pregnant. She didn't like the fact. The thought of the physical hell she had gone through mere months before was still fresh in her mind, especially when added to the grief of the dead baby. To face that again… Her thoughts turned to Henry. He wanted another child. He wanted her, and she had given in to their passion as much for her own sake as for his. She needed to feel his strength, his love. She knew it could lead to pregnancy, but she had shoved the thought from her mind for the sake of the moment, never allowing herself to consider how easily it could happen. Had they not tried month after month to start their family when they were first married? Pregnancy didn't happen every time, and the chances for occurrence had been few since the stillborn.

Emma shook her head in disbelief. She thought her moments of passion with Henry had been too few, too infrequent. But she was pregnant, Calista had examined her. Tears rose in Emma's eyes. She did not want to face the torment of labor. She did not want to loose another child. She looked around the small room through tear-filled eyes, wanting, but fearing the very thing that she would now have to face once again. She was pregnant.

She suddenly reached through the crib bars, pulling the blanket from the bed. This she held tightly to her breast as tears streamed down her cheeks. She was going to have another baby -- and she wanted it, she wanted it alive. This time she would protect it better, before it was born. Emma had not been sick a day all spring, all summer. Maybe this time… Hope rose within the young woman. She would not go down to Deer Lodge City, not now. They had a whooping cough epidemic there, they had had since late spring.

Emma's thoughts turned to Henry. Repeatedly she had suggested a visit to her mother's house, and he had forbid it, claiming he could not spare her. At the time she had thought he would simply miss her too much, and had used her tincture work as an excuse. But he knew about the whooping cough, her brother had made repeated orders for their cough syrup, a newly developed product from Emma's hands. Whooping cough was a danger Henry did not want her exposed to, not while there was any chance of something occurring like the year before.

A soft smile rose to Emma's lips. She would have a healthy baby. She would have it for Henry. She rose to her feet, re-placed the dust sheets over the baby furniture, and left the room.

By the time Henry got home from the store that night, he was hot and sweaty. Summer was fully upon them; and despite opening what doors and windows City Drug had, it was still stifling hot. He was exhausted as he sat down at the dinner table. Emma had prepared a simple meal, refraining from any more cooking than was absolutely necessary.

"I wish this was lakefront property," Henry complained as he ate. He noted the two new cases of cough syrup ready to be shipped against the wall.

"I could prepare a bath for you," Emma responded. "It wouldn't be the same, I know, but it would cool you down."

"It wouldn't be the same at all," Henry replied as he finished his meal, "but I will take it. You could cool off too."

"I don't think my day was as hot as yours," she stated as she rose from the table. "The downtown gulch can get awfully stifling. We had some breeze up here."

"I'll get the tub," Henry offered.

Emma went upstairs, and got her husband a towel and his nightshirt. When she returned, the tub sat in the kitchen, the curtains were drawn, and together she and Henry pumped water on the back porch as dusk settled in for the night. It was late. Henry always worked late.

Within minutes the tub had two inches of water in its bottom, and Henry turned to his wife. "Why don't you go first?"

"I don't have my nightgown," she responded. She didn't want to go first. She didn't want to go at all. The thought of Henry seeing her without clothes was not something she wanted, not after Calista's visit that morning.

"I'll run up and get it," Henry offered.

Emma watched him go, and panic swept her. He wasn't taking "no" for an answer. She was going to get wet, that was all there was to it. In desperation she tore off her clothes, and got in the tub, splashing water all over. Then she stopped, and listened for Henry's footsteps on the stairs. All was quiet. He was taking longer than she had expected. Cautiously and quickly she began to wash. Then as she heard him coming back downstairs, she grabbed the generous towel and rose, wrapping it around her middle.

"You're through?" Henry exclaimed as he walked into the kitchen. "What's your hurry?"

"I know how much you're looking forward to the cool water. I didn't want to hold you up," Emma replied as she stepped out.

"Here's your nightgown," Henry offered.

As he sat down to take off his shoes, Emma quickly slipped into her night clothes. "I think I'll go on up to bed," she commented.

Henry made no response as she gathered her things and slipped from the room. In bare feet Emma escaped upstairs. Adrenaline flowed through her body as she pondered her narrow escape. Her hand slipped to her middle, feeling its extra bulk. She was going to have to tell Henry about her pregnancy.

Emma entered their room, and dropped her clothes in the rocking chair. Then she wandered into the nursery. But this time she did not remove the dust covers, she felt the wood of the crib through the cloth, pondering her situation. To tell Henry the truth, to admit Calista was correct, was to admit aloud her greatest fear, but she was nearly through her third month, and more people would soon suspect the truth. She was surprised in a way that Henry had not said something already.

Emma returned to their bed and climbed in, pulling the sheet up over her as she faced into the darkness, away from Henry's side. Within twenty minutes he crawled in beside her. He lay still for a few moments.

"Business has been really good lately," he noted aloud.

"How good?" she asked over her shoulder, glad that his mind was not on her.

"Really good," he replied.

She rolled onto her back. "Good enough to make up for the last six months?"

"And then some," he added.

Emma rose up on an elbow. "Then you and Wood can get the loan and start building the new store downtown."

"I could if the down payment was only half as much as it is," Henry responded. "I'm afraid Wood has had some unexpected expenses."

"He doesn't have his share?" Emma cried.

"It doesn't appear that way," Henry answered. "I'm afraid the downtown store just isn't meant to be built yet."

Emma knew that Wood had been scrambling for money. She didn't know the particulars. Henry didn't confide everything he knew. He respected his partner too much.

"Emma, your medicines have really started to take off. We should be able to afford a little wallpaper and paint."

She knew he was smiling even though it was too dark to see. "I enjoy my work," she replied.

"Maybe we can even order a new bed, and fix up your mother's room so she can come for the holidays," he suggested. "I want you to be happy."

"I am happy," Emma responded.

"Yes Emma, you are happy on the surface," he agreed, "but we both know that you won't be completely happy until one thing happens." His tone had suddenly shifted into grave seriousness.

A wave of alarm swept Emma. Here it was. She had to tell him. She had to tell him the truth. Her jaw trembled. Her eyes watered. No words came to her lips. She didn't know how to even begin.

"Emma, I know you are scared." Henry's voice was suddenly very tender. "But we have to face it."

Emma grabbed his hand, pulling it to her stomach. She took it and flattened it against her like when she wanted him to feel their unborn kick.

"Emma…" Henry's voice fell off. His hand now moved on its own, touching and feeling. "Emma? You're late?"

"Over two months late," she replied quietly.

"Why didn't you tell me?" he demanded.

"I never kept track. I didn't think…"

"Emma, is this true? Do you know for sure?"

"Yes," she answered. "Calista was by this morning."

"Calista? Then it is true," he declared as he rose up on an arm. "You are really with child!" His breath exploded from his lips in sure pleasure, and he gasped like a man in disbelief, blessed disbelief.

Emma's heart sank within her. Her husband's joy was her fear, and it caused a ghastly, hollow feeling.

"Emma, what is wrong," Henry demanded.

"I'm scared," she replied simply.

"Don't be," he responded. "Second babies are always easier. Everyone says so." He laid his head then on her stomach, and kissed it. Then he took her into his arms, smothering her with the joy of his caresses. His love was hard to resist, and slowly, very slowly Emma found herself responding to him, her fear sliding into the background. Maybe he was right. Maybe second babies were easier. Maybe this child would be born alive and well.

The following day after church, Henry and Emma walked home. The weather was muggy. Scattered clouds lingered overhead, but the weather had not cooled. With relief they entered their home. Emma dropped her hymnal on a small table, and headed upstairs to change into something cooler. Henry was removing his necktie.

"Emma, are you planning to write to your mother this afternoon?" he asked.

"Yes," she replied as she climbed the stairs.

"Are you going to tell her about the baby?"

"No."

"Why not?" he demanded. He stood at the base of the stairs as she continued climbing.

"Because I don't want to write her about it," Emma answered.

"Then how do you plan to tell her?" Henry inquired.

Emma stopped. She was a good seven feet above him. "I don't know."

"You will be big with the baby by Christmas," Henry commented.

Emma felt a wave of fear sweep her. What he said was true.

"Emma," Henry continued as he now climbed the stairs between them, "you have to tell her."

"I don't want to do it by mail," Emma responded.

"You can't go down there, not with the whooping cough," Henry stated.

"I know," Emma replied quietly.

"She will be hurt if you don't tell her reasonably soon," Henry told her. "Your mother sets great store by babies."

"Yes she does," Emma agreed quietly.

"Perhaps you should invite her to Helena," Henry coaxed.

"The spare bed was borrowed," Emma noted. "We gave it back."

"Then perhaps we should go shopping," Henry offered. "It is summer. It shouldn't take too long to order in a bed." He paused momentarily. "Invite your mother to Helena. We will figure something out."

"She will get suspicious if I invite her for no reason," Emma replied evasively.

"Is that so bad?" Henry asked with a smile.

"Yes," Emma decided. "I don't want her jumping to any conclusions."

"Well, the fair is coming up in September," Henry suggested. "I'm sure your sister would like to go. Invite them both."

"I would like to see them," Emma continued as they finished climbing the stairs together. "Maybe they would come."

"It might even cool down a little by then," Henry offered as they entered the bedroom. He purposely stepped on the hem of her skirt as she dropped her shawl on the chair. "I don't know why you took a wrap to church," Henry commented as Emma discovered her skirt confined her. "You surely were hot enough without it."

"It was to cover up my extra weight," Emma replied as she turned. She was suddenly in his arms.

"Just because my wife is becoming more voluptuous, is no reason to hide the fact." He grinned.

"I don't want people to know," Emma responded as her fingers paused in their task of unbuttoning the bodice of her silk blouse. It had been a mistake to wear it. The silk didn't breathe, and she was dripping with perspiration.

"The whole world should know," Henry countered. "We are going to have a baby. That's good news."

"Not if it doesn't live," Emma replied. She grimaced. She had spoken without thinking.

Henry's levity vanished. He grabbed her hand, pulling her after him. They descended the steps and exited the house.

"Where are we going?" Emma asked as she hurried after him.

"You'll see," he answered.

Henry led the way for several blocks, and then turned in at the Ingersoll house. Aromas from Calista's Sunday dinner met them at the door along with her son. The house was full with their extended family.

"Ed, is your father home?" Henry inquired.

"Dad," he called over his shoulder as he opened the screen door for them.

Cy Ingersoll appeared from the kitchen. "Henry, Emma, it's good to see you," he greeted. "What can I do for you?"

"It's Emma," Henry began.

"In here," Cy automatically responded as he indicated his office. He closed the door behind them. "What seems to be the trouble," he asked as his gaze settled on the young woman.

"You know she's pregnant," Henry stated.

"Yes, congratulations," he replied with a soft smile.

"Emma is afraid she's going to loose the baby again," Henry continued.

Cy focused sharply on the young woman. "Are you having problems?"

"No problems," she answered quietly.

Cy studied her a moment, and then his eyes shifted in confusion to Henry. He sat down in his desk chair. "I'm afraid I don't understand. Calista said everything looks fine."

"I have no doubt," Henry agreed, "that everything is fine."

Realization dawned on Cy, and his attention shifted back to Emma. "You had me scared for a moment." He smiled. "Just because you had a stillborn, Emma, doesn't mean it will happen again. From what Calista tells me, you are the peak of health, and have been. Don't worry. The baby will be fine."

Emma made no reply.

Cy rose from his chair and took Emma by the shoulders, looking her squarely in the eye. "There is no reason you should loose this baby. It wasn't your fault."

"Then whose was it?" Emma replied.

"I don't know, but it wasn't yours," Cy responded. "Believe me, it wasn't yours. This baby will be fine."

Henry walked over to the office door, and opened it. The commotion outside died into silence. Cy's family gathered, concerned over the sudden interruption. They all knew Emma from the previous Thanksgiving, and Henry from long before that.

"Is everything all right?" Calista asked.

"Yes," Henry answered, "but Emma has an announcement to make, if you haven't already told your family." He turned to his wife.

Emma felt heat flush her neck and face. Her heart beat widely as Cy took her by the arm and led her out of the office. Emma was suddenly standing before all his family.

"I...ah, I..." Emma's voice broke. "I'm expecting," she finally blurted after several moments.

The Ingersoll family excitedly descended upon her, congratulating her and asking questions.

Emma looked around for an escape, but there was none as Henry stood nearby with a smile on his face. Emma answered one excited question after another as her eyes repeatedly returned to her husband. She wanted to leave; but before she knew it, Henry had accepted an invitation to dinner.

"So does your mother know?" Calista asked as she and Emma cleared the table.

Emma's attention swung to the woman.

"I imagine she has been waiting for the news," Calista continued as she handed Emma an empty bowl to take with them to the kitchen.

"No, I haven't told her yet," Emma answered.

"Why on earth not?" Calista demanded.

"I don't want to tell her in a letter, and Deer Lodge City has had all that whooping cough," Emma replied.

"Oh yes, the whooping cough," Calista acknowledged, "but a letter is better than nothing...or you could invite her over."

"We thought we might do that in September, so she and my sister could come to the fair," Emma offered.

"September?" Calista repeated. "You will be half way through your pregnancy by then."

"Yes, and she will have half the time to worry," Emma stated.

"Oh Emma, mothers always worry, don't concern yourself about that. It's their job. Besides, this could be your tenth baby, and she would still fret over you as if it was your first. I know. I have watched it a thousand times. The only instance when it doesn't happen, is when there is no mother, and that's worse." She smiled. "You have a great mother. Tell her."

"So you are finally writing to Deer Lodge," Henry noted quietly over Emma's shoulder that evening.

"I'm not telling her," Emma responded as she looked defiantly up at him.

"Just invite her to the fair," he replied.

"It's too soon for that," she retorted. "Besides, we haven't a room prepared yet."

"I will match some paint to the wallpaper you like, and bring it home tomorrow. We should have a new shipment of the paper by next week."

"And the bed?" Emma demanded.

"I will look into it," Henry promised.

"I didn't appreciate what you did earlier. It was none of their business."

"Calista already knew," Henry replied. "So did Cy."

"But not the whole family," Emma countered. "They didn't need to know, not like that."

"It wasn't their need I was concerned about. It was yours," Henry responded. "Emma, I love that you are carrying our child. You should love it too."

"They didn't need to know," Emma repeated.

Henry squatted down beside her. "Emma, you are carrying our baby."

She looked into his eyes. She felt his love. Suddenly she rose.

He rose too, pulling her into his arms. "Emma, you have to let the past go," he whispered to her. "You are carrying our baby, our Adele."

Emma focused sharply on him. The name hadn't been spoken since their tragedy. "Our Adele?" she repeated.

"Yes, Adele is here," he said as he cradled her growing stomach in his hands. "You are carrying our daughter, and she will be as beautiful as her mother. She will probably be a singer too, like Jenny and your grandfather." He smiled.

"Adele," Emma repeated.

"Yes, Emma. Our daughter. She is in your womb now, but she will be in your arms by February. It's not so long to wait, not for Adele."

Emma's jaw quivered. She wanted a daughter so much. She wanted Adele.

Henry's lips touched hers as tears flowed from her eyes.

True to Henry's word, he brought home paint the following evening; and wallpaper the next week. Before many more days had passed, the local furniture store delivered a new oak bedroom set, complete with bed, chest of drawers, and shaving stand. Henry was on hand for its arrival, and instructed the men to take it up to their room, while he and Cy moved the old furniture into the guest bedroom. Emma hadn't asked her mother to visit yet, but she had hinted in her letters that the fair was coming up in September.

As the men from the store left, Henry and Cy stood at the bottom of the stairs. Emma joined them.

"What do you think?" Cy asked.

"The new furniture is beautiful," Emma answered.

"Cy knows of a cabin not far from a little lake up the gulch," Henry told his wife. "What if we take off a couple days for a little vacation? I could do some fishing."

"I like fish," Emma responded, "especially trout."

Cy smiled. "And you can swim and cool off. And when you are too bored, there's always hiking. Exercise is good for expectant mothers. Just don't over do it."

"I'm too lazy to over do it," Emma replied.

"Yes, of course," Cy laughed. "You and Henry are two peas from the same pod. How late did you stay up last night with your tinctures?"

"Only eleven," Emma answered. "I had to shake them."

Cy turned to Henry. "The cabin is only free next week. So don't put off going. Emma, I have to run. Calista wants me to drop in on one of her midwife visits. Something about a complication."

As Cy left, Henry turned to his wife. "I will make arrangements with Wood to get off early Saturday, and we can spend Sunday and Monday up there. All right? You finished your tinctures?"

"Yes," Emma agreed. A few days off sounded wonderful.

By five o'clock Saturday afternoon, Henry was gathering things to take up to the cabin. Fishing poles, a tackle box...he handed his wife a compass. "Stick that in your pocket, and keep it with you at all times," he instructed. "It's easy to get turned around in the woods."

"Okay," Emma replied as she tucked it away, and put her nightie in the carpet bag. "Do you want anything besides your nightshirt and razor?" she asked.

"Just some extra socks. I might get my feet wet, fishing." Henry pulled out two pistols and a rifle.

"What are those for?" Emma asked in surprise. "Are you going hunting?"

"Do you know how to use a gun?" Henry inquired.

"No."

He briefly showed her the basics.

"Henry, I don't want to hunt," Emma responded.

"You don't have to," he countered. "They're for protection. We don't know what animal's territory we might be invading, and bears... Well if they even smell food, they're ready to take it from you even before you get a chance to taste it. The guns are just to keep them at bay. I'm not going up to hunt. I'm going fishing." He smiled, and threw a few last items on the pile. "Do you want anything else?" he asked. "If not, I'll load this stuff into the buggy."

"Don't forget the food in the kitchen," she reminded him.

Forty-five minutes later Emma was seated beside her husband as the horse pulled them up Rodney to State Street. They passed below the crest of the hill where the dirt road joined Davis and extended into the gulch. The horse trotted rhymetically through the steeper terrain. The hills now rose on either side with trees reaching down to the lane. From time to time, kilns would appear where industrious men were carving a living from the soil. Humble domiciles also existed nearby, but all these became less and less frequent as they climbed farther into the green hills.

Suddenly their pace slowed, and Emma's attention returned to the road. A herd of deer grazed on either side. Emma turned to Henry, and he put a finger to his lips as a smile lit his eye.

Chapter Ten

The buggy continued to approach the herd of deer. Emma watched spell bound as the horse pulled them closer and closer. The deer didn't seem to mind the horse at all, but drifted causally out of the way.

Henry pulled on the reins, and the horse stopped. The deer continued to graze unconcerned as Emma stared in amazement. Then one doe looked up, curious. Emma extended her hand. The deer was so close, she could almost touch it. In eager surprise, Emma turned to Henry. He smiled, and silently raised a forefinger to his lips as a reminder to maintain their silence. Emma stared around her. Never had she been so close to deer. Never before had she watched them proceed with their lives as if she wasn't even there.

Henry now tapped the horse lightly with the reins, and they again moved forward. Heading up the road, they soon left the deer behind. After about forty minutes, Henry again slowed the animal, and pointed to two chipmunks running across the road and up a tree.

Emma was fascinated as her husband again urged the horse onward. After another hour they approached a junction in the road. Henry turned left, and slowed the horse as they now entered a narrow lane.

"How do you know which way to go?" Emma asked.

"I know these hills," he replied. "Before I met you, I used to come up here on Sundays, and spend the entire day, usually on foot. Then once in a while I would take an extra day or two off like now, and hike as far as I could get."

"Why?" Emma cried.

Henry smiled. "Why not? The hills are beautiful, and there is always something unexpected around the corner, a deer, a new wild flower, something."

"The tinctures," Emma gasped. "You get the plants up here, don't you?"

"Some of them," Henry agreed. "There is plenty of horsetail and fireweed. But some of the stuff you want doesn't grow here. I order that, once I find out where to get it." Henry pointed. "There's the lake."

"We're here already?" Emma exclaimed.

"It doesn't take long, not when you're enjoying yourself."

The buggy passed the lake within minutes. Two tents were erected near its shore. Emma pointed to them, and Henry responded, "Probably John and Platt. I think they were coming up this weekend."

"Who are they?" Emma asked.

"Oh just a couple of businessmen and would-be politicians." Henry grinned.

"Are you going fishing with them?"

"That kind of depends," Henry replied. "Maybe."

He directed the horse on past, and turned off the road a quarter of a mile beyond. There, picking their way through the trees, the lane turned into hardly more than wheel tracks. Emma could hear a stream gurgling close by, and the soil became more rocky. Henry directed the buggy through the brush, and suddenly there was a cabin at the foot of the hill.

"Used to be a miner's cabin," Henry offered as he pulled the horse to a stop. A lean-to barn stood nearby.

"It's beautiful here," Emma responded.

"I'm afraid the cabin is very primitive," Henry stated, "but I told you that this morning. It will make the Frenchwoman's place look luxurious."

Emma smiled as he helped her out of the buggy. The reference to their wedding trip did not go unnoticed.

Henry grabbed Emma's carpet bag and a basket of food. Then he led the way inside. It was completely empty.

"Good, it's been swept out," Henry noted.

Emma looked around her. The building was small. It had a fireplace, and nothing more. "We sleep on the floor?" she asked.

"On the bed rolls we brought," he answered. "It's getting dark. I'd better hurry and get this stuff unloaded."

Emma walked over to the single window. It looked down the slope toward the lake. She turned and went out, helping Henry get the stuff inside. Then he took the horse to the barn.

Emma spread their bed rolls on the floor. The baskets of food she placed near the fireplace. Henry came in.

"Are you hungry?" she asked as she offered the bakery rolls he had purchased for the occasion.

He reached for the bread, and collapsed comfortably on the bed roll. "I thought I would go fishing first thing in the morning. Do you want to come?"

"Are the chokecherries ripe?" Emma inquired. "Calista told me there are tons of them up here."

"There's a patch just north of the cabin."

"Maybe I will do that instead," she decided.

"Wait until I get back," he warned. "Bears love chokecherries. If I get lucky, I should have a couple nice fish by breakfast; and we can go after that."

In the morning Emma rolled over as bright sunlight poured from their single window. She was alone, as usual. She vaguely remembered Henry getting up while it was still dark. Emma reached for the bakery goods, and then rose to her feet and went outside to eat her breakfast on the front step, still in her nightgown and bare feet. It was a beautiful summer morning, warm and fresh with the scent of trees and grass.

When she finished, Emma returned inside to dress. Henry had left a pistol on top of her clothes. She set it aside as she dressed, and then strapped it obediently to her waist. She had heard plenty of stories about wildlife not wanting to share their beautiful habitat. She looked at her shoes and socks. They looked confining and tight in her pregnant condition. She was on vacation. Why shouldn't she enjoy herself?

Emma went outside, and headed to the barn. If Henry hadn't taken the horse, she would hitch it to the buggy and go to the lake. She reached the shed, rounding the corner to the door. The long grass at her feet jerked explosively, and two small creatures darted away. The movement ignited movement farther on, but this creature did not follow the others' flight. It was bigger, and ran straight at Emma.

Alarmed, she glanced quickly around for safety. A ladder, built into the side of the barn, rose to the opening over the main door where hay was deposited for the winter. Emma leaped onto it, ascending three or four steps in her haste to get away from the animal. The wood rungs were rough, and Emma adjusted her stance as she now looked down. The creature stood at the base of the ladder, it's thin quills pointing up at her, a low agitated noise rising to her ears. The animal searched the trampled grass.

"A porcupine," Emma gasped in surprise. The animal's head rose momentarily as Emma noted its small shiny eyes. "Go away," Emma demanded.

The creature pondered Emma, its forepaws rising against the side of the shed.

Emma watched in alarm. She had never considered whether the animal was capable of climbing a ladder.

The porcupine tried to grip the wood with its claws. But as it could not get a foot hold, it dropped back to the ground.

Emma let out a sigh of relief. The porcupine again looked at her. Every time she made noise or changed her position on the crude ladder, the animal's attention sharpened on her, and its quills rose in defiance. In between, however, the animal would become distracted, chewing on grass and pine needles, or digging for roots at the base of a nearby bush.

Emma was stuck. Henry's pistol caught on the ladder side, and reminded her of its presence. She could just shoot the animal, and then she would be free to leave. But she remembered the small creatures that had raced away at her approach. The porcupine had young, and the death of the mother would leave them helpless and hungry. Emma could try to jump off the ladder and run to safety, but the porcupine had moved with incredible speed; and with Emma's bare feet, she wasn't positive she wouldn't falter at a critical moment. It was better she just waited for the animal to leave.

Emma hung off her crude ladder as moments turned into minutes, and minutes turned into an hour. Still the porcupine lingered. Emma made as little noise and movement as possible, but her feet hurt from the wood of the crude rungs biting into her flesh. Her muscles ached too. Still she waited. Clouds came over the tree tops. A brisk little wind had picked up. Emma was starting to get cold, but the porcupine didn't seem to notice. Emma glanced down the road. If only Henry would come home...

Another twenty minutes elapsed as Emma hung from her perch. The sun no longer shined, and the breeze was steady as she waited impatiently. Then she felt the first drops of rain hit her forehead. Then came more, big drops, splashing against her as she realized she was going to get very wet. She reached for Henry's pistol. She was not going to let a porcupine put her health in danger, not when she carried an unborn child. Her eyes dropped to the base of the ladder, but the porcupine was not there.

Emma descended with caution. The grass could hide many things. But once Emma's feet hit the ground, she took off at a dead run for the cabin. The pistol rode forgotten at her waist as heavy rain now fell on her. By the time she reached the cabin door, the downpour had soaked her to the bone.

Emma broke into the cabin as she stripped off her wet things, wrapping a blanket around her. Then her attention turned to the fireplace. The wood had already been laid. Matches rested in their tin box on the mantel, and she promptly secured one, setting the kindling on fire. Within minutes a nice fire was warming her, and she turned to dry her hair with a dish towel she had brought with. Now she relaxed. She was warm. She was dry. The porcupine was gone.

Emma heard footsteps outside, and suddenly the cabin door slammed open. Emma's blanket instinctively rose to cover her. Who was this intruder that was catching her only in her underwear? In her pregnant condition, the camisole barely covered her bosom, and her pantaloons were pulled tight.

A water drenched man came through the door, moisture dripping from his hat, from his clothes, leaving puddles around his feet. Suddenly he straightened.

"Henry, you're soaked," Emma exclaimed as her blanket fell to the floor. She was instantly with him, setting his bucket of fish aside, leading him to the warmth of the fire as she removed his hat. "Take off your wet things," she admonished as she picked up her blanket to keep it from getting dripped on.

Henry obeyed. Both knew the danger of catching a chill.

"Where is the horse," Emma asked as she dried him with her towel.

"In the barn," Henry answered. "He's fine. That rain surely came out of nowhere."

"Right over the tree tops," Emma agreed. "A blame porcupine had me cornered out at the shed. That is the last time I go without shoes up here."

"A porcupine?" Henry repeated with a smile. "Why didn't you use your gun?"

"It had young," his wife responded. "I couldn't kill it."

"You didn't have to kill it," he replied with a grin. "The noise would have frightened it away."

Emma stared at him.

"Is that why you are barely dressed?" Henry asked softly.

"I got drenched," Emma explained as she pointed to where her clothes lay to one side of the fire. "I don't know how long it's going to take them to dry."

"Or mine," Henry decided as he took hold of his wife at the waist, "but I have an idea how to pass the time."

After a nice lunch of fried fish, potatoes, and onion, Emma and Henry found their clothes were merely damp and put them back on. Outside, the sun shinned once again on the sparkling wet world.

"Do you think the weather will last?" Emma asked as she and her husband stood studying the patch of sky overhead. "It's become awfully hot and muggy."

"It should last for ten minutes anyway," Henry responded with a chuckle. "The chokecherries aren't far. We don't want to sit in the cabin all day."

Emma turned. "Oh, I don't know. At least you aren't off somewhere, or working." She smiled.

Henry smirked as he pulled his wife closer. "I want four kids you know," he whispered in her ear. "Boys."

"Not boys, not the first one at any rate," Emma retorted as she pulled away with a grin.

"But after," he insisted as he grabbed for her again. She waltzed free just beyond his reach as they danced around the small clearing in front of the cabin.

"What about the chokecherries?" she asked now as it became harder and harder to escape her husband's fervor.

"Chokecherries?" he laughed as he grabbed again for her, and latched onto her arm. "What about chokecherries?"

Emma dropped theatrically into the damp grass. The moisture felt good against the heat of the summer day. "You promised."

Henry pulled her unceremoniously to her feet. "Then chokecherries you shall have." He disappeared momentarily inside, returning with two buckets and his rifle. The two set off under the summer sun as their frivolity resumed. Emma had her husband's attention, and she wasn't about to lose it.

Suddenly Henry's mood changed. He instructed his wife to pick from the nearest bush while he went beyond, his eyes alert, his ears listening. Then he hastened back to Emma.

"There's a cougar upwind of us," he whispered quietly.

Emma's eyes rose in alarm. "Where?"

Henry positioned her so she could make out the enormous cat some distance away. A second one appeared, and the first took a swing at it. Soon the two cougars were wrestling.

Emma gasped.

Henry put a finger to his lips to indicate silence. Then he took her arm, leading her away. They retreated the distance to the cabin. There, Henry took the horse from the barn and hitched it to the buggy. Helping Emma in, he headed toward the lake.

"Those were the biggest cats I have ever seen," Emma commented finally.

"There are more chokecherries down by the water," Henry offered. "They aren't as big, but at least we won't have to worry about cougar."

"Don't they come down to the lake?" Emma asked.

"Those two have the creek," Henry answered, "and I don't remember seeing cougar at the lake. Too many people maybe." Within minutes, Henry pulled the horse off the road, and they approached the water.

"Where is everyone?" Emma demanded. "There were two tents here yesterday."

"Gone home. Tomorrow is a work day," Henry responded, "and it is getting on toward supper."

"Is it that late?" Emma asked. It was still hot, and perspiration trickled down her neck.

"Yes, are you hungry?" Henry replied. "We can pick some chokecherries."

"I want them for cooking," Emma countered.

Henry drove the buggy through the grass. Chokecherry bushes grew close to the water, loaded with fruit. Emma jumped from the vehicle, grabbing a bucket as she went. Within minutes Henry joined her. He laid the rifle at his feet as he began to pick. His chokecherries, however, never made it to the bucket.

"Henry, you're eating them all," Emma noted.

"I'm hungry." He smiled.

"So am I," she replied, "but chokecherries don't taste very good right off the bush."

"A little dry," he agreed as he offered her some.

Her mouth never opened. "Henry, you're smashing them on me," she complained. She reached into her bucket, grabbing a handful of chokecherries that she promptly smashed against him.

He pulled away, quickly picking a few more, throwing them at her.

Emma threw back, waltzing closer and closer to the water's edge. Suddenly she held up her hand. "Stop," she demanded, "the juice is going to stain our clothes."

Henry's closed hand fell to his side as he approached the water. Emma was already at its edge, washing her face and hands. Suddenly Henry bent over her, smashing chokecherries again into her mouth. She squealed as both fell onto the bank.

"Stop," she cried, "we're getting all wet and muddy."

"Then let's get all wet and muddy," he laughed.

"No, our clothes," she protested.

"Take them off," he responded. "No one is around. We can go for a swim. You can swim, can't you?" he asked.

"Of course," Emma retorted. The water would feel good in the humid heat.

Henry's demeanor suddenly quieted. "Maybe it's too cold to swim, I mean..."

"I doubt that," Emma replied as she pulled free. Within moments she plunged into the lake, her clothes hastily hung on a chokecherry bush.

Henry quickly followed.

The mountain water was cold enough to invigorate them. Henry chased his wife as she swam parallel to the bank. He swam with long, powerful strokes as he quickly overcame the small distance between them. Then he dove. He came up beneath Emma, grabbing her at the hips, lifting her into the air. Surprised gasps and chuckles broke from his wife as she slid back down into his arms. Suddenly his lips were against hers, and they kissed until Emma suddenly broke away, laughing.

Henry swam after her again, catching her by the ankle. She turned, doubling over as she rose into the air and then landed on him. They crashed into the depths of the water amid explosions of more laughter.

Emma's face suddenly rose. "Is the horse okay?" A small bear was approaching the water as the former noticeably become nervous.

"Oh heck, I forgot about the horse," Henry complained as he jumped to his feet, running along the shore to the buggy.

Emma stifled a laugh as she watched her husband's cheeks catch the glow of the evening sun. Then she rose as well, hurrying the distance to her clothes.

The small black bear took one look at Henry, and turned tail, bawling as he went. Henry immediately retrieved his rifle, and then calmed the horse before turning again to his clothes. Emma had already claimed the bushes and was nearly dressed. Henry joined her. She smiled. Suddenly he realized his nakedness, and blushed.

Emma reached over and planted a quick kiss on his lips. "You'd better hurry. It will be dark soon, and we need to get back to the cabin."

The following morning Henry joined Emma outside the cabin as she took a morning walk through the meadow. The grass rose well above her ankles as she strolled through it, stopping now and again to pick the wildflowers that grew randomly in its midst: Rocky Mountain Blue Bells, Crane's Bill, and Water Hemlock.

"Are any of these good for tinctures?" she asked Henry.

"Water Hemlock is poisonous," Henry pointed. "As far as the others go, you would know more about them than me."

"I guess they're just pretty then." She smiled.

Henry slipped his arm around her shoulder. "We really should leave pretty soon."

"I hate to go back," Emma responded. "You will be down at the drug store until late, and I have enough paperwork to keep me busy for a month."

Henry smiled. "Your tincture business is doing well."

"Thanks to the whooping cough in Deer Lodge City," she replied. "I'm not sure I like making money off the sick."

"But without you, they wouldn't have your medicine," he countered, "and you should be paid for your work."

"The medicine does seem to help, but... Deer Lodge has had the epidemic for three or four months now. You'd think they would kick it."

"Individuals have. It's just that everyone keeps passing it around. You know little children, they share everything."

"Well I'm going to watch ours," Emma decided. "If an epidemic hits Helena, they are not going to school. I will teach them myself."

"And take care of all your orders too?" Henry asked with a smile. "You can't protect our children from everything."

"But I can try," Emma responded with determination. "Sick people suffer too much." Her head turned suddenly. "Where is the mine, anyway? You said the cabin used to be a miner's."

"There was a cave in." Henry pointed. "The entrance used to be behind the cabin, there in the hill. But there's nothing much left, just a hollow full of rock and dirt and broken timbers."

Once a week Emma wrote her mother, and over the next two months plans were made for a visit to Helena. Emma's mother and sister would come for the fair while her brother, Harry, would take the opportunity to go back East to visit their old home in St. Louis and his familiar trampings in New York where he had resided during the Civil War.

The Fourth Annual Fair at Helena promised to be exciting. Six whole days of festivities were planned with the best exhibitions to be given in the entire territory. The whole city was caught up in anticipation of the event. Henry and Wood were busy preparing their exhibition and sales booth.

"Mother, have you forgotten your parasol?" Jenny demanded early Wednesday morning. Her face turned eagerly to Emma. "We're meeting Henry at the fair?"

"Yes," her sister responded, "at the booth. Then we will watch the ball game together."

Jenny waited impatiently for Emma to finish shutting up the house, and then the three women began the walk downtown where they caught the omnibus for the fair grounds. The vehicle was crowded and vocal as the city residents anticipated the day ahead. The horse drawn vehicle let Emma and her mother and sister off at the fair amid a throng of people who slowly made their way in.

"Where is Henry's booth?" Jenny asked.

"Over by the women's displays," Emma answered as she pointed to an exhibition tent.

The three walked through the mob of people, excitedly talking about what they wanted to see. Within minutes they were at the women's displays, and only with effort did Emma manage to keep her mother and sister from becoming distracted.

Emma wished she hadn't bothered as they drew near City Drug's booth. Voices were coming from the back of Parchen & Paynter's stall, masculine voices, angry voices. Emma glanced at her mother and sister. There was no question who the voices belonged to.

Chapter Eleven

"Emma, dear, perhaps Jenny and I should walk on over to the bleachers ahead of you," her mother suggested. "You could meet us there."

"Yes," Emma responded, "okay."

"I don't think that Paynter fellow likes us much," Jenny whispered quickly to her sister.

Emma watched the two disappear into the crowd. Now she turned to the booth. The voices faded into silence as she approached the back. She waited several moments, seeking the courage to go inside.

Wood Paynter had said some things she didn't like. He had all but accused her husband of cheating him, of devoting more time to Emma's tincture sales and the Deer Lodge store than to Helena's City Drug. Emma couldn't see how that was possible. Henry was always downtown. ...and it wasn't like Wood hadn't had the opportunity to be a part of both. He had sold his interest in Deer Lodge to her brother, and had refused the tincture business outright. If he wasn't interested in expansion that was his right, but he shouldn't restrict Henry.

Emma opened the door, and stepped inside. Henry was out in front with customers. Wood looked up. His face was still slightly flushed as he turned back to what he was doing. Emma's arrival would not draw a friendly greeting from him today.

Emma walked through the tiny structure to her husband's side.

"Oh Emma, is it that time already?" Henry asked in surprise.

"Yes," she responded quietly.

Her husband glanced behind him. It was only momentary. "Where are the others?"

"They went on ahead," she answered.

"Maybe you should do the same," he commented. "I'm afraid I can't get away like I hoped."

Emma was quiet momentarily. "Shall I bring you something to eat later?"

Henry's eyes flashed to her. Gratitude was there. "Yes, please." He paused momentarily as he took hold of her hand. "I'm sorry about all this. Can you make my apologies to your mother?"

"Yes," Emma replied.

Emma's mother was only two booths down, purchasing scones for everyone. Jenny stood idly waiting as she listened to the music from Groshon's booth. Her eyes drifted to the fiddler playing his violin. Several people were dancing as others, including Jenny, moved to the beat. Emma joined her sister as she recognized several of her husband's customers.

"You and mother haven't made it to the baseball game, I see," Emma commented.

"How is Henry doing?" Jenny asked.

"He can't get away," Emma answered. "I have to pick him up some lunch later."

"I never liked Paynter," Jenny replied quietly. "Ever since we came to Deer Lodge, I have felt the tension. Maybe it's because our brother knows more about medicine than he does. Maybe it's because our father was an actual doctor. But whatever it is, Paynter doesn't like us, and never has."

"Wood has always been very nice to me," Emma responded.

Jenny smiled. "You are married to Henry. He has to be."

The Grand Baseball Tournament commenced at ten o'clock, but Emma's thoughts were not on the game as she watched the players with her mother and sister. Her thoughts were on the friction between her husband and Wood Paynter.

Emma knew Henry and Wood had never seen eye to eye on certain things, but they had been partners for a long time. How often had they had quarrels she knew nothing about? How often had these quarrels happened as a result of her family? Harry had introduced her to Henry, and had worked for City Drug in Deer Lodge. Is this when the friction between the partners really began?

Wood sold out his partnership in the Deer Lodge City Store...to Harry. He had refused to join Emma's tincture business. Did all this have to do with who Emma was? Did her brother's medical training, and the fact that their father had been a doctor make Wood uncomfortable? Questions upon questions rose in Emma's head. Was it her fault that Henry and Wood were at odds? Where would it all lead?

"Emma, you are awfully quiet," her mother commented as the crowd's enthusiasm finally faded. The game was over. The winners had converged on the field, and the fans were already dispersing from the stands.

"I was just thinking about Wood Paynter," she responded quietly.

"I imagine he has cooled off by now," her mother offered.

"Jenny doesn't think he likes us," Emma stated.

Marie glanced momentarily at her other daughter.

"Well, he doesn't," Jenny asserted. "He never has. It was Henry who hired our brother, before we moved out to Montana. Harry told me so."

Her mother turned her attention back to her oldest daughter. "Emma, you know full well that sometimes people just don't get along. Your brother and Wood are two of these, just like Harry doesn't get along with that Bowie fellow down in Deer Lodge. I think it's competition, or something. Anyway, don't take it personally. It happens. Your husband and Wood will work things out eventually, one way or another." She smiled. "How about something to eat?"

Emma took Henry some hot food for lunch. He ate on the back step of the booth. Wood had gone back to the downtown store, and a young clerk was taking his place.

"I can go with you to the parade," Henry offered. "I'm sorry about this morning."

"Do you and Wood quarrel often?" Emma asked.

"From time to time," Henry admitted. "Where are your mother and sister?"

"Over looking at the quilts," Emma answered.

"Have you told them about the baby?"

"No, not yet," Emma replied.

Henry smiled softly. "Don't put it off too long."

Henry Parchen accompanied his wife and her family to the Grand Parade at one thirty, and then returned to City Drug's booth. The horse races didn't hold his interest like the preceding afternoon. Then Klein's horse, Belmont, had won all three heats in the trotting race.

Emma, her mother, and her sister strolled the fair grounds after that, taking in the displays of produce. The ponderous size of the potatoes, cauliflower, melons, and squash challenged their kitchen garden ambitions, but any increased zeal would have to wait until the following spring. The displays of embroidery, lace, needlepoint, braiding, quilting, millinery, and general sewing made a more immediate impression. Ideas from these could find their way into upcoming winter projects.

"Oh look," Emma's mother noted as they walked past Mc Farland's booth of books and pictures, "a baby-jumper. These are so terrific," she exclaimed as she went over to it, "and this is a good one."

Emma and Jenny followed more slowly.

Marie looked up with a smile. "Shall I buy you one, Emma?" she asked. "They are hard to find, and you will probably need one sooner or later."

"But she's not even expecting," Jenny retorted. She turned to her sister. "Mother isn't pushy or anything," she blurted in exasperation.

"Of course I want a grandchild," Marie responded as she focused on Emma. "You and Henry are trying again, aren't you?"

Emma flushed.

"Mother," Jenny cried.

"Well, they should be," the older woman stated. "One misfortune shouldn't stop them. Babies are all wonderful miracles. You girls wouldn't even be here if I had let tragedy stop me." She turned to Emma again. "Shall I buy one?"

"If you wish," her daughter answered quietly.

Jenny turned to her sister. "Emma, don't let her push you like that!"

Emma smiled self-consciously. "It's okay, Jenny."

"Okay? What will Henry think?" she demanded.

"He usually agrees with mother," Emma replied simply.

Henry worked late, and the women of his family went home ahead of him as the sun sank into the warm dusk of the fall day. Jenny and her mother were tired from all the walking, and headed upstairs to bed. Emma followed within minutes. But as she slipped into her nightgown, mischief entered her thoughts. She returned downstairs to the ice box where she had chocolate mousse prepared and waiting in three pieces of the crystal stemware she and Henry had received for their wedding. She had made the chocolate dessert only the night before, and had hidden it behind the ice block hoping for an opportunity like this to be alone with her mother and sister...and to announce her news.

Balancing the cool, rich chocolate dessert between her fingers, she grabbed three spoons, and headed upstairs in her bare feet. Voices were still audible from the guest room as she hesitated outside, and knocked.

Jenny appeared in her nightgown. "Oh, sweet secrets," she exclaimed as she opened the door wider, and pulled her sister in. A single kerosene lamp illuminated the room as Jenny shut the door behind them.

"Sweet secrets," their mother repeated as she turned with a big smile, dressed only in her camisole and bloomers.

Jenny took a chocolate dessert, and pulled her sister to the floor. Marie promptly joined them as they sat facing each other on the round, rag rug.

"Oh let me go first," Jenny cried as she tasted the mousse and let the smooth sensation run down her throat. "Wow, this is better than usual."

"It's the rum." Emma smiled.

"It is good," her mother agreed. "I swear every time you make it, Emma, it gets better."

"Chocolate and rum mix well together," her daughter replied.

"And she should know," Jenny laughed, "with all the medicine she's been making. I understand mothers can actually get their children to take Emma's whooping cough syrup without so much as a groan."

"I try." Emma smiled again.

"Now about your secret," Marie prodded.

"Let Jenny go first," Emma suggested.

"Yes, my secret," Jenny laughed as she rose to retrieve the lamp, and placed it in the center of the rug. As she sat back down, she began. "Last night I had a dream."

"What kind of dream?" Emma asked.

"I was lost in the middle of a corn field. I couldn't find my way out. Everywhere I looked there was just more corn."

"Where was this cornfield?" their mother inquired.

"Outside Deer Lodge, I think," Jenny replied. "Anyway, I walked through the stalks, and I walked some more...but it must have been in circles, because I just could not find my way out. I was starting to get scared, and I shouted for help. But none came. So I walked and walked, becoming more and more frightened. The corn was so tall I couldn't see anything. And the air was so hot and still, I felt like I was suffocating."

"Corn fields can get hot and humid," Marie agreed.

"I was getting really desperate," Jenny continued, "when suddenly out through the stalks walks this young man. He was fair-haired, good looking, and had strong, broad shoulders."

"A man?" Emma burst.

"Yes," Jenny responded with a broad smile, "and he was dripping wet."

"With sweat," their mother asked.

"No, with water," Jenny giggled. "He kept asking if I'd seen the river, that he had lost the river."

"The river? He had been swimming?" Emma laughed. "If your corn field was so close to the river, why couldn't you hear it?"

"I could, but I didn't know which way the sound was coming from."

"So what happened?" Emma demanded.

"The young man turned into a bear," Jenny chuckled.

"A bear," their mother repeated in surprise.

"You know dreams," Jenny responded.

"So did your dream end?" Emma cried.

"Well almost," Jenny replied. "The bear lumbered away, leaving broken corn stalks in his wake. So I followed, thinking bears could probably smell water, and sure enough, he led me through the corn until I could see the river. Then I woke up."

"I wonder if it means anything," Marie pondered.

"Just that Jenny needs to find a bear of a man," Emma laughed.

"You said he was handsome," their mother noted. "Maybe this fellow is in your future, Jenny."

"My future," Jenny responded with a laugh, "I doubt it. No good looking fellow is going to be interested in me, not with all my small pox scars."

"He will see beyond the dents in your face to the goodness of your heart," their mother replied. "Don't worry, Jenny, in time it will happen."

"He will probably fall in love with your voice," Emma offered, "like the ancients that fell captive to the sirens and their sweet songs."

"So mother, it's your turn to tell a secret," Jenny decided as she had enough of such talk.

"Me? A secret?" the older woman retorted in apparent innocence. "What secret could I tell...that I haven't told already?"

"If I can come up with one, so can you," Jenny replied with a laugh. "How about back in France? Did you see anyone guillotined?"

A shadow fell over the older woman's expression. "I was only a child, but my father did leave me at the church one time when we went into town. I love churches. They are so beautiful. I was supposed to stay in the pew and say prayers while my father was gone, but he didn't come back for a long time, and I remember the most peculiar sound. It came repeatedly, a whine that ended in a sharp thunk. Strange, I haven't thought about that in years."

"Do you suppose it was..."

Jenny was abruptly cut off by her mother. "No, Jenny. It was just the bell rope in the wind, slapping against the wall. That is what the priest said."

Jenny didn't look convinced as she turned to her sister. "Your turn," she proclaimed as she finished off the last of her chocolate mousse, and set the crystal dish by the kerosene lamp.

A smile grew on Emma's lips, but she said nothing.

"Emma," Jenny responded as she forgot about her mother's story, "what have you got to tell?"

"She has something," their mother decided with a knowing look.

"I'm expecting," Emma stated.

"Pregnant," Jenny exclaimed. She leaped to her feet, and pulled her sister up, her eyes examining the folds of white fabric hiding Emma's stomach. "When?"

"The first of February," her older sister answered.

Happy giggles exploded from Jenny as she now began swaying and singing little nursery rhymes. Then she grabbed Emma's hands, waltzing around the room in the lamp light, and casting shadows against the wall which only made the mood merrier. Their mother placed the empty dishes and lamp on a nearby table, and joined in.

It was nearly midnight when Henry crawled into bed with his wife. She had been asleep nearly an hour, but came to briefly as her husband curled up against her.

"I see you told your mother about the baby," he noted softly.

Emma turned. Henry pointed through the moonlight to the baby-jumper hanging in the doorway of the nursery.

"Yes," Emma muttered sleepily.

Henry kissed her softly in approval.

On Sunday Henry Parchen took his extended family to church, and then after a quick lunch headed for the fair grounds to pack up the last of the booth. Jenny decided to go to an impromptu choir rehearsal that afternoon, and Emma found herself alone in her mother's company for the first time since her arrival.

"Jenny seems to be making friends at church," Emma noted.

"Yes," her mother agreed. "She is good with people, and has her grandfather's ear for music." She paused momentarily. "Emma, do you think your brother's trip east caused that argument between Henry and Paynter?"

"Harry's trip?" Emma repeated as she thought over the question. There had been reference to the Deer Lodge store. "Wood thinks Henry spends too much time on things outside our drug store here," she offered quietly.

Marie was thoughtful as they finished up the dirty dishes. Then she turned. "Emma, maybe I shouldn't bring this up just now, but something has been bothering me, and I don't know who else to talk to. Jenny's heart is good, but she doesn't really understand things of this nature, not like you."

"What is it, mother?" Emma asked.

"It's your brother. I know his trip east wasn't exactly well timed. I don't think Henry really appreciated him taking off like he did. But once your brother makes up his mind, there is no room for discussion. I may even have been to blame for the whole thing. It was my idea. I just never dreamed he would go now, before winter."

"We will all survive." Emma smiled.

"I know, I know," her mother responded, "only you don't know but the half of it. Your brother has been working hard at the store all year, putting in long hours...but he isn't seeing the return he was hoping for. You must remember, Harry plans on being rich. When he gave up the gold fields, he didn't give up his dreams. I've tried to talk some sense into him, but it really hasn't done any good. I suggested the trip back East to give him a little perspective. Life is not a bed of roses, and even roses have thorns."

"Harry is restless again?" Emma questioned.

"Yes, and that Bowie fellow in Deer Lodge isn't helping," Marie continued. "Having a second drug store is cutting sharply into City Drug's profits. Harry has to price his wares competitively now, and he hates it. On top of that, Deer Lodge isn't growing as fast as other towns. Your brother, I think, feels left behind...that, and where there are more people there is more demand for merchandise."

"So what are you saying?" Emma asked. "Harry wants to sell his share of the drug store business?"

"I don't know," her mother replied as she wrung her hands. "He was happy as a clam when he first started. You know the trade fits him like a glove, but he isn't taking these new challenges well. He is getting restless again, like when he went on his 'long tramp'."

"The 'long tramp' settled him down," Emma noted.

"Yes it did, and that's why I suggested his trip east. I just thought he would wait until spring."

"But you are worried this time," Emma decided. "Last time you weren't."

"Harry is visiting his buddies in New York. Most of them are 'old money' people. Buying and selling businesses are an everyday thing to them."

"You are worried that he will want out of the Deer Lodge store, that he will move east again, aren't you?" Emma suddenly gasped.

"Yes," her mother responded.

Emma stared at the older woman. "Will you go with?"

"I don't know," her mother anguished. "I'm not the New York type."

"He might go back to St. Louis," Emma suggested.

"Yes," Marie agreed.

"Would you go back there?"

"I might," she replied. "Your father is buried there...and the children."

"But..."

"But I don't want to see your brother buried there, and Jenny would probably go with, and she is better off out here."

"She could stay with us," Emma offered.

Her mother's face softened. "I'm afraid she would eventually follow. She hasn't your sense."

"So what do we do?" Emma asked.

"Wait for your brother to come home," her mother responded quietly, "then we'll know where the cards lay. But I would bet a change is in the air."

Over the five weeks of Harry's absence, Emma's sister became a vital part of the music at the Methodist/Episcopal church where the Parchens attended. Emma's mother watched all with approval as she worried about her son. She had no idea what the future held for her small family, but she met each day with faith and strength. She had faced difficulties before.

The older woman seemed to understand too, the difficulties of others, and interceded for Emma more than once, finding some reason or another to extract Jenny and herself from the house. Emma's love for her mother swelled as she found herself alone with her husband whenever she felt the need to talk with him. This happened within the week. Henry and Wood found themselves in another argument over the proceeds from the fair. It seemed Emma's tinctures had done better than anything else they carried in the booth.

Emma sat down at the dinner table with her husband. He had come home late, and was eating alone.

"Where is your mother?" Henry inquired as he picked up his fork.

"She and Jenny went for a walk," Emma replied. "She loves watching the seasons change."

Henry was silent as he began to eat.

"You and Wood had another argument?" Emma asked.

Her husband's eyes rose. "Yes."

"Was it better or worse than the last one?"

"Worse," he answered reluctantly.

"Will it get better?" she probed.

"I don't know," Henry replied truthfully.

"It is because of me, isn't it?"

Henry set his fork down as he chewed his food thoughtfully. "Why would you say that?"

"Because of the tinctures," Emma stated.

"We are making a good profit on them," Henry countered.

"But does that make Wood happy?" she questioned.

"It should," Henry responded.

"But does it?" Emma pressed.

Henry stopped eating, studying his wife momentarily. "No."

"Do you want me to stop making the stuff?" Emma asked.

"No," Henry replied.

"Then what are we going to do?" she implored.

Henry picked up a slice of bread in silence.

"Henry?"

He looked at Emma. "I don't know," he admitted softly.

Both fell silent now.

"Henry," Emma began again quietly, "I'm afraid we have more problems than just my tinctures."

"What do you mean?"

"My brother's trip east – it wasn't just because he hadn't been home in seven years."

Her husband focused sharply on her. "It wasn't?"

"No," she replied quietly.

"Then why?" Henry asked.

"Harry's worked his fingers raw over the past year..."

"Yes, I know," her husband interrupted. "He's had a good year."

"Not good enough," Emma responded.

"Well, he can't expect miracles with Bowie's Drug Store going in. Competition always cuts down on the profit line," Henry countered.

Emma rose from her chair. "You don't know Harry," she stated as she turned to face him. "He has dreams. He gets restless. He won't stay in a job that's just a job."

"What is that supposed to mean?" Henry demanded. "City Drug in Deer Lodge is a good viable business, and he is half owner. Are you saying he wants it all?"

"No...no," Emma replied. "He doesn't want your half."

"Then what does he want?" Henry demanded in surprise. "Your brother is good at what he does, but..."

"I think he wants out," Emma interrupted.

"Out?" Henry suddenly gasped. "You mean he wants me to buy him out of Deer Lodge? Wood is going to love that. He thinks I spend too much time over there as it is."

"I know," Emma agreed miserably. "But if we don't figure some way to keep Harry here, mother thinks he will go back to St. Louis or New York."

Henry's chair moved backwards. He had lost all interest in his food. "Your brother is that discouraged with Deer Lodge City?"

Emma nodded silently. "Harry doesn't think Deer Lodge is big enough for two drug stores."

"It's big enough, but not by much," Henry replied. "I did the calculations when Bowie moved in."

"Well I wouldn't count on Harry staying," Emma stated softly. "He has dreams of big money."

"We all have dreams of big money," Henry responded.

"But some people have more patience," she offered quietly.

Silence again fell between them for several long moments.

"Do you have any suggestions, Emma?" Henry finally asked.

"Maybe you could offer him a partnership here," she suggested softly.

"Over Wood's dead body," Henry retorted.

"You and Wood haven't been getting along," Emma reminded him.

Chapter Twelve

Henry stared at his wife. "You want me to end a partnership that's worked for six years?"

"You and Wood haven't seen eye to eye for months," Emma reminded him softly. "Maybe it's time to part ways."

"Wood and I are having some rough times, granted," Henry responded, "but that doesn't mean we throw six years to the wind."

"Harry may move to New York anyway," Emma decided. "It was just a thought." She picked up the dirty dishes, and took them to the wash pan. "Jenny was chosen to play the organ at church next Sunday."

For a month, little was said around the Parchen house concerning City Drug Store. Henry focused on the family and the upcoming baby. He smiled and laughed and essentially forgot about work at every opportunity. Emma sighed with relief. Maybe tension between the partners had eased. At any rate Henry was more relaxed than he had been in months.

Late that afternoon, Emma heard noise outside on the front porch and opened the door.

"Harry, you're back!"

"Emma," he responded as his sister burst through the screen door.

"We weren't expecting you until tomorrow," Emma cried as the siblings hugged.

"I caught an earlier train out of New York," Harry D'Acheul explained.

"It feels like ages since I've seen you," Emma noted as she drew back. Her brother was looking at her middle.

"Maybe it has been," he replied. His eyebrows lifted. "Do you have news?"

"Of course I have news," she responded happily. "Jenny is singing up a storm at church, and mother likes Helena. She has made friends left and right."

"That's not what I meant," he objected.

"I know," Emma commented as she took his arm, leading him inside. "Yes, I have news, hopeful news, but let's not talk about that now."

"Why not?" he asked.

"Because everyone is gone, and I want to hear all about your trip," Emma answered. "How was St. Louis?"

"Good, good," he responded. "Everyone is gone?"

"Henry is at work, mother is at a church circle, and Jenny is off shopping. I told you we didn't expect you until tomorrow."

"Yes, I know," he replied, "but what is a trip, compared to expecting a baby?"

Emma's levity vanished. "If I can keep this one," she added.

"You aren't having problems, are you?" her brother asked.

"No, but I didn't think I had problems last time," Emma answered.

"Last time was a freak thing," Harry stated. "It won't happen again, Em."

"I hope not," she responded quietly.

Harry noted his sister's demeanor, and changed subjects. "The East was hot and crowded."

"And you loved every minute of it," Emma encouraged as her face brightened.

"Of course," he laughed.

"Mother is afraid you will want to move back," Emma noted.

A cloud crossed her brother's expression. "No, Em, I don't want to move back. I don't belong there anymore. You wouldn't believe how things have changed, how St. Louis has changed, even our old neighborhood. I felt like a stranger."

"Changed how?"

"New buildings, new people... The familiar things look dull and drab. They haven't been kept up. It's not the same. You knew about our old house, didn't you?" he asked.

"Yes," Emma responded with a wave of resignation. "So what now? What are your plans?"

Harry focused on her. "Mother really has been talking to you, hasn't she?"

Emma met his look. "She has been worried during your absence, really worried."

"The trip was her idea," he exclaimed.

"Yes," Emma replied, "but she always gets concerned when you're restless. You know that."

Harry D'Acheul smiled softly.

"So if you don't want to move back East, what do you want?" she asked.

"Emma, for heaven's sake, can you get more blunt?" he retorted.

His sister grinned. "A month of wondering craves relief."

"All I know is that I don't want to move back East," he replied. "There is no future there. Everyone is already situated, and the competition is fierce."

"You have a bit of your own competition in Deer Lodge City," Emma noted.

"Yes, I have," Harry agreed, "and I've learned how the East would deal with it, only I don't like their methods. I would rather move."

"Where?" Emma asked.

"Did I say 'move'?" her brother repeated, and then smiled.

"You did," Emma answered. "Where would you like to move?"

"I don't know, Em," he replied. "I own a drug store, remember."

"I remember," she responded quietly.

"Is that what this is all about?" her brother suddenly demanded. "You want to know if I'm going to leave Henry in a lurch, don't you?"

"The thought has crossed my mind," Emma replied. "Wood Paynter is jealous of the Deer Lodge store as it is."

Harry D'Acheul's brow furrowed. "Jealous? There isn't anything to be jealous of. He sold out before Bowie moved the second drug store into Deer Lodge."

"He is jealous of the time Henry spends on it, and he hates my tinctures," she stated.

"Paynter hates your tinctures?" Emma's brother responded in disbelief. "You're kidding! The profit line on them beats out anything he can order, and the kids like your cough syrup. They actually take it."

"It doesn't matter," she replied quietly.

"It does matter," Harry repeated. "You and Henry are doing everything right."

"Wood doesn't think so. You don't either," Emma objected, "or you wouldn't be so unhappy with your job."

"My job could be done by a clerk," her brother stated, "and it has been during the last two months, hasn't it? Henry hasn't made any emergency runs to Deer Lodge, has he?"

"No."

"Look Emma, whether I sell out or not isn't really important. The store could run itself. And as for Paynter, he was right about getting out. There really isn't enough profit line to divide two ways, especially now with Bowie's store."

"So you're going to just quit?"

"Quit the drug business? Hell no," Harry responded. "I'm just going to find a bigger town, or at least one that is growing faster."

"What do you mean?" his sister cried.

"Emma, I like my work. I'm just not getting rich...and I want to be rich." He smiled broadly. "Actually, I spent a good chunk of my time in New York learning about new things coming out in medicine, and I think the doctors here will be eager to get their hands on them once they are introduced. But Deer Lodge is not the best place to be located for this. It's not big enough, and its expansion rate is slow. I need a better location, some place that has a little hustle and bustle, someplace that's growing and eager for new things and new ways."

The front door opened behind them, and Jenny appeared. "Harry," she screamed in surprise, "we weren't expecting you until tomorrow."

Within the hour their mother also returned home; and amid a fury of questions and excitement, Harry told them all about his adventures in the East. By supper Emma's husband had also joined in, and the family spent a long evening catching up on the past couple of months.

Emma watched her husband listen to her brother's news. His interest was intent, his questions poignant.

Within two days Harry D'Acheul, his mother, and Jenny had returned to Deer Lodge City. Emma felt the loss as she straightened up the house, and then turned to the number of tincture orders that had piled up over the last week or so. She barely finished with them when an order from Deer Lodge arrived. Many in the town were suffering from bronchitis and heart palpitations. Emma's thoughts turned to Dr. Ingersoll's favored tincture, Lilly of the Valley, but her orders were not for this. The doctors of Deer Lodge preferred tinctures of digitalis.

Emma packed up the requested heart medicine and cough syrup, sending them off to her brother as she thought about all he had said concerning the East and his dreams.

That evening Henry Parchen also brought home an order for more of Emma's tinctures. The weather was growing cold, and with it came an increase in tincture demand. But this was not all. Without the diversion of Emma's family, Henry's conversations with Wood Paynter were coming home to Emma as well. Things had not improved.

By the middle of December, Henry was starting to question his loyalty to a man that for six years had been his partner, and now was making his life hell.

"Wood can't be all to blame," Emma responded after her husband vented the day's frustrations on her.

"You're right," Henry retorted in exasperation, "it's a crime to work hard and be honest."

"Wood is honest," Emma replied, "and if he doesn't work as hard as you, maybe it's because he has different priorities."

"I'll say," Henry agreed. "I wish I knew what they were."

"I thought he spent most of his time with his family," Emma commented.

Henry smiled softly. "He does...and Jennie misses the East. Sometimes I think she unwittingly makes Wood discontent with everything that is not old and established. She often remarks about some cultural event her family attended. I think she feels her children are growing up too wild and unrefined."

"Why would that make Wood upset with you," Emma asked.

"I have asked myself that a thousand times," Henry replied. "City Drug is the only thing I know of that is putting grocery money in his pocket, yet he treats the store like it's his prison, and me like I have betrayed him or something." He shook his head despondently. "I don't know."

"Maybe the store is his prison," Emma suggested.

Henry's eyes rose. "What do you mean?"

"Evidently Paynter rather be doing other things. Maybe it's time he did just that," Emma stated. "Maybe it's time to cut each other loose."

"Emma," Henry countered quietly, "do you have any idea how long it takes to build a business like we have?"

"Or how much mental torment the two of you give each other in a day's time?" she replied evenly.

Henry said nothing.

Emma's mind wandered to her brother. He was all for doing business someplace larger than Deer Lodge City, someplace that was growing. "Is Helena's population growing much?" she suddenly asked her husband.

"Some," he answered. "Why?"

"Harry said he wanted a drug store somewhere larger than Deer Lodge."

"Helena is definitely larger than Deer Lodge City," Henry replied. He became thoughtful now. "Harry wants to move?"

"I told you that a long time ago," Emma responded.

"Yes, I guess you did," he agreed. "Maybe he and I could make it work," he considered thoughtfully.

Emma stifled a grin. "You seem to get along well with him."

"Most of the time," Henry replied. "Maybe I should talk to him."

"Maybe," Emma encouraged.

Christmas approached with increasing snow as the thoughts of the populace turned to the holidays and to their families. The friction between Henry and Wood eased, and Henry never talked to Emma's brother about moving to Helena. Everyone was focused on Christmas, and Wood reverted to his old self, asking after Emma's condition.

"Her baby is due when?" Wood asked as he finished with a customer, and Henry took money from another.

"The first of February," Henry answered.

"Then you will be a father," Wood responded, "and things will never be the same again. Right, Mrs. Stoakes?"

"Yes, Mr. Paynter," she agreed as she turned to Henry. "The first baby takes 95% of your wife's time. The second one takes the rest, and after that it doesn't matter any more. There is no way under heaven for her to maintain order in your house like you have know it up to now. So enjoy the holidays this year because they will be the last quiet ones you will know for a good many." Then she broke into a wide smile. "But the little ones are the biggest blessing you can ever have." She reached for her parcel, and turned to leave.

Henry turned to Wood. "Is that right?"

"Absolutely," he laughed. "You won't know what hit you...or your house, Parchen."

"You make it sound so wonderful," Henry retorted facetiously.

"Don't worry, old man, you will survive." A broad smile lingered on Wood's lips as he retreated from behind the counter.

Henry watched his partner for a moment. It had been a long time since Wood had called him "old man". Would a baby in Henry's life make a difference in their partnership? It seemed unlikely. Yet a baby at least could give them some common ground again.

City Drug closed at six Christmas Eve, and with wishes for a good holiday, Paynter, Eichler, and Parchen parted paths, each heading home over the frozen ground crisp with the light snow that had fallen since four that afternoon.

Henry trudged his way up the Broadway hill, grateful that it hadn't turned slick. Sleighs made their way across the street at intersections. No one wanted to brave the steep incline head on.

Lights glowed from his house as Henry approached. Emma had decorated the porch with evergreens and ribbons. He climbed the steps and stomped heavily, knocking the snow from his shoes. He reached for the brass door knob, and entered the warmth of the light. Wonderful smells met his nose. Emma was busy in the kitchen. He shut the door, and hung up his coat and hat.

Henry glanced at the front room where a green Christmas tree stood. He had fixed it in the stand the evening before. He and Emma would decorate it tonight, all except the base. His eyes focused on it. Emma had been busy. The stand was no longer visible. Green moss covered it, trimmed in tiny silk flowers and other woodland delights. The Christmas tree looked as if it had grown up right there in the front parlor.

"Henry, you're home," Emma greeted as she handed him a cup of hot cider. "How was work?"

"Good," he responded. "People were really nice, including Wood." He smiled. "I think he's looking forward to our baby."

"He's not the only one," she retorted with a grin. "Are you hungry?"

"No, not much," he answered. "We munched on Christmas treats all day."

Emma set her cup of cider down on a nearby table. "Well if you want, we can start stringing popcorn."

The Parchens finished decorating their Christmas tree late that evening, and then turned in for the night. It was quiet as Henry momentarily drew back the curtain. A light snow was falling, and only a few lights twinkled in the distance over the small city.

"Oh," Emma exclaimed quietly as she joined him, "it's beautiful."

"Yes," Henry agreed as he shared the view, "much better than the years I spent living over the store."

Emma smiled as her husband put his arm around her, and pulled her close.

Christmas morning dawned clear and beautiful, but Henry and Emma didn't notice until nearly eight-thirty. The holiday afforded a leisure neither had enjoyed for some time, and together they went downstairs in their slippers, arm in arm. Emma stopped at the parlor. The tree glistened in the morning light, decorated and adorned like something from a fairy world.

"Shall I light the candles?" Henry asked.

"Do you think it would make it any prettier?" she countered.

A soft smile rose to his lips. "No."

"Then let's save the candles," Emma suggested. "They are pretty just as they are."

Henry led her over to their couch, and together they sat down, enjoying the beauty of the tree. Then he reached down and retrieved a wrapped package from the several resting there. This he handed to her.

"What is it?" she asked as she accepted the gift.

Henry smiled broadly.

Emma slowly unwrapped the present. It was larger than a shoe box. She lifted the lid, and pushed away the tissue paper to reveal a porcelain doll with real human hair and a Christmas dress. "Oh Henry," she exclaimed in surprise.

"It's for our daughter," he noted softly.

"For our daughter?" Emma cried. "How do you know our baby isn't a boy?"

"Because God wouldn't do that to us," Henry responded. "The doll is for Adele."

Emma smiled at her husband. His faith in their future was absolute. Adele was already a fact to him. "She won't be here until February," Emma commented.

"I know, that's why you opened the doll. It's for her room. It should be there when she comes. This is your gift." He now offered a smaller present from his pocket."

Emma reached under the tree, and retrieved a package which she handed to him. "Happy Christmas."

The holiday for Emma and Henry was peaceful, quiet, and happy, and the mood extended into the following weeks, although a major fire again broke out in Helena during the first week of January. The fire started in China town and consumed 150 buildings before it was finished. Yet this fire did not destroy City Drug, though it did considerable damage to its plaster walls, and took the rear structure where Henry and Wood stored some of their back stock. Emma and Henry breathed a sigh of relief. At least their house was spared, and they hadn't lost everything.

But Wood Paynter was rattled. He had watched his interest in Deer Lodge go up in smoke a mere two years before, and now he had witnessed actual flame and smoke destroy much of Helena. Money was suddenly tight in the city, and even if this fire did not financially ruin Paynter, he knew all too well it could have.

In broody silence Wood worked at City Drug. When customers bought Emma's tinctures, he said nothing. He said nothing when Henry arranged for repairs. Wood Paynter acquiesced to everything. He disputed nothing.

Then after work on the thirteenth, Wood asked Henry if they could talk. Henry Parchen readily agreed. The two of them had gotten along better since the fire than they had in months; and if Wood Paynter wanted to talk things out, then Henry was all for it. Maybe Paynter was even ready to discuss building their new fireproof store.

Henry walked into the back office, and sat down on the crate, leaving the desk chair for Wood. Paynter was a mere two steps behind him. He took a deep breath, and turned to Henry.

"I want out," he stated succinctly.

Henry focused sharply on him. "You want out of what? We carry a pretty broad range of merchandise – drugs, paint, mining chemicals..."

"I want out of City Drug," Paynter interrupted. "Maybe you can get your brother-in-law to buy my share...like Deer Lodge."

Henry stared at him. "You want out? We've been doing better than we have in months. You want to throw six years away?"

"I want out," Paynter repeated.

"Why?" Henry gasped.

Wood Paynter strode across the small space. Then he turned back, his eyes flashing. "The fire could have taken us again."

"It could have," Henry agreed, "that's why we pay the insurance premiums."

"Yes, and the money just keeps draining away."

"That's why I keep pushing for a brick building," Parchen replied.

"Yeah, more money," Paynter retorted.

"We have to protect our interests," Henry stated quietly.

"You have to protect your interests," Wood corrected. "I want out."

Silence reigned between them for several moments.

"What will you do?" Henry asked quietly.

"I'm going to liquidate everything I have, and go back East," Paynter answered. "I'm tired of working my fingers to the bone every day, and for what? To have some fire burn me out? I'm sick of it."

"Is there anything I can do to change your mind?" Henry inquired.

"No," Wood replied quietly. "I should go. I'm sure my wife has supper waiting."

Henry Parchen stared after his partner as Paynter left the store. He was in a state of shock. He had worked so hard to make the business profitable, to make Wood feel a part of it all despite his incessant distraction. Henry had even resisted his wife's urgings to break things off with Wood, and for what? Paynter had just up and quit. Henry couldn't believe it.

He glanced around him, mentally tabulating if the store had been fully closed for the night. Then he grabbed his coat and left.

The walk home was cold, but not any colder than the night before. Henry's breath crystallized in the air as he strode forward. The physical exertion felt good as his mind wrestled against the fact of Paynter's exit.

Henry felt anger and betrayal. Yet as he considered his options, the possibility of Emma's brother came to mind, and with it a breath of fresh air. The possibilities of a partnership here would have none of the road blocks he had suffered. The future would be theirs to claim. Could it be that Paynter was actually doing him a favor?

Henry climbed the steps to his house. Emma was reading in the parlor. At a glance, he saw it was a baby book. "Paynter just quit," he announced bluntly.

Emma glanced up, her eyes freezing on his. The book slid off her lap unnoticed as she rose to her feet, her middle protruding in front of her. She had less than a month of pregnancy left. "How are you?" she asked as she now helped him off with his coat.

"Fine," Henry replied. "I think I had better get in touch with your brother."

Henry Parchen sent a brief telegram to his brother-in-law the following morning, following it up with a letter of explanation. Emma's brother responded immediately, sending a wire that of course he was interested. He asked several crucial questions. Each party managed to receive a lengthy letter from the other before the snow storm of January 23rd set in. The mail slowed to a stand still for a few days, but not the dissolution proceedings of Parchen & Paynter. It was officially set for the 29th. Emma's brother sent more telegrams than she cared to count, and her husband wasn't much better, hardly noticing that the big, district wide conference at their church was scheduled to convene the same day.

Emma finished off an order of tinctures for the store, and left the heavy box where it sat. Henry had moved all her supplies up to the attic since Paynter's announcement. Both knew Emma's family would soon be moving to Helena, and staying with them at least for a while.

Emma went downstairs to start supper. As she entered the kitchen, she heard the front door open. She glanced at the clock. Henry was home on time for a change.

"Well, it's done," he announced as he joined her.

"You and Paynter," she asked.

Henry nodded an assent as he embraced his wife. "The baby is getting big. What do we have, a week left?"

"If our calculations are right," she answered. "When is Harry coming?"

"The first of next week. I have some paper work to get ready for him," Henry noted. "He can only stay a few days. He has to inspect the Deer Lodge penitentiary the following week, and make a report before the new warden arrives." He smiled softly. "I imagine your mother and sister will accompany him, but I am afraid they will miss most of the church conference."

"I didn't think you had even noticed it," Emma responded. "Mother is very excited. She writes about the conference all the time."

"There has just been a lot else on my mind."

Chapter Thirteen

Two hours passed, and Emma's stomach began to cramp. Dismissing the discomfort as having resulted from dinner, Emma turned her attention to the church work she had volunteered for, preparing special little extras for the banquet the influx of preachers would attend the following night at the Rocky Mountain Church Convention.

Emma finished the place cards, and shifted her position as another cramp gripped her middle. She rose to her feet, ignoring it, picking up her supplies and putting them away. Five minutes later it came again, harder.

Henry looked up from his newspaper. "Are you all right?"

"I think so, though these preliminary contractions are getting to be a nuisance...even if they don't mean anything. Calista told me they might show up a week ahead of time, and show up they have."

"You are sure they aren't something more?" Henry asked.

"I'm not sure of anything," Emma responded with a smile. She hesitated only momentarily, and then proceeded with her task as if the cramps had never occurred.

Henry went back to his newspaper.

By bedtime Emma's contractions had not diminished, and Henry now pondered his wife with concern. "I think I'll see if Calista is home," he decided as he went for his coat.

"I hope these things don't last all night," Emma complained. "I will never get any sleep."

Henry lingered at the door. "Do you need anything before I go?"

"No, I don't think so," Emma replied, and mustered a smile, "but don't be gone too long, all right?"

"No longer than I have to," Henry told her, and disappeared.

Emma glanced at the kitchen. She had let her dishes go to finish up the church work. She headed back, placing two dish pans of water on the stove to warm. Cramps came and went as she put in the soap and washed the dishes.

"Emma," Henry called as he came through the front door. Calista followed on his heal.

"I'm in the kitchen," Emma responded as she hung up her towel. The dishes were done.

Calista followed Henry Parchen through the house, noting the tidiness of everything. When they got to Emma, she smiled. She knew the signs. The floors were spotless, no mess lingered anywhere, and even the windows sparkled. "How long have your contractions been coming, Emma?" Calista asked.

"Since about eight," she answered.

"And how often do they occur?" Calista Ingersoll inquired.

"Oh they didn't come often at first, probably as much as a half hour in between, but now... I guess every five or ten minutes," Emma replied.

Calista turned to Henry. "Is everything ready?"

"Sure, but Emma isn't ready to deliver yet, is she? I thought her discomfort was just that preliminary stuff. She isn't due for another week."

Emma was intently watching the older woman.

"Second babies often come a little early," Calista informed them. "I suggest we get ready, and..." She looked at Emma as she doubled with another contraction. Calista took hold of Emma's arm at the elbow. "Come on, let's walk it off."

"Where is Cy?" Emma asked as they headed out of the kitchen.

"Away," Calista answered. "He is tending a miner down with consumption. I doubt he will be home before late morning."

"I'm glad you are here," Emma responded.

Three hours later a cry pierced every recess of the house. Tears of joy rose in Emma's eyes as she reached for her daughter. Adele Marie was a healthy, vibrant little baby with good lungs and a marvelous pink color. Perfect tiny toes and perfect tiny fingers flagged the air incessantly as the miniature human being was nestled into Emma's arms. Adele stared up at her mother with all the intensity and wonder that was typical of such little eyes. Emma was exhausted from the ordeal, but she had never known such euphoria. Her baby was alive and well. Emma glanced joyously at Henry. He stood behind Calista, pleased and happy.

Suddenly cramping again gripped Emma, and she handed the newborn to Calista who immediately passed the child to its father. Calista's attention settled squarely on Emma. Within minutes the afterbirth passed, and the midwife drew Emma to her feet. "Come on, let's get you cleaned up. Adele is fine with her father."

Henry was sitting in the rocking chair, cradling their newborn in his arms, watching her every movement as if transfixed. Emma smiled, and followed Calista from the room. Twenty minutes later, she returned alone to find Calista had already stripped the bed and remade it with fresh linens. Henry had not moved. Adele was sleeping in his arms.

"Is she all right?" Emma asked as she approached.

Henry looked up. "She's perfect. Calista says that you need to feed her soon, though, that Adele needs your colostrom."

"All right," Emma agreed as she reached for their daughter. Henry rose from the chair, vacating it for his wife as he handed the baby to her.

Emma gratefully sat down. She had not yet recovered much strength.

"What is that great smell?" Henry asked moments later as his nose lifted to the faint aroma drifting up the stairs. He sat on the end of the bed.

"I don't know," Emma murmured as she offered Adele her breast. "I suppose we should wire mother."

"What time does she get up? I hate to send telegrams in the middle of the night," Henry responded.

"She is usually up by six," Emma replied.

"Then I'll send a wire on the way to work," Henry decided. "I would take the day off; but without Paynter, I don't dare. Do you think Calista can stay with you during the day?"

"Of course," Calista declared as she waltzed into the room with a plate of food. She offered it first to Henry. "How long do you think it will be before Emma's mother gets here?"

"Knowing Marie, she will take the first coach out of Deer Lodge," Henry answered with a smile.

Calista turned to offer Emma nourishment. "Then I don't see any difficulty," she replied. "All my expectant mothers are months away from their delivery dates."

"Calista, this is good," Henry decided as he ate. "What is it?"

"Meat cakes," she responded. "They are very special. I only fix them after a baby is born." She reached to fondly stroke Adele's small cheek. Then she smiled broadly at Emma. "I told you there was nothing to worry about."

Marie arrived the following evening as excited as Emma had ever seen her. The woman was bubbling with conversation as she took Adele into her arms and briefly held her new granddaughter. Then returning the baby to Emma, she took over her daughter's chores in the kitchen, peeling the potatoes and placing them on the stove to boil. She then retrieved a glass of water from the pump. This she gave to Emma. "Drink. You are drinking for two now," she told her daughter.

Emma accepted the water. She was thirsty. "Do you and Jenny like the idea of moving to Helena?" she inquired. "I don't think anyone has really asked you."

"We love it," Marie declared. "Our family will be all together again."

"Harry will be over on Tuesday?" Emma inquired.

"Yes. He about had a kitten when he found out I was leaving this morning," Emma's mother related with a grin. "He sends his congratulations, by the way."

"I will have to thank him," Emma replied.

"I will have to organize this move, I'm afraid...when I get back," her mother continued. "Harry's mind is so wrapped up with business, he won't tell me or your sister what the schedule is for moving out of the house, or even where we will be staying once we get here."

"You will stay with us," Emma responded.

"Of course we will stay with you," Marie agreed, "for a while. But there are three of us, and I don't think Henry is the type to take in boarders, do you?" She smiled. "I would like to find a nice little house close by." She paused only momentarily. "Emma, I was thinking on the way over, that you and Henry could use the furniture from your old bedroom. There is a bed and dresser. Maybe Adele would eventually like having her mother's old things, and in the meantime your brother could use that room -- until we find a house."

"That sounds fine," Emma responded.

"I have some other furniture too that I really don't want to leave behind, you know, like Jenny's piano, grandmother's spice cupboard, and daddy's rocker. Could we keep them here for now?"

"Of course," Emma replied.

"Oh good," the older woman sighed in relief, "that simplifies things a great deal. I think I can handle the rest with your brother's help." She smirked slightly. "I will just tell Harry what my schedule is," she declared. "Would you like another glass of water?"

Emma's brother and sister arrived in Helena on Tuesday. Harry D'Acheul spent the rest of the week at the drug store, while the women of Emma's family fussed over the new baby. By Saturday Harry was on the coach back to the west side while his mother and sister stayed in Helena. They would return the following week, after Emma's brother had made his inspection and report on the Deer Lodge penitentiary. Together the three would pack and move.

Emma's mother had already put the word out that their home was for sale. But as the moving date drew ever nearer without any serious buyers, Harry finally made arrangements for Thomas Napton to rent the house. He was an attorney in Deer Lodge City who was looking for a larger place. With all the arrangements finally settled, Harry D'Acheul immediately left for Helena. His mother and sister followed on February 23rd, thankful that the intense cold of the preceding week had eased for their coach ride over.

Emma welcomed all into her house. Having her family around her and a new baby was everything she could have dreamed of. Everyone she loved was at hand, happy and excited. Her brother was all smiles as he anticipated doing business in a town the size of Helena. Her mother was happy for him and for Adele, who was never without someone to dote over her. Even Jenny was caught up in the enthusiasm, anticipating more opportunity to share her musical talents.

It took several days for the household to settle into a routine. By then, Emma again had tincture orders to fill. She returned to the attic to work below the wonderfully large skylight of paned glass. Here she crushed her dry plants, cured her tinctures, and bottled her creations.

Emma took a scoop of crushed hyssop from a large jar, placed it in one of her quart jars, and filled it with gin. Then she fastened on the lid, marked the label, and placed it with the other jars setting under the skylight. In two weeks she would filter out the herb and bottle it for shipping.

Emma now began shaking each of the quart jars as part of her daily routine. Footsteps were audible on the stairs, and within moments her mother appeared. The older woman looked around her in amazement.

"You have a blessed factory up here," Marie noted aloud.

Emma smiled. "The orders keep me very busy."

Her mother wandered around the outskirts of the room, peering in under the eaves. "What are in all these boxes?"

"Dried herbs, mostly," her daughter answered. "I need to grind them up."

"What about all the boxes of tincture you had last year? You had them stacked in the dining room."

"Gone," Emma replied. "I can't seem to get that far ahead anymore, which is probably good since demand shifts with the current epidemic." She smiled softly.

"Then your orders haven't diminished?" her mother asked.

"Just the opposite. I supply drug stores all across Montana, and one in Corinne, Utah. Somebody from Fort Benton took one of my tinctures with on a trip, and ran out. So when they went to the Corinne drug store, and couldn't get it, they special ordered it from us and have continued ever since. So now I supply them too."

Emma's mother settled on a nearby stool. "So it's turning out to be quite a little business," she surmised thoughtfully.

"Oh yes," Emma responded. "Henry plans on doing a little marketing in Utah on the way home from his buying trip back East. But he keeps wishing the railroad would come up this way. Shipping would be so much easier, you know, with all our little glass bottles. Now we depend mostly on the Overland Coach."

"A train would make shipping easier, wouldn't it," Marie decided. "They say the railroad will really open up the West."

"That's what Henry thinks."

"He leaves when?"

"Not until the first of next month," Emma answered.

House hunting went slow for Emma's mother. She didn't think she was being particularly fussy, but then again she did not want to live in a log, mining cabin either. The available dwellings were anything but acceptable to her. In frustration she considered the possibility of building, but spring's arrival was awfully slow, and she literally threw up her hands in despair when the deepest snow of the year fell on March 18th.

"Don't worry, Marie," Henry Parchen consoled as he finished breakfast. "I am counting on you and yours being here while I am away. I would really be miffed if I found you had moved out while I was gone, and left Emma and Adele without family in the house."

"Oh Henry," Emma's mother exclaimed as a smile finally emerged in her face, "I don't think you have to worry about that."

"Not likely," Emma's brother laughed. "Builders don't like snow."

Within days Henry left on his trip East with plans to take full advantage of what Emma's brother had learned the previous fall. They had spent many hours discussing the potential of modern medicine, and the potential of increasing their store's profit line.

As a result of Parchen's departure, Harry D'Acheul now spent long hours at the drug store while Emma concentrated on the spring demand for her tinctures. With her mother and Jenny both in the house, Adele's needs were never left wanting. Jenny seemed especially fascinated by the infant, often entertaining the little one with singing. Meanwhile, Emma's mother busied herself in the kitchen. Each seemed content with the new roles they now played.

Emma appreciated the chance to disappear into the attic. As much as she loved her family, the sudden increase of people in her house was a dramatic change from the past year or two. In the attic she found opportunity to have time and goals for herself.

Emma crushed the dried herbs into a coarse powder and placed them in the large jars that were steadily replacing the boxes lining the eaves. This would save her time later, and gain space for the spring plants she would soon be preparing for dehydration. On top of this, the attic air was cool enough to make the work pleasant. Later, the attic heat would make such labor miserable while drying plants in record time.

Emma looked up as her mother appeared. Without a word Marie sat down on the empty stool.

Emma smiled. "You are getting to be a regular visitor up here."

Her mother pulled her sweater tightly around her as her eyes settled on Emma's work. "I think your father would be absolutely fascinated with all this," she commented after several moments. "He never liked prescribing mercury and colomel. They are so harsh. Yet sometimes they were the best medicine he could lay his hands on."

"I always liked your ways better," Emma responded. "I think colomel probably would have killed Jenny during her small pox if you hadn't taken things into your own hands."

Marie smiled softly. "I wasn't so sure at the time. I hated going against the doctor's advice."

"I'm glad you did."

"I'm glad you brought me Dr. Ingersoll's medicine at Deer Lodge City two years ago," her mother replied. "Nothing else did any good."

"I have developed several tinctures for Dr. Ingersoll," Emma offered. "He and Henry have encouraged me at every turn."

"So I see," her mother commented as her eyes again surveyed the attic. "You say your orders are increasing?"

"Yes," Emma answered, "pretty steadily, though Henry thinks they would go right through the roof if we ever got a railroad to Helena."

"But you are making money," Marie asked.

Emma smiled. "I'm not making as much as the store yet, but I'm working on it."

"The store? You could make that much?" her mother inquired.

"I could make more, a lot more," Emma replied, "especially if we secure the western market."

"What do you mean, dear?"

"The west coast – if they ordered from us, they could get tinctures faster and cheaper. They wouldn't have to come from the East."

"Then your business really is a gold mine," her mother commented slowly, deep in thought, "with or without the railroad."

"It's not as dirty as mining." Emma grinned.

"No," Marie agreed. "Could you supply California from your attic here, or would you need more space?"

"I would probably need a factory if we shipped that far," Emma decided.

"...and people. You would need help," her mother added.

"Probably."

"If you had a larger place," her mother began, "and help..." Her voice faded into thought.

Emma finished with her box of herbs, and put the jar back in the eaves. "What are you thinking, mother?"

Marie's eyes rose. "I was thinking how a venture like this could support the whole family. It could give you and your sister a living, so that neither of you would ever lack in life. You just don't know when a catastrophe could leave you, or her, destitute."

"I doubt Jenny would like the work," Emma responded.

"No, it's not music," her mother agreed, "and she has too much of her grandfather in her. That's one of the reasons I worry about her. She doesn't have the practical sense you have." She paused, and then her eyes fixed intently on Emma. "But if you had the factory, she would always have a livelihood she could fall back on. She wouldn't starve, not while you had a job to offer her."

"Factories cost a lot of money," Emma replied. "Where would we get that kind of money? I can't ask Henry. He is saving to build a fireproof store downtown."

"The house," Marie responded with sudden inspiration.

"The house, what house? I'm not giving up my house. I have a child to raise."

"Not your house...mine," her mother retorted.

"Your house? Your house is still over in Deer Lodge, and where are you, Harry, and Jenny going to live without a house?" Emma demanded.

Suddenly her mother shrugged. "Maybe it's a silly idea," she decided. "Oh, I hear the baby."

Emma was already at the stairs. Her mother followed. Adele had grown considerably over the last couple of months, and now lay on her back screaming with arms and legs thrashing the air. Emma immediately reached into the crib and took her daughter to the changing table. Within moments the wet diapers were off, and Adele began to coo.

"Emma," her mother began now, "you know that over the years I've sent your brother to college, and helped him financially with his partnerships. Jenny has had her music lessons, but you...you have never asked for anything. You helped me with the boarding houses in St. Louis, and with the chores at home. You have been the joy of my life, always there, always ready to help."

"I just did what any daughter would," Emma responded as she took Adele into her arms, and retreated into the bedroom where she sat down in the rocker to feed the baby.

"Honey, you aren't just any daughter," her mother replied. "I don't know what I would do without you."

Emma smiled. "I don't need anything, mother. I'm content as I am."

"Yes," her mother sighed, "and you should be. You have everything I ever dreamed of for you. God be praised."

"If you want to do something for me," Emma offered now thoughtfully, "put a little money aside for Adele...so she can go to college. I think she should get training of some kind, so she has something to fall back on if her life doesn't turn out to be as rosy as we all would wish."

"Yes, that is a good idea," her mother agreed, "but what if you have more than one child, and what if the next one is a boy, Emma. Henry would want him to go to college too. And what if there is only enough money to send one?"

"I see your point," Emma responded as she adjusted her daughter, "though hopefully we will have a few extra dollars by then."

"If things go well, you will...and if you plan ahead," her mother replied. "That is what Henry has been trying to do, but with the fires and a growing family, it isn't easy. I know. If it's not fires, it's illness, or something just as bad."

"You have endured so much," Emma commented thoughtfully.

"Yes, and I want things easier for you," her mother stated. "I have been thinking about this for some time, and I think you have hit on the very solution. Your factory can provide everything you will ever need or want. It can help your husband and Harry by giving them a product with a good profit line, and Jenny, well, it will give her a living if she should ever have need of it. Emma, you and Henry Parchen are the salvation of our family. He was right to get you started making tinctures, and he is right about supplying the west coast."

"If the train comes through," Emma added.

"Even if it doesn't," her mother responded. "Emma, you have already proven there is a demand for your work. All you need is a factory and more help."

"That takes money," Emma replied, "and it will have to wait. Henry gets his new store first. He might have even had it by now if... We had burial expenses," she finished quietly.

An understanding expression settled in her mother's face. "An honorable man, truly honorable," she noted quietly, "and proud, I dare say."

"Yes," Emma agreed.

"That is why I'm offering to help you, not him," Marie continued. "If you prosper, so does he. But the store... I dare not meddle there."

"What do you mean?"

"Emma, the best I can do for your husband, is help Harry help both of them. I am Harry's mother, after all. But I am not Henry's. To help him would be to interfere, and I won't cross that line. But you are my daughter, and you have at your fingertips the most marvelous opportunity. If you had your factory..." She just smiled broadly.

"But there is no extra money."

"So what if I help?"

"Mother, do you have any idea how much a factory would cost?" Emma demanded. "You don't have that kind of money."

"But I have some," the older woman responded, "and the drug store property extends back quite a ways. Henry has talked about building a fireproof warehouse, hasn't he?"

"He has talked about building a fireproof store," Emma replied as she finished with Adele, and the baby began to play with the rattle her grandmother offered. "Plus, your house down in Deer Lodge didn't sell. You need your money."

"Emma, what if Henry builds a warehouse, and I add a floor to it...for you, for your tincture business?"

"No mother, his new store comes first," Emma objected.

"The warehouse would be for his store," she countered.

"The old store. If he builds the warehouse, he may never get the new one," Emma responded.

"Perhaps you are right," her mother agreed. "Still, if you don't mind, I would like to speak to him about it."

"It won't do any good," Emma replied. "Henry is very stubborn about his priorities."

By the end of April Henry Parchen was in Corinne, and sent a telegram home. Emma read it in silence.

"What does it say?" Marie asked.

"Henry is bringing someone home," Emma replied as she looked up, "his nephew."

"Good," Jenny exploded. "Our brother has been spoiled having that room upstairs all to himself."

"I suppose the young man wants to see the West," their mother surmised. "Do you think he will stay, Emma?"

Chapter Fourteen

Henry Parchen arrived in Helena on Thursday evening, the seventh of May. He wanted to be back in time for Wood Paynter's auction sale scheduled for the following day. Henry Parchen and his nephew got off the Overland Coach as wind tore at their clothes. Small clusters of dark clouds threatened rain. Henry looked up. Emma was running toward him. Within moments they were in each other's arms.

Emma's brother made his way to them with a large smile on his face. "Well Parchen, how did it go?" he demanded.

"Fine. Fine," Henry replied as he turned to his partner. "I would like you and Emma to meet my nephew, Henry Duerfeldt. Henry, this is my wife, Emma, and her brother and my partner, Harry D'Acheul."

"It is nice to meet you," Emma responded as she offered her hand.

Young Henry Duerfeldt took it briefly. "I understand you already have a house full. I hope I'm not putting you out too much."

"Nonsense," Emma retorted, "you can share Harry's room." She turned to indicate her brother.

"It's good to meet you, Duerfeldt," Harry stated. "Are you going to join us down at the drug store?"

"I don't know for sure," young Henry Duerfeldt answered. "Uncle Henry said he had some work for me, but he didn't say exactly what." He turned to Parchen.

"My nephew wanted to see Montana," Emma's husband announced, "so I invited him out." Then he smiled. "Harry and I need a reliable sort to look after things, especially when shipments come in."

"Henry, Harry, Henry... How are we to keep you three straight," Emma cried in exasperation.

"Just call me Duerfeldt, Mrs. Parchen," Henry's nephew offered.

"Dir...what," Emma floundered.

"'Duer' will be just fine," Henry's nephew decided.

"That's not a name," Emma fretted.

"Then how about the Prussian pronunciation? Henrick?" he asked.

"Henry, Harry, Henrick... How about if I just call 'supper'?" she resolved.

"That should work just fine," Henry Duerfeldt agreed with a smile.

"So who were you named after," Emma's brother inquired as they picked up their luggage, and started walking up Broadway.

"Uncle Henry, of course," Duerfeldt replied. "My mother was heartbroken when her little brother moved so far away."

"Then we can just call you 'Junior'. All right, Parchen?" Emma's brother asked.

"And what happens when we have a son," Emma countered.

"A nephew?" her brother exclaimed. "Are you expecting again, Em?"

"No, not yet," she answered, "but we do have plans to name our first son Henry."

"That will make three Henrys on the Parchen side of the family alone. It's a good thing mom nicknamed me, Harry," Emma's brother teased with a big grin.

The gusty weather did not let up with nightfall, but brought rain by morning. Wood Paynter's auction was postponed until Monday while the members of Emma's family hung on her husband's every word, listening intently to his descriptions of the East, and of his recent visit to family in Nebraska. Here his nephew also joined in, possessing much more knowledge than his uncle could gather from such a brief stop-over.

On Monday Emma's brother left for Deer Lodge, and Henry Parchen returned to the store with his nephew. After acclimating the young man to normal customer demands, Parchen left for a short time to attend Wood Paynter's auction. Emma secretly feared that if prices did not bring the expected money, her husband might end up purchasing something major, maybe even the Paynter house. He had already bought Wood's share of the business property, and Emma would not be happy if he spent more money. She was still waiting for construction to begin on the new store property. They needed a fireproof building.

That evening Henry and his nephew came home with a wood box. It was covered due to the rain. But with a smile, Parchen presented it to his wife.

"What's this?" she asked warily.

"Open it."

Emma set the box down on a chair, and removed the cover. Colored porcelain met her eye. "What is it, a lamp?"

Her husband smiled. "You need something decent to read by, and this one puts out a lot of light."

Emma brought out piece by piece, assembling it on the table as her family gathered around to watch.

"It's beautiful, Emma," her mother noted.

"Yes, it is," she agreed. Her eyes shifted to her husband. "Is this all you bought?"

"There is just one other thing," he added.

"What?" she asked worriedly.

Henry Parchen took her by the hand, and led her out to the back porch. There tied to a post was a small kitten. "I thought we could use her, and Birdie Paynter begged me to give her a good home," he stated softly as the fur ball backed away from the human intrusion.

Emma knelt momentarily over the small cat, freeing it from the post. "You brought us a kitten?" she asked as the creature climbed her blouse.

"We don't want mice," Henry told her.

"Maybe not, but she's a tom cat," Emma decided.

"Adele should like him," young Duerfeldt offered as he reached for the kitten.

Harry's trip to Deer Lodge was brief, and he was home Thursday night. Emma's mother said little as she watched her son join the family at the dinner table nearly twenty minutes late. The conversation hardly broke. Her eyes shifted to Emma. She was finally getting an uninterrupted meal. Adele had eaten early, and was asleep.

The older woman watched the ease in which Henry's nephew fit into the family circle. She assumed the same spirit existed down at the drug store. All three men spent their days there. Marie's gaze shifted to her son-in-law. She would have to go down to Parchen Drugs if she wanted to talk to him.

A small bell rang as Emma's mother entered the drug store. Two customers lingered in the aisles as she passed. Henry's nephew greeted her briefly as he waited on one of these. Her son was on a ladder, retrieving a box, and Henry Parchen was working on an account book at the cash register.

"Good morning, Marie," he greeted with a smile. "I was just thinking about you? What did you say Adele needed?"

"Salve," Emma's mother answered. "We seem to have lost our tin. It's really odd."

"Would you like to take it with you," Parchen asked as he left the counter momentarily, and returned with the item.

"Yes, it might be a good idea," Emma's mother replied. "But that is not why I came by. Could we talk?"

Concern instantly rose in her son-in-law's face. "Certainly," he answered as he escorted her back to the office, and closed the door. "What's wrong?"

"Oh nothing's wrong," his mother-in-law responded as Parchen offered her the chair, and found a seat on the nearby crate. "I just haven't had an opportunity to talk with you since your trip, and I've had a few things on my mind. You haven't any pressing store business, have you?"

"Nothing that can't wait," he replied.

"Well you know, my hunt for a house has not gone well," Marie began.

"Yes. In fact I was just discussing the situation with a builder who stopped by the store. He has some pictures. If you want to pick out a house, he can give you a price estimate."

"Thank you, Henry, but I think I have changed my mind about all that, and I want to see what you think of my new idea."

"Certainly," he agreed.

"While you were away," she continued, "I spent a little time up in your attic. Emma has a pretty good little business going up there."

"Yes, she does," Parchen affirmed.

"I am wondering if it isn't time for her to expand."

"We have been expanding as money will allow," Henry Parchen replied. "I just brought her orders from three new stores."

"Your attic is going to get a little tight if you plan on building her any more shelves."

"True," Parchen agreed.

"May I be frank, Henry," his mother-in-law asked.

"Please."

"I have the money I was going to use for the house, but I see such potential in Emma's tinctures. It's a virtual gold mine, especially if you secure the market in California, and I would rather invest my money in my family. I've helped Harry already, and Jenny, well, she has had the best music instruction I could find her. But Emma... It's time Emma had something. Listen, Henry, I know you have a house full with all of us under your roof, but Jenny takes care of Adele a lot, and I would feel lost without a kitchen...and all this frees Emma to work on her tinctures, only just think if she had a real factory with employees."

"You want to build her a factory?" he asked.

"I wish I could," Emma's mother responded, "but I'm afraid I don't have that kind of money. No, what I'm suggesting is for the two of us to put our heads together to find a way of making the most of what we do have."

"By using the money you were going to buy a house with?"

"Yes. If I live with you, Emma would never have to worry about the kitchen, and you and she could have the money."

"What about Harry and Jenny? We only have three bedrooms, and Emma and I are planning on more children," Henry replied.

"Don't worry about Harry," Marie laughed. "He will move on before you know it, especially with your nephew sharing his room. I would be more concerned about young Duerfeldt. As far as Jenny goes, we can share the room until you need it for the children, and then I'll take the space under the stairs, if you don't mind. Rheumatism is starting to affect my knees, and I'd like to be close to the kitchen. And then with any luck, Jenny will have had enough time to find herself a husband." Marie smiled.

Henry Parchen rose to his feet, turned around, and sat down again. His eyes returned to his mother-in-law. "Even if we did that, what about Emma's factory? You said you didn't have enough to build it."

"By myself, no. But Henry you own property, you are looking to build. What if we just add another floor, you know with skylights for Emma's tinctures?"

"I can't build the new store yet," he replied, "even with your house money. And Harry can't come up with the difference. He just joined me in Helena."

"But you own property," Emma's mother insisted, "behind the store here. A fireproof warehouse would be a much smaller investment. And didn't you just loose your extra storage space with the fire?"

"We are planning on a new store," Henry objected, "a fireproof store."

"Yes, but think. If the warehouse was fireproof, you would have the same protection you do in Deer Lodge. All of your back stock would be safe, and isn't that better than nothing? Plus, if Emma was on the upper floor, making money..."

Henry's eyes focused sharply on her.

Emma's mother smiled. "Think about it, Henry. I think there's real potential here, otherwise I wouldn't be offering my pittance. Well, I'd better run along. I have taken enough of your time," Marie declared as she rose to her feet. "Talk to Emma if you wish." Henry's mother-in-law excused herself and retraced her path to the front door, waving a greeting to her son who was now sorting through several boxes in a frantic search for something.

Henry Parchen followed as far as the counter where his accounting books lay, but his thoughts lingered on Emma's mother long after she was gone.

Reverend Shippen's sermon on Sunday stormed the congregation of the Methodist/Episcopal Church with all the bluster of the past week's weather as he propounded the Christian's duty to overcome the evil of the world -- not withstanding the politics that would put the Deer Lodge penitentiary under territorial jurisdiction.

Emma's brother couldn't agree more with the Reverend as the family finally gained the out of doors. Emma was relieved to see everyone. Adele had not been quiet during the service, and she had spent the majority of the time outside as she tried to quiet her daughter. Now she joined her husband as Jenny offered to take Adele. The walk home was hardly more than a block long. But as the various family members disappeared inside the house, Henry detained his wife.

"Let's not go in yet," he suggested. "Jenny has Adele, and your mother won't have lunch ready for a little bit yet."

"Okay," she readily consented. "What would you like to do?"

"I would like to walk," he answered, "toward the hills, if you don't mind."

"All right," she replied. They turned up Rodney Street.

"Your mother came by the store to see me this week," Henry Parchen informed his wife.

"She did?"

"Yes," he affirmed. "She thinks it's time for your tincture business to expand."

"I know," Emma responded, "but your fireproof store comes first."

"That's what we have always said," Henry agreed.

"We have insurance," his wife responded. "We can wait until we can do things right."

"But what Marie said made sense," her husband countered.

"Like what?" Emma asked.

"Like making the most of what we have now," he answered. "If I build a fireproof warehouse behind the store, we could make up for the storage space we lost in January, and have at least some fire protection. When Deer Lodge went up in smoke it was nice having the back building, and I don't know when I can get the new store built. My partners never seem able or willing to come up with their half of the money."

"Give Harry a chance," Emma retorted with a grin. "He has only been your partner for a few months."

"True," Parchen replied, "but he has made quite an expenditure already, and it may be a while before he can make any more. In the mean time we wait as one fire after another comes along."

"So you want to build a fireproof warehouse?" Emma asked.

"I want to protect our interests, and we both could use more space," he answered. "Your mother wants to add a floor to the warehouse for your tincture factory. I think she feels the attic is getting too crowded." He smiled.

"If mother spends her money on the warehouse, she will have to live with us, probably forever, maybe even Jenny and Harry."

"Harry will probably move out eventually," Henry noted.

"Yes," Emma decided, "but not mother. And we will have Jenny until she marries, if she ever does."

"I told Marie we wanted more kids," Henry offered, "and she thought when the time came, maybe we could fix her a bed under the stairs so she would be close to the kitchen, considering her rheumatism. By then, maybe Jenny will have found herself a husband."

"Mother lives in that kitchen," Emma commented.

"Your kitchen," her husband replied. "Would you give up your kitchen for a factory?"

"She does save me a lot of time by fixing the meals," Emma noted.

"And Jenny is good with Adele," Henry added. "So what do you think? Is this what you want?"

"I don't know. Could it work?" Emma asked. "What about you? Do you mind all my family underfoot?"

"They are family," Henry stated.

"But would you rather have it like before, when we first built the house?"

"I miss our privacy," he confessed.

"I do too," she agreed, "but if they left, I would miss them."

"Yeah," Henry affirmed. They walked in silence for several minutes. Suddenly Henry turned. "What do you think? Should I build the warehouse?"

"It would help in case of fire," Emma responded, "and you do already own the land."

"I do, don't I?" her husband agreed. "Actually, I don't know why I didn't think of this sooner." A smile crept into his face. "I could actually afford to build the warehouse."

"But if you build the warehouse, it could keep you from building your new store later, couldn't it?" Emma questioned.

"I need more space," her husband replied, "especially after the January fire. Our old living quarters have become floor to ceiling crates and boxes, and none of them are empty." He smiled. "If my business is to continue growing, I have to have warehouse space. The same goes for you."

"You think it's a good idea then?" Emma asked.

"Yes," he answered without hesitation, "but I'm just not sure about your mother giving up her house."

"My mother has always had a house," Emma commented now, "usually a boarding house with other income property, anything that would keep us when daddy got sick. But she is getting older, her rheumatism won't let her run stairs now like a boarding house requires. Yet if she had just a small house, I think she would miss the people and the money. She has always invested in income property of one sort or another." Emma paused. "It's not surprising, really, that she changed her mind about getting a house. I just didn't expect this."

"I have always liked your mother," Henry confessed softly. "She has a head on her shoulders."

"She's had to have," Emma replied. "Life has not been easy on her."

"So maybe her idea is good," he offered.

Emma grinned. "You need a fireproof warehouse; she needs her family; and I...I guess I need more space for the tinctures."

"And some more help," Henry decided. "Do you like my nephew? Maybe he could work for you."

"I thought you brought him out to Montana for the drug store," Emma countered.

"I did, but I can always find someone else for Harry and me. I want someone reliable, someone I can trust to help you. Warehouses are lonely places."

"So you have decided?" Emma asked.

"About what?"

"About my mother's offer," she replied.

"Have you?" Henry questioned.

"Yes."

"You can live with your mother in your kitchen?"

"Yes," Emma replied. "Can you live with my family in your house?"

"Yes."

Plans were drawn up for the Parchen warehouse, and excavation began June 1st. Emma often walked downtown with Adele to meet Henry after work so she could watch the progress of the bricklayers. By mid July the structure had risen into the air, and excitement grew within her as it neared completion. Skylights were already installed in the roof as the carpenters worked on the finishing touches. Henry, on the advice of his mother-in-law, had also arranged for the carpenters to build twice the number of shelves and drying racks as Emma had in her attic. Still, his wife could only marvel at the quantity of space as cases of jars and bottles began to arrive. Then the carpenters carried in an enormous desk.

Emma turned to Henry. "You ordered a desk?"

"Your mother did," he replied.

"Mother?"

"I think she saw your mess of order forms in the attic," he responded with a grin.

"And she thinks a desk will solve the problem?" Emma asked.

"Apparently she thinks it might help," Henry laughed. "You do need to organize things better if you are going to have employees."

"I will manage," Emma replied in a disgruntled tone. A matching oak chair now followed the desk inside.

"I have a wagon coming by the house tomorrow to unload the attic," her husband offered. "I hope you are ready to move. You don't have much time before the mass of green herbs arrives."

"The drying racks aren't finished," Emma noted. "We will need them before we need all the shelves."

"Talk to the carpenters," Henry suggested.

Emma handed Adele to her husband, and went inside.

Crates of green plants arrived the following week as the carpenters struggled to complete the order of drying racks. Emma made do with the small units from her attic for the first few days. Then as the taller units emerged from the carpenters' hands, Emma's factory took on more order. She spent long hours getting her things organized. Jenny often helped, bringing Adele along for a few hours, depositing her on a blanket with a few play things. The child was walking now, toddling into drying racks, pulling green plants onto the floor. The herbs now rose to the higher rods as the women worked. Without realizing it, Emma was now putting in as long of hours as her husband, coming home exhausted.

But the house was a respite. Emma's mother kept it picture perfect, while Jenny made sure Adele was more than adequately cared for. Life was good that fall as the family worked industriously together, finding reprieves in the harmless pranks and humorous stories they shared. Laughter often invaded the dinner table as Emma's brother would relate stories about their pastor's incorrigible cow. It hated fences, and found the most incredible escape routes. Laughter often exploded around the table as Jenny then picked up the story, twisting it around until her brother became the object of teasing.

"Hattie cornered me the other day," Jenny recalled with a grin. "She wanted to know whether our brother, Emma, knew how to sing. Can you imagine! Everyone in our family can sing, just not all of us care to." Her eyes flashed to Harry. "You should join the choir."

"If I had as much time as you," he retorted, "I would."

"As much time as me," Jenny repeated hotly. "I work. I look after Adele, and I help Emma downtown. I even give piano lessens twice a week."

"And you sing in the choir and for weddings, and you are volunteering all the time for one social or another. It's a wonder Adele even sees you."

"Well if you spent any real time at church, you would probably be married by now," Jenny countered. "Isn't that right, mother?"

Marie turned to her son. "She is right, you know. Everyone is very nice. It wouldn't take long before you met someone."

"I haven't time for a wife," Harry D'Acheul scoffed. His attention shifted to Emma. "I think we are running low on your cough syrup in Deer Lodge. School is back in session, and the nights are getting cold. Our man, Triaberger, will probably be screaming for a shipment very soon."

"I will get a case ready to ship," Emma responded.

The holidays were the best Emma could remember, though she missed decorating the house. These jobs had become the responsibility of others as she worked downtown. Cy Ingersoll came by the warehouse regularly now to discuss her tinctures, especially those destined for his wife. Calista had fallen ill, and was in some discomfort as Cy struggled to find a cure for her. Emma scoured her books, looking for something that might make a difference, but as time slipped by all she and Cy could do was watch and pray. Meanwhile, Emma's sister was involved in countless seasonal productions, and grandma often watched Adele as her daughters went in opposite directions.

"Emma, did you hear about Wood Paynter," her husband asked as he slid the door of the loading dock shut against the winter cold.

"No," she responded as she shivered. The January air was frigid.

"He had a son."

"He did," she exclaimed. "Are they still back in Michigan?"

"Yes," Henry replied. "I haven't heard from him in a long time, but there was an announcement in the paper."

"There was? I must have missed it," Emma concluded. "Do you think the tinctures will freeze on their way to Fort Benton?"

"Possibly," Henry acknowledged. "That's why we used the larger bottles. I don't think the Overland Coach driver would appreciate corks randomly popping off."

"No," Emma agreed. "When are you leaving for Deer Lodge?"

"Next week."

"I hope it warms up some," Emma noted.

"Me too," her husband responded.

Henry Parchen took a shipment of medicine to Deer Lodge when he went. He spent ten days there, closing out the books from the previous year, checking inventory, and placing orders for the coming months.

He had not been back in Helena for two weeks when Harry was called to Deer Lodge to give the annual report at the penitentiary. Jenny was not pleased. Her brother had finally joined the effort to stage a benefit for the Helena Library Association. Being instrumental on the Music Committee, Harry was now prevented from attending the Mardi Gras Hop he had contributed so much too. Emma and Henry went to the dance on Tuesday night without him.

Chapter Fifteen

Emma enjoyed being in her husband's arms. The Mardi Gras music had finally slowed, and she was glad. With all the family in the house, and all the things at work dominating her thoughts, moments alone with Henry were becoming too few. Emma laid her head against his shoulder and dreamed of the days when they lived in the house alone. What she wouldn't give to have him chasing her around the bedroom again, full of fun and spontaneity!

Henry held her close, and Emma's thoughts drifted to his upcoming trip. It seemed like her husband was on the road more and more. This trip, however, was not to Deer Lodge. It was to Pleasant Valley. Emma frowned momentarily. Pleasant Valley might be pleasant in the summer, but it was not a place one wanted to be in the winter time. Storms seemed to be excessively treacherous there, and the one that had descended on the valley the week before was not something anyone dismissed lightly. Emma snuggled closer to her husband.

"What's wrong?" Henry inquired quietly.

"Pleasant Valley," Emma answered.

"Oh," he replied. They danced silently for several moments. "You know I have to go."

"Yes," she agreed, "but I wish it was a different time of year."

"I know," he responded. "I'm not looking forward to the trip either."

Hewin's band shifted into the final lively piece, and Henry led his wife off the dance floor.

"You two are going to the St. Louis Hotel for our late supper, aren't you?" John Kinna asked as they passed the hardware store owner.

"Don't know, John," Henry answered over the music. "Got to work tomorrow."

"We all do. You should come," he coaxed. "Anton and his wife will be there."

"Holter and his wife left an hour ago," Parchen replied. "Their son is down with the croup."

"They did?" John Kinna responded. "I wish they had told me."

"Take care, John. Maybe we can get together for lunch tomorrow," Parchen offered. He and Emma walked out into the foyer.

"Are you hungry?" Henry now asked his wife. "We could go over to the St. Louis for something to eat."

"I'm more thirsty than hungry," she answered as the two wandered over and claimed their coats. Arm in arm, they left the building.

"I really don't want to go home," Henry noted quietly. "Tomorrow is just another day."

"Another day closer to your trip," Emma agreed.

"Pleasant Valley really has you bothered, hasn't it," Henry commented.

"After the storm last week, yes," Emma responded. "But it's not just that, you will be leaving for New York then. It seems like you're never home any more."

"But you know how important it is for the railroad to come to Montana," Henry maintained. "You know how important it is to our future and our children's future. A couple months apart will be a sacrifice well worth it in the years ahead."

"Yes, I know," Emma agreed reluctantly.

"And you won't be alone. We have family here now."

"Yes," she agreed, "all five of them. But it won't be the same without you."

Henry smiled as he took her into his arms. "Tell you what," he suggested softly in her ear. "What if we do something wicked? What if we don't go home tonight."

Emma stared into his face. The light reflecting off the snow revealed an unusual mischief in her husband's face. "Where would we go?" she asked.

Henry's smile grew. "Come on. I'll show you."

Emma walked with her husband as curiosity grew within her. As thoughts of his trip faded from her mind, Henry led her to the back of their warehouse, and unlocked the door, letting them in at the loading dock.

"What are you up to?" Emma cried with interest.

"You'll see," he replied as he lit a lantern. "Wait here a minute," he told her as he momentarily disappeared. Then motioning for Emma to join him on the lift, he mechanically pulled them toward the upper floor and the tincture factory.

"Don't I spend enough time up here already," she asked with a grin.

"Ah, but I bet you have never seen the pulley platform at night," he declared. His eyes twinkled in the lantern light.

Emma followed him to the narrow ladder, and one after the other they climbed up to the skylight, passing the massive mechanics of the lift. As Henry gained the platform, he motioned Emma over on her knees, and then put out the lantern.

"What are you doing?" Emma demanded in the sudden blackness.

Henry's arm encircled her. "Look," he stated softly as he pointed.

Emma's eyes slowly adjusted as she strained to focus first on his outstretched finger, and then on the darkness beyond. "Stars," she exclaimed softly, "lots and lots of stars."

"Do you see the Little Dipper?" Henry inquired.

"Yes, there," Emma answered. "The sky is so blue."

"Midnight blue," Henry agreed as his cheek brushed hers. "You smell good."

"It's my lavender soap," Emma responded. Her eyes turned to him.

"Are you still thirsty?" Henry asked.

"Yes."

He pulled back then, fumbling with his coat. Within moments Emma heard the soft pop of a cork. "Here," he offered as he shoved the bottle at her.

"What's this," she asked.

"French wine," he replied.

Emma stared at the hazy dark image of the bottle. "Is it good?"

"Of course it's good," Henry retorted. "You should know that by now."

That was not what Emma meant. She had never drunk wine from the bottle, not good wine. Somehow it seemed sacrilegious.

"It's the same stuff we had over the holidays," Henry offered as his wife still lingered.

"I didn't mean it like that," she finally commented. "I just have never drunk from the bottle."

"You said you were thirsty."

"Yes," Emma agreed. She took a sip. The smooth quality of the grape rolled over her palate. She swallowed, the liquid soothing her dry throat as her body craved more.

"Okay Emma, save some for me," Henry objected as his wife indulged herself. He pulled the bottle gently away from her.

Emma sat down on the floor, relaxed. Her eyes lifted to the heavens. "I think I see the dragon constellation," she commented after a moment.

"Where?" Henry asked.

"There by the Little Dipper," she answered. "It's supposed to be between the Little and the Big Dipper, and I think those two stars, there, are part of the Big Dipper." She pointed.

"The skylight isn't big enough," Henry decided as he positioned himself snugly against his wife, and tried to see.

"It's marvelous," Emma responded as she turned to him. "I have never seen the winter sky like this. It's big and beautiful. There's nothing in the way. And it's warm." She laid back, staring at the sky. "We haven't laid under the stars since...Deer Lodge, in mother's back yard." She propped herself up on one elbow. "Remember, it was the Fourth of July. You, me, and Jenny tried to name the different constellations, only we couldn't, so we made up new ones."

"I remember," Henry replied.

Emma turned at his voice, and smiled.

"I remember how much I wanted to touch you," Henry confessed softly. His fingers reached to brush her cheek. His lips followed.

Within the week Henry Parchen left Helena for points west. The corridor between the Rockies and the Bitterroot Mountains was the object of the first leg of his journey. The Utah Northern Railroad was considering an extension of their line north, but the feasibility of the terrain was in major contention. To alleviate these fears, Henry Parchen and others had consented to undertake the winter travel necessary to determine certain points of fact before attending a railroad meeting scheduled for March 15th in New York. Their contacts there needed this information for the strategies they planned to present at the Railroad Convention convening April 22nd.

Emma straightened her aching back. It was nearly six o'clock Monday evening. She was alone on the upper floor of the warehouse. It had been a quiet day. She finished shaking a quart jar, and reached for another. She had a half dozen to go yet. Then she could go home.

She set the last jar back on the shelf, noting that she would have to bottle up five different tinctures in the morning, and make labels. This was good. It would be a break from grinding herbs.

Cy Ingersoll appeared from the stairs. "Need some tinctures," he stated.

Emma smiled softly. "How is Calista?"

"About the same, maybe a little better," he replied with a tired look.

"It's been what, five months now?" Emma asked as she took the short list from his hand.

"Five months... It seems her illness has turned chronic, doesn't it," he responded. "You would think I could cure my own wife."

"Cy, you of all people should know doctors are not miracle workers," Emma reminded him kindly.

"Some think we are," he replied.

"And some believe in ghosts." Emma smiled. "Do you think the rosemary helped at all?"

"Maybe a little," he responded, "but it was precious little. With all the herbs and plants we deal with, why can't we find the solution?" he lamented.

"I don't know," Emma answered, "but healing takes time. You know that."

"I also know when things take too long, the chances of recovery aren't good." He turned momentarily aside, overcome.

"Cy," Emma responded as she placed her hand on his arm.

"She helped so many people," he exclaimed suddenly. "Why should she have to suffer like this?"

"I don't know," Emma replied.

"I had better go," Cy decided.

"Mother baked yesterday," Emma offered as she hastily retrieved a full basket. "I was planning to drop this off on the way home."

"Thank you...again, as always." Cy Ingersoll mustered a smile. "Calista enjoys your visits, and you don't have to bring something to stop by."

"I know," Emma responded. "Tell her I will try and stop by later tonight."

"I imagine Henry should be on his way to New York by now," Cy stated as he abruptly changed the subject.

"Yes," Emma replied quietly.

"I hope his trip goes well. This has been one severe winter. Well, I'm off."

Emma said nothing as she watched Cy retreat down the stairs. She keenly felt her husband's absence, especially on top of the disheartening news of Calista. She had received a telegram from Henry. It was from Pleasant Valley. Henry said all was well, including the weather.

Emma finished her tinctures, and locked up for the night. At least now she could go home to her daughter.

Easter came and went, and Emma began to get used to life without her Henry. Adele was growing so fast that Emma spent every free minute with her, watching her progress with utter fascination. Her mother often dropped the child off at the factory when she had a church meeting to attend. Emma enjoined the companionship, and Adele loved to play with the dried herbs, picking them apart, crushing them between her hands. Emma worked until the child became tired and bored, and turned her attention to more dangerous preoccupations, like climbing the shelves. At these times Emma would take her daughter aside, and tell her a story or sing a little song until the exhausted child fell asleep. During Adele's naps, Emma tried to make up for lost time.

Then on the 26th of April, Harry burst into Emma's factory. "Henry was in Cheyenne on the 18th," he announced.

Emma looked up from her work. "Then he is finally on his way home," she replied with relief.

"Yes, but the road was washed out so they may be delayed several days," Harry continued. "Preuitt and Rosser are with him."

"That was over a week ago," Emma decided.

"Yes, so he can't be too far away," Harry agreed. "I bet he is here by Saturday."

"Saturday," Emma repeated as hope rose within her. "I hope so."

Harry's prediction came true. Henry Parchen arrived home, exhausted, but happy to see Emma and the family. Exclaiming over and over how much Adele had grown in his absence, his eyes now turned to his wife. He had missed her.

Emma smiled. It was the same smile that had captivated him so completely when he first met her. It was a shy smile, but alluring at the same time. Henry put his arm around his wife, and led her upstairs to their room. The family chuckled in amusement, and turned to other things.

"Emma, what are all these evergreens doing in here," Henry asked as he closed the bedroom door behind them.

"I thought you would like them," Emma replied.

"It smells good," he responded. "Adele is getting big."

"Yes," Emma agreed, "and she loves playing with other little children."

Henry took his wife into his arms. "Is that what this is all about? You want to give Adele a baby brother?"

A smile grew on Emma's face.

Calista's condition improved only slightly from time to time alternating with frustrating regressions. For nearly ten months Calista fought against her illness, and her husband with her, but by August things looked hopeless. Emma's heart sank. She was pregnant again, and it did not look like Calista would be around for the birth or their little chats or anything else. The woman was dying; and as much as Emma grieved for her, Calista's constant pain was something she wished relieved at any cost. She would miss her friend.

"If I have another daughter," Emma told the now frail Calista after sitting with her for some time, "I shall name her after you."

A faint smile formed on the tired lips. "What day is it?"

"I'm not due until late February," Emma answered.

"I meant today," Calista whispered. Her strength was failing.

"It's August. The third," Emma replied with concern.

"And is the sun shining?" Calista asked.

"It was," Emma responded. "It's almost dark now."

"Then you best start for home," Calista noted. "Tell Ed I would like to see him on your way out, would you?"

Calista Ingersoll died at 9:45, Tuesday evening, August 3, 1875. She was 59 years old. Friends and family gathered for the funeral at her home on Union Street, Thursday afternoon.

Emma sat beside her husband as the minister related how Calista had been born in South Orange, Massachuetts. She had fallen in love with Dr. Cy Ingersoll, and had married him in Fredonin, New York. While raising their family, Calista often assisted her husband in medical matters until finally she had become a midwife in her own right. Then in 1864 the Ingersolls had emigrated to Montana where she was greatly loved for bringing Helena's earliest babies into the world, often by candlelight.

Strains of the hymn, "Nearer My God to Thee", rose from the lips of those gathered. Tears crept into Emma's eyes. She had managed to stay dry-eyed until now, despite the tremendous loss she was feeling, but Calista had hummed the hymn repeatedly the morning following Adele's birth. Calista had been such a good friend, and had seen Emma through all the fears and doubts of the stillborn until Emma not only had brought Adele into the world, but another was on the way as well.

Emma pulled her shawl carefully up to conceal her weight gain as she wondered if she would have another daughter. The service ended, and Henry rose to join the pall bearers. Emma wiped her eyes.

An old gentleman sat down beside Emma as his hand covered hers. Emma looked into the wrinkled face she had often seen around town.

"Mrs. Ingersoll carried water from the stream in Last Chance Gulch to bathe my wife with before she died," he noted quietly. "There never was such an angelic woman." He patted Emma's hand momentarily, and then rose and silently melted into the crowd.

Emma's hand covered her mouth. Her loss was not the only one. Her eyes drifted to Calista's son, Ed. He had returned to Helena a few weeks before. Young Ingersoll's arm was around his own wife. His expression held awful grief.

Emma rose to her feet. The pall bearers were picking up the coffin. Everyone would be following them to Benton Avenue Cemetery where Calista would be laid to eternal rest.

A son was born to Emma and Henry on the 26th of February 1876. They named him Henry George – Henry after his father and his maternal grandfather, and George after his paternal grandfather. Now officially there were four Henrys in the family, though Emma was prompt in conferring the nickname of her brother on the baby, reducing the problem to two Henrys and two Harrys. "Uncle" was the title given to the elders. This helped distinguish between the age groups.

With mixed feelings, Emma watched her brother move out of the house, freeing up a bedroom for Adele. Harry took rooms at the Rumleys, a few blocks away on the corner of 6th and Rodney. Mr. Rumley's mine was looking very promising, and he had daughters. Whether any of this was an enticement for Harry, Emma couldn't determine; but her brother always did gravitate to money, or at least potential money.

Henry's nephew, on the other hand, moved to the attic. Emma couldn't say she didn't like this. She had gotten rather used to having men around the house, and in all honesty she would be glad of young Duerfeldt's company in the absence of her husband.

Because of the new baby, Emma's brother took the store's annual buying trip east that spring. When Harry returned home on April 29th, he was in the company of Mr. Shirley Ashby. Mr. Ashby's mother had fallen critically ill and died in his absence. The funeral was scheduled for the following morning at the Ashby residence on Rodney Street.

Emma cradled her two month old son in her arms as her mother expressed her profound sympathies to Mr. Shirley Ashby. "Hebe was a 'god send' to me," Marie told him quietly. "Since I moved to Helena two years ago, no one has been more kind. She was a gentle, gracious, and pious Christian. My life has been blessed by knowing her. I only wish it could have been longer."

"Thank you, Marie," S.C. Ashby replied. His eyes were red, and his voice was much subdued.

Harry D'Acheul offered his hand. "Ashby, I'm sorry for your loss."

"It seems so impossible," he noted quietly. "All the times I have taken risks, huge risks, and survived. And now this..."

"It was all unexpected," Henry Parchen commented as he now took Ashby's hand in turn. "No one could know something like this would happen, especially while you were gone. No one but God." He smiled gently. "Chin up. There is reason in what God does, and when He does it. Don't blame yourself for not being here."

S.C. Ashby nodded, unable to reply. He turned his attention instead to Emma, his eyes focusing on the baby. "How old?" he asked simply.

"Two months," Emma replied quietly. It had been two months since she had given birth. It had been eight since Calista's death.

The family filed outside, joining the largest cortege Helena had ever known as it followed the sixty-nine year old woman's remains to the grave.

Within weeks measles hit Helena, and then scarlet fever. Henry Parchen went to Fort Benton where the Missouri River steamships unloaded their freight for points overland, but he could find no transportation to carry his loads south even though trade at the fort was good. It seemed that various local tribes had taken large numbers of buffalo robes, and agents had destined these cargoes for a demanding East, securing priority in all matters of transportation.

Meanwhile illness in Helena became epidemic, making inroads into the schools. Emma again turned to her sister and mother to watch her children as she returned full time to her tincture business. Parchen Drugs was constantly demanding more medicine; and this, added to her growing shipping orders, slowly cleared out Emma's back stock.

Young Henry Duerfeldt stacked one crate of tinctures on top of another at the loading dock. Then he turned to his aunt. "Did you hear about the Indian Massacre?"

"Indian massacre, no," Emma replied as her attention left her paperwork. "Where was this?"

"The Big Horn Mountains. The Cheyenne massacred an emigrant train on Willow Creek. The store has been buzzing with the news all day. I guess Crook's Command out of Fort Kearney is coming, but everyone thinks they will be too slow, probably on purpose. I think they are scared." He paused as he straightened his crate. "This makes thirteen people dead from what I've heard," Duerfeldt continued, "and everyone thinks there will be a big Indian war soon."

"I hope not," Emma responded as her thoughts drifted to her husband. He was on his way home from Fort Benton, and there was a lot of wilderness between them.

"I hope there is a war," Duerfeldt countered. "Maybe then we will get some decent soldiers out here that aren't afraid of doing their duty."

"There has to be a better way," Emma noted quietly. "Wars are so costly."

"Maybe," her nephew replied, "but it's better than living in fear."

Through the summer of 1876, Indian scares continued to mount while Helena took time out to celebrate the Centennial Fourth of July. Emma grinned as she watched S.C. Ashby's growing interest in Miss Guy. Romance was in the air, and evidently Emma's brother was also falling prey to its spell. Of late, Harry had frequently been found in the company of a certain Hattie Rumley.

"I think we're going to lose a brother," Jenny confided to her sister as the family walked down off Tower Hill. It had been a day of parades and festivities, ending with a torch procession up to the fire tower.

"I think we already have," Emma responded as Adele took her hand.

Jenny's eyes turned. "What do you know that I don't?"

Emma smiled. "I think it's time for sweet secrets, don't you? Mother made pudding last night."

Jenny's face brightened. "Yes, sweet secrets," and she ran off ahead.

"I suppose you want me to put the kids to bed," Henry commented with a grin.

"...and occupy your nephew," his wife laughed.

An hour later a kerosene lamp was set in the middle of Jenny's bedroom rug as dishes of pudding were passed among the women of the family. Marie shut the door, and then sat down between her daughters.

"How is your rheumatism, mother?" Emma asked.

"Not bad," she answered as she made herself comfortable. "I think the warm weather helps."

"Okay, Emma, spill what you know about our brother," Jenny cried.

Emma arranged her skirt attractively over her folded legs, and then looked up. "I saw Harry and Hattie at the reading of the Declaration of Independence," she began thoughtfully, and then grinned. "I don't think they heard much of it."

"Why not?" Jenny demanded.

"Because they were kissing," Emma replied as she took a spoon of pudding.

Jenny squealed. "When do you suppose the wedding will be?"

"I don't think your brother is in any hurry," their mother commented.

"But if they were kissing..." Jenny responded.

Marie shook her head. "No, Harry won't rush things." She grinned then. "Not like Mr. Ashby."

"Mr. Ashby, what do you know about Ashby?" Emma asked in great delight.

"I heard," their mother continued, "that wedding bells will ring before you know it."

Jenny squealed again. "Do you know when?"

"Next month, so I hear." Marie smiled.

Silence fell momentarily as the women indulged in a little pudding.

"Your turn, Jenny," Emma finally coaxed.

"Oh...um, I saw Wood Paynter the other day," she offered with a look of consternation. "I don't have anything as exciting as you two."

"Did he see you?" Emma asked.

"No, he was walking with a group of men, mine owners, I think."

"Henry says he has run into him a couple of times since he came back to Helena, but they don't talk much," Emma commented.

"Busy with his investments, probably," their mother replied. "I understand he arranged for some pretty significant backing while he was in Michigan."

"He probably thinks he's too good for the likes of us anymore," Jenny responded.

"He is probably just busy," her mother noted.

"Mining is awfully risky," Emma worried.

"It's not much worse than the freight business these days," Marie offered. "This Indian War could cost your business hundreds of dollars, Emma, not to mention the loss of life."

"If the railroad extends north, it could help a lot," her daughter replied.

"Are you putting up as many herbs this year?" Marie asked.

"I'll make what tinctures I can," Emma answered, "but it doesn't look like Henry will order greens from too far away. Thank goodness, mother, you planted what you did in the garden."

"Yes, most of them are doing wonderfully, though I did loose the Meadow Sweet. But I'm awfully glad Reverend Shippen finally sold his cow. Another disaster like last October would be awful. That blame cow devastated my entire flower garden."

"I understand there are several people who aren't too happy with Reverend Shippen," Jenny confided quietly, "including Mr. Wilbur Sander's friend. What is his name? X?"

"Oh you mean Mr. Beidler," Emma replied.

"What is the X for?" Jenny asked.

"It's his middle initial, I guess," Emma answered.

"What is wrong with his first name?" Jenny demanded. "Do you know what it is?"

"I think it's John, but I'm not sure," Emma replied. "It's my understanding that the man just goes by 'X' or 'X Beidler', nothing else."

"I have heard something else," their mother offered quietly, "usually a four letter something else."

"Oh a real rough type," Jenny concluded with a smile. "Do you suppose we could get him to make a call on Aunt Renard?"

A gasp escaped their mother, and then laughter. "Perhaps it's best," she continued after a moment, "that Reverend Shippen seems to be spending more and more time in Butte."

"I understand Hattie Rumley hasn't attended our church since Reverend Shippen cornered her at Mr. Gamer's social," Emma offered.

"What did he say to her?" Jenny cried.

"I don't know. Harry wouldn't say. But I got the distinct impression it was more how he said it, than what he said," Emma related. "Harry has been taking Hattie to the Presbyterian Church."

"Well ladies, I am exhausted, and it's getting late," their mother decided. "Jenny, would you mind taking the dishes down to the kitchen?"

During August, S.C. Ashby married Emma Guy in a quiet little ceremony held at Daniel Floweree's home. Only intimates of the family were invited to share the exchange of vows. Emma and Henry Parchen rejoiced in their friend's union. The new bride was everything her new husband had lost in his late mother, and more. Young and pretty, Emma Ashby had all the charm, beauty, and accomplishments that suited Mr. Shirley Ashby. It would be a blessed union.

Meanwhile Reverend Shippen took up permanent residence in Butte where the population was steadily growing. Bishop Marvin of the Methodist/Episcopal Church promptly wrote that a new minister was already appointed, and would soon arrive in Helena.

But the fair came and went, as did the preachers at the M/E Church. Sometimes a minister from a nearby town conducted the services, sometimes an elder from the congregation. But what happened to the appointed minister Bishop Marvin had written about? This was a matter of speculation. Most credited a change of heart on the minister's part. After all, the Sioux had attacked General Cook and Terry's men after being refused supplies, and there was much talk among the tribes that the whites needed to be driven out of the area entirely.

By October Governor Potts and General Smith needed a breather from the tense situation with the various Indian tribes. They gathered a party of hunters, and headed to Muscleshell to hunt a few buffalo. Henry Parchen was among these. The trip was an experience.

"I left the robe at the tanners," Henry announced as he collapsed comfortably into his mother-in-law's rocker. "It should make a fine 'great coat'."

"Did everyone get a buffalo?" Emma asked.

"Everyone except Ben Stone," Henry related. "We had a little accident. He broke his leg."

"What kind of accident?" his nephew demanded.

"We left him at Camp Baker. He is doing fine," Emma's husband continued as he ignored his nephew's question.

"Did a buffalo charge Ben Stone?" young Duerfeldt asked.

"No," Henry answered. "Governor Potts took a fine big bull. I think he's going to have the head mounted."

"What about yours, daddy?" Adele cried.

"Mine? Mine was a big ugly fellow," Henry responded as he pulled his daughter onto his lap. "I left the head behind for the buzzards. I didn't want him to scare you."

"I wouldn't be scared. Little Harry might be, but not me," Adele claimed.

Her father smiled. "I brought home some meat. Do you like buffalo, Marie?" His eyes lifted to his mother-in-law.

"Indeed yes," she exclaimed. "It is far better than cow."

"Good, the bundles are out on the porch with my stuff." He turned to his nephew. "Could you help bring it in?"

"Sure, Uncle Henry," he replied.

"Henry, about the Indians..." Emma interrupted. "We have been worried sick. You heard about the Custer Massacre?"

"Yes, but we were fine – aside from the coach accident," he related.

"Coach accident?" Emma repeated.

"It overturned near Camp Baker. It was quite a ride."

"The coach overturned," his nephew exclaimed as he grabbed his coat. "What happened?"

"The horses hit a bad section of road. They were going pretty slow, but the wheel must have slid over the edge, and it came off. The driver, Ben, was thrown from his seat. The horses broke loose, of course, but then the coach started to roll. Governor Potts ended up under all of us. There wasn't much anyone could do."

"But you were all okay?" Marie asked anxiously.

"All except Ben Stone," Henry answered. "We just got a little bruised. Nothing serious."

"The day Custer's Massacre hit the newspaper," Emma related, "a large party of Nez Perce Indians came through Helena. I guess they were just returning home from their annual buffalo hunt, but everyone stopped and stared at them, wondering if we were going to be scalped right there on the street. I was taking Harry some medicine at the drug store."

"They probably felt as strange as you, being stared at," her husband replied. "I wonder if they even knew about the Custer Massacre."

"I didn't wait to find out. I ran for home," Emma responded. "Mother was alone with Adele and little Harry."

Chapter Sixteen

With the colder weather of fall, Helena settled back into her normal routine as numerous flocks of geese headed south over the city. A quiet election was conducted on schedule, and the normal social events again kept the long evenings from becoming too solitary.

But it wasn't until the family sat down at Thanksgiving Dinner that Emma's brother made his announcement concerning his intentions toward Hattie Rumley. She was also present, and the family exploded in approval.

"When?" Jenny squealed in delight.

"Sometime before Christmas," Hattie replied.

"I need to go to Deer Lodge before Christmas," Henry Parchen noted. "Have you decided on a date?"

"Not yet," his brother-in-law answered. "We have to talk to our minister."

"You are planning to be married in the Presbyterian Church?" Marie asked.

"Yes, is that all right?" Hattie responded.

"Well yes, I suppose so," Marie decided. "At least you have a minister there."

"We like the Presbyterians, mother," Harry offered now. "The church suits us."

"That's good, son," Marie affirmed. Her eyes shifted to Hattie. "What do you plan to wear?"

"Mother is making my dress," Hattie responded with a smile. "I'm going to have a long, lace veil." Her eyes shifted to Adele. "Would you like to carry the end of it? I might need a little help walking down the aisle with all that yardage."

"Yes," the three year old declared. The child's enthusiasm was so great, the table broke into immediate laughter.

At eight o'clock on the evening of December 14th, the family and friends of the Parchens and the Rumleys gathered at the Presbyterian church to witness the exchange of vows between Harry and Hattie. They were not disappointed. The bridal ceremony united two esteemed members of Helena's society as Mr. and Mrs. D'Acheul.

Hattie turned to walked down the aisle as her dress and veil twisted around her ankles. Adele lifted the veil high into the air as she bent to free the dress from around her aunt's ankles. The long, white veil settled over her, trapping her within a beautiful lace shroud.

"Look," Harry noted, "your dress came with a cute little bijou."

Hattie broke into a gracious smile as the three year old looked helplessly through the lace. The new bride pulled her veil aside, and Adele stepped out to the delight of the entire congregation. Hattie immediately bent and presented Adele with her bridal bouquet.

Big eyes turned upward. "For me?" she asked.

"For you." Hattie smiled. "You are the best little helper I could have."

Adele beamed.

Hattie took her new husband's arm, and together they walked down the aisle as husband and wife. The congregation followed the bride and groom to the Rumley home where a reception was held for them. The food was good; the company was excellent; and the gifts were many. As Hattie surveyed the numerous packages waiting to be opened, she noted Adele's large eyes. "Why don't you bring me yours?" she suggested.

Adele instantly retrieved the first gift the new Mrs. D'Acheul was to open, and presented it to her.

"Thank you," Hattie responded.

Harry sat down beside his wife. "What do you have?"

"A present from our little bijou," she answered. Hattie pulled the wrapping paper free, and opened the box. A butter dish rested inside. "Adele, how lovely!"

The child instantly retrieved another gift from the table, but was intercepted by her mother. "Adele, this might be breakable. Carry it carefully."

The little girl obediently slowed down, carrying it very formally to her new aunt. Hattie threw Emma a smile, and accepted the gift. "Thank you."

The gift turned out to be a cake basket from Mr. and Mrs. F. Gamer.

Over fifty gifts followed which Hattie personally opened. When the task was finally finished, it was late, but no one seemed to mind. They had thoroughly enjoyed themselves.

After the wedding, Harry and Hattie took rooms at the Cosmopolitan Hotel, and readily accepted Emma's Christmas invitation. The Rumleys were also invited. Emma enjoyed the fuss. She joined her mother and sister in the preparations. Tincture orders had slowed with the holidays, and never had she anticipated having so many in her house.

Emma chuckled to herself as she thought how the newspaper had gone on about Harry and Hattie's wedding and the brilliant reception held at the Rumley's spacious mansion. Their house was one of the nicer ones in Helena, but it was no mansion. Emma had seen mansions in St. Louis, and the house at 6th and Rodney was not even a large one by such standards. Still, compared to the many one or two room log homes many people lived in, the Rumley house was nice. Emma smiled. Her house was nicer.

Emma turned her attention back to the garland she was making. Henry was bringing candles home for the window sills, and this year they would light them. Emma's contribution to the family's income was making a difference, and even her careful husband was starting to relax.

Christmas morning dawned white and cold as Emma woke to her son's cries. She rose from the warm bed, and wrapped a shawl around her shoulders as she hurried to the crib. Lifting little Harry into her arms, she drew back a curtain, noting the small flakes of snow quietly descending over the already white world beyond.

Out in the hall she heard her mother on the stairs, and Jenny's voice broke the stillness as she quietly hummed a Christmas carol. Within moments Adele broke into her parents' room.

"It's Christmas," she declared as she ran straight for the bed, and pounced on her father.

He pretended to be asleep, and Adele crawled on top of him. "Wake up, daddy," she called urgently. "It's Christmas."

"Christmas? No, that's not until tomorrow," Henry Parchen teased as he rubbed his eyes sleepily.

"No it's not, it's today," Adele exclaimed. "Come on. Get up."

Henry allowed himself to be pulled into a sitting position, and then Adele suddenly lost interest, running from the room with a squeal. "Grammy, grammy, I want to help with Christmas."

"Adele, wait for your brother," Emma shouted after her.

The little girl reluctantly returned to the room where Emma was dressing Harry. Adele handed her mother the toddler's last shoe.

"There," Emma concluded, "you are dressed, Harry."

"Drressssed," the child sputtered.

Emma smiled. "Now Adele, you can take him downstairs with you."

"Yesss," little Harry replied as his mother set him on the floor. The two children ran for the stairs. Adele promptly sat down before taking little Harry into her lap, and sliding the bumpy distance to the first floor. Their father had risen from bed, and kept a watchful eye on his children's adventure. Then he returned to the bedroom, shutting the door as he stripped off his nightshirt. Emma was already washing up. Suddenly, warm hands wrapped around her middle.

"Merry Christmas," he whispered in her ear.

Emma turned, and they kissed. "Merry Christmas."

"Harry is almost a year old," Henry reminded her. "It's time to get busy on the family again."

"We are always busy," Emma laughed. "Between the store and the tinctures, it's hard to find the time, let alone the energy." Henry drew his wife snugly against him. His warmth felt good in the chill winter air.

"What about tonight?" he asked.

"We'll see," Emma chuckled as she broke away, waltzing just beyond his grasp.

"All right, we'll see," Henry agreed with a smile as he lunged for Emma, purposely letting her escape. "Tonight, we'll see."

Breakfast was light, consisting of the family's fill of coffee cake and tea. Then the Parchen family hastened to ready things for the one o'clock dinner. Marie had a goose roasting in the oven, and kettles of vegetables waited for last minute cooking. Meanwhile young Henry Duerfeldt was outside, chopping wood with his uncle while Emma and Jenny dodged children and set the dining room table.

"Hattie, Harry, come in," Henry Parchen welcomed as he met them at the door.

"Merry Christmas, Henry," Hattie greeted. "Oh it smells wonderful in here. I bet Emma's mother has been cooking since dawn."

"Nearly," Henry agreed. "Let me take your wraps."

Harry handed over his buffalo coat, and then took their Christmas gifts over to the tree. Adele and little Harry instantly appeared.

"Here, this little one is for you, and this is for your brother," Uncle Harry told Adele quietly. "Don't tell anyone, but you can open these now while I put the rest under the tree." Then he put his finger to his lips. "Shh now, it's our little secret."

Adele handed her brother's gift to him, and then tore the paper from her own. A small cigar box was revealed, and Adele instantly opened it. "Oh," she squealed as she found a large chunk of sapphire, "a treasure."

"It's the real thing," her uncle stated as he bent down beside her, "so don't lose it. When you get older, you can have jewelry made from it."

Adele threw her arms around her uncle's neck. "Thank you, Uncle Harry."

She turned to her little brother. "Harry, just rip the paper off. Like this..." she instructed as she grabbed the edge of the paper, giving it a small tug. It ripped a hole four inches long.

Little Harry was immediately intrigued, and pulled more until the new ball escaped the wrapping and his hands. The young boy promptly chased the rolling toy across the room.

"You shouldn't have," Emma noted quietly to her brother.

"Sure I should of," he retorted with a smile. "Now they have something to occupy them until dinner."

"It's good to have you here," Emma responded as she gave him a hug. She looked up as her husband opened the door. Hattie's family had arrived.

The magic of Christmas worked its spell. Never had food tasted so good, or one's stomach felt so small. Dinner was followed with the excitement of giving and receiving gifts, and then by Christmas carols. After that, everyone indulged in a late, scrumptious dessert.

It was during times like this that Henry Parchen truly enjoyed his in-laws. Marie had created wonders in the kitchen, and Jenny sang like an angel with the others joining in. Everyone enjoyed the day. Before Henry met Emma, he had known some pretty bleak holidays, holidays when he was just too far away from his family in Nebraska.

As the day drew to a close, the families walked down Broadway to the peal of church bells. At the Methodist/Episcopal Church, Santa Claus distributed goodies from under the tree to the numerous children. Laughter and joy were on everyone's lips as snow fell with increasing ferocity. After all the fun, parents pulled their exhausted children away, leading them home to bed. It had been a day to remember.

"Harry says Wood Paynter has joined Brown & Weisenhorn," Henry remarked as he climbed into bed next to Emma.

"The carriage makers?" she asked sleepily.

"Yeah. His Michigan money must be running a bit thin if he has taken on another line of work."

"Must be," she replied softly. Her thoughts had already drifted elsewhere.

Emma's life was as happy as she had ever known it. Her children were handsome and healthy and vivacious. She had a fine house, and enough family around to never let her experience a dull moment even when her duties at the factory grew monotonous. This was one of the two slow times of year in tincture production. The winter weather curtailed most deliveries, and only towns in epidemic need ordered anything. The other slow time was early summer when spring deliveries had already been made, and the new herbs were still growing, and not yet ready for harvest.

Henry too had a respite. Business down at the drug store had slackened after Christmas. He, of course, still had customers, but the demand for chemicals and paint was low this time of year, and Christmas had depleted any desire for the extras in life. Demand at the drug store was now limited to the basic and practical needs of its customers, a bottle of tincture for a cough, or a few tacks for something that had broken.

To Emma's delight, Henry came home promptly after six. He spent the evening working on the space under the stairs for his mother-in-law's bed and dresser. Marie's rheumatism had kicked up again, and was demanding relief.

Emma picked up little Harry, and turned to Adele. "It's time for bed."

"No mama, I want to stay up," the little girl objected.

"You need your beauty sleep, young lady," her father countered.

Henry had finished his carpentry for the night, and he swept up his daughter as she shrieked in delight. The two parents headed upstairs with their children squirming in their arms. Half an hour later both little ones were tucked into bed.

"Adele was so tired," Henry whispered as he joined his wife in the hall, "she could not stop talking."

"Little Harry went out like a light," Emma responded.

"Too bad we haven't a hideaway somewhere," Henry commented as he drew his wife close. "The house has people everywhere."

"Including the attic," she retorted in good humor. Emma leaned forward, kissing her husband lightly. He responded with a more passionate kiss, and fire ignited between them. Emma reached for her husband's hand, leading him quietly back into their bedroom. Pulling the curtain across the nursery, she unbuttoned her blouse.

Every night for the next couple of weeks, Henry and Emma retired early as they found pleasure in each other and hoped for yet another child. Meanwhile talk was growing in town. The Sioux Indians were moving along the Marias

River in large numbers. An attack was feared, and the threat only seemed to spur Henry and Emma's passion.

Then on the 26th of February, the Parchens celebrated young Harry's first birthday. Following his sister's recent example, he tore into his presents... without any thought of propriety. While everyone was busy talking in the entry, he was busy in the parlor tearing wrapping paper ruthlessly from his new treasures.

"Harry," Emma exclaimed as she suddenly darted around the corner. Her young son longed up with large, innocent eyes from a periphery of mess.

Chuckling uncontrollably, Emma's brother joined his young nephew, and took the toy from the small hand to admire.

"You are supposed to wait until after supper to unwrap your gifts," Emma scolded as she whisked up scrap after scrap of paper.

"He didn't know, Em," Harry laughed. "Let him enjoy them."

"I think he already has," she responded in disgust.

Within moments the family gathered around the year old child so he could finish the task of unwrapping his presents, but young Harry now only wanted to play with his new things, totally ignoring the packages he had missed. Only with Adele's help, did he finish unwrapping the last of them. The little girl neatly arranged her brother's new things in a pile, playing momentarily with one or two. Then with the air of someone too old for such nonsense, she rose to her feet and left the room.

"She is getting big," Hattie commented to Jenny.

"Too big for her own good," Jenny laughed. "Before you know it, she will have her own business." Her eyes swung to her older sister.

"She could do worse," Hattie replied. "Jenny, did you teach Adele that new song you told me about?"

"Yes."

"I would love to hear it," Hattie responded. "Wouldn't you, Harry?"

Her husband turned. "What?"

"Adele's song. I told you about it. Wouldn't you like to hear your niece sing?"

"Yes I would," he answered. His attention turned back to his brother-in-law. They were discussing some last minute items for Parchen's upcoming buying trip.

Later that night, Henry sat down on the bed next to his wife. "Emma, how about coming east with me this time? We could stop in St. Louis," he offered.

Emma's fingers fell from the small ties of her nightgown. "I don't want to leave the children."

Henry smiled. "They have your family."

"But if I went, it would cost more," Emma replied.

"Not much," her husband responded. "We would share the same bed."

"No," Emma decided, "not until you get your new store. We have to be frugal. Then I will go, if you want. Then perhaps, we will even be able to afford our wedding trip."

"Our wedding trip..." Henry's head cocked. "You wanted to see the Pacific Ocean, didn't you?"

Emma's eyes grew dreamy. "Yes, I would love to see it. ...and California. I understand oranges and lemons grow there. ...and flowers in the winter time."

A smile grew on Henry's lips.

"But the store comes first," Emma stated as she left her thoughts behind. Her fingers began tying her nightgown again.

Henry's hand rose to hers, halting her progress. Then he blew out the lamp.

Henry Parchen was on his way to Utah by the first of March. He paused there only long enough to send a letter to his brother-in-law, expressing how many former Montanans claimed they would gladly move back if there was but a railroad reaching that far north.

Emma did not know exactly where her husband was. By the time the letter arrived, Henry could be in Chicago or some other city.

Emma woke. It was dark. She looked around her in the blackness as an eerie feeling gripped her. But before she could climb out of bed, the entire house began to shake. The windows rattled in their casings; the furniture creaked; and the drawer pulls bagged loudly against their plates. Then as swift as the shaking began, it was gone.

Emma's heart pounded within her, and she instantly jumped to her feet, flying across the floor to little Harry. At his crib she stopped. The child had not awakened, but slept peacefully. Assured of his well-being, Emma headed out into the hall to Adele's room.

Marie appeared from the bedroom she still shared with Jenny. "What was that?" she cried.

"I don't know, Mother, maybe an earthquake," Emma answered, and disappeared into Adele's room.

The girl's eyes flickered momentarily open as Emma bent over the bed, but within seconds she rolled over and was fast asleep again. Emma straightened. Her children were safe.

Back in the hall, Emma's mother, sister, and nephew had gathered. All had felt the quake, and their excited whispers told what each had experienced. It took several minutes before they had calmed enough to go back to bed.

Emma climbed into her empty bed. Where was Henry by now? Had he felt the earthquake? Without much further thought, she covered herself up with the heavy quilts, and shivered. The sheets had cooled considerably in her absence. She rolled over as she pulled the covers tightly around her. Within minutes she drifted off.

Three hours later the house shook again, harder. Emma bolted out of bed in the darkness. This time the noise was louder, and she nearly lost her balance on the way to the nursery. Little Harry woke too, crying as Emma whisked him into her arms. She had no sooner accomplished this than the shaking stopped. A grinding noise ensued. Then suddenly it was gone as well.

With her heart pounding wildly within her, Emma now stood clutching her small son as the bedroom door banged open. "Mama," Adele shouted as she ran to her. Grandma followed on her heals with Jenny and Henry Duerfeldt not far behind.

"That was a big one," young Henry gasped.

"Yes," Emma agreed. "What time is it?"

"Nearly five," Jenny offered. She had managed to light a candle.

"Do you suppose there will be any more shaking," Emma's mother worried.

"I don't know," Emma replied quietly. She glanced at her sister. She was shivering with cold. "My shawl is on the chair, Jenny," she offered. Jenny passed the candle to her mother, and snatched up the shawl, flinging it around her shoulders.

"What do we do now?" young Henry Duerfeldt asked. "Would you like me to go downstairs, Aunt Emma, and see if there is any damage?"

"Please," Emma responded, "but be careful."

"You can count on it," he replied, and disappeared.

Emma's mother reached over to the dresser, and shoved the mirror back away from the edge. "I think we should put our breakables on the floor for the night."

"Good idea," Jenny agreed. Her eyes turned to her sister. "Do you think we will have any more quakes?"

"I have no idea. I didn't expect these." She became thoughtful now. "It's practically morning. I suppose if the earth moves again, it might wait for daylight."

Her nephew re-entered the room. "You have some broken glass downstairs, Aunt Emma, in the dining room. Two plates fell off the shelf. I shoved everything else back against the wall."

"Thank you," Emma responded.

"Should I go down and clean up," her mother asked.

"No, let's wait until daylight so we can see," she answered. "It won't be long. In the mean time, I'll put the children in bed with me so I'll know where they are. We can clean up later."

Once again the family returned to their rooms as Emma tucked her children comfortably into bed with her. Emma did not fall back to sleep though. Aside from fearing another earthquake, her children tossed and turned so violently she often found a little arm flung across her face. Startled anew with each occurrence, Emma waited patiently for daylight.

Emma hurriedly finished breakfast the following morning. No further earthquakes had shaken their world since five that morning, and taunt nerves had begun to relax. But all Emma could think about were the glass jars she had down at the warehouse. How much loss had her tincture business sustained? Why hadn't she thought to have the carpenters put side rails on the shelves?

Emma grabbed her heavy cloak, and headed for the door.

"Aunt Emma, wait. I'll walk with you," Henry Duerfeldt offered. He hurried out the door behind her, and joined Emma as she now gingerly stepped through the pile of snow that had slid from the roof.

"I wonder how much stuff fell off the shelves at the drug store," Emma pondered aloud as they walked briskly down Broadway.

"I doubt very much," young Henry replied. "Most of the merchandise is too heavy for that little quake to budge."

"Don't you have breakables up by the windows," Emma asked.

"Oh heck, I forgot about that stuff," her nephew responded.

Emma left her nephew's company at the warehouse, and circled to the back door. Cy Ingersoll waited there.

"Cy, I didn't expect you first thing this morning," Emma greeted.

"I came by to see how all your jars faired with the earthquake," he replied with an encouraging smile. "Plus, I promised Mrs. Cullen that I would drop a bottle of your cough syrup by her house when I passed on my way to see another patient. Her little boy, Ernie, has an awful hack."

"I have been thinking about you," Emma commented.

She let herself in, and waited for Cy to follow. Both now headed for the lift. As they gained the upper floor, several jars lay broken and spilled in the aisle ways. The floor boards were wet, and the air smelled of alcohol and herbs.

"Oh no," Emma breathed.

"I don't think it's as bad as it looks," Dr. Ingersoll offered as he coaxed Emma forward. "Look how many jars are still on the shelves."

"But what about the little bottles of tinctures," Emma worried.

"Aren't most of them in crates?" Dr. Ingersoll asked.

"Yes, but..."

"Come on," Cy coaxed. "You have them in the store room, right?"

Emma followed the man. As light flooded the dark insulated space, all was well. The earthquake had not disturbed the crates.

Emma and Cy returned to the area under the sky light. "Have you a mop?" Cy asked.

Emma pointed toward the stairway. "There is a closet on the left."

By the time he returned, Emma had picked her way through the debris. "I lost fourteen quarts," she concluded.

"It could have been worse," Cy responded.

"Yes, but you better pray your heart patients improve on their own. I lost all my new stock of the Lilly of the Valley and half my digitalis...along with what was to be my back stock of our scarlet fever medicine."

Cy grimaced. "What about your hawthorn? Do you have that?"

"Yes," Emma responded.

"We will just have to substitute then," he concluded. "Why don't you get the trash barrel, and pick up the broken glass? I'll mop up."

Chapter Seventeen

The one good thing about Henry's buying trips east, was that he took them so early in the year. By then most of the stock was out on the shelves, and the customers could almost help themselves. Only Emma's tinctures could readily be re-supplied, that is if she had any back stock. On top of this the Indian situation was pretty quiet. Most tribes were still in their winter camps, and if they stirred at all, it was to hunt food. This allowed Henry's travels to take place in relative safety.

By the first of May, Henry Parchen was not only back from his buying trip, but intrigued by much of what he had seen, especially in the town of Butte. Emma's brother had told him how much Helena's neighbor had grown, but Henry was stunned by what he saw...so much so, he had to go back. Taking John Kinna with him, Henry returned to Butte for a fast visit. Emma's brother smiled, stayed behind, and tended the store. He knew the potential of Butte. He had looked the place over pretty carefully the year before.

Emma turned the page of Helena's *Daily Independent* one July evening. The children were all in bed. Her mother was darning socks by the light of the kerosene lamp, and Henry was at a meeting.

"Governor Potts has sent 60 guns to Missoula County, and received a wire for more from Beaverhead," Emma noted aloud.

"Tragic," Marie responded, "it's simply tragic people can't come to some kind of understanding without the use of guns."

"General Howard was out maneuvered by eighty-five Indians at Salmon River," Emma continued. "They passed along a bald mountain opposite the camp in full view of the soldiers. The general pursued in haste, and telegraphed for a regiment of regulars." She paused as she read further. "He now has 500 men, 3 howitzers, and 2 Gatlin guns." She looked up from the paper.

The summer was pretty well focused on the Idaho Indian War, culminating the following month in the Big Hole Battle where General Gibbons and three of his lieutenants were wounded, and one killed. The Nez Perce also suffered heavy losses, and finally withdrew.

The soldiers and their families were instantly elevated into heroes. The daughters of General Gibbons were visiting Helena at the time, and a social gathering was promptly thrown at Samuel Hauser's Benton Avenue residence. A hundred invited guests thronged the parlors to meet these ladies -- along with General Sherman, members of his staff, and Lieutenant Jacob, the one hero from the Big Hole Battle.

"Oh Emma, you should have been there," Jenny cried as she joined her sister on the upper floor of the Parchen warehouse.

Adele looked up from her doll, listening to her aunt.

"The party was absolutely wonderful," Jenny continued as she brought over another box of herb greens to replenish Emma's supply. Now she dug in as well, hanging the plants on the drying racks.

"Were a lot of people there?" Emma asked.

"Oh yes, tons of them, and no one wanted to go home, not even the band," her sister related.

"What time is it now?" Emma inquired as she worried about getting far enough along before her next shipment of herbs arrived.

"Nearly ten," Jenny answered. "I'm sorry I'm so slow getting down here, but I didn't get home until five this morning, and I thought I should probably get an hour or two of sleep before I came. Mother is at church?"

"No, Mrs. Rumley's. Several ladies are meeting there this morning to discuss plans for their displays at the fair," Emma replied as she glanced to her son, sleeping in the baby carriage. He stirred with all the conversation.

Jenny lowered her voice. "Harry and Hattie were there too, of course. It seemed like Harry was always talking to General Sherman, or his son. Hattie had a devil of a time getting him to dance with her."

"So who did you spend the evening with?" Emma asked quietly.

A smile grew on Jenny's lips. "Lieutenant Jacob," she announced. "He was awfully quiet at first, just letting his friends introduce him and what not. But as the others fell into conversation, he seemed to fade into the woodwork. So I joined him."

"In the woodwork," Emma teased quietly.

"You might say that," Jenny chuckled.

"So what did the two of you talk about?"

"Mostly his family. He is awfully homesick. But I think my talking to him made the other girls jealous," Jenny continued. "They were always staring at us, smiling whenever he looked their way."

"And did he return their smiles?" Emma asked.

"No," Jenny laughed, "that was the funny part. He kept his eye on the general. I think the girls were just hoping they would catch his attention."

"It sounds like you had a lovely time," Emma decided as she lost interest.

"Don't pout," Jenny objected. "You will be able to go to the parties again in three or four months. Besides, you have your Henry, and pretty soon a new baby. I would swap last night's party for a husband and family any time."

Emma smiled, but it wasn't that she missed the party as much as she felt the pressure of tending her herbs. More plants would be arriving that afternoon, and she still had boxes from her last shipment to finish up. Plus, Dr. Ingersoll wanted to discuss a new medicine for diphtheria with her. The man was willing to talk while she worked; but the fact was she was so tired, she couldn't think straight. Repeatedly, she had put him off.

"Nettie Chumasero is going to throw a Farewell Party for the Gibbon girls on Wednesday," Jenny added. "Governor Potts should be at that one too."

Emma said nothing. Jenny had enjoyed last night's party so much, she would be sure to attend the Chumasero's. Emma loved to see her sister happy, but at the same time it meant one more day of low production at a critical time in the tincture business. The herbs had to be tended properly, or they lost much of their medicinal properties.

By the first of September, Emma's mother began to note her eldest daughter's fatigue, and suddenly her other commitments disappeared. Taking her grandchildren under her wing, she helped downtown whenever she could, and regimented Jenny's life into a much more organized schedule that contributed some regular hours into Emma's business.

The 1877 territorial fair came and went. Indian affairs intensified, and snow fell on the evening of September 30th. During the following month, Chief Joseph surrendered 350 Nez Perce prisoners, and a son was born to miner and hardware store owner, Anton Holter. October was essentially a very busy month as everyone anticipated the approach of winter -- none more than Henry Parchen.

Butte's potential as a new drug store location fascinated Henry, especially in light of the stagnation in Deer Lodge. Urged on by Emma's brother at every opportunity, Henry Parchen decided that a trip to the west side was needed, and should be made before the weather got any colder. In addition, Emma's third baby was due in November. Henry headed out, and spent the first three days of his trip in Butte. The final four were spent in Deer Lodge, and confirmed his thoughts. Emma's brother was right. Butte was a better place for a store.

"A healthy baby boy," Dr. Ingersoll declared the twelfth of November as he sat down on the edge of the bed, watching Henry hold his newborn son. "Congratulations."

"Thank you," Henry responded. He glanced at the doorway. Adele and little Harry lingered there, wanting to come in. "It's okay," their father reassured, "come meet your new brother."

Adele broke into an eager run with little Harry on her heels. As she came to a stop at her father's knee, her eyes were big.

Little Harry tried to push her out of the way. "Let me see," he demanded in a toddler's slur.

Adele stepped to the side as she pulled her little brother next to her. Then she pressed down on the blanket so he could see. "Harry, this is Albert D'Acheul Parchen," she announced with great importance. "God decided you needed a little brother more than I needed a sister." Her eyes turned to her father.

"We were blessed with a son," he acknowledged in quiet gratitude, "a healthy, baby boy."

Adele suddenly turned. Her mother was slowly climbing the steps, and she ran to meet her.

"You met Albert?" Emma inquired softly as she gained the second floor.

"Yes," Adele replied.

"What do you think?"

"He is awfully small," Adele answered.

"So was Harry when he was born."

"That tiny?" Adele asked in disbelief.

"Yes, so were you," Emma affirmed with a smile.

Little Harry came running to them, and grabbed his mother around both knees. "Baby, baby, baby," he babbled.

Emma reached down to her son as Marie appeared behind her. "Don't pick him up, Emma. You are too worn out."

Emma turned slightly. "Yes," she agreed, and sat down on the floor, pulling little Harry into her lap. "So what do you think of having a new brother?" she asked the small boy. Her mother went into the bedroom.

"I play wid him," he answered with a childish grin.

"Not right away, he is too small," Emma replied. "Isn't he, Adele?"

"Greatly tiny," she agreed. She sat down on the floor next to her brother. "We have to wait until he gets big like you, Harry. Then we can play chase, and you won't be the smallest any more. He will."

Little Harry's eyes grew large. "Me win?"

"Maybe," Adele responded. "Maybe."

Cy Ingersoll appeared at the door. "What are all of you doing out in the hall?" he asked. "The baby isn't sleeping."

"Course not, I right here," little Harry retorted.

"Not you, dummy," Adele admonished. "You aren't the baby any more. Albert is."

"I not?" the little boy replied in surprise.

"You are the big brother," Cy corrected with a smile. He wandered back into the bedroom, and reappeared with little Albert, placing him in Emma's arms. "He needs your colostrom," he reminded her quietly.

Adele and little Harry both nestled up to their mother. A smile crept into Cy's face.

Work on the tinctures faded to nothing as Emma spent the next couple of weeks with her children. Her nephew, Henry Duerfeldt, was instructed how to make shipments, and the rest waited for Emma. Then just before Thanksgiving, Emma returned to the factory, taking baby Albert with her as she mailed out additional orders, and turned once again to her tinctures. Shipments would slacken off soon, but it would only be temporary. Once the snow and frigid air of winter descended in earnest, so would illness, and it often lasted well into spring. Emma placed dried yarrow in a quart jar and filled it with gin. This she shook and placed under the sky light to cure. She repeated this five more times. Then she turned to her next recipe.

She heard the noise of the lift. Someone was coming up. She measured out the herb for the next jar, and looked up. Dr. Ingersoll walked toward her.

"I didn't expect you." She smiled.

"I need some of your willow bark," he replied. "The cold weather is causing the rheumatism in my older patients to kick up."

"How much do you need?" Emma asked as she headed for the store room.

"Just a bottle or two," he answered. "Most of them buy it from Parchen Drugs, but I have a few patients who don't get out much."

Emma smiled. The truth was when Cy came around and got medicine from her, he often took it to individuals who couldn't afford to buy it. He and Emma had long ago worked out a method of splitting the cost between them. Neither had the heart to turn their back on someone who really needed help. There was too much suffering in the world as it was. Emma had worried at first that her husband would not approve, that is until she caught him practically giving medicine away to a widow with six children. It was then Henry told her how everyone in town helped this lady when they could. In turn, she made sure that she and hers repaid the kindness with honesty and generosity in whatever ways they could. This, Emma was to find out, was not an isolated case.

"Have you thought any more about preparing a special diphtheria medicine," Cy inquired. "It has been weeks since we talked. Sulpho carbonate of soda is so harsh. I can't imagine what else it does to the body besides attacking the diphtheria fungus."

"What do you want the tincture made out of?" she asked.

"We need something for the throat," he replied, "for the fungus...and we really need to boost the immune system. It will have to be strong, though, or we haven't a prayer against something as fatal as diphtheria. We have to halt the progress of the disease before gangrene sets in, or there's no hope."

"Well anise works well on the throat," Emma responded.

"Anise? Which part?" he inquired.

"The seed," she answered. "I have often used it for sore throats."

"You make tinctures of anise? I didn't know that," Cy replied.

"Not tinctures," Emma corrected. "I make tea. It's something daddy used to make me when I was sick. You crush the seeds with a rolling pin, then put them in a cup, and fill it with boiling water. He would often add a little honey."

"That makes sense," Cy decided. "The throat is too sore for the burning effects of a tincture, or harsh chemicals."

The two talked for close to an hour, working out the combination of ingredients that would best make up the new medicine. Then as little Albert began to cry, Cy left. Emma took the infant into her arms, checking his diaper, and feeding him.

On Thanksgiving, Emma spent the morning shaking her tinctures, and then returned up Broadway as far as their church. Everyone was already present as she slid into the pew. Reverend Hewitt of the Presbyterian church was filling in until their new pastor arrived. This suited the family. Reverend Hewitt was already Harry and Hattie's pastor.

The holiday dinner that followed was accompanied by much talk of Butte. Hattie's parents had mining interests there, and only added to her husband's eagerness to establish a store in the town. But their enthusiasm wasn't necessary for Henry Parchen, he had already done the calculations. The store was a good idea.

By February the new drug store in Butte was becoming a reality. Emma's husband and brother had long since decided that the contents of the Deer Lodge store would better serve all, if they were moved to Butte. The building in Deer Lodge would be closed down. Harry and Hattie were especially excited over the prospect. The move held such promise.

Emma left her children with Jenny while she and Marie crossed the street to attend the church social. It was Monday evening, and Henry and Harry were both gone, so it was up to Emma and her mother to put in an appearance at Wood Paynter's new house on Rodney. For despite all the ill feelings that had passed between them, Wood still thought enough of his old partner to build a house directly across the street from them. It wasn't a fancy place, much more basic than the Parchen house, but it was an economic way to provide space for Wood's growing family. Emma was glad she didn't have to make beds in it, though. The second floor ceilings slanted with the roof.

Wood gave the devotional for the social, and refreshments were served. There was a nice crowd of church members, miners, and customers of the carriage makers. Many were also customers of Parchen Drugs, and Emma suddenly found her advice was being sought by more than just occasional women. It seemed nearly everyone, including some pretty impressive mine owners, had questions concerning health related issues. Emma tried her best to offer what knowledge she could, when suddenly she looked up. Wood Paynter was watching. He smiled as she saw him. It was his warm smile, and it was almost proud. Whatever bad had passed between them was gone. They were again friends.

"So where is Henry these days?" Wood inquired as people finally drifted away from Emma. "I hear he's hardly ever in the store any more."

"He and Harry are moving the Deer Lodge store to Butte," Emma answered.

"Butte? Humm, that's probably a good idea. The town is growing like a weed," Wood acknowledged. "Is Mr. Triaberger going with?"

"Yes, I believe so," Emma replied.

"Well keeping the same clerk ought to keep things on an even keel," Wood decided. "How do you like the idea? You're from Deer Lodge."

"I only lived there a very short time," Emma stated, "and I think the move makes sense. Deer Lodge really doesn't need two drug stores."

"Well I wish you and yours the best in the venture," Wood responded with a smile.

"I understand your venture is doing well. Your company seems to be making one vehicle after another, and they are all sold," Emma commented.

"Yes, we are," Wood agreed. "There seems to be a constant demand, and that's good." He smiled. "If you will excuse me, Emma, I see two of my children are demanding my attention."

Wood hasten to his two squabbling offspring as Emma's mother joined her. "You two seem friendly."

"Yes," Emma replied. "It is easier to talk to him now than when I first came to Helena."

Her mother smiled. “I told you things would work themselves out.”

By the end of the month, the move to Butte was complete. Henry sat across the kitchen table from Emma as he finally had a chance to read the Helena newspaper.

“Henry,” Emma began tentatively, “I have been making tinctures in the warehouse for four years now; and well, if my calculations are anywhere near correct, the money I have made should just about cover the construction cost.”

Her husband looked up. “Construction cost? Of what?”

“Of the warehouse,” she answered, “and that isn’t figuring in what you saved by buying in bulk and having the warehouse space to store the drug store’s back stock, nor is it taking into account any profits you made in the last few years.”

“The profit was used to offset the Deer Lodge drain,” her husband responded. “The move to Butte wasn’t cheap, but at least we should now have a positive cash flow.”

“But what about your business here,” Emma asked. “You planned to build a new store years ago.”

“I built the warehouse instead,” Henry reminded her as he took a sip of coffee.

“But it has paid for itself,” Emma countered, “and the drug store has had a couple of good years, despite Deer Lodge. Couldn’t you and Harry think about building the new Helena store? We must have your half of the money, maybe even a little extra, and Harry has a little tucked aside. I know he has.”

“I can’t even think of an expenditure like that right now,” her husband responded, “not after Butte, and not until after our spring orders begin to recoup.”

Silence fell between them as Henry Parchen returned his attention to the newspaper, and Emma sipped her coffee. The house was quiet. The children were in bed. Emma’s thoughts drifted.

She had worked long and hard to recoup all the money tragedy had cost her husband. The graveyard and the coffin for their stillborn child had long since been recovered, and now the cost of the warehouse was essentially back in their pockets. Both of these things had interfered with achieving the dream of Henry’s new store. Years had passed. Then, when Emma was just starting to think it might again be possible, the Butte store had burst upon the scene. It made a lot of sense to move the Deer Lodge stock to Butte, but would it push Henry’s dream back yet more years?

“The carnival and masquerade are coming up Friday,” Henry noted as he looked up from his newspaper. “Would you like to go, Emma?”

Thursday morning Emma hurried down Broadway, clutching Albert tightly against her. The wonderful weather they had been experiencing was suddenly gone. Clouds covered the sky, and the air was brisk. As Emma let herself into the warehouse, she pulled the heavy door shut and crossed to the lift. Setting little Albert down beside her, she worked the pulleys, and both ascended to the upper story.

Emma deposited her child on the floor with his rattle, and glanced up. Snow was falling on the skylight, melting as it touched the glass. Emma began to shake her tinctures as she thought about the carnival scheduled for the following day. Helena had not seen snow since October. The fact had made the move to Butte possible so early in the year for Parchen Drugs, but to have snow now when the carnival was to take place tomorrow... A lot of people would be truly disappointed.

Emma worked furiously. Her time was short when Albert wasn't fussing, and tincture demands had been high all winter because of the good roads. She made her way through the numerous shelves of jars, and thought about her decreasing supply of herbs. Hopefully, spring demands wouldn't be as great.

Albert began to cry for attention, and Emma looked wistfully at the two jars she hadn't managed to shake. She went over to her tearful son, changed his diaper, and then rocked him to sleep as she wondered whether her husband would remember to pick up her costume at the rental shop.

Friday morning dawned clear and sunny as all of Helena breathed a sigh of relief. The carnival procession was scheduled to begin just after one o'clock, and nearly all the businesses closed for the day. The parade commenced at Bridge Street with four richly clad Roman couriers clearing the way. The Third Infantry Band with its thirty musicians followed. Then a grand triumphant with chariots, soldiers, prisoners, athletes, and gladiators made their way down the street as vendors heckled the crowd, selling snacks and treats. Wagons then appeared, depicting scenes of claim jumpers and wood seizures, and these drew tremendous applause. Helena's brass band followed, comfortably quartered in one of Helena Brewery's mammoth tubs.

Over three hundred people attended the masquerade ball that evening at the graded school. Dancing commenced at eight-thirty and continued until half past four.

As usual, Emma loved dancing with her husband, even if their costumes made movement awkward. She was dressed as the Six of Diamonds. Henry had rebelled at the thought of paying good money for costumes, and had taken two pair of sign boards, and painted one like playing cards and one like dominos. Then wearing only black clothing, he and Emma had slipped the straps of the boards over their shoulders.

Emma's brother had been more creative. Dressing like a Chinese, he had a long, black braid of hair that dropped down his back.

"Where do you think Harry got his pigtail," Emma asked as she danced with her husband.

"Harry? I rather think he stole it off some poor horse," Henry chuckled.

"He is wearing a horse tail?" Emma gasped.

"Well I did notice that a horse outside Weir & Pope's Drug Store had a short black tail the other evening when Harry and I were down that way on an errand."

"Harry stole a horse tail?" Emma repeated.

"Ask him, if you don't believe me," her husband laughed.

"But a horse tail?" Emma shook her head in disbelief. The song finished, and they wandered over to the punch bowl.

"Harry," Henry greeted, "Emma wants to know where you got your pigtail."

Emma's brother grinned. "Can't tell you that."

"But I can," Hattie snickered as she pulled her sister-in-law closer. She whispered something in Emma's ear.

"Hattie," Harry exclaimed, "you are ruining all the fun."

"Not on your life," she responded with a smile she couldn't keep off her face. "It was terrible," Hattie now related to Emma. "I washed and washed it, trying to get out the smell. Then Harry made me braid the darn thing. But if all that wasn't bad enough, we had to figure out a way to make it hang down his back." Hattie burst into chuckles. "I finally had to tie a black ribbon around the end of it, and pin it up under his little skull cap."

"Then it stayed all right?" Emma asked.

"Only with the help of a whole card of hair pins," Hattie laughed. "Emma, it was awful."

At the end of the month, Harry took Hattie to Butte to check on things there. They spent ten days. The following month, Henry made the trip. Both found the town of Butte was proving to be everything they had hoped for. They had a thriving second store once again.

In June and July major freight shipments arrived for them at Fort Benton, and were seen to their destinations. Harry took the responsibility of the Butte merchandise, not returning to Helena until the end of July. More freight was expected in August.

Emma was busy with the summer's shipment of herbs. She had two temporary workers helping as her husband and nephew moved crates of wallpaper in from the Bentley house. He had purchased the property years before as the site for the new store, and they were trying to empty the structure so demolition could take place. Emma smiled to herself. Finally after all this time, the new Helena store was becoming a reality. It didn't hurt that all over town there was considerable building going on. The fact had kept frugal Henry from dismissing her idea of starting the new store.

Emma glanced at the watch pinned to her lapel. Her help was quitting for the day, and she needed to pay them on their way out. As her employees left, Emma turned back to her work. Her mother wouldn't have supper ready until eight.

"Emma," Henry called as he emerged from the stairs, "are you alone?"

"Yes," she answered.

"Good," he responded as he took her arm. "Come on, I want to show you something."

Chapter Eighteen

Henry pulled his wife over to the nearest table, and spread out the plans he carried in a roll. "Look," he pointed, "if I extend the new building back, I can get two more stores the size of ours, or four small ones, with offices and warehouse space above. Do you know how much income that could bring?"

"How much more will it cost?" Emma inquired.

"Well, that's just it. It will probably double the price. But the interesting thing is, it will pay for itself in five years."

"Five years," Emma repeated. "...if we keep it rented."

"Yes, but that shouldn't be hard. Everyone who has seen the plans, wants to know how much office space I will have left to lease."

"But we don't have that much money," Emma worried.

"No, but the bank does, and they will put up the rest. What do you think?"

"How much is the interest?"

"The same as everyone else is getting in town. I understand Sam Hauser has some investors back East who are banking on the railroad coming through here." He smiled. "In five years the whole thing could be ours, especially if we sell the old store."

"Do you think it's worth the risk?" Emma asked as she tried to consider what things could go wrong. The addition was huge.

"Hauser is a pretty straight guy," her husband replied, "and the return on the money is so good." He smiled again. "It would be crazy not to build the extra square footage."

"Then I guess the decision has already been made," Emma decided as she began to relax. A smile crept into her face. Her Henry had waited years to build the new store. Why shouldn't he have a building that would run half a block up Broadway?

"What's the matter?" Henry asked.

"Nothing," Emma grinned. "You will just have a shorter distance to walk home in the winter cold."

"Building interiors aren't connected."

"They should be," Emma responded. "Even the miners have tunnels to shelter them from the winter elements when they go to work, and downtown Helena isn't without a few old mining tunnels that have been converted into service entries."

"I won't have any farther to walk than I do now," Henry laughed, "and I don't think the city would approve of any more tunnels."

"I wasn't talking about digging more tunnels. I was thinking of connecting the entry ways," Emma replied.

"It's a nice thought, but no shop owner would agree to forfeiting his prime sales space for an indoor corridor. That's what the sidewalk is for."

"Maybe not," she responded, "but no one in their right mind likes to walk outside in inclement weather."

Diphtheria invaded the territory that fall, killing two in Butte. Dr. Ingersoll and Emma struggled to improve their medicine as Henry and Harry finally moved into their new store in early November. Setting on the southeast corner of Main and Broadway, it was considered a very eloquent brick building with tall glass display windows, handsome wood doors, and a wonderful classic cornice that ran above the two additional stories, extending back over the Broadway shops and offices.

Emma followed three customers into the new Parchen Drug Store. Handsome wood display cases lined the walls, the glass sparkling with Henry's typical cleanliness. No longer was his merchandise stacked on rugged open shelves. Farther back in the store, the formality of the woodwork eased, allowing freer access to the broad range of merchandise they carried. The shelving units were shiny with new varnish with cans of paint and mining chemicals finally finding order and a degree of sophistication.

"I love this store," a woman remarked.

Emma's attention shifted. She didn't know the woman, but she seemed to be enthralled with the perfume counter.

"Aunt Emma," Duerfeldt greeted with a broad smile, "you haven't been in since we got things arranged, have you?"

"No," she replied.

"Well, what do you think?"

Emma's eyes swung slowly over the interior as pride swelled within her. "It's nice," she responded in pure satisfaction, "really nice."

Her nephew beamed. "Uncle Henry ordered stationery with a picture of the drug store on it, did you know?" he exclaimed.

The new store was a dream come true for Emma. For as much as Henry had wanted a new store all these years, she wanted it more. She had never forgotten how he postponed his dream in order to pay the expenses of their stillborn child, and she wasn't naive to the fact that most postponements never happened at all. How many years had Henry struggled with a partner who didn't share his hopes for the future?

But now they had it all: a nice house, three healthy children, a brick warehouse, a new store in Helena, and one started in Butte. Life was good. And aside from the diphtheria epidemic that closed the public school the first of December, Emma was suddenly free of her old worry. It had taken time, but her dreams had come true. So had the dreams of many others around her. With a light and happy heart, Emma observed how much Helena had grown the previous year with all the promise of the same continuing into the next.

A white Christmas settled over Helena, and the Parchen family enjoyed its richest blessings as the children squealed with delight over the new treasures under the tree. Adele was nearly five years old. Young Harry was almost three, and Albert was one. Plus Emma's brother was married, and Jenny was now employed as a music teacher. Everyone was happy, including Marie, who looked with pride on her family.

Emma sat down next to her mother. "It's a good Christmas," she commented as she watched the children dog pile on her brother. Hattie was trying to get out of the way as Emma's husband came to Harry's rescue.

"Yes," Marie agreed. "After all these years, it looks like my father was right to bring us to America."

"Mother, was grandfather as foolish in business as it seems? Sending you to that market in France, to sell all those cows at your young age, well, it seems a bit like idiocy."

"Yes, I suppose it does look that way," the elder concurred, "but it really wasn't. You see my father trusted the man who went with me. Our foreman knew cattle, and he knew the market, or at least he should have. I went with, first because my father wanted me to learn, and second because my presence legitimatized the sale. It said without words that the cows were being sold for us, and my father was tied up elsewhere."

"Still," Emma responded, "you got a bad price."

"Yes," her mother stated. "My father's trust in our foreman was misplaced. Papa was naive when it came to people. He thought everyone had the same honesty he had, except of course criminals. But his trust in this man was not his biggest error, it was his trust in the French government. He didn't understand the power plays that went on continuously between the French officials in those days, how fickle the bureaucrats could become, how petty. And it wasn't just the money they siphoned out of him at every turn, it was all their regulation. He spent hours learning and meeting their requirements, and then when it looked like he had everything under control, they would suddenly come up with some new restriction. By then it had become the straw that broke the camel's back, but it was too late. We had to sell our home with its beautiful saloon."

"Was that their plan?" Emma suddenly demanded. "Was it a deliberate fleecing?"

Her mother's eyes settled on her. "I don't know that they even knew, or cared."

1879 arrived with excellent sleighing. The snow, covering Helena by the first of January, was fine and light, gusting up in clouds of fairy dust at the first hint of breeze, glittering and sparkling in the sunlight. It was cold. It was clear. It was beautiful.

There was a quiet peace setting over Helena. It was as if everyone was quietly waiting for the winter cold to pass to resume their more vigorous activities, and yet the reprieve was welcome too. It allowed time to rest, to recoup, and to plan for the future.

Emma tended her tinctures, but often cut her days short. With three young ones at home, she was drawn by their incessant demands; and if she could relieve her mother some before supper when childish attention spans grew especially short, she felt she should.

Emma's brother, Harry, was thankfully taking on the major responsibility of the Butte Store, freeing Henry from his normally heavy load. As a result Emma often shared the evenings with her whole family, including her husband. The time was often spent on games and stories for the children, and then it was off to bed.

As the household grew quiet each night, Emma and Henry crawled into the cold sheets of their bed. They snuggled together for warmth as they pulled the numerous blankets and quilts over them. Already in each other's arms, it was only a matter of moments before the fire ignited anew between them. Their passion, however, was no longer explosive and feverish. It was warm, and as natural as eating or drinking. Their union was now just a wonderful part of life, warm and intimate; and as their desire found satisfaction, they fell into peaceful sleep, no longer shivering from the cold.

By the following week, however, life again became more complicated. Henry Parchen came home from work in a state of consternation. "Triaberger has quit! He's been with us for six years. He even moved from Deer Lodge to Butte. He liked the move, but now he has up and quit."

"How did you find out?" Emma asked as she finished changing little Albert's diapers, and set him on his feet. Her young son promptly crawled to his father.

"He's in Helena. He told us," Henry cried as he picked Albert up.

"In Helena?" Emma responded. "Who is tending the Butte store?"

"He says he has some young kid watching shop, but Harry about had a fit. He is leaving on the return coach tomorrow."

Emma stared at her husband. "Is Mr. Triaberger going to work here?"

"Not in my store," Henry retorted, "not after a stunt like this."

"So why did he quit?" Emma asked. "There must have been some reason."

"Well..." her husband replied as he set his squirming son back down on the floor, "he did say something about opening his own place."

"What are his chances?" Emma inquired.

"Of opening his own store? Here? Now?" Henry choked. "Not good. This is the slowest time of year. You can't even get shipments in."

"Then something drastic must have forced him into this," Emma decided. "Mr. Triaberger would know the odds would be against him."

"We have always treated him well," Henry stated.

"Did he ever talk about quitting in Deer Lodge?"

"Never," Henry responded.

"Then perhaps something happened in Butte," Emma suggested.

"Like what?" her husband demanded.

"I don't know," Emma answered, "but something must have happened. Maybe a miner threatened him."

"Why would someone do that?"

"Maybe the miner was desperate for medicine, and didn't have any money," Emma hypothesized. "Harry always hated giving credit. Maybe he made a new rule or something."

"He would have told me," Parchen replied.

"Maybe he forgot," Emma responded. "You know how my brother is when he gets caught up in something. Everything else goes to the wind."

"I just hope Harry gets to Butte all right. The weather could turn nasty."

Emma's brother made it to Butte just ahead of a snow storm, and stayed for its duration. But as the weather eased, Harry D'Acheul did not feel he could leave the new store, and instead sent for his wife. She packed up their few belongings, and went. Emma felt for the young woman. She remembered well her February journey to Helena. She just hoped the trip would go faster for Hattie, and without incident.

"You write to us when you get there," Emma told her sister-in-law. "This is the worst time of year for travel. You don't know what can happen, and there have been slides everywhere."

"I will," Hattie responded. "Don't worry."

Emma smiled. "I will try not to as long as you promise not to get out of the coach until it stops at a station. No walking on down hill ice."

Hattie grinned in recognition of the story Henry Parchen had often told at family gatherings. "I rather stay in the coach where it's warm," she replied.

Emma gave Hattie a quick hug, and then retreated, allowing the young woman's parents to have the remainder of the time before the coach left.

Emma's husband left to join his partner in Butte on the 27th of February. He planned to stay a few days, and then would head east on their annual buying trip. Hattie's father would look after the store in Helen with the help of Emma's nephew, Henry, who would divide his time between the store and the numerous tincture shipments that were going out. Scarlet fever had broken out in Fort Benton.

Two weeks after his departure, Emma had a sudden realization. She tried to catch Cy, but the man was on the run. His son, the doctor of Vestel, was in jeopardy of losing his stock of goods by confiscation of the sheriff.

Emma sighed, and turned back to her work. She had been pregnant before. She knew what was advised, and Cy Ingersoll had his hands full. It was hard to believe that anyone could accuse Cy's son of any wrong doing. Yet the young man did have a streak of rashness about him, and he was always borrowing money. Had it gotten him into trouble, real trouble? Four and a half weeks later A.E. Ingersoll was arrested and indicted for taking $14,800 of Mr. Bristol's money while it was stored in a safe at Cy Ingersoll's office.

By the time Henry Parchen got home in May, his wife was four months pregnant, and looked it.

"Emma, why didn't you tell me?" he cried as he pulled back from their embrace. "When is the baby due?"

"As far as I can figure, October or November," she answered.

"It was all those wonderful cold nights," her husband decided on the spot. Then he squatted down to young Albert, who had both arms wrapped around his legs, and whisked him into the air. "How would you like a baby brother, Albert?"

"Baby," Albert repeated.

Henry turned to Adele and young Harry. "That's right. We're going to have a new baby."

"Another," Adele sighed in resignation.

"Yes, Adele, another baby. Won't that be wonderful?" her father cried as he left Albert on the floor, and now whisked his daughter high over his head until she squealed in delight. "Another baby, another brother or sister."

"Sister," Adele responded. "I want a sister. I already have two brothers."

"All right, we will see what can be done," her father laughed. He glanced at Emma. "We forgot the fir boughs."

"So we did," she agreed.

Adele was now placed back on the floor as Henry Parchen turned to his oldest son. Young Harry stood straight and proper alongside his mother. "We will take good care of the new baby, father, just like we did while you were away."

"You knew about it?" his father asked.

"Yes sir. We made sure mama...mother did not get sick," he replied.

"So you did," Henry noted as he stifled a grin. "Good job, son."

"Thank you, sir," the boy responded. Now he turned to his siblings. "Time for snacks," he decided as he caught his sister's hand, and herded his younger brother toward the kitchen.

Their father glanced at Marie, quietly standing in the background with a large smile on her face. She turned to follow the children.

"Harry has certainly grown," Henry Parchen told his wife. "They all have, including you."

"Yes," she agreed as she slipped her hand into his. "You have a lot to catch up on."

Henry Parchen reached for his luggage, and followed his wife up the stairs. "Harry and Hattie have decided to stay in Butte," he told her. "It looks like they have made it their new home." He paused momentarily. "Have you been seeing Cy?"

"No," Emma replied quietly.

"Why not?" Henry asked as he drew to a stop.

"His son, Ed, was indicted on robbery charges. The timing hasn't been good." She smiled softly. "I've done this before."

"Ed was arrested? I knew he was always short on money, but robbery?" Henry gasped.

"It seems he borrowed a substantial sum from a family friend, without telling him first," Emma explained as they left the hall.

Henry placed his bag on the floor inside the bedroom door. "How much did he take?"

"Ed claims it was $10,000, but Mr. Bristol says $14,800 was missing," Emma replied.

Henry shook his head sadly in disbelief. "Poor Cy." He closed the door, and then turned to his wife, taking her into his arms. "I missed you," he stated softly as his lips met hers.

Within the week Cy began making regular visits to Emma, taking time to discuss various tincture preparations. Over the summer Emma continued to grow in the middle as her work load dramatically increased.

"You have got to stay off your feet more," Cy scolded as he stopped by, and found Emma hard at work among the several employees now racking the fresh herbs coming into the factory. "Your ankles were swollen the last time I examined you."

Emma handed her friend a cup of coffee, and sat down on a nearby stool. "I know, but we have so much work right now; and when my help gets done with one task, unless I'm there to move them directly to the next one, they end up standing around. Can you imagine standing around with all this work?"

"No, but I can imagine ankles swelling up to the size of turnips, big fair turnips," he stressed as a smile crept into his face.

"I will try and stay off my feet more," Emma promised as she took a swallow of coffee. "Maybe I should hire an assistant."

"Two, if necessary," Cy advised. "You don't want to endanger the baby."

"No, I wouldn't want to do that," Emma agreed.

"Then see about an assistant," Cy advised again. "Listen Emma, I've got to run. I have two more stops to make before supper." He rose. "Remember, stay off your feet, and cut back on your salt. Fresh food is great this time of year."

Emma rose to see him out.

"No," Cy objected as he swung around, pointing his finger at her. "You stay off your feet. I'll see myself out. Thank you."

Emma obediently sat back down.

"Mrs. Parchen, should we hang the new shipment in with the last one," a young woman asked.

"If the herb is the same, yes," Emma answered. "But when it changes, we have to post the rack."

"Okay," the woman replied, and hurried off.

Emma sat a moment longer, enjoying the respite as she thought how Cy had encouraged her business from the very beginning. The factory had grown year after year until now the floor was crowded with drying racks. Most of their bottled tinctures occupied the dark cool basement, and they shipped year around with only inclement weather limiting their efforts. Still, she had a baby on the way. Maybe she should cut back on her work for a while.

Like Adele, Emma hoped it would be a girl. Three boys in one room could become tight. Eventually there was the attic, but they would have to share the space with Henry's nephew. But aside from this, a baby girl in the nursery might prod Emma's sister along. She had dated the same fellow for the last month without any great catastrophe, and maybe with a little added incentive, the relationship could blossom. It would certainly please their mother, and solve the bedroom situation for the children. Jenny would still have a good six months before they needed the extra space in Adele's room.

Otherwise she and Henry had better have a little talk. The house wasn't that large, and where would they ever put more children? Emma loved being pregnant. She loved Henry, and the thought of restraining their desire was not something she wanted to even think about. She loved the touching, the having, the pure unadulterated pleasure of quenching the thirst of their desire.

Someone dropped an empty crate, and Emma's attention shifted back to the factory. She set her empty coffee cup aside, and rose to her feet.

The fair came and went, and Emma cut back her hours at the factory by nearly half. She felt fat. She waddled when she walked, and suddenly she wondered what it was about pregnancy she loved so much.

"Are you staying off your feet?" Cy Ingersoll asked again as he always did on his visits.

"Yes, as much as I can," Emma answered.

"Well it shouldn't be for much longer. The baby has dropped."

"I thought I wasn't due for another two weeks," Emma responded.

"A week at the outside," Cy replied.

Emma fell silent.

"Everything looks fine," Cy continued as a matter of course. "I would say this one will probably be your largest. Maybe another boy."

"We were hoping for a girl," Emma offered quietly. "Then she can share the room with Adele."

"And if it's not?"

"Then the boys' room will become more crowded, I guess," Emma decided.

"Well you can always build a larger house," Cy laughed. "It's not like your tincture business has shrunk at all."

Emma looked up. "A larger house? We have a fine house."

"And a fine large family. It's not like you couldn't afford to build a larger place," Cy replied with a grin.

On October 21, 1879 Ruehling Achille Parchen was born to Emma and Henry. The wonderment of a new baby completely captivated Adele who promptly forgot she wanted a sister. The newborn captivated its parents too as both wondered how three growing boys would manage in the same bedroom.

Emma now spent every available minute with her children, taking the baby downtown to the factory with Adele, who was now old enough to start grinding herbs. It was good experience for the little girl to be away from home from time to time as she would be enrolled in school the following year.

Emma worked on her tinctures alongside her employees. They had enough accounts now to keep everyone busy all year. Emma disappeared into her office. It was time to feed Ruehling, and she wanted to be alone.

A knock came at the door, and it cautiously opened.

"Henry, what are you doing here?" Emma exclaimed.

Her husband let himself in, and closed the door. His eyes settled on their newborn feasting in Emma's blouse. "I need to talk to you," he responded. "I think I have a buyer for our old store."

A smile emerged on Emma's face. "That would certainly help our finances. Who is it?"

"Gans and Klein," Henry answered, "but they want the whole lot, the warehouse included."

"I have to move?" Emma asked.

"It looks like it," Henry replied. "How about if I move you across the street into the back section of the new store building. That way you would have alley access for shipping."

"Henry, I need sunshine remember," Emma cried.

"I have already talked to our builder. He says he can put some sky lights into the third floor unit."

"What if I just stay here, and rent from Gans and Klein," Emma suggested. "This place may not be as roomy as it once was, but at least it's set up for me."

"Gans and Klein are going to level everything. They want a new store, and they like this location."

Emma frowned.

"Look Em, suppose you move into my building temporarily. I will have to build another warehouse soon anyway, especially with you on the third floor."

"You paint such a rosy picture," Emma responded facetiously.

"What I thought we might do," Henry continued patiently, "is eventually build you your own building. It can't be this year -- maybe not for a couple yet. It really depends on when the railroad goes through, because then your market is going to grow so fast you simply won't believe it." He smiled. "In the meantime if we can sell this property, and put away a little money... We do own that land on Broadway behind the parcel Gans and Klein want."

"Maybe we should have built this warehouse there," Emma commented.

"No," Henry replied, "not a warehouse. When your building goes in, it's going to be nice."

"My building?" Emma repeated.

"Your factory." Henry touched his baby's small hand. "John Kinna and I have decided to resign from the fair board," he announced as he now changed the subject. "I feel as if I have missed a good chunk of our older boys' lives, going to so many meetings all the time. But at least there isn't another government wood seizure going on like a couple years ago."

"No," Emma agreed.

"Besides, this may be our last baby," Henry commented with a soft smile. "The house is getting full."

"Maybe we should build a bigger one," Emma suggested.

"A bigger one," Henry responded in amusement, "and where is the money going to come from?"

"Gans and Klein... What if the railroad never comes through?" Emma countered.

"It will." Henry grinned.

"I can't imagine three boys growing up in that bedroom," Emma decided as she met her husband's eyes, "and I think I would like another daughter."

"Another daughter? What if it's another son?" Henry replied in good humor.

"Then we will really need a bigger house," Emma stated.

"We will manage with the one we have," Henry laughed. "There is always the attic."

"And what do you plan to do with your nephew," Emma asked.

"Marry him off?"

"I want more children," Emma responded evenly.

"The number of children in a family should be a matter of reason and rational thought," Henry declared. "Our house is full."

"I would like another daughter," Emma urged.

"We will see," Henry replied as he kissed her gently.

Chapter Nineteen

That night Emma and Henry shared the passion of their bed as Ruehling slept peacefully in the nursery. Emma now fell blissfully asleep as Henry watched over his wife, stroking her arm as she lay beside him. At the moment a larger house was out of the question. They had four years of debt to pay on the new store, and though their businesses were doing well, they could not depend on the future going as grand as the past two years had. Henry's hand dropped. They now had four children. They also had two solid businesses, both of which would soon be bursting their seams for want of more space.

If they were careful, they might be able to pay the new store off a year early. Then perhaps they could think about the new warehouse. But a new house...not yet, they couldn't afford it. Henry would simply have to make sure their family did not grow any more. His eyes dropped to his sleeping wife. He loved her. He loved her more than anything. How could he deny her when the fire ignited between them? His eyes dropped. He knew how. He was just going to have to curtail his desire, but he wouldn't tell Emma, not if she didn't ask.

In a year's time the new store on Main Street was doing so well, Henry made a substantial increase in his inventory. But with bulk shipments coming in only during the summer months, he found himself wondering where he would put everything. Crates were stacked to the ceiling, occupying every spare inch of space. Still, maybe he could move the rows closer together while the profit line helped remove their debt.

May 5th Ed Ingersoll died in prison. Bright's kidney disease was blamed. Yet as Emma pondered the situation, she couldn't help wondering how the man's kidneys could suddenly become so weak and vulnerable that it would lead to death.

But Emma couldn't talk about it with Cy, he was so distraught over the situation that even a hint of the subject brought immediate withdrawal. It had been five years since Calista's death, but now the man's grief was again fresh and new, and much more volatile.

Emma closed up the warehouse as Henry met her. They headed up the hill together.

"I saw Cy today," Henry noted quietly.

"I was just thinking about him," Emma commented. "How did he look?"

"Pale. I don't think he is taking care of himself like he used to," Henry answered.

Silence fell between them for nearly half a block.

"Henry, I don't get it," Emma cried suddenly. "How could Ed's health go bad so fast? He was just fine during all the tension of the allegations."

"You know illness can sneak up on you," Henry responded.

"Yes, but there is usually a cause," Emma replied. "What causes Bright's disease?"

"I don't know. Isn't it a form a kidney failure?" Henry asked.

Emma thought about his statement. "What would cause his kidneys to fail?"

"How about a beating?" Henry suggested quietly.

"A beating?" Emma abruptly stopped. "At the prison?"

"Stranger things have happened."

"The guards get that rough?" Emma cried.

"I think the other inmates are more likely," Henry offered softly. "Ed wasn't always the most tactful person, but he did have a good heart for all his faults. Maybe he tried to stick up for someone, and caught it instead."

"You think so?" Emma asked.

"There is a good chance," her husband replied. "I have written to your brother, asking him to look into the matter." He smiled briefly. "It can help when you know someone who has been on the penitentiary's Board of Directors."

It took several months for Harry D'Acheul to find out anything regarding Ed Ingersoll's death. Even then, it was only sketchy, limited to stray comments overheard by the guards, and their observations. It seemed that Ed Ingersoll had found use for his skills as a doctor inside the prison walls. Helping the less fortunate, he frequently encountered the antagonism of others while earning the fierce loyalty of a growing few. Fights resulted, but never under the eyes of the guards. The only thing they saw were the results, a limp here, an obviously sore middle there.

Another Christmas came and went, and again tragedy struck. On the 17th of January, Emma and Henry were abhorred to learn that Wood and Jennie Paynter had lost their infant son. Tears sprang to Emma's eyes. Her breath choked within her. The innocent baby across the street had died from congestion of the lungs.

At two o'clock on Wednesday, the Parchens joined the gathering of friends at the baby's funeral. Wood's wife was pale, and coughed from time to time as she tried hard to maintain composure. Emma felt only a hollow emptiness. She and Henry had a son that wasn't much different in age from little Paul. Would illness steal their child as it had the Paynter's?

"Emma, you remember Mrs. Brown, don't you?" Henry offered.

Emma looked up, and forced a smile. "It's nice to see you again," she responded.

"Oh Mrs. Parchen, isn't this the most sad of times. Dear little Paul, he was such a darling, and to think..." She paused. "Oh well, my grandmother always used to say that God moves in mysterious ways. Heaven must be full of beautiful little children, children that are simply too good for this world."

"Yes Mrs. Brown," Emma agreed with a slight smile. She really wasn't paying the woman any mind. Lots of things were said at such times, lots of things nobody really wanted to think too much about.

Emma caught a glimpse of the little coffin through the numerous people. The wood box was hardly bigger than their still born's.

"Emma, everyone is going out to the cemetery. Do you want to go?" Henry asked quietly.

"Yes."

Emma missed nearly a week of work as she became vigilant at little Albert's bed. The child had a bad case of the croup, Harry had a runny nose, and Adele complained of a sore throat. On top of this, Emma's sister was down with a fever cold. Only Ruehling seemed healthy, and Emma abandoned the latter to her mother's watchful eye as she forbid the two access to the upper floors where she confined the sick. Then finally one by one, the family recovered and returned to normal life.

Henry finished supper, and reached for the newspaper, placing it in front of his wife. He pointed to a column.

"Ed's youngest," Emma suddenly cried. "No!"

"I'm afraid so," Henry responded.

"Ed Ingersoll?" Marie asked as she began picking up dirty dishes.

"Yes," Henry answered as Emma continued to read. "It was diphtheria, and very quick. It took his youngest, and the Dearborn girl who was staying with the family. Their funerals were yesterday."

"I should have gone," Emma decided.

"You had your hands full here," Henry replied. "I put in a brief appearance, and excused us."

"You talked to Cy?" Emma inquired. "Did he say whether our diphtheria medicine helped at all?"

"I talked to him, and no, he didn't have much to say about anything."

"Is he all right?" Emma responded.

"Shook, but he will survive," Henry answered. "He's used to death."

"But not in his own family," Emma cried.

"He is becoming used to even that," Henry added quietly. "Where is your sister? I thought she would be at dinner tonight."

"She went out," Emma replied as she continued to stare at the paper. "Louis Walker came by."

"The cold air won't help Jenny's cold," Henry cautioned.

"She wrapped up warm, and they were just going down to the Rumley's," Emma offered. "I think she and Louis are getting serious."

A month later Emma's mother smiled mischievously when Jenny informed them despondently that her Louis would not be by Friday evening. He had to work late.

Marie turned to Emma. "The children are in bed?"

"Yes. Why?"

"And Henry is meeting with those men from the Board of Trade?" Marie asked.

"He probably won't be home until late," Emma responded.

"Good," their mother replied as she pulled fudge pudding from the pantry.

Jenny's face brightened. "Sweet secrets," she cried.

Marie smiled. "Why don't you run up and get Adele, Emma? She's in school. She's old enough to join in."

"And she can sleep in tomorrow," Jenny exclaimed excitedly. "Go get Adele, Emma."

Emma slipped upstairs, and through the door into her daughter's room. The girl looked up from her pillow as her mother put a finger to her lips, motioning for Adele to come with her. The young girl quickly put on her slippers and robe, and followed her mother to the stairs.

"What's wrong, mama?" Adele whispered anxiously.

Emma again put her finger to her lips, covering a smile. Then she led the way down. Marie and Jenny were already in the parlor, sitting on the floor around the kerosene lamp. Four stemmed dishes of pudding were spaced at equal distances around the circle. Emma sat before one, and motioned for Adele to sit at the other.

"Adele," Marie began, "we thought you were old enough now to join us."

"Yes," Adele exclaimed with wide eyes as she plunked herself down. "What are we doing?"

"Sweet secrets," Jenny answered. "From time to time the D'Acheul women get together for 'sweet secrets'. It's time you joined in."

"Secrets," Adele repeated. "What kind of secrets?"

"You had better ask your mother," Marie responded.

"What kind of secrets, mother," Adele asked eagerly.

Emma grinned mischievously. "Secrets you wouldn't tell your father or your brothers...at least not like this." She giggled.

Adele's dark eyes widened, but she said nothing as she turned to look at her grandmother.

"This is a time, Adele," Marie began quietly, "when you can let your French spirit loose and say anything you want. You can talk about boys, or about the life you fancy."

"You can tell about bad dreams or bad girls or just stuff," Jenny laughed.

"Or good stuff," Emma added, "don't forget the good stuff, like things we remember about daddy...your grandfather, Adele."

"Or my daddy," Adele responded.

"Or your daddy," Jenny agreed with a smile.

"Then I want to go first," Adele cried. "Do I eat the pudding before or after I tell?"

"It doesn't matter, dear," Marie replied.

"Good," Adele exclaimed as she put a quick spoon into her mouth. She took a moment to swallow. "There is this boy at school, and he kissed me," she stated as she suddenly turned to her mother in embarrassment.

"A boy kissed you," Jenny squealed. "Adele, you do start early."

"Is that okay, mama," Adele asked now in a much quieter tone.

"Where did this boy kiss you?" Emma countered.

"On the cheek," Adele answered, "where else?"

"And how long ago was this?" Emma continued.

"Oh ages ago, long before we all got sick," Adele told her.

"Has he tried to kiss you since?" Jenny inquired.

"No, he seems to have lost interest," Adele replied with a small frown.

"Probably just a dare," Jenny decided as she turned to her sister. "You know, like the kiss I got after I was over the small pox."

"Probably," Emma agreed.

"A dare? What does a dare have to do with my kiss?" Adele cried.

"Boys sometimes dare each other to do things," Jenny responded. "It's kind of a lark for them. They do it just for fun. It doesn't mean anything."

"Do you like this young man?" Emma asked now.

"I did," Adele answered, "but now he has turned into an awful bore."

Emma smiled. Adele sounded like a woman ten times her age.

"Typical," Jenny laughed. "It's all right, Adele. Don't waste another thought on the boy. He doesn't deserve it. But when the girls corner you someday and want to know if you have ever been kissed, you can say 'yes'. Just don't mention how young you were at the time."

"All right," Adele agreed slowly. Her eyes rested on her aunt. "What is your secret?"

"Louis," Jenny replied as her eyes beamed. "He really likes me."

"Tell us something we don't know," Emma retorted.

"All right, Em," Jenny responded, "he loves me."

"We are still waiting for something new," Marie told her.

Jenny's eyes shifted to her mother as Adele sat entranced, watching her aunt's every move.

"Well he kissed me the other night," Jenny offered.

Adele instantly squealed, and her aunt smiled.

"Does he talk about your future together?" Marie inquired.

"Of course," Jenny giggled. "I wouldn't be surprised if he doesn't pop the question soon."

"Marriage?" Adele cried.

"Yes, marriage." Jenny's eyes were glowing as her niece squealed again.

"Not so loud, Adele," Emma rebuked. "You don't want to wake your brothers."

The girl instantly quieted, but her face beamed as she listened to the exchange of information between her aunt and mother and grandmother. Finally though, Adele lost interest as her eyes swung to her mother. "What is your sweet secret?"

Emma stopped mid-sentence as her eyes focused on her daughter. "You mustn't tell your father, ever," she admonished.

"I won't," Adele promised.

"I went down to Chinatown once," Emma stated.

"Alone?" Three voices cried the word simultaneously.

"I went with a young Chinese girl," Emma answered. "Calista was down there tending a pregnant woman, and she needed medicine. It was an emergency."

"What did you see?" Jenny demanded.

"A lot of shanties," Emma answered.

"Did anyone bother you?" Marie asked.

"I got a number of looks, but no one stopped us," Emma replied.

"Okay, grandma, your turn," Adele decided.

Marie smiled. "You must be enjoying yourself, Adele. You are the only one with pudding left."

Six months later Louis Walker married Jenny. Harry and Hattie came over from Butte two days prior. Emma's brother took the opportunity to discuss with Henry the latest medical supplies available on the market as the women became lost in all the preparations for the upcoming event. Even Hattie's mother pitched in, offering the many showy flowers from the Rumley garden. Marie was pleased. The Parchen garden, which she personally oversaw, was magnificent, but more medicinal in blend. It's often wild appearance contributed more to the foliage of the bouquets than to the featured flowers. Jenny was pleased. The bouquets were stunning and symbolic at the same time, with rosemary for remembrance and hyssop for the blessings of good health.

The ceremony took place at the Parchen residence the morning of September 21st, 1881. Only at the last minute was it decided that Harry, rather than Henry, would walk Jenny down the aisle. Jenny had lived with Emma and Henry for seven years, and Henry had been the father image in her life during this time. However blood is considered thicker than water, and when it came down to the last minute, Harry D'Acheul claimed his sister's arm.

Reverend Reed did the honors of uniting the couple before a small crowd of family and friends. The Parchen house had never seen so many people within its walls. Jenny's face glowed with happiness, causing everyone to forget about her numerous pox scars. Louis stood by her side tall and proud.

Emma glanced at her mother as the minister pronounced the couple man and wife, and saw a look of utter satisfaction in her face. All her children were now married.

"Mama," young Albert called as he tugged on Emma's sleeve, "are they going to kiss?"

The little voice carried loudly through the room as Reverend Reed looked past the couple in front of him to where the Parchens occupied the first row of chairs. A benevolent smile rested on his lips. "You may kiss your bride now, Louis," he instructed with a grin.

Young Albert's mouth dropped open as he watched his aunt and new uncle do just that. The little boy was still staring at the couple as the crowd now rose to offer their congratulations. Within moments Albert Parchen's view was cut off.

"Albert, come on," Adele urged. "There's cake."

"Did you see that," the young child demanded.

"See what?" Adele replied.

"They kissed. They did it for me."

"Not for you," Adele told him. "All married people do that."

"They do?" Albert asked as he now followed his older sister. "How come?"

"They just do," Adele answered.

"Well I think they did it for me. I think I'll ask Aunt Jenny to do it again. Want to come?"

"Albert, if you bug Aunt Jenny, I'll cream you," Adele warned. "Besides, the cake will be all gone. Everyone is getting there ahead of us."

"Cake?" Albert abruptly forgot about the kiss.

By noon Jenny had thrown her bouquet. Then hurrying off, the newly married couple headed for Deer Lodge before they went on to Butte and other towns on the west side. The wedding trip was in the opposite direction from Emma's, and was by private conveyance, and during good weather. Louis was combining their travel with the rounds he needed to make to various mines. The company was paying for the trip, and the two would be gone several weeks.

"Is Aunt Hattie throwing Jenny a party too?" Adele asked as her mother picked up a stack of dirty dishes.

"Of course," Uncle Harry offered as he came to his sister's aid. "Your grandma is going to be there."

"I wish I could go," Adele pouted.

"You have school," Emma responded as she handed Harry the dishes, and picked up more.

"Couldn't I skip a couple more days?" Adele begged. "I am missing today already."

"Yes, and Adele could go to school in Butte," Harry teased. "She could become our daughter."

Adele suddenly turned to stare at her uncle. "Your daughter? Who would I play with? You don't have any kids."

"No, not yet," Harry responded more quietly.

"Adele, school is important," Emma stated, "and grandma is going to stay at Harry's for a few weeks. You don't want to miss your spelling bee next Friday."

"No, I want to be here for that," Adele decided. "Okay, I'll stay home." With that, she ran off to the kitchen.

Bad colds seemed to overtake Helena that fall, followed by a small pox scare. Two were dead by December, another wasn't expected to be far behind. Butte's Chinatown reported thirty cases. Emma put in long hours as she filled one order after another.

To complicate things, Dr. Ingersoll departed for the East on December 10th to spend the winter there. Emma knew he had a brother in Corning, New York, and suspected Cy could really use the time away, considering the tragedies that had befallen his family during the past year or two. But Emma couldn't help feeling regret. Cy had always been there, discussing medicines with her, trying to concoct the best possible combination of resources for his patients. Emma loved that about the man. His passion for healing was remarkable. It gave her energy when the hours got long.

Emma's mother returned to Helena just after Thanksgiving, and Christmas was spent much like the preceding year with the addition of Jenny's new husband. The couple was very excited. Louis had received a letter from his mother stating that she would come for a visit in August, possibly bringing her other son with her. This was especially good news as Louis's family had not been able to attend his wedding the preceding September.

"Louis and I are thinking about building a house," Jenny confided to her sister as they washed the holiday dishes.

"Really," Emma exclaimed. "When?"

"Oh not for a year or two," Jenny replied, "but we are looking at lots."

Emma broke into a warm smile. "Where?"

"Well all over, but I especially like the parcels on North Rodney. I'm not a big one for hills." She grinned.

"I could do without them as well," Emma responded warmly. "But with the drug store, our location is good."

"Thank goodness the assay office where Louis works, is not clear downtown," Jenny laughed. "I would die if I had to climb all the hills you do, and you do it with kids."

The snows of winter were followed by the winds of spring and the sunshine of summer as Helena's residents again began to enjoy the great outdoors. Henry had twisted an ankle during the early months of the year. It wasn't serious, but it still troubled him from time to time, especially if he was compelled to climb ladders in his back room quest for merchandise.

Coupled with the sudden realization that the town of White Sulfur Springs was not one that patronized Emma's tincture business, Henry Parchen decided that a few days in that part of the country, soaking his ankle in mineral water and talking to businessmen, could prove beneficial. So in June he set out, availing himself of the Overland Coach.

Emma saw him off as usual, and returned to work where new crops of herbs were already arriving. Adele was with her. School had finished the preceding Friday, and Emma's daughter had participated in the final program.

Several days later, Emma noted how much Adele's focus on work had improved. The young girl was keeping up with the slower of the Parchen employees, and with a smile Emma decided she should reward her daughter.

Crate after crate of herbs took their place on the upper floor of the new store building, and space again became prime. Skylights were opened to encourage air flow in and around the drying plants. The humidity was great, and often grew oppressive during the hot June days.

Emma wiped her brow, and turned to her daughter. "That finishes this shipment, and we shouldn't have another until the first of next week. Why don't you go on home while I finish up a few things."

"Gladly," Adele responded with a sudden smile. "Do you suppose Grandma made cookies?"

"She usually does on Fridays," Emma replied cheerfully. "But you save me one, okay?"

"Okay," Adele agreed as she stacked her empty box, and turned to go. She was at the stairs when she passed her cousin, Henry Duerfeldt. "I get to go home," she declared gleefully.

"Wish I could," he retorted as he reached to poke her playfully.

Adele dodged him, and continued down and out of sight.

"Henry, have you got some more orders for me?" Emma asked as her nephew appeared.

"I wish I did, Aunt Emma," he answered.

Emma glanced at him. "You are too late to help."

"I didn't come for that," young Duerfeldt agreed.

Emma set down the paperwork she had gathered. Her employees had left a mere half hour before. "Is something wrong?"

"I don't know. Maybe," her nephew replied.

"What is it?"

"I heard a rumor. I don't know if it's true, but I thought you should be aware of it," Duerfeldt stated.

"A rumor?" Emma repeated.

"We had a customer in from Meager County, not a regular, just a guy traveling through."

"And this rumor?"

"I guess they've had some Indian trouble over that way," her nephew continued. "The man said a guy got killed, a city fellow, not anyone from around there."

"So..." Emma prodded with growing uneasiness.

"The man said the dead guy was from Helena. Ran a drug store."

"My Henry?" Emma gasped.

Chapter Twenty

"We don't know that," Henry Duerfeldt objected. "We don't even know if the man had his facts straight, or if he was just spinning a yarn."

"But he said the victim was from Helena, and ran a drug store," Emma responded. "How could he know that?"

"Maybe it's just coincidence," Emma's nephew suggested.

"A pretty unlikely coincidence," she replied.

"Aunt Emma, maybe he stayed at the same hotel in White Sulfur Springs as Uncle Henry. The place isn't that large. He may have overheard someone talking, and just made up the story. I haven't heard of any Indian problems lately, have you?"

"No," Emma answered.

"See, so it's probably just some tall tale. I'm sorry if I've upset you. I just thought you should know. It's hard telling whose ear that man may yet bend before he leaves town, and I didn't want you to hear it from someone else."

"Thank you," Emma stated quietly.

Henry Duerfeldt looked into his aunt's face. "Are you all right? Maybe I shouldn't have alarmed you."

"I'm fine," Emma replied, "and I'm glad you told me."

"It's getting late. Can I help you close up," her nephew offered. "I've already finished down at the drug store."

"No, I'm fine. I just have two things I should file, and then I am going home," Emma told him.

"Okay then," he responded. "I'll see you there later on. I'm having dinner at a friend's tonight, remember."

"Yes." Emma watched the young man leave, picked up her papers, and headed back to her desk. But instead of doing any filing, she merely shoved the pages into a drawer and slammed it shut.

Could she really be a widow? Emma stared at the wall in front of her. The thought was almost beyond comprehension. This was not a trip back East where Henry would be gone months. It was merely the short jaunt to White Sulfur Springs. The distance to Deer Lodge wasn't much different.

Emma picked up her sweater and lunch pail, and headed to the stairs.

"Emma, you are awfully quiet this evening," her mother noted as the children finally left the dinner table. The pie plate was totally empty.

"Our Duerfeldt came by the factory," Emma responded. "I guess there is a rumor going around."

"Yes, I've heard it too," her mother offered. "But I honestly can't understand why a man, who has once quit the drug business, would ever want back in."

"What are you talking about?" Emma replied in confusion.

"Evidently not what you are," Marie decided. "What is this new rumor?"

"That Henry, my Henry, is dead," Emma answered bluntly.

Her mother's eyes widened. "I hadn't heard that one. When was this supposed to have happened?"

"I don't know," Emma retorted as she rose from her chair to put her dirty dishes in the wash pan.

"Then how... Where..." Marie's voice fell off.

"There was supposed to be Indian trouble somewhere around White Sulfur Springs. They were supposed to have killed him." Emma suddenly turned to her mother. Her eyes were glassy wet. Worry rested heavy in her expression.

"I haven't heard of any Indian trouble," Marie offered quietly.

"Neither have I."

"Then maybe it's not true," her mother suggested hopefully.

"But what if it is?" Emma demanded.

"I'm sure it's not," Marie decided.

Anger flashed within Emma. It was possible that her husband was dead, and her mother wouldn't even consider the fact. Her eyes landed angrily on the woman. "You lost two husbands."

Marie visibly faltered. "Yes," she agreed quietly, "it can happen."

"What would I ever do without Henry?" Emma asked in a still voice.

"Go on," her mother replied. "You just go on."

For two and a half days Emma lived with the awful dread, wondering if her husband was alive or dead. For two and a half days she hoped that a reply to her telegram would arrive, and yet feared it too. To know the truth would in some measure be relief, even if it meant facing a truth she didn't want to learn, but nothing came, Emma found no rest. Henry Parchen was due back any time now, and Emma met the coach on Monday and Tuesday without gaining any further clue to her dilemma. Then as she waited on Wednesday, and the door of the coach opened, Henry Parchen stepped out into the sunshine.

"Henry," Emma exclaimed as she threw herself at him.

"Emma, hi," he responded in surprise. "What's wrong?"

"They said you were dead," she cried as she clung tightly to him.

"Dead? Who said I was dead?" he demanded as he pulled her over to the side so the other passengers could get out.

"Some drifter came into the drug store. I tried to wire you on Saturday, but I didn't get an answer."

"Probably because I was at the hot springs," Henry replied. "Still you would think I'd get my messages."

"I was so worried," Emma exclaimed. "Did you see any Indian trouble?"

"Indians? No," Henry answered. "Where is your mother?"

"At home with the children," Emma responded.

"Duerfeldt, how is business?" her husband greeted as his nephew appeared.

"Great, now that you're back," he returned with a wide smile. "The drug store is already closed for the night, Uncle Henry. Let me help carry your things home."

Henry Parchen reached for the bag the driver was now unloading from the coach, and passed it to his nephew. When he turned, Herman Gans was passing.

"Parchen, it's good to see you back alive," the man welcomed.

"You heard the rumor too?" Emma's husband demanded.

"I think all of Helena heard it," Gans noted, and grinned. "I told John Kinna not to believe such garbage."

In August Jenny's mother-in-law came for a visit, bringing Louis's brother, and in September Adele returned to school. But before November was over, Henry Parchen had installed a telephone at the drug store. Telegrams, he had personally found out, could be misplaced or lost, and the message never received. Of course the modern convenience of a phone was not bad for business either. Once his customers had the same installed in their homes, medical prescriptions and other orders could be filled and delivered without the person ever leaving the comfort of their home, a very appealing thought with snow arriving in Helena as early as October.

Emma walked down the store aisle. She was picking up a few things her mother needed, stopping to inspect a new hot water bottle near her tincture shelves.

"Emma, I think I've got the dye your mother wanted," Henry announced as he joined his wife. "She wanted lavender for the rags?"

"Yes, she is working on a new rug," Emma agreed as she examined the rubber bottle. "What's this?"

"You put hot water in it, and then put it in bed with you, under your feet," Henry told her. "It stays warm for an hour or more."

"It certainly is a funny shape," Emma noted.

"That way it doesn't roll around and leak," her husband responded. "Harry sold three cases of them last month."

"How many have you sold?" Emma asked.

"Probably close to a dozen," Henry answered. "Helena is not quite as game for new things as Butte."

Emma raised an eyebrow. "I think Harry could sell a blind woman spectacles if he thought they were modern and new."

Her husband grinned. "Yes, you are probably right, especially when it comes to the latest in medical science. He claims doctors back East are already experimenting with the idea of using this rubber, hot water bottle in conjunction with a tube for their patients with congested bowels. According to him, in five years or so, there won't be anyone dying from such an affliction."

"I think I read there were two last year," Emma replied. "I wish they would find a cure for congested lungs instead. There were twice as many that died of that, and I still feel bad about Wood Paynter's son."

"Yes, little Paul," Henry agreed. "Still, what I've heard about this hot water contraption sounds dangerous to me. It defies nature, and that can't be good."

"So are you and Harry going to carry the rubber bottle and tube affair when it comes out?" Emma asked.

"Your brother definitely will," Emma's husband answered, "and I suppose a lot of people will think it's a gift from heaven." He paused momentarily. "I don't know. The hot water bottle seems to be popular, and there's nothing wrong with that part."

"True," Emma noted, "if you don't mind rubber." Then she smiled. "I'd better get these things home to mother. She wants to dye those rags this evening."

"Emma, you didn't tell me you and Henry are rich," Jenny declared as she waltzed into the tincture office the following morning.

"Rich?" Emma repeated in disbelief.

Jenny threw her newspaper down in front of her sister, and pointed to a column. "You are considered one of the 'rich' of Lewis and Clark County." She grinned. "You are even listed twice."

"Tax tables," Emma gasped. "I thought what we paid in taxes was a matter of privacy."

"A matter of public record," Jenny laughed. "You and Henry can build a mansion."

"A mansion?"

"Not that you need one any more," Jenny continued. "Adele has her own room now." She smiled. "But wouldn't it be grand?"

"We are still in debt," Emma replied.

"Oh bosh," Jenny retorted. "I bet Henry already has the store paid off, what with all that rent he gets." She grinned.

"We have to settle the loan first," Emma responded.

Jenny pointed to the newspaper. "I bet the banks wouldn't worry a bit about that old loan, not with you being rich and all." She smiled. "The kids are getting big, and everyone can always use more room. Besides if your children follow our example, they will take their time getting married."

"We are not building a house," Emma stated firmly, "not yet, at any rate."

After her sister left, Emma returned to her desk. Jenny's newspaper still lay across the space, and she picked it up, focusing on the tax column. They really were listed twice, once as individuals and once as a company, and both entries were in the upper quarter. Sam Hauser paid the most tax, $2,204.20, but he was making money hand over fist. He had to be.

Emma sat down in her chair. She remembered reading that the Deer Lodge tax for the previous year was 19 mills. She wasn't sure on the exact figure for Helena. Henry always took care of the books, but she was certain it was in the neighborhood. Emma picked up her pencil, and did a quick tabulation. Sam Hauser made in the neighborhood of a hundred and sixteen thousand dollars. She inhaled sharply. That was a lot of money, and that wasn't counting First National Bank's income.

Then pulling the newspaper over, she read what Henry paid in taxes, and did a similar calculation. All together they made forty-one thousand two hundred and forty-seven dollars...or at least in that neighborhood. Emma stared at the figure. She hadn't realized how much their income had grown. She smiled. They could afford to pay two cents on the dollar in tax. Protection from an Indian attack was worth it, not counting all the help the government had given to the railroads. Once they were connected by rail to both coasts, they would make even more money. Their tinctures and cough syrup were becoming very popular.

That evening Emma crawled into bed next to Henry, and gave him an affectionate kiss.

"What's that for," he asked as he turned slightly.

"For all your hard work," she replied with a smile he could see even in the dark.

"You are welcome, I guess," he responded.

"Do you realize how fortunate we are," she exclaimed. "Oh, of course you do. You take care of the books."

"Emma, what has gotten into you?" Henry puzzled.

"Jenny came by and brought by the tax article from the newspaper," Emma offered. "We made forty-one thousand dollars last year."

"Yes," Henry agreed, "about that. The newspaper listed it?"

"Just the taxes paid. I did a quick calculation," she stated, "but we are rich."

"I wouldn't say that," Henry retorted, "but we are making ends meet."

"But we have this house, the new store, our children, and our health. What could be better?"

"Having it all paid for," Henry answered.

"But we could build a mansion," Emma continued undaunted.

"Is that what this is about?" Henry asked.

Emma beamed even through the darkness.

"We have needs, and they aren't a new house," Henry told her firmly.

"What needs?" Emma demanded.

"Storage space," her husband replied. "Your tinctures are stacked in crates to the ceiling, and my back stock is starting to overflow into the rear aisles of the store."

"Yes, we could use more space," Emma agreed.

"A new building costs money, and we are just getting out from under the debt on the store building."

"True," Emma decided. "It seems crazy that we owe so much when we make so much."

Henry chuckled lightly. "It's the way of the world, my dear. You should know that...spend money to make money."

"Yes, of course. So a bigger house is out of the question?"

"I'm afraid so," Henry responded as he took her into his arms, "but maybe we can afford a trip soon. Would you like that?"

Emma pulled herself up onto an elbow. "A trip? Where?"

"I thought perhaps when the railroad is finished, we should take the kids some place. They have never ridden on a train."

"Where would we go?"

"Where do you want to go?" he asked.

"The Pacific Ocean," Emma answered automatically.

"Wait a minute," Henry retorted with a chuckle. "I was offering a short jaunt for the kids, not a full blown holiday to California. If you want our wedding trip, you will have to wait at least until February and our twelfth wedding anniversary."

Emma stared at her husband in the dark. Had she heard him correctly? Had he actually said the words? They were going to California in February?

"Emma, say something," Henry coaxed.

"We are going to see the Pacific Ocean?"

"That's what you've always wanted, isn't it?" he asked.

"Yes, but..."

"Yes, and it's about time, don't you think?" he responded. "It's been almost twelve years."

"The kids should see the ocean too," Emma decided. "Can we take them?"

"Possibly...if you don't mind sharing the trip with a little business," Henry replied.

"The California market, of course," Emma exclaimed. "Of course we want to do business while we're there, the more the better."

"It is kind of a dream," Henry agreed. "There are several in town who are talking about spending next winter down there."

"I would love to spend a winter away," Emma responded, "but can we afford it. We need more warehouse space."

"The whole winter is a bit out of the question," Henry decided, "but we do need enough time to capture as much of the coastal market as possible. Let me think about it."

Talk of travel was in the air that spring as work on the railroad progressed closer and closer to Helena. In March Harry and Hattie arrived in Helena. They stayed just a few nights. Emma's brother was on his way east for the stores' annual buying trip, and their mother had decided to go along as far as St. Louis. She would stay there visiting relatives and friends while her son went on to his regular destinations. Then Harry would stop again in St. Louis on his way back, and spend a few days before the two of them would start the journey home.

Hattie, meanwhile, would go home to the Rumleys and stay. Her sister, Birdie, had just returned from Denver where she had spent the winter, and it was rumored Julia was seeing more and more of a certain young man. It was a chance to be just sisters again in their old stomping ground, a circumstance they were gradually outgrowing.

Harry and Marie left for St. Louis, and on Monday morning Emma saw Adele off to school. As she watched her daughter walk up the street, a squabble broke out behind her. Young Harry and Albert were in a dog pile, fighting over a toy soldier.

"Enough you two," Emma scolded as she whisked the metal figurine from a small hand. "No fighting."

"But mama," Albert cried, "I had it first."

"But it's mine," the oldest retorted.

"It is Harry's," Emma agreed as she handed the toy back to its rightful owner. "Did you ask permission to use it, Al?"

The small boy declined to answer.

"Okay, you two," Emma replied, "go play quietly somewhere else. I have some paperwork to get done this morning. Aunt Jenny will be by later to baby-sit."

By four o'clock, Emma was stationed at work, packing up orders alongside her employees. Most of the medicine was being shipped out of town. After the last couple of winters, Helena was enjoying a reprieve from epidemics like diphtheria. If only congested lungs would disappear. The Holters had just lost their five year old son that February.

At seven o'clock that evening, Henry Parchen sat at the dinner table watching his young family finish their meal. Emma sat across from him. Duerfeldt sat at the diagonal. Jenny had gone home to her husband.

Adele finished her dessert, and asked to be excused. Soon each of her brothers followed suit, pulling their older cousin with them. All were excited about a game of Chinese checkers they wanted to play.

Henry moved to a chair closer to his wife. "They say the railroad will be finished this summer."

"Can our California trip wait until our next anniversary?" she asked. "We don't want to loose the market to someone else."

"I don't think we have to be in that big of a hurry," Henry responded. "The Mullan tunnel isn't going to be an easy job. The blasting alone could delay things substantially. Plus the first few weeks will be loaded with excursionists. I think the railroad office is even planning to raffle off tickets for the first through trip from St. Paul to Portland."

"So we have time to build a warehouse," Emma surmised.

"We have time," her husband concurred. "I'm already looking for property."

"You're not going to build on the land we bought down by the depot?"

"The property down there is going to be worth a fortune, and besides, we need a warehouse closer to the store. I don't want to hire a wagon to go clear out to the depot for a lousy can of kerosene. It would be better to have the warehouse within walking distance."

Then his eyes shifted. "By the way, how do you like having your kitchen back? It's all yours again...at least for a month or two."

"It was Jenny's domain tonight," Emma replied with a grin. "She fixed supper."

Emma's husband secured land on Jackson Street for a new warehouse, and by July work had commenced.

Jenny and Louis also bought a lot on Rodney Street where they planned to have a house constructed across from Major Davenport. This pleased Marie very much. She liked the Davenports. But work was slow getting started on the Walker residence, most of Helena's builders were already employed on the new Northern Pacific Railroad Depot. Work on the house's foundation wasn't even started until August.

"John Kinna, Will Muth, and I thought we would take a yard train out into the Prickly Pear Valley Wednesday, and do a little hunting," Henry informed his wife as they got ready for bed.

"Mother would love some venison," Emma replied. "I imagine she would put off her pickles to can meat."

Henry smiled. "I wish you weren't so busy. I often think of the year we went up the gulch together, just the two of us, and stayed in the cabin. I wish I had seen the old porcupine tree you up that ladder."

"Maybe someday we can do it again," Emma responded. "It was kind of special, though I could have done well enough without the porcupine, and the cougar, and the bear. We saw more wildlife than if we'd gone to a zoo."

"Well I hope we see as much on our hunting trip. Bear meat is absolutely delicious."

"And absolutely dangerous to get," Emma replied. "I would prefer venison, or maybe a rabbit or two."

"My wife," Henry declared with laughter, "the shy huntress. If you ever went hunting we would be lucky to get a fish."

"Without a doubt," Emma chuckled. "I like my bears and cougars in pictures, not on my dinner plate."

Wednesday morning, Henry Parchen and his friends hazarded the depot's construction crews, and caught the yard train out into the valley. Emma was impressed with the railroad building. The fine brick structure gave a legitimacy to Helena, an air of permanence Eastern cities took for granted. She couldn't wait until the passenger depot was built. It was supposed to look like St. Paul's, just a little smaller.

Emma headed back into town. It was the busy season at work.

The following day the newspapers announced the Northern Pacific Freight Depot was finished. Five days later the papers announced the railroad was finished. Nine days later they announced that Helena's hotels were packed with a growing influx of strangers.

Henry Parchen was glad his hunting trip hadn't lasted long. The increased flow of visitors was good for business, and everyone was excited about the ceremony the railroad had planned for September 8th. Henry smiled to himself. Emma kept asking if the Northern Pacific really planned to drive in the last stake and leave it there. It was supposed to be gold.

Chapter Twenty-One

Despite the ten new passenger cars the Northern Pacific brought west into Helena, Henry Parchen seriously doubted there would be enough room on board the train for all who wanted to journey to the formal opening of the transcontinental line, fifty miles west of Helena. Dignitaries and distinguished guests from the East and Europe were expected: President Arthur, Hon. William Evarts (ex-Secretary of State), Generals Sherman and Grant, Henry Villard (President of the Northern Pacific), and journalists from American, English, and German newspapers. With a crowd like that, Henry Parchen quietly secured means of private conveyance. Helena's Board of Trade might secure train seats if they were lucky, but there wasn't a chance under the sun that there would be room for their families. This was a monumental event, an event the Parchen children could tell their children and grandchildren about.

Harry and Hattie also planned to attend the occasion, traveling from Butte to Deer Lodge where they would stay the night with friends. This was where the Parchens would meet them, and then together they would travel the remaining distance to Gold Creek the following morning.

Excitement hung in the air as Emma herded her three youngest children into their rented buggy. Henry was exchanging some last minute information with her brother, Harry, and their friends, the Naptons. Meanwhile Hattie made room for Adele in their buggy by moving the picnic basket outside the vehicle, and strapping it on. It was a number of miles to Gold Creek, and they couldn't dawdle.

"Mama says your sister got married last week," Adele announced as she climbed in beside her aunt. "You must feel terrible, missing it."

"Yes," Hattie agreed, "I wish I could have been there."

"Why weren't you?" Adele asked.

Hattie stared at her young niece. "Didn't your mother tell you?"

Adele's eyes turned upward momentarily, then they shifted back to her aunt. "Nope."

"I wasn't feeling well."

"Oh. I thought sisters had to be at weddings. Who took your place as bridesmaid?"

Hattie was quiet momentarily. Her niece's audacity surprised her, but she had wondered the same thing. "I don't know, a friend perhaps."

"Julia married a government lawyer, didn't she," Adele asked unabashed.

"A U.S. District Attorney," Hattie answered quietly.

"Will they be at Gold Creek too?"

"No, they're in Denver," Hattie replied quietly.

Harry climbed into the buggy, and picked up the reins. But before releasing the brake, he turned to Adele. "Well young lady, are you ready to go make some history?"

Adele broke into a grin, and eagerly nodded.

Her uncle shifted the brake out of the lock position, and slapped the horses with the reins. The buggy jerked forward.

The closer the buggies got to Gold Creek, the more people appeared. What was once a pristine piece of countryside was now a maze of milling people and horses. One train had already arrived, but the other, from the opposite direction, was still in route. Henry pointed out the small cabin where Granville Stuart had lived when he found gold in the creek. The buggies proceeded as more and more people converged along the tracks near the speaker's platform.

"Let's park the horses under those trees," Henry suggested, "and then we can take our picnic lunch over and lay out our blanket near the platform. That way we should be able to see all the proceedings."

As Emma readily agreed, he shouted their intentions to her brother. The two buggies pulled up side by side under the shade of several saplings. Excited children flowed from the vehicles as the adults grabbed the picnic baskets. Then together they walked over to a likely place with a view of the speaker's platform. Within moments the blankets were spread, and the children were pulling food from the baskets.

"I'm starved," young Harry exclaimed. "I want the biggest piece of fried chicken mom brought with."

"Oh no you don't," Adele declared, "that's for daddy. You get what I give you."

"I don't want your old chicken neck," Harry cried as he threw the bony piece to the ground.

"Harry, you pick that up and dust it off," Emma responded. "We don't waste food."

Harry scowled, but was about to obey when his uncle reached for the chicken, and picked off the small pieces of grass. "Do you want it?" Emma's brother asked.

"Not really," young Harry answered.

"Hmm," Harry D'Acheul mussed, "I love chicken skin." He took a bite. "So crunchy and tasty, and you know I've been told the meat on the neck is the most tender of any on the whole bird." He took another bite, this time ripping off the narrow strand of meat running the length of the piece. "Hmm, I think they're right."

"But there isn't much there, and the bones are always in the way," Emma's son complained.

"Prizes are never for the faint of heart," his uncle replied. "Thanks for the treat."

Young Harry scowled, and turned back to his sister. "Uncle Harry took the neck. What else you got?"

Adele handed her brother another piece of fried chicken as her Uncle Harry glanced mischievously at their mother, smiling. Emma mouthed silent words of thanks as a train whistle blew in the distance, becoming ever louder and closer.

Young Harry immediately turned to his father. “Can we go see the train?”

Henry Parchen noted his son’s excitement, reached for a roll, and rose to his feet. “Come on then.”

The formal opening of the Northern Pacific Transcontinental Track pivoted around the Honorable William M. Evarts’ oration. As the former Secretary of State, he was a worthy and rather long winded speaker whom the Parchen children were more than happy to see finish. They were waiting impatiently for the “golden spike” to be driven into the tracks. Even when Emma pointed out the President of the United States and the two generals from the Civil War, they only briefly took note. Comments from their father regarding the presence of Anton Holter, Charles Broadwater, or Sam Hauser drew more interest, but not much. At least these names the children had heard from time to time.

“I think, Emma, the golden spike is probably just gilded,” Hattie decided as the crowd migrated to where Henry Villard was about to drive the last hob into the tracks.

Emma’s husband lifted young Harry onto his shoulders as her brother did the same for Adele. Then the women lifted Albert and Ruehling up so they too could see. Mr. Villard swung the sludge hammer again and again, slowly pushing the yellow spike into the ground. Suddenly cheering and applause broke out. The Northern Pacific Transcontinental Railroad was now officially open.

“Emma, I think I see President Arthur,” her husband exclaimed as he bent to talk into her ear. “Maybe he will shake our son’s hand. I’m taking Harry.” Emma watched her husband disappear into the crowd as the boy slid off his father’s shoulders.

Emma turned back to their family. Hattie was pointing out the fine fashion of several women to Adele as Albert pulled on his mother’s arm.

“Can we go see the trains again?” he pleaded.

Emma glanced at her brother. He and Ruehling had a small piece of paper laid across a comb, and were blowing on it, producing buzzy noises.

“Albert and I are going to look at the trains,” Emma decided.

“We’ll come with,” Uncle Harry offered. The comb disappeared into a pocket.

The group wandered to the tracks, and followed them to the nearest train. The iron horse sat quietly as the locomotive rose over their heads. Little Albert reached out to touch the grate of the cow-catcher.

“Wow,” he breathed.

They walked alongside as the boys looked up with awe. As they passed the sleek passenger cars, Emma pulled her children to a stop. “How would you like to ride on a train?”

All three turned to her with wide eyes. “Can we?”

"Not today," Emma responded as she noted their enthusiasm, "but maybe soon."

"Can I ride in the caboose?" Ruehling cried.

"They don't let passengers ride in the caboose," Uncle Harry replied. "That's just for railroad men."

Reuhling's expression fell.

"Did you know you can sleep on trains?" Hattie asked as the children all turned to her.

"Daddy and Uncle Harry have," Adele declared. "The train has dining cars too, with linen table cloths and flowers in vases and everything."

"Yes, Adele," her Aunt Hattie agreed. "Everything is very nice."

"I'd like to sleep on a train," Ruehling decided.

"And let the clickity-clack lull you into slumber," Uncle Harry responded.

"But not the whistle," Albert interrupted. "That could wake you up."

Uncle Harry smiled.

The following evening the Parchens arrived home as darkness crept over Helena. Emma's mother met them at the door as young Harry suddenly blocked the path.

"I met the President," he announced. "Shook his hand and everything."

"President Arthur?" his grandmother asked.

"Yes."

"And what did you think of him," Marie inquired.

"Do all presidents have gray hair?" her grandson responded.

Marie smiled. "They all seem to by the time they leave office."

Young Harry looked puzzled. "Maybe it's because they are all old."

"Not as old as me," Marie countered with a grin.

"But you're our grandma. You're supposed to be old," Albert insisted as he pushed his older brother in. "Come on. If we get ready for bed fast enough, she might bring us cookies."

"I touched a train," Ruehling declared as he came in the door on his father's shoulders. "It was big. And it made a lot of noise."

Henry set his son down as Adele reached for his hand. "Come on, Ruehling. We have to get ready for bed right away if we want cookies."

The young face looked up as a huge sigh escaped his lips, then he trudged inward. His father returned outside to look after the buggy.

Marie turned to her daughter. "It looks like everyone had a good time. How were Harry and Hattie?"

"Fine, mother. They send you their best," Emma replied.

"Did Hattie say anything about her sister's wedding?" Marie asked as she took her daughter's coat, and hung it up.

"Not to me," Emma answered. "I think she felt bad about missing it, and I didn't want to bring it up. I'm just glad she felt well enough to join us at Gold Creek."

Within the month Adele was back in school for the fall term, and most of the excursion parties left as the weather turned increasingly cool. The carpenters, however, continued their hard work on the passenger depot of the Northern Pacific Depot, and on various other construction projects going up around town, including the new Montana National Bank building. Wood Paynter had purchased the building next door, and was adding a second floor and a new front to it in connection with Charles Broadwater's bank. Incredibly enough, Jenny and Louis's house managed to get finished despite everything.

Henry Parchen stood in the doorway of his store that September as he watched the stone arches being set into place on Montana National Bank. Emma joined him.

"What is Wood thinking of," he asked quietly, "putting in a drug store right there, across from us?"

"It's a good location," Emma replied.

"Yes, for one drug store, but two?" Henry turned to her. "Does he hate me that much?"

"Maybe it was the only available site," Emma suggested.

"Or the best considering he wants to take back the business we used to share," Henry worried.

"Well, there is a whole dirt street between us," Emma responded with a grin, "and it will get good and muddy with a little rain or snow."

"I always hate that," Henry grumbled. "But Wood's location is right next to the new bank. Any of my customers that bank there won't want to cross through the mud this winter."

"But all the rest are used to doing business on this side of the street," Emma offered as she tried to cheer her husband up. "Besides, it's a little late to get many more shipments in, and I doubt Paynter & Comstock have the inventory you do, especially with your new warehouse." She smiled.

"Why couldn't Paynter have stayed with the wagon business?" Henry groaned. "He made good money doing that."

"His company didn't make anywhere near what we did, and it was divided three ways," Emma replied.

"How do you know that?" Henry asked.

"The newspaper," she answered. "Remember last December when the article came out on who paid the most taxes?"

"Yes."

"Well, it was in there. Paynter, Brown & Weisenhorn paid only two hundred dollars tax as a whole company."

"As a whole company?" Henry repeated. "I thought they were doing well."

"At least they were listed," Emma responded. "That's more than some. Well, I'd better get back to work. Thanks for lunch."

By the 12th of October, Wood Paynter and Charles Comstock had moved into their new store as Henry Parchen and his nephew watched with concern.

The streets were muddy as Emma had predicted. A recent light snow had followed on the heels of a two day rain deluge, and pedestrians did not cross through the mud without good reason. The result was that Parchen Drugs saw little change in their flow of customers. However two weeks later a crew suddenly appeared in the middle of Main Street. They put in a three inch thick, six foot wide plank crossing, and Paynter & Comstock were hailed as public benefactors. Now would come the true test of whether this corner of downtown Helena could reasonably support two drug stores.

Meanwhile on October 27th, Colonel and Mrs. Wilbur Sanders celebrated their silver wedding anniversary amid two hundred guests, and a daughter was born to Charles Comstock's on the 18th of November. Life was good in Helena as Henry Parchen tallied and re-tallied each day's sales. Everything seemed to be okay. Sales were down on certain days, but the decrease was not significant, and finally Henry started to relax as his sales began their normal increase before Christmas.

"Emma, are you writing to Aunt Renard?" Marie asked on a snowy Sunday evening.

"Yes, mother," Emma answered without looking up from her letter. "You know I write her twice a year like clockwork, once for her birthday and again at Christmas."

"Yes, so she told me when I visited last spring," Marie replied.

Emma now paused. She looked across the kitchen table at her mother. "Was she complaining?"

"Probably." Marie smiled. "She said your letters have become very predictable, both in content and in their arrival."

"Is that bad?" Emma asked.

"Your aunt wishes you were more involved in society, that's all," Marie offered. "I think she feels you would get out more then, maybe even travel. She wishes you would visit her."

"Visit her," Emma repeated. "I have my work, the children, Henry..."

"I know," her mother responded. "My sister just misses you, that's all. It has been a good number of years since you stayed with her."

"And since you pulled me home," Emma added.

A sympathetic expression rose in Marie's face. "She wonders why you don't come east on Henry's buying trips. I think she wants you to stay with her while he attends business -- like Harry and me."

"And what do you think?"

"I think she would shower you with all possible attention," Marie laughed, "but my opinion is unchanged. She would do it for herself, not you."

Emma smiled softly. "That's why I stay home, and write letters."

Marie grinned. "I wondered. Oh, there was one thing she made me promise to ask you." She paused momentarily. "What was it? Oh yes! She wants to know if you are still planning to take a marvelous wedding tour someday, and see all the sights? Do you know what she means by that?"

"Yes, I know what she means," Emma replied quietly. "When I married Henry, I didn't think she would be very impressed if she thought we were just coming home to Helena after the ceremony, you know, without a real trip. So I told her Henry's promises were as good as having gold in my pocket."

"Now I understand," Marie responded, and then paused. "You know, you won't have any peace from my sister until you and Henry do take a trip somewhere -- together."

"That may happen soon enough," Emma offered.

Her mother's interest perked. "Really?"

"Henry has something planned for our Twelfth Wedding Anniversary in February," Emma told her, "but that's all I'm going to say for now." She smiled, and turned her attention back to her letter.

Emma wanted very much to see the Pacific Ocean, to walk along its beach, to collect shells, and to build sand castles with her children. That wasn't exactly what her aunt would consider a romantic wedding trip, but it was what Emma wanted. After working so many years, day in and day out, the Pacific Ocean simply sounded like fun.

...and this was the anniversary gift Henry wanted to give her in February. Love swelled in Emma's heart. For despite the serious misgivings she had felt their first night in Helena, Henry had given her the world, the whole world on a progressive day by day basis. They had a house, a family, and two businesses. ...and she was a part of it all. She had truly shared Henry's life and Henry's love. A warmth rose within Emma as she again returned her thoughts to her letter.

Christmas was celebrated at Jenny and Louis's new brick home on North Rodney. Jenny beamed as she welcomed her family in the door. Evergreens decorated the porch, the entry, and every nook and cranny Jenny could find, making up for the lack of furniture. The Christmas tree sat in the front window, creatively decorated with a few glass blown ornaments, but mostly with bits and pieces of nature – pine cones, a bird's nest complete with tiny eggs, dried berries, and more. Emma could only marvel at her sister's ideas. She, herself, had used food to decorate their first tree.

"Adele, what a beautiful dress," Jenny exclaimed as her niece entered the house.

"Grandma made it for me," she responded with a big smile.

"Are you ready for your duet?" Jenny asked.

"Yes," Adele answered, "but I don't think my brother is. I can't get Harry to practice with me at all."

"Harry," Jenny cried as she grabbed her nephew's shoulder, "is this true?"

"Adele's too bossy," the boy complained. "I don't want to sing."

"Oh Harry, just this once...for me?" Jenny begged as she reached to tickle her seven year old nephew.

"I don't want to," the boy replied as he dodged his aunt.

"Oh Harry..."

"Oh Harry, what?" Jenny's brother demanded as he now came through the door.

"Not you," Jenny retorted with a smile. "I'm trying to get our nephew to sing a Christmas song with Adele."

"Sing with girls," her brother repeated. "Ugh!" His eyes twinkled as he then turned to his nephew with a worried expression. "You know, Harry, we may not get dinner unless you sing. How about if I join you? Will you sing then?"

"Okay," his nephew agreed reluctantly.

"Okay," Harry D'Acheul repeated, satisfied. "We're all set, Jenny. What are we singing?"

"A carol," she replied, "a French carol."

"What about a Prussian one?" Henry Duerfeldt demanded as he and his uncle came in.

"Not this year, Henry," Jenny laughed as she finally shut the door. "The packages go under the tree. Wow, you have some big ones. Louis, can you take their coats? Mother, let me help you with that."

Jenny and her mother disappeared into the kitchen. Emma followed as she felt a little envious of Jenny's style. It permeated everything, and made Emma's own house seem a bit dull. Most of Jenny's walls were decorated, most surfaces; and where there wasn't anything, the space looked as if it had always been intended for bare tidiness.

Dinner was delicious. Emma never realized Jenny even knew how to cook, but here it was, steaming and tantalizing. Had their mother taught Jenny when she wasn't around?

"This is so good," Emma commented aloud as she indulged in a second forkful of dressing.

"Yes, what did you put in it?" their mother asked.

Emma looked up. "You didn't give her the recipe?"

"No," Marie replied. Both sets of eyes turned to Jenny.

"I got it from a lady at church," Jenny offered, "but I thought it needed a little perking up, so I added honey."

"Honey? I would never have thought of that," her mother responded.

"Louis's mom adds it to a lot of dishes," Jenny stated. "His uncle kept bees."

"It is good," Hattie agreed. "Can I have your recipe, Jenny?"

"Certainly," Jenny answered proudly.

Dinner was followed by gifts, and everyone watched as the Parchen children opened the largest packages under the tree.

"A wicker case to carry things in," Adele exclaimed as she ripped the paper from hers. Her eyes swung to her parents. "Are we going some place?"

"Maybe," her father answered, "maybe."

"I got one too," her brother, Harry, announced.

"Me too," Ruehling cried.

"What about you, Al?" Adele demanded.

"I don't know, maybe," he answered.

"Well open the package," Adele responded.

"Not yet," Albert objected. "I want to open Uncle Louis's gift first."

Everyone watched young Albert open the box. He lifted out a toy train as a broad smile lit his face. "Thank you," he exclaimed as he turned to his elder.

"Open the big one now," Adele cried.

Albert ignored his sister, reaching instead for another package.

"Open it, Al, or I'll eat your dessert," their brother, Harry, muttered under his breath.

Albert looked up with startled eyes, and obediently reached for the big present. Within moments he unwrapped his own wicker case.

"Hurray, we are going some place," Adele squealed.

All the children turned to their mother.

"Don't look at me," Emma responded. "Your father is doing the planning."

Four pairs of eyes shifted to Henry. He smiled. "I thought we might go for a train ride, a long train ride."

Ruehling jumped up, a smirk on his lips as his little hands landed on his hips. "I want to sleep on the train."

"You will. We all will," his father affirmed.

"Do we get to eat in the dining car?" Adele demanded.

"Yes."

"Where are you taking everyone?" Emma's brother asked.

"California."

"California," Adele squealed, "for the winter?"

"For a month or so," Emma replied.

"California, really?" Adele exclaimed. "Genett Kinna is going to California."

General commotion broke out as everyone asked questions, and eventually returned to unwrapping their presents.

Chapter Twenty-Two

Tired children walked home through the ice and snow Christmas Eve. For despite the festivities that had accentuated their day, sleep at last demanded its claim on them. Adele and Harry managed to carry their new wicker cases most of the way down Rodney, but eventually their mother had to add them to the sled she pulled. Henry Parchen carried Ruehling, and the exhausted children made their way home to bed.

As the children were tucked in, Marie appeared with cups of hot coffee.

"Are you coming to California with us, mother?" Emma asked as the three wandered into the front room where they could sip their coffee and chat in the company of the Christmas tree.

"I would like to see the Pacific Ocean," Marie replied as they sat down, "but I don't think I'm up to the trip. St. Louis was enough for me."

"But you wouldn't have to take a coach, and the trains are warm," Henry offered.

"I know," his mother-in-law agreed, "but I think not. Jenny says I can stay with them, and it would probably be best. Besides, the six of you could use some time together. It would be good for your family."

"You are part of our family," Henry responded. "It would seem funny without you."

Marie smiled. "Thank you, Henry, but your trip will give me some time alone with Jenny and her husband. I would like to get to know Louis better."

On New Year's Eve, Emma's brother and sister, and their spouses came to her house. Harry D'Acheul was excited about the Parchen trip to the coast, for this was not a buying trip east, but a selling trip west. The potential market sparked all his interest and ambition.

Emma grinned as she listened to her husband and brother talk. They were discussing their marketing strategy -- which cities were key locations, which stores were the largest, who the proprietors were, and on and on.

"Emma, do you plan on spending any time on the beach?" Hattie asked her sister-in-law.

"Oh yes," she replied as her attention shifted. "The children and I are going to play in the sand and surf for an entire month, getting wet and running bare foot." Emma smiled broadly.

"Good," Jenny responded. "The way those two are talking," and she indicated her brother and brother-in-law, "I wasn't sure. It sounds like a business trip to me."

"You must realize, Jenny, that business isn't all drab and boring like you think," Emma informed her sister. "Those two are really excited about California, and they are enjoying themselves."

"You must need a certain mentality then," Jenny decided as she shook her head in bewilderment. "It all sounds awfully dull to me."

"That's because your interests lie in different areas," Hattie pointed out. "My Harry loves the challenge of something new. You love music."

"Yes, Aunt Jenny," Adele agreed as she joined the ladies, "I want to grow up just like you."

Jenny turned to her niece. "You want to teach music someday?"

"I want to make music," Adele exclaimed. "It is so beautiful."

Emma stared at her daughter. Adele did have talent, but she did not have her aunt's style, nor her uncle's zeal, despite the ease in which she could play and sing. Adele, however, was a pretty child, and she was definitely a Parchen. Emma glanced at her mother. Marie was watching Adele too.

"Emma, when you go to California, you should look into buying scents and oils for your new lotions," Uncle Harry interrupted. "You know they grow all kinds of things out there, a lot of citrus. Maybe you could develop a new line, and add soaps, or maybe even a men's cologne. Why should we import anything from France when you can make it here?" her brother demanded with a smile.

"You are getting ahead of yourself, Harry," Emma responded. "I know I've mentioned making lotions from time to time, but my tinctures and cough syrup keep me very busy."

"So hire on more help," her brother retorted. "It wouldn't be hard to expand our market in that direction, and the profit line has to be terrific, the way we sell the imported stuff."

"He's right," Emma's husband agreed, "and California is a regular market place for all sorts of things you won't find here in Montana."

"I bet they even grow lavender," Harry offered.

"I grow lavender here," Marie objected.

"You do?" her son replied. "Can you produce its oil?"

"I don't know," his mother answered.

"Lavender oil," Emma repeated. Her eyes flashed to her brother. "You are talking about a whole new line of products, cosmetic products."

"Sure, why not?" he asked.

Emma glanced at her husband. He was watching them intently. Emma now turned. Adele was standing beside her, and placed an open book across her lap.

"Mother, see here," Adele pointed. "My geography book tells all about California. They grow citrus fruit, coconuts, bananas, rice, and all sorts of things." She looked up.

"I see," Emma responded. "What about nut trees? I like almond oil."

"They grow nuts in Oregon," Adele answered as she turned some pages in her book.

"Outside Portland, I think," Uncle Harry agreed as he came over, and looked over his niece's shoulder. "A customer was telling me about this farmer who is putting in a huge nut grove over there."

"Yes," Adele asserted as she showed her mother the page.

"Maybe we should stop briefly in Portland then," Henry Parchen decided as he caught his partner's eye. "It would at least be a good place to do a little selling."

"Would you like to see a nut grove, Adele?" Emma asked.

"Oh yes," her daughter exclaimed eagerly. She turned as Albert came into the room. "You like nuts, Al. Would you like to see where they grow?"

"Peanuts?" the six year old asked.

Adele looked at her Uncle Harry. "Do they grow peanuts there?"

He smiled. "No Adele. Peanuts are grown in the South, in the dirt, kind of like potatoes. Nut groves are trees -- trees of walnuts, filberts, almonds, and things like that."

Adele turned to her brother. "Sorry, no peanuts."

"No peanuts," young Albert repeated with a frown.

"No peanuts," their uncle repeated again as he grabbed the young boy, tickling him until his nephew was laughing so hard, tears ran from his eyes.

"I think we need more cookies," Emma decided, and rose to her feet.

Emma's company left just after midnight. Her mother had excused herself and followed the children to bed shortly after nine. Their nephew, Henry, was still at a friend's party. So when Emma and Henry closed the front door, they were alone.

"Happy New Year," Henry whispered as he grabbed his wife around the waist, and pulled her close.

"Everyone seems excited about our trip," Emma noted, "even the children."

"They should be," Henry replied. "It's going to make us rich."

"I remember when my brother went on his 'long tramp' to find gold," Emma responded. "He never got rich."

"He was looking in the wrong places," her husband informed her. "More gold is found in opportunity than in rivers and mines."

"When did you turn into a philosopher?" Emma grinned as she now twisted out of his grasp, picking up the empty cookie plate.

"Since the railroad came through," Henry replied as he joined her effort. "It has brought opportunity. By the time our children are old enough, we will be able to send them to any college they want, and maybe even buy that mansion you seem to think we need." He smiled. "...maybe I'll even buy a big ranch. A lot of people in town own ranches." He paused momentarily. "Then in our old age we can travel wherever and whenever we feel like it. Maybe even France, if you want."

"I don't want to go to Europe," Emma declared as she pushed a chair back into place, "at least not now while the children are so young."

"But maybe later..." Henry grinned. "The fact is, Emma, California is ripe for the picking, and if we don't take advantage of it, someone else will, probably with an inferior product. So the way I see it, we will probably double our market, maybe more, all in a year's time."

"Double," Emma gasped as she straightened. "We are going to ship that much?"

"Yes," he replied.

"How?"

"That's why we built the warehouse," Henry answered. "And just as soon as our cash flow allows, just as soon as our new market stabilizes a bit, we are going to build you that new building on Broadway."

"My factory?" Emma cried.

"Yes, your medicine has always produced a good income. It's time we had a building that looks like it. I think maybe a three story structure. You could cure and bottle your herbs on the third floor under spacious skylights, dry and grind them on the second." He smiled. "The basement could be your stock area, and you can ship out through the back alley."

"What about a Broadway entrance?" Emma asked.

"I think perhaps we might fit one in...a small one, maybe in conjunction with the two Broadway shops we could rent."

"You have really thought this through," Emma responded.

Henry grinned. "You better keep your eyes open for some good help. You may be needing it." He took the empty glasses from her hands, and set them together on a nearby table. "We can finish this in the morning. Let's go to bed."

Getting four children ready for a long trip was not the easiest task Emma had ever undertaken. Her idea of things to pack did not correspond to her mother's, and her kids managed to get their clothes dirty faster than Emma could take inventory. Repeatedly she took one or another of the children downtown to see about getting something decent to take south, but usually it was in vain. Albert didn't like the color, Harry thought it didn't look grown-up enough, Adele was simply bored and didn't care, and only Ruehling liked shopping. He wanted everything, including a new wagon.

"Relax Emma," Mrs. Ashby encouraged as she bent to whisper something in Ruehling's ear. The small boy nodded eagerly, and immediately quit fussing.

"What did you say to him," Emma demanded as her son now stood like a gentleman beside her.

Mrs. Ashby smiled. "I told him my husband might give him a ride on a freight wagon when he gets back from California...if he's good until then." Mrs. Ashby looked down at the little boy with a questioning look.

"I be good," Ruehling replied, "real good."

"He won't forget your promise," Emma laughed.

"Good," Mrs. Ashby responded. "I will tell Mr. Ashby that when he brings down Parchen Drug's freight from Fort Benton next time, Ruehling wants to sit on the wagon while they unload it."

"He will love it," Emma declared. "Is your husband in town?"

"Oh yes," Mrs. Ashby answered. "He is attending the Board of Directors meeting at Montana National Bank. They have to iron out some details for a proposal they are submitting to the National Treasury."

"It sounds like he is busy," Emma noted.

"Mr. Ashby is always busy," she laughed, "but at least he takes time for the family." Mrs. Ashby broke into a soft smile. "He really appreciated your husband's kindness back when his mother died. Dr. Ingersoll told him how Henry did everything in his power to get the medicine mother needed, even the time when it was in the middle of the night. Well I had better not keep you any longer. I'm sure you have plenty to do before you're off to California." She turned to Ruehling. "Remember, you promised to eat an orange for me, a big round one, all right?"

"Yes ma'am," Ruehling replied in his most polite voice.

"Hurry up, Albert," Emma admonished at the breakfast table, "you are going to be the last one finished." She wiped Ruehling face clean, and then told him to tie his shoe again and go get his coat.

"Adele, have all you children got your wicker cases?" her father demanded.

"I don't know," she replied. "Ruehling was playing with the stuff inside his before grandma called us to breakfast."

"Ruehling!" Emma responded.

"Don't worry, mother, I picked up everything," young Harry announced as he entered the kitchen with four wicker cases in his arms. "Shall I take them out to the wagon, father?"

"Mama, I was going to put some more stuff in mine," Adele cried.

"Too late, young lady," her father declared. "Harry, take the cases on out. That will help a lot. Emma, I think all we need now are our coats." He pulled his pocket watch out through his coat. "We've got to leave immediately. The eight o'clock train waits for no one."

Emma smiled briefly to herself as she thought how Henry had used practically the same phrase twelve years before, that first morning in Deer Lodge...and ever since. Henry hadn't changed much. He still got impatient before trips, he still worked too hard, and he still had dreams. Emma glanced at her husband, remembering why they had to rush so to make the Deer Lodge stagecoach. Now they rushed because of the children. The more things changed, the more they stayed the same. Who was it that used to say that? Oh yes, it was her father.

Louis and Jenny appeared at the door. "Good morning," Jenny greeted as they came in.

Emma finished stacking several dirty plates together.

"Dont' worry about the dishes, Emma," her mother admonished. "I will see to them once I get back from the depot."

Emma caught Albert before he flew out the door, and buttoned his coat. Ruehling was next.

"Harry get your mother's coat for her," Henry Parchen instructed. He tied Adele's scarf tightly around her throat.

Within moments the Parchens were leaving the house, and climbing into the wagon Henry had rented for the occasion. Marie climbed into the buggy with Louis and Jenny. The horses immediately headed north down Rodney.

"Brrr, it's cold," Jenny commented.

"Only about twenty below," Louis chuckled. "We are going to have numb fingers and toes by the time we reach the depot."

"Can't you hurry the horses any faster," she cried.

"Not on all this ice and snow," he replied. "Relax, we are making good time."

Within twenty minutes Emma was standing inside the new passenger depot with her family, warming themselves at the wood stove as they waited for Henry and Louis to see to the luggage. Emma surveyed the building with its new walls and floors. The varnish of the benches and ticket counters gleamed, and a man stood on top of his ladder, making adjustments to the large clock. Emma glanced at the schedule board. Their eight o'clock departure had been moved back to eight thirty.

"Emma, Henry and Louis are back," Marie announced.

"The luggage is taken care of," Henry declared. He pulled their tickets from his pocket.

"Our train departure has been moved back to eight thirty," Emma informed him.

"Eight thirty, good," Henry responded. He pulled out his pocket watch. "That's good. We were running late anyway." He turned to the children. "Why don't you all go over and sit down while I confirm our schedule."

"Is the train here? Is it here?" Ruehling demanded.

"I don't know," his father answered as he shooed his flock over to the benches. He went up to the ticket counter.

Moments later he returned. "The train hasn't come in yet from Bozeman." He sat down next to Louis.

"You be sure to write us," Marie instructed. "We want to know that you get to California safely."

"And bring us something from the ocean," Jenny added with smile. "I would love to see the Pacific."

Conversation flowed freely within the family as Emma glanced again at the schedule board. The time of departure was being changed again. As she watched, their departure was moved back an entire hour.

"Henry," Emma called softly, "the schedule board."

Her husband looked up as a scowl rose into his expression. But oddly enough, Emma did not share his consternation. She settled back into the bench and relaxed. All her worries were over. Her family was here. Their luggage was here. All the responsibility of getting a family of six ready for a trip clear to California was over, and it felt good to sit and relax. For the first time since Christmas, Emma had nothing she should be doing, no other place she should be. A smile emerged on her face as she realized they were essentially on their way already. The trip was fact. Their dreams were becoming real.

"What are you thinking about?" Henry asked as he noted her smile.

"California...the Pacific Ocean," Emma responded. "All we have to do now, is wait for the train."

"If it ever gets here," Henry complained as he caught Albert before he ran into a passing gentleman.

"It will," Emma stated, "and California really exists."

"You doubted it?" Henry questioned.

Emma smiled. "Until now, it only existed for others."

An hour and a half later, the train pulled into the station as its whistle broke the din of conversation within the depot. Ruehling jumped off the bench in eager excitement, and would have run straight for the door if his father hadn't caught his coat tail.

"Whoa there, son," Henry laughed. "We have to wait for the passengers coming in from Bozeman."

With a huge, impatient frown, Ruehling sat back down. To the young boy an eternity seemed to pass before people came through the door. Then with an expression of patient martyrdom, Ruehling politely asked his father if they could board.

"Not until the whistle blows again and the conductor announces it's time," Henry told his son. He glanced at Emma with a smile.

A frown took up residence on Ruehling's face as his mother tried to distract him.

But because of the intense cold, passengers were not allowed to board the train until a maintenance check was run on the engine, and ice removed. It was nearly eleven thirty before the whistle blew again, and the Parchens headed for the passenger cars.

"Ruehling, slow down," Henry Parchen called as his young son pulled and tugged on his hand. The two were already well out in front of the others.

"Daddy, daddy, come on," the little boy cried urgently. "The train is waiting."

Suddenly the boy stopped. A conductor stood at the steps where people were boarding. The man's uniform seemed to check Ruehling's enthusiasm.

Henry took the opportunity to wait for the rest of his family. As they arrived, Emma and Jenny hugged as Marie did the same with each of her grandchildren. Even Ruehling was pulled into the family farewell. Louis waited patiently, shook hands with the adults and pressed silver dollars into the palms of the children. "Have a good time, okay?"

The Parchen children nodded vigorously as faint "thank you's" left their lips.

"Okay, Ruehling," Henry called. "Do you want to be the first one on the train?" He was handing the conductor their tickets.

The small boy straightened, walked over to the tall step, and climbed on. He waited just inside until Albert and the others joined him. His eyes were still wide as Henry and Emma followed. Then the family filed through to where they would sit. Henry placed the children side by side in the seats with the oldest in front, then the younger two, and he and Emma behind.

Still they waited for their journey to begin. But as Henry's patience was tried, Emma did not suffer from anything except anticipation. Excitement was growing steadily in her as the minutes ticked by. They were going to California. They were leaving behind the awful cold of the past few days. They were going where it was warm, where flowers grew in February. Emma's spirit soared. She was going to see palm trees. The promise Henry had made her exactly twelve years ago to the day was becoming real. She was going to see the sights. She was going to see California and the ocean.

The noon hour approached, the locomotive fired up, the whistle blew...and Emma thought she was going to explode.

"You are more excited than Ruehling," Henry decided with a grin. The train slowly began to move. Young faces pasted themselves against the windows as they waved to their grandma, and their aunt and uncle.

"He hasn't waited for this as long as I have," Emma responded with a smile.

"Happy Anniversary," Henry offered warmly.

"Yes, our anniversary," Emma sputtered as her hand dove into her pocket. It emerged with a small wrapped box which she gave to Henry. "Happy Anniversary."

* * * * *

The Parchens built a handsome, three story, brick building on Broadway in 1886. The children were offered good educations, i.e. Adele attended the Conservatory of Music in Cincinnati. They also acquired a ranch in the Judith Basin, and in 1904 bought the Italian Renaissance mansion that used to stand on the corner of Rodney and State Streets, Helena. Henry and Emma lived here the remainder of their lives.

The cemetery where Calista and Cy Ingersoll are buried is one that is in great need of funds. Maintenance is only performed at this time by the volunteer efforts of local citizens who cut back brush, pick up trash, and raise fallen markers. Calista's tombstone is one of those that has fallen, and has sadly broken in half. Dr. Cy Ingersoll has no stone at all, although he "only laid down his life's work when the great master said: 'It is enough.'" He was ninety years old.

If you would like to contribute to our historic heritage, and provide toward the repair and/or placement of historically correct gravestones, some of which are wood, please contact:

The Benton Avenue Cemetery Association
P.O. Box 4212
Helena, Montana 59604

I would love to see our past appreciated, wouldn't you?

Ann Cullen